BROKEN

a novel

Paige K. Palmer

BROKEN
a novel
Paige K. Palmer

Copyright 2012 by Paige K. Palmer
Cover Image by Bryan Palmer
Cover Design by Gideon Fisher & Bryan Palmer

TABLE OF CONTENTS

For my father, who told me I could be whatever I wanted to be, and to Bryan, for accompanying me along the way.

THE PRELUDE: FRIDAY, MAY 25TH, 1973

Addie

It seemed like an odd day. I thought it weird how you can feel an odd day coming. And it wasn't that anything was out of place. Except for a dream, the events of the day seemed like any other. But as I walked up the stairs to our bedroom I felt a change was about to happen to me. The small, delicate hairs on the back of my neck tingled as I reached the top of the stairway. Whatever the change was, it was going to be big.

It was actually a refreshing feeling. For so long now I felt as though my life was insignificant; life had come to have no meaning. The loss of Ean left me empty and broken. Ean. That's what I would have named him if he had been born – if he would have lived, if he would have grown and married and had children and died an old man. But he didn't. And the months since had been filled with pain, tears, and misunderstanding. Family and friends preached hope to me, but hope only existed in my few dreams, which is what I planned to do when I reached our bedroom. Instead, I turned and stopped at the nursery and opened the door.

A rush of coldness danced across my cheeks and lingered there until I submerged my entire body into the room. It was such a cold room. I thought it fitting that the temperature of the room matched that of my lost child. When I wanted to feel the cold and emptiness – which was often – I would come into this room, to the middle of it, and just sit, breathing in the solitude and welcoming the loneliness I had woven around me as a safety-net. But with the feeling of change surrounding me, I walked to the window above Wyatt's drawing desk and opened it, letting the early summer afternoon breeze of May slip into the room and warm it. I watched as the breeze scattered my husband's drawings across the room. They were tiny floating stories circling above his desk. That desk had been the cause of so many fights the last couple of months. I never believed Wyatt when he told me he moved his office home to be closer to me. I never believed him when he argued that the nursery would be the only room he could work in because of the natural light that came in from the window. As I grasped a few papers in mid-air, I remembered how talented my husband was and now thought perhaps he was right. The light in this room was beautiful. I let the page go and watched as it floated to the ground and rested on the pages of my chaotic scribblings scattered around the room – ramblings that came to me in the night. *My dream...*

It was Friday, almost 4:30. Lesley would be here in approximately three hours. Lesley – my supposed savior and friend. There was something about Lesley that was different now. I noticed a change in Lesley about a month ago but couldn't pinpoint exactly what the change was. Lesley and Wyatt's relationship seemed to have changed as well. They laughed more together, appeared more at ease around each other, and yet there was still a child-like nervousness about them that made me wonder if this was the way Wyatt and Lesley acted when they were children, before their college years together, before Wyatt and Lesley were married, before Wyatt and Lesley were divorced. But that was before my time, so I tried not to speculate on it.

But how interesting that would be, I pondered, to have an insight, a reference explaining Lesley and Wyatt's behavior over the last six years. Did I want to know what their life was like before I entered the picture? *Curious,* was the only answer I gave myself. That was enough for now.

I walked over to the rocking chair and sat down, letting the breeze off the lake try and cool my mind. I was incredibly thoughtful today: Dream thoughts, life thoughts, thoughts about Wyatt, thoughts about Lesley. Perhaps that was the change. Since the loss of the baby my mind had only been full of that day, moments leading up to it and moments following; a whirlwind of moments beaten against each other to comprise one day. How life can change in one day.

CHAPTER 1: POINT CANEISSA

Saturday, May 25th, 1974

"Damn it!"

Wyatt had forgotten to go grocery shopping.

Today was the last Saturday in May. Wyatt always went to town on Fridays and had planned on going yesterday, but the news of his sister's visit made him somewhat distracted. He wrote the errand on his calendar: *May 24th, grocery shopping.* It was even circled in red – granted, that was for an entirely different reason – but it was marked and planned. Nowhere was there penciled in a planned visit from his sister Prue.

Wyatt threw down the morning paper to the empty space in front of his breakfast, crossword puzzle side up, half completed. He had just filled in twelve across – seven-letter word for supermarket. Wyatt stared into his day old, reheated cup of coffee and contemplated what he was going to do with his sister while she was visiting. Tapping the last piece of bread, toasted and lightly jellied, on the rim of his plate, Wyatt realized that feeding Prue would be a necessity. Annoyed, he turned around and grabbed his car keys off the counter, hoping the holiday weekend had pushed the crowds to the lake instead of Harrisman's Grocery. He would be grossly disappointed.

Point Caneissa was a small town and had been since its inception in 1844. Even now there were not more than 5200 residents living in the quaint Lake Michigan town. Set on a rocky, weather-beaten bluff that sloped down to create a small, white sand beach, Point Caneissa was divided into two parts – the old part of town that held the shipping yard and workers' cottages and the touristy part of town. The shipping yard and its cottages were no more than a ghost town now, its residents long driven away by the pursuit of modern progress, though a few of the neighboring town's factory workers took up residence in the houses farthest away from the lake that could be salvaged. The paint on these houses had peeled long ago and the wood underneath resembled that of driftwood, causing one to wonder if the houses themselves had once been boats or ships lost in the tumultuous waters of Lake Michigan. Either way, death seemed to linger in the air in this part of town, on the buildings and the leaf-less forest surrounding them, and people only drove by quickly now, never entering the lamp-less section of this decayed boomtown. The second part of Point Caneissa was the complete opposite.

What once had been Point Caneissa now had given birth to what was Point Caneissa: Summer beachgoers', antique seekers', art lovers' big city getaway. A hundred years ago, Point Caneissa's shipping yard was the fastest, easiest route to transport consumer goods from Chicago to Detroit. It didn't take long for the consumer to follow, making Point Caneissa a destination playground for the wealthy. Along the beach they built a boardwalk with carnival games and booths filled with the smell of fried and barbequed delicacies. A wooden carousel and roller coaster – Bailey's Comet – sat behind the boardwalk with Point Caneissa Casino and Burlesque on the end, built partially into a small cove. Hotels and restaurants sat on the bluff overlooking the boardwalk with bed and breakfasts' located on the north side but still within walking distance. There were art fairs and summer festivals that lined Main Street, bringing in crowds that overpopulated the small town between May and September. And when boat was no longer the favored mode of transportation, planes, trains, and automobiles brought the snowbirds in droves, causing one part of the town to die while the other part continued to thrive. And the cycle was about to start all over again.

Driving down Pine Street, Wyatt searched both sides for a parking spot. The businesses and townhouses along the street had hung American flags on porch posts for the Memorial Day celebrations – the official start of summer. Harrisman's lot was full with unfamiliar cars, and as he parked his car three blocks away, Wyatt laughed smugly as he passed the wall of license plates from Indiana, Illinois, Ohio, and other places in Michigan – out-of-towners fooled by the beauty of this place in summer. *Let them come to Point Caneissa in the gray of January,* Wyatt thought to himself. *They'd crawl over each other just to get out.* He smiled as he pictured men in shorts and women in sunhats horrified by the frostbitten wind creating three-foot snow hills on the normally warm, sandy beaches of their memory. And if the weather didn't drive them away, the never-ending gray that intertwined with the lake, no doubt, would. Wyatt picked up his reluctant pace as he realized he didn't recognize any of the cars parked up and down this street, or, for that matter, in Harrisman's parking lot. Could he be so lucky as to not run into anyone he knew? The idea almost sent him into a sprint.

Wyatt entered the small grocery store. Grabbing a cart, he began slowly maneuvering around the large quantity of people in the first aisle of fruits and vegetables, searching the faces of a crowd he did not recognize. *Could this really be happening?* Wyatt optimistically wondered. *Could I walk through this store and not be awed at or met with questioning eyes?* So far, so good, and Wyatt became hopeful that his shopping trips could be increased from every two weeks to once a week, at least through the summer when he could blend in with the steady stream of out-of-town traffic. Wyatt casually continued walking around the whole store, relishing in his newfound anonymity. But, as is the usual case, all good things must come to an abrupt end.

Wyatt made his way to the front of the store, steering his cart to a line that had thirty people in it. It seemed that only two of the three cash registers were manned this morning, and the line that Wyatt had found himself in diverged into two about twenty people up. Until then, his fate was in the hands of the grocery gods and he prayed he would find himself unscathed from this visit. If he made it out of the store safely, he promised he would produce a bountiful summer of patronage. Wyatt waited patiently as he reached the fork in the line, relieved that no one had spoken to him or even recognized him. But then the third register opened to help with the overflowing traffic, putting fate parallel to the left of Wyatt's cart.

"Wyatt? Wyatt Trilmon?"

Wyatt looked up and found a blond, stocky man and his wife looking at him. Though the man was balding, Wyatt recognized a face from his past.

"Bill Morningstar."

"Look, honey, it's Wyatt Trilmon."

The woman, trying desperately to prevent her child's oncoming temper tantrum, glanced up at the man her husband was speaking to, smiled politely, and quickly returned her focus to the little girl sitting in the cart. This was a face Wyatt remembered, also.

"Wyatt, you remember my wife Lu – "

"Lucy Everson. I remember," Wyatt said calmly, forcing a small smile. "I didn't know the two of you had gotten married."

"Yep, yep. Lucy pinned me down almost eight years ago. I think it might have been around the same time you and Lesley got hitched."

The line moved up one.

"That was eleven years ago," Wyatt said sharply, looking down to the ground, all signs of a smile having left his face.

"That long? I guess time flies."

"Yeah, I guess."

"You ever talk to Lesley?"

Wyatt focused his attention to the right wheel on his cart.

"No. We don't talk to each other anymore."

"Oh," replied Bill Morningstar. "Too bad. She was always a looker, that Lesley. Ow!" Lucy had shoved her heel into Bill's foot, glaring at him. "Well, she was!"

Wyatt smiled as he watched Bill quickly rub his toes on the back of his calf.

"Say, Wyatt, I was real sorry to hear about your new wife, what was her name?"

"Addie."

"Yeah, Addie. I was real sorry to hear about what happened."

The line moved up one again.

"Thank you, Bill."

Wyatt began to place his items on the counter.

"So, did they ever figure out why she did it?"

"Bill!" Lucy said shortly, punching him in the side.

"Excuse me?" responded Wyatt, shock and anger filling his eyes.

"What?" Bill looked down at his wife. "It's a legitimate question." He returned his focus to Wyatt. "I mean, did they find a note or anything, explaining why she did it?"

Wyatt didn't say anything as he shifted his body forward, quickly emptying what was left in his cart onto the counter.

"Bill, keep moving," his wife commanded.

"What? What was so wrong with what I asked?"

Wyatt kept his focus forward, waiting for the person in front of him to finish paying. When the woman moved out of the way, Wyatt realized why his line had been moving so slowly. There, behind the register, was Gladys Garvey, the high school's retired librarian, and the slowest cashier in Point Caneissa.

"Hey Wyatt," Bill called. Wyatt did not respond.

"Wyatt! It's so nice to see you," said Mrs. Garvey, her voice giddy with sincere surprise.

"Hello, Mrs. Garvey."

"So, how are things?" Gladys Garvey smiled, her aged, worn down teeth peeking through at him as she punched in the prices on her register.

"Things are fine, Mrs. Garvey."

"That's good. You know, sweetie, we don't see – "

"Hey, Wyatt!" Bill called again.

"Mrs. Garvey, I'm kind of in a hurry today. My sister's coming to town."

"Prudence is coming? How lovely! How long – "

"Would you like me to help you bag?" he asked, annoyed with her questions and delicate age, though relieved she didn't seem to notice Bill Morningstar's invasive questioning.

"You were always such a nice boy! Here, let me get the bags for you."

"No, no. I can get them. You just keep punching in numbers." Wyatt smiled and winked at her, trying to keep the situation under his control.

"Okay, Wyatt."

Wyatt went to the end of the counter and began to bag his own groceries. "Is that Wyatt Trilmon?" he heard someone whisper down the line. He continued to bag as the sound of his name began to hush through the crowd, coming from all directions.

"She seemed like a pleasant-enough girl."

"Poor Wyatt."

"He should have stayed married to Lesley."

"Lesley was such a nice, *local* girl. And real successful now, I hear."

"Where was that other girl from?"

"New York, I think. Big-city girls."

"Such a shame."

"Yes, he could have been happy."

Wyatt's ears stopped on the last comment he heard.

I could have been happy? Wasn't I happy? I could have been....

Wyatt placed his bagged groceries in the cart.

"That'll be thirty-four twenty-one."

Wyatt handed Mrs. Garvey his payment.

"Thank you, Mrs. Garvey."

"Have a happy Memorial Day, Wyatt, and tell Prudence I said hello."

Wyatt didn't say anything, just smiled and nodded, and headed out the door. If Bill Morningstar attempted to retract any of his comments, they fell on deaf ears.

As Wyatt stopped outside Harrisman's, struggling to hold all four grocery bags in his arms as he maneuvered the shopping cart toward its pen, he spotted Sheriff Roberts across the street at the ice cream shop, staring at him. Sheriff Roberts grabbed his triple scoop ice cream cone from the Tasty Freeze vendor and ran to catch Wyatt before he left town.

"Hey, Wyatt!" Sheriff Roberts yelled, waddling towards him, trying to lick his ice cream and say hello at the same time. For a middle-aged pudgy man, he did both quite well. "You need some help with those?"

Wyatt let go of the bags, letting them fall back into the cart, and waited for the sheriff.

"Hey Wyatt, I haven't seen you in a while," he said as he leaned slightly on the cart, catching his breath and taking a lick every two seconds or so. "About four months I think?"

"Yeah, I've been keeping to myself, trying to get things done and settled."

Sheriff Roberts took another long lick from his ice cream, then looked up at Wyatt.

"Seems like enough time has passed to have things settled."

Sheriff Roberts picked up one sack, leaving the remaining three for Wyatt to juggle. He nudged Wyatt to the sidewalk, leading him down the rows of cars as he took a lick of ice cream every few yards, balancing the groceries on his hip as he walked. Wyatt, however, stumbled under the load as he followed, his anger being aggravated by this current annoyance.

"I was kind of hoping I'd run into you," Sheriff Roberts said somewhat nervously. "I saw your car parked down a ways and couldn't believe it. Never would have thought you'd come to town on a Saturday, especially this Saturday of all Saturdays. The only thing stranger would be to see you here on the Fourth of July."

"I didn't have a choice," Wyatt said quickly as they crossed Market Street. *One more block to sweet salvation,* he thought.

"What do you mean?" asked the sheriff.

"I ran out of food, Richie."

"Oh." Sheriff Roberts looked down at his sack, then at Wyatt's load. "You must eat a lot. There's enough here for two, maybe three people."

"Is there a reason you wanted to talk to me, Rich?" Wyatt snapped.

Sheriff Roberts stopped while Wyatt continued his quick, labored pace. After about twenty feet, Wyatt realized the sheriff was no longer beside him. Wyatt took a few steps backwards and sighed.

"Prue's coming up to the house for the week. She'll be here sometime today." Wyatt turned and began walking toward his car again, motioning with his head for the sheriff to follow. A little overly delighted, Sheriff Roberts shadowed Wyatt as they closed the distance between themselves and Wyatt's car.

"So, Prue's coming to visit!" the sheriff squeaked jovially. "Is there any special occasion?"

Wyatt set his bags on the trunk as he searched for his keys, his eyes never reaching Sheriff Roberts' face.

"I can only think of one."

"Oh, right." The sheriff took a step back, taking a long lick off his ice cream cone.

Wyatt unlocked the car, pushed the front seat forward, and began loading the groceries into the backseat. He noticed the sheriff standing there awkwardly, licking his ice cream cone as he fervently tried to come up with something to say. In his attempt, Sheriff Roberts was almost breaking a sweat.

Wyatt smiled as he placed the last bag into the car, chuckling to himself as he walked to the sheriff, knowing he had caused the discomfort so obvious on the sheriff's face.

"I think she's checking up on me," Wyatt said as he grabbed the last bag from Sheriff Roberts' arms and placed it in the back seat with the others. He noticed little splotches of chocolate on the one side of the bag and frowned. "She's making sure I haven't gone crazy or something." Wyatt pushed the front seat back and got in.

"Probably not a bad idea," Sheriff Roberts replied, smiling as he leaned against the 1970 Buick Gran Sport 455, dark green paint still shining like new from the factory. He ran his hand across the smooth top, then patted it like it was a dog. "With all the stories floating around town, I'm sure she's heard at least one of them. Heck," he laughed, "I'd come check on you too if I heard some of the local gossip going around."

Wyatt sighed and laid his head back against the seat. Sheriff Roberts could tell he was not amused.

"Look, Wyatt, I know this hasn't been an easy year for you. God knows I know it."

"Is that what you wanted to tell me, Richie?" Wyatt's voiced cut him off violently. "Because if it was, I could have saved you the three-block walk. If I wanted sympathy, I could have walked into any store downtown and gotten it. *God knows* I could have."

Sheriff Roberts stepped away from the car, his eyes falling to the ground, his lips ignoring the melting cone in his hand.

"I didn't mean it like that, Wyatt." His voice was small and disjointed. Wyatt began to relent, remembering that this man was his friend – his oldest friend, actually – and never once had Sheriff Roberts ever looked at Wyatt with the same judgmental eyes that the rest of the town seemed to hold for him.

"I know you didn't," Wyatt responded softly. "I'm sorry, Richie. I just got a lot on my mind."

Sheriff Roberts turned to face Wyatt again.

"I tried to find anything on why she did it," Sheriff Roberts said slowly, almost pleading. "I really did."

"I know you did, Rich."

Wyatt's sincere response gave the sheriff the little bit of courage he'd been waiting for.

"All I'm sayin' Wyatt is that I know you had nothing to do with it. I know it in my heart, Wyatt. I know," the sheriff paused, concentrating on his words, "I have a feeling you think you had something to do with why she killed herself."

"Richie – "

"No, Wyatt. I've got to say this. I've known you a long time. You're a good man, a good friend. That mornin', all those scattered, nonsensical papers we found, they were ramblings of a crazy person."

"Richie – "

"I'm just sayin' Addie's death had nothing to do with you, alright? Nothing."

A drop of chocolate rolled down the cone and fell on Wyatt's arm.

"I've got to go."

"Wyatt – "

Wyatt started the car and put it in reverse. Sheriff Roberts grabbed his arm.

"Come into town more often. You, living in the old side of town with no one around you…it may do you some good being around people."

"I'll think about it."

Wyatt floored it, causing Sheriff Roberts to lose his balance and drop his ice cream.

"Addie needed help, Wyatt! She was crazy! That's the only explanation," he yelled at the speeding car.

Sheriff Roberts thought about chasing after Wyatt in his squad car, but he knew he'd never catch him. And if he did, what would be the point? Wyatt wouldn't talk to him. He didn't talk to anyone. Sheriff Roberts sighed as he began to walk the three blocks back to the Tasty Freeze. "Maybe butter pecan this time," he muttered. "Nuts give a better consistency."

CHAPTER 2: BABY BOOM

Wyatt

"Wyatt!"

I had just finished hanging the last strip of wallpaper when I heard screams coming down the hall from our bedroom.

I'd been working in the nursery all weekend, trying to finish it as a gift for Addie. Tomorrow is her 27th birthday. Addie had picked out the shades of pastel blues, greens, pinks and yellows for the walls, the Winnie-the-Pooh wallpaper border and Pooh accents for the crib, changing table, and rocker a month before and swore she wouldn't peek until I had finished it. After I started the nursery, Addie expressed her thoughts about changing the décor to a baby jungle animals theme. But, with the help of a few other opinions, she was persuaded back again by how cute the baby would look surrounded by Pooh, Piglet, Tigger and Eeyore. People told her, "What good childhood friends you've picked out for your baby!" I told her it would take two months to finish, but the excitement of the baby made me work harder. So I decided it would be a surprise for her birthday, since it was the one thing she wanted more than anything – except for the baby.

"Wyatt!"

I rushed down the ladder, slipping on a stuffed Piglet as I stepped off and fell to the floor, breaking my right hand as I braced for the impact. I pushed myself up with my other hand and ran down the hallway into the bedroom, looking around to find Addie, seeing only the bathroom door shut halfway. Her screams were coming from there. I pushed the door open and found her slightly hovering over the toilet, tears streaming down her face.

"We have to go to the hospital."

"What?"

"Now!" she screamed. She reached her hand towards me for balance as she gathered her nightgown between her legs. As she stepped forward I looked behind her at the toilet. It was filled with blood.

*****

Addie waited five years before trying to get pregnant. Looking back on that short space in time, I remembered Addie once told me that she had read a psychological study while attending Barnard College that said couples who were married for four years or more before having children had a better chance of not getting divorced. Not wanting to take any chances, Addie hid her true ambition from me during those first five years of our marriage, and then, without telling me, she went off her birth control. So far I had been very successful in my illustrating career. The move to San Francisco after graduating from NYU was paying off, and Addie felt now was the perfect time to start a family. I, on the other hand, had no idea what she was planning.

The night Addie told me the results of her scheme, we had just gotten home from celebrating my thirty-second birthday. Although I was more than slightly hammered, I didn't find it unusual that my wife had not partaken in the same activity. I followed her into our bedroom and watched as she began to take off her clothes, my drunkenness making me more aroused as the thought of her naked body swirled around in my head. I walked slowly over to her, grabbing her from behind, and began kissing her neck.

"Wyatt, no," Addie said, pushing my hands gently away from her.

"Com'on." I grabbed her again. "It's my birthday."

"No." She turned around and began leading me back to the bed, smiling and excited. "Okay, sit down. I have something to tell you."

I sat on the corner of the bed and wavered, waiting impatiently for some sexual act to come – my birthday present.

"I know this may come as a shock," she began, "but it's something that I've wanted for a long time and it will make us both *sooo* happy. Ready?" She paused for dramatic effect. "I'm pregnant!" Addie squealed as she said the words. It made my ears ring.

My brain tried to grasp the thought of having a baby, of being a father, but it was too much for my sloshed state and I passed out. Addie was disappointed but blamed herself for letting me drink so much later rather than earlier in the evening. She tucked herself under the covers, leaving me lying awkwardly on the floor for fear that picking me up would put too much strain on her fragile, developing baby.

When I woke up I was still on the floor, face planted downward into the carpet, drooling. The room was still dark; the curtains hadn't been drawn. I remained on the floor, not sure why I was there, with the distinct fear that a dream I had while in my drunken stupor was true – a dream that Addie was pregnant. I couldn't remember anything from the night before, just the feeling that something in my world had been horribly and irrevocably disturbed. But then the smell of sizzling bacon entered my nostrils and my thoughts from the early morning were then pushed away.

I walked into the kitchen just as Addie was finishing filling my plate with my favorite breakfast foods. I sat down at the table and waited.

"Good morning sleepy head!" Addie said cheerfully. "Did you have a good night's rest?"

"I don't know," I replied. "I'm not sure. I woke up on the floor."

"That's because that's where you passed out," Addie explained as she placed the full plate in front of me.

"I take it, then, I had a really good night." I spoke with a forkful of eggs in my mouth.

"I like to think so," she answered. "I think it will be a birthday you'll never forget."

"Good." I paused to chew a piece of bacon. "Because I had the distinct feeling when I got up this morning that something was wrong, that something bad had happened." I smiled at my wife, putting the rest of the bacon in my mouth. "But I guess everything's fine. Everything seems normal."

"Everything is perfect."

I continued to eat my breakfast. At the stove I watched my wife make her own breakfast of an egg white omelet and a bowl of freshly cut fruit on the counter next to where she was cooking. Everything was normal. I started to chuckle a little at my own unwarranted paranoia. How could anything be wrong? Addie was right. Everything was perfect. I remembered the pregnancy dream and laughed even harder. How silly, now, it had all made me feel.

"What are you laughing at," asked Addie.

"I was just remembering a dream I had last night. A nightmare, really. At least I think I dreamt it last night."

"What was it?"

"It's silly," I continued smiling. "Not anything I'd really expect to be afraid of or should be afraid of. It's kind of embarrassing, now that I think about it."

"Tell me what it is."

"I can't believe it freaked me out like that." I put another fork full of eggs in my mouth. "And it was only a dream. I hate to think about how I'd react if it really ever happens."

"*What?*"

I was a little embarrassed confessing this fear. It was ridiculous that at thirty-two the idea of having a baby would scare me. Perhaps it was the dream itself, the way it happened, so unexpectedly, that threw me off. I always thought that when Addie and I decided to have children, the news of conception would make me overwhelmingly happy. I just wasn't ready for it yet.

"Well? Are you going to tell me?"

Addie was facing me now with her hands on her hips. She reminded me of my mother, waiting for me to tell her whatever bad thing had happened at school that day. That image, Addie as a mother, also made me laugh, so I decided to divulge the whole hilarious idea to my wife.

"I dreamt you told me you were pregnant. I dreamt we were going to have a baby. How ridiculous is that?" I continued eating my breakfast, chuckling through the crunching piece of toast.

"It was not a dream," said Addie, still standing with her hands resting on her hips, across the kitchen.

"What?" I was still laughing to myself, not yet comprehending what my wife was telling me.

"I told you last night. It was my birthday gift to you. I'm pregnant. We're going to have a baby."

I let my fork drop quickly to the plate and leaned back in my chair, staring at her. Addie didn't look pregnant. Nothing seemed to be different about her. Wouldn't I have noticed if she was pregnant? Wasn't there some kind of change I would have seen? Addie stood there waiting for me to say something.

"That's…wonderful," I answered, pretending I was excited this new, unwanted chapter was starting in my life, but I knew she could tell there was something wrong. Addie folded her arms around herself in a hug and looked down to the floor. That was my signal. I stood up and walked over to my wife, placing my arms around her and pulling her in. "I'm so happy, Addie. You've made me so happy."

Addie began to cry.

"I'm sorry, Wyatt. I'm so sorry."

I pulled her closer and squeezed. "There's nothing to be sorry for." I pushed her away to look into her face. "We're having a baby. That's wonderful! It's the best birthday present I could have asked for."

"Really?" she sniffled.

"Really."

"You're not mad at me?"

I had no words. In truth, part of me was mad. Part of me wondered how she could have let this happen. Part of me wanted to run out of our third story apartment screaming. But I didn't. It was the look on Addie's face that kept me rooted, tethered to the floor like a misbehaved puppy. She had terror in her eyes, that questioning flicker of "Is he going to leave me?" that I despised and feared myself. I had ignored a look like that once before, and I promised myself I would never be the cause of it again, for fear of the consequences.

I placed my hands on Addie's cheeks, cradling her face.

"You did nothing wrong." I moved my hands down her neck, resting them in her lower back, pulling her in close to me again. "I love you, Addie," I whispered. "So much." I moved to kiss her cheek, then pulled away to look into her face. "Now, go wash your face and get ready. We need to celebrate."

"Okay!"

Addie went to the bedroom and I heard the shower start. I walked back to the table and sat down in front of my plate, unable even to look at it, let alone eat it. I picked it up, walked over to the trashcan, lifted the lid and began scraping the food into the plastic bag. It was ironic, I thought, that this was the second time in my life I was throwing away a celebratory breakfast my wife had made into the trash. The first, cooked by a different wife, completely and utterly changed my life in every way. I wondered, while scrapping the last of the eggs off, what this one would do to me – if it would be as painful as the last. But I didn't have time to wonder, so I placed the greasy plate in the sink and headed to our bedroom, preparing for the big day ahead of me.

When Addie and I got back from our day of celebrating I was exhausted and laid down on the couch to close my eyes. Addie sat on the edge and held the phone up to my ear. When I heard it ringing on the other end, I opened my eyes and looked at Addie.

"It's your sister, so you can tell her the good news."

The good news. That was the last thing I wanted to think or talk about right now. I had been trudging through it secretly in my thoughts all day, passing by baby boutiques and smiling at the differently styled rompers I soon would be paying for. I wondered, while walking through the sea of baby items, if I would ever get to pick out anything, or if all that would be left up to Addie. Seemingly, she had decided to have a baby without me – no discussions, no planning had been involved, at least none on my part – so would I have a say in anything? What clothes would he wear or toys would he play with? What schools would he attend? Would he eat eggs and bacon like his father or would he be forced egg white omelets and fresh fruit like his mother? Or would he make his own choices? I wondered if I had any choices at all anymore.

"Hello?" I heard someone on the other end answer.

The familiar questioning tone of my sister's voice cleared my thoughts and relieved me. All I had to do now was say one sentence, and the conversation would be out of my hands. No more thinking, no more speculating, just short responses. That would be easy.

"Hey, sis, it's Wyatt. I don't know quite how to tell you this, but Addie and I are going to have a baby."

My tone was calm and cool, almost robotic. I waited for the elated congratulations to stop, all the while saying "Thank you...Thanks.", before saying "I'll let you talk to Addie," and handing my expectant wife the phone.

An hour later Addie walked into the bedroom to find me lying there, hands behind my head, staring at the ceiling.

"Your sister is so happy for us," Addie said as she crawled in next to me, laying her head on my chest and finding her spot in the groove of my upper-body. She fit so perfectly there, between my chest and arm. If we were to switch positions, I wouldn't fit quite so well in Addie's arms, and both of us would feel unrelaxed. For this one reason, I often thought God really did make woman for man, no matter how difficult it was sometimes dealing with them.

"What did Prue say?" I asked, half listening.

"Oh, just that she's happy for us and can't wait to be an aunt. It just made me feel really good talking to her. Didn't you?"

"Sure," I said, sounding uninterested. But Addie continued.

"She asked me all kinds of questions, like how I was feeling, if I was excited, how far along I was – "

"Wait," I interrupted. "How far along *are* you?" I lifted myself up, pushing her to my side so I could look at her.

"About a month, maybe a little more, from what the doctor can tell. Why?"

"It just occurred to me that I didn't know. I mean, I should know how far along my baby is, right? Because people are going to ask. I didn't think about people asking."

"Of course they're going to ask. This is a big deal, and we're at the center of it."

Addie put on her biggest grin, placed my arm around her shoulders, and leaned the both of us back against our pillowy bed. We laid in silence until Addie spoke again.

"You know, Prue asked something very interesting."

"What's that?"

"She asked if we were going to stay in San Francisco. Of course I hadn't even given that any thought. I mean, we've made a home for ourselves here. It caught me a little off guard I guess."

"Why'd she ask that?"

"She said that she thought since we were going to have a baby, maybe we'd move somewhere else…somewhere less big, less crowded, less city. I never even thought about it."

"Me either."

"Maybe we should," Addie trailed off.

A week went by and after watching how happy Addie was and getting congratulatory phone calls and cards from family and friends, I decided this new chapter in my life was a good thing. Life was full of unexpected happiness. After all, I never thought I'd love someone like Addie, and now I didn't know what I'd do without her.

The week had produced many new developments, one of which were piles of housing brochures scattered through the apartment at all of my favorite spots: my recliner, my nightstand, my place at the table, and even the bathroom. Addie was sending a very loud hint. Wanting to accommodate our new life, I decided that San Francisco was not the place I wanted to raise my family. Though beautiful, as my sister so politely suggested, it was becoming too crowded – a cultural melting pot of what seemed to be every idea ever thought. I looked through all the real estate magazines and housing brochures Addie had so delightfully placed in the apartment. They were from all over the country. Cities with the best schools, towns with wholesome values and little crime, and picturesque properties anyone would fall in love with. But nothing caught my eye. I found myself looking at each brochure or magazine and finding different aspects I liked, but not a whole picture. There were certain things about San Francisco that I loved – the hills and the bay surrounding them, the architecture, the art scene – but that wasn't enough. All this searching made me think back to my own childhood and what it was exactly that I loved so much about it. What was it that made me want to give my children the same experience? My friends, my family close by, my school, my house, Lake Michigan. Of all the places I'd been, I'd felt my hometown was different, special in some secret way that no one really could put their thumb on. That's when it hit me; I wanted to move back home. I wanted to raise my family in the same place I was raised. Point Caneissa had so many good memories for me, why wouldn't it produce good memories for my children? Excited, I called my sister.

"You know that little thought you put into Addie's head?" I asked after Prue said hello. "Well, I've been thinking about it and maybe you're right. Maybe we should move away from San Francisco."

"And greetings to you, too, Wyatt," responded Prue. "What exactly are you thinking now?"

"I'm thinking I would like to move home. I want to move back to Point Caneissa."

"Really? After all that gallivanting across the country? What brought this on?"

"Besides your suggestion to my wife?" Prue giggled. "I started thinking about all the fun we had as kids growing up there. It just seems like the perfect place."

"Are you sure you're remembering things correctly," she asked. "As I recall, you couldn't leave Point Caneissa fast enough. I mean, you didn't even say good-bye to Lesley before you left for college."

Lesley. Why did she have to bring up Lesley?

"Perhaps you're getting just a little sentimental with a baby coming and all."

I could tell Prue was goading me, little jabs leading me along, trying to provoke a reaction out of me. She knew this new attitude on life – on family – wasn't like me.

"It's not that I was in a hurry to leave Point Caneissa," I started slowly. "It's just that I was in a hurry to start my adult life. And there were certain things that at the time seemed too hard to face. So I just left." My voice grew stronger now. "Besides, I was just a stupid kid then. I'm a grown man now. I see things differently."

"*Right*," Prue replied, dragging the word out in disbelief.

"It's true."

"Well, that's great," said Prue. "Point Caneissa: 'Practically Perfect in Every Way'."

"Aren't you rich."

"I have my moments," she laughed. "What does Addie think about all this?"

"I haven't told her yet."

"So, you're relocating without telling her? Smooth move, Wyatt. Let me know how that turns out."

"I didn't say that," I retorted. "We've been looking at different places, I just haven't told Addie about Point Caneissa."

"Stellar."

"Anyway," I began again, "I was just wondering if you knew of anyone back home trying to sell their house. I'd like to have an idea of places before Addie and I make a trip all the way out there."

"Why don't you move into mom and dad's place? That would make the most sense to me, since you already own it, and you're having such fond memories of it and all."

I could tell by her tone that Prue wasn't done making fun of me.

"Cute, Prue, but I'm serious. Besides, I can't move into mom and dad's. I've been renting it out to Jeff Stokley and his family the last seven years. I can't just ask them to leave because I want to live there now. It wouldn't be right. Mom and dad would have never done that. Besides, Addie wouldn't live there anyway."

"Why not?"

"Because it's not on the water. Wherever we decide to move, Addie insists that it be by water. Something about space and balance, I don't know. Do you know of anyone or any house?"

Prue paused for a moment, then answered.

"As a matter of fact, I do. Me."

"What are you talking about?"

"Well, I never told you because I knew you would make fun of me or think it was crazy, but, do you remember Persephone?"

"That old witch-lady who lived in the old part of town?"

"She wasn't a witch and she wasn't old!"

I could tell I had struck a chord. I knew Prue had been friends with Persephone but I never realized how close they were. By the sound of Prue's voice, I could have been insulting our own mother.

"I remember Persephone," I tried again. "She was very nice. Always looked out for you, from what I can recall."

"Yes she did," Prue replied, sounding a little heartbroken. "Anyway, she died a few years back – "

"I'm sorry to hear that. Why didn't you tell me?"

"I thought I did," she answered, annoyed.

"Maybe you did. I must have forgot."

"Anyway," she started again, "after Persephone died, I received a letter from a lawyer about her will. He was going around giving people the items that she left for them."

"What did Persephone give you?" I asked, thinking it a ring or necklace, or perhaps her crystal ball. The last made me smile.

"A set of keys."

"To what?"

"Her house."

The conversation paused. I couldn't believe that this strange woman who was the cause of so many rumors in town bequeathed my sister a house. Every scary story or urban legend that surrounded Point Caneissa had to do with that witch Persephone or her creepy old house. Persephone was what campfire stories were made from. It was ridiculous. But then again, so was Persephone.

"I don't believe it," I said finally. "She left you her house? Why?"

"The lawyer said it was because she thought of me as a daughter, and because she had no children of her own, she wanted me to have it. Crazy, right?"

"A little, yeah. So what did you do with it?"

"Nothing. It's just sitting empty."

"Why didn't you tell me about this before?"

"I didn't need to before."

I was finding her answers a little cryptic.

"So, when can we take a look at it?" I asked.

"Whenever you want. I'll send the keys tomorrow to Aunt Ginny. You can pick them up whenever."

"Okay. Sounds good."

"Wyatt," she said suddenly. "If you like the house, I mean, if you and Addie like the house, perhaps we could come up with some kind of trade."

"What do you mean?"

"I mean, if you both like it and want it, maybe we could trade houses, Persephone's house for mom and dad's. What do you think?"

"I don't know, Prue. Why this sudden interest in mom and dad's house? Is there something wrong with Persephone's?"

"No," she said quickly and reassuringly. "I just think it's time I've moved on from that. I can't bring myself to sell it, and I don't want to give it away, but if we traded, I'd get something and you'd get something. I will even promise never to sell mom and dad's if you promise the same about Persephone's. It's a win-win."

"I don't know, Prue. This is happening all so fast. Ten minutes ago I didn't even know you owned a house, let alone Persephone's. I don't know what to think."

"Look, no pressure now, just go look at it. You might not even like it. Addie might hate it."

"I doubt it."

From what I could remember of Persephone's house, it was big, white with dark blue shutters, and quaintly antique looking. And it was right on the lake. It was straight up Addie's alley.

"Just go look at it. Look at others, too. Don't make any haste decisions. You're a real putz when it comes to that, you know."

"That's what you think." Prue laughed when I said this. "I guess it wouldn't hurt to look at it. I'll call a realtor tomorrow and set up some appointments. Send Aunt Ginny the key and tell her I'll be calling her. This is crazy, Prue. You know that, right?"

"All depends on how you look at it, I guess. When your life is full of craziness, you expect everything. For us, it's just another normal day."

"I guess," I sighed.

"Look at it this way," Prue continued. "Five years ago you were on a plane to Vegas to get married. Three years ago your art career took off soaring. A week ago it was just you and Addie, a happy couple living their life as they always have, taking what it gave them. Today you're going to be a father. Heck, ten years ago you were married to a completely different person with your life on a completely different path. Craziness, I tell you. Full on craziness."

Again with the talk about Lesley.

"Huh, I guess you're right." I drifted away from the conversation. Ten years ago I was married to a completely different person. *Lesley.* I'd forgotten about Lesley in all this recent "craziness". What would she think about all this? Usually, when something terrific happened in our lives, Lesley was one of the first names mentioned to share the good news with. But this time I had forgotten her. I wondered if Addie had forgotten her too.

"Hey," I said, interrupting Prue's babbling on about my new life. "Do you know if Addie told Lesley yet? I mean, did she mention it to you at all?"

"She didn't mention it to me. Why?"

"No reason. Hey, sis, I have to go. I have some things I have to get back to."

"Okay. Let me know what you think of the house."

"All right."

"Talk to you later."

"Bye."

I hung up the phone, reached for it again, and moved my fingers over the numerals in Lesley's phone number, never pressing any of the buttons down hard enough to dial.

*****

I followed the lamp-less streets until I found the Red Arrow Highway. It would only be twenty miles now to the hospital, and I drove them as fast as I could, shifting and steering awkwardly with my left hand. It was January and no one was on the road this late at night, so my swerving went unnoticed. I wondered if it was good to be this alone, no one knowing the pain and fear we were going through – what I was going through – no one there to help us. *What if we had stayed in San Francisco?* In San Francisco there would have been people to help, but Point Caneissa was small and isolated. Strange how my memory depicted this place. I began to regret moving my budding family here. Life didn't seem so picturesque at the moment.

I looked over at my wife. In the darkness that surrounded me Addie was the only thing illuminated by the moonlight. Her white nightgown glowed in the darkness. She was still grasping the tufts of cloth between her legs, clenching the blood-soaked knot she had made, hoping it would hold everything in. She no longer cried but just sat and stared ahead into the night.

When we got to the hospital I ran in and begged for them to help me. A male nurse rushed out with a wheel chair, took Addie out of the car, placed her in the chair and wheeled her through the automatic doors. The front desk nurse told me to please park my car in the patient parking lot and then return to the emergency room. When I returned to the desk, the nurse escorted me to exam room three, where a doctor would see me shortly.

"Where's my wife?" I asked the nurse as I entered the room and found Addie wasn't there.

"She's in the maternity ward upstairs."

"Then why am I here? I need to be with her."

"There's nothing you can do for her now. Just sit down here and the doctor will see you about that hand."

"But – "

She walked out of the room and said nothing more. I had forgotten about my hand. I looked down at the limp mass at my side, then back at the door. *What did she mean there's nothing I can do for Addie now?*

I tapped the cast on my hand with my left forefinger as I walked down the hall of the maternity ward. It was my version of a nervous twitch. It had been two hours since I saw Addie. The desk nurse made an exception letting me into the ward so late, but I guess she felt sorry for me. She looked at me with pity. It was a small hospital and in-patient stories traveled fast. I searched the hallway for room 213. It was the very last room in the corridor.

I took a breath before opening the door.

Addie was in bed, completely covered by a pink knit blanket. A gray-haired man stood over the foot of the bed writing something on a chart. Addie looked like she was dreaming.

"Is she okay?"

The doctor jumped a little, causing his pen to draw a squiggly line down the rest of Addie's chart.

"Oh, my goodness!" The doctor smiled at his own jumpiness and then looked at me. "I didn't know anyone had walked in."

"I'm sorry." I walked over to the bed and touched Addie's hair. "Is she going to be all right?"

"Oh, yes. She'll be fine."

"Really? Are you sure?"

"Quite sure. I gave her a sedative so she'll sleep. We'd like to keep her overnight, of course, for observation."

"But you just said she was fine."

"Yes, but it's standard procedure here to keep miscarriage patients overnight to make sure there's no hemorrhaging. She was bleeding quite a bit when she came in. More than normal. But there's nothing to be alarmed about now. She'll be fine."

"Miscarriage?"

"Yes. I thought they told you downstairs." A look of concern washed over the old man's face. "Oh, I'm terribly sorry. This must come as quite a shock to you then."

"I don't know that I understand."

"I'm afraid your wife has lost the baby. It's not uncommon for first-time pregnancies to be lost. She was just into her fourth month, about 17-18 weeks, correct?"

"Yes, but – "

"That's what I thought. Don't worry though. She can still have another. All hope is not lost."

"I don't understand what's happened." I could feel myself losing the air in my lungs, as if I'd been sucker-punched and now all the oxygen was slowly slipping out of my mouth as I desperately tried to breathe. "Everything was supposed to be fine."

"Well, I did a rudimentary exam of her pelvic region and I believe that the placenta attached too low in the uterus. Her body just couldn't hold on to it any longer. Some type of extreme jarring movement may have contributed to the detachment also. It's hard to tell, really, but there was nothing we could do. If not today, it would have happened eventually."

It was hard to comprehend what he was saying so matter-of-factly. I didn't understand. I couldn't. He had lied. All hope was lost.

Seeing my non-reaction, he set Addie's chart down and walked to the door.

"I'll see you both in the morning."

"You didn't tell me your name."

"I didn't? Well then. I'm Dr. Mortenson."

"Thank you, doctor."

"I'll see you both in the morning." His words faded as the door closed behind him.

"It is morning," I whispered.

In the briefest of moments I had lost everything I never wanted. I walked over to the window and sat on the ledge against it, watching the stars fight the sun's coming day, and cried.

Addie

I lost Ean in January. January was the perfect month. Not that we get to choose such things, but if you can, try and pick January. It's cold and silent, dark and lonely. And dry, despite the snow.

Spring would be hypocritical.
Summer is the opposite of January, alive.
Autumn is too late, the bounty having already been reaped.

But January is consumed by winter, the gray beating against the trees, blending with the melting snow. It hurts.
In January, nature isn't sleeping. It's dying.

CHAPTER 3: INDISCREET INTERRUPTIONS

Lesley

"Hello?"

"Lesley?"

"Yes."

"It's Addie."

I already knew who it was before I picked up the receiver. Addie was the only person who called me this early in the morning.

"Hi Addie. How are you?"

"Well, I've got some big news. Really big!"

"Okay, let me have it." I wondered what celebrity Addie had seen lately, or which pair of high fashion boots she saw in a store window and just had to have. That seemed to be Addie's obsession lately: celebrity gossip and shoes.

"Are you sitting down?"

"Uh-huh."

"I'M PREGNANT!"

I pulled the phone away from my ear. The screaming on the other end was too painful for my eardrums. As I waited for the shrieking to stop, I started to ask myself how I felt about this obtrusive announcement. About thirty seconds into my internal questioning, I was distracted by the faint sound of my name being called through the telephone.

"Lesley?"

"I'm, I'm here. I'm here."

"Good. I thought I lost you."

"No, I'm here."

"Sooo, what do you think? Isn't it great news?"

"Yeah, really great news."

"You don't sound very happy about it. Is something wrong?"

"No, no. I just...well, I just woke up. I mean, when you called I was sleeping. The phone woke me up. You know, you're the only one that calls me this early."

"I know," she giggled. "That's why I do it, sleepyhead! So what do you think?"

"I'm still a little groggy, but happy. Very happy."

The words came pouring out of my mouth. I wasn't even sure if I meant them. I mean, part of me had already lied. I hadn't been asleep when Addie called. In fact, I'd been up for the last hour-and-a-half procrastinating the start of my day. I had just poured myself a bowl of cereal when the phone rang. And now I regretted the idle effort I had put into my breakfast. The shock of hearing my ex-husband's new wife tell me she was pregnant was too much to take in over a soggy bowl of corn flakes. It was morning, and too hard to think. I didn't know how I felt yet. Happy, sad, mad, depressed, hatred, melancholy. I didn't know.

"I'm glad you're happy, Lesley, but I've got more big news!"

"More big news? What could be bigger than you and Wyatt having a baby? That's the biggest kind of news there is." I sounded cheerful enough now. I was actually starting to believe that I was happy for Addie and Wyatt.

"Wyatt and I are going to move to Point Caneissa!"

"What?"

"Yeah! Isn't it great? Wyatt and I've been talking and we both agree that San Francisco is too big of a place to raise a baby. People lose themselves in such a big city and we don't want that to happen to our family."

"It's not *that* big of a city."

"Sure it is," Addie protested.

"It's not like it's New York, and we've all lived in New York. And Chicago's bigger than San Francisco and I never feel lost here in Chicago. Even Wyatt's lived in Chicago." I wanted to forget that part of his life – my life – but I had to throw it in for the sake of argument. "He didn't seem to mind it."

"Well, San Francisco's too big for us."

Us? Ugh! I wanted to vomit.

"Besides, all of Wyatt's family's there."

"Prue's not there," I interjected. "She's in Cleveland. You should move to Cleveland. Cleveland's not too big."

"Lesley, what are you saying? That's crazy-talk. Besides, Point Caneissa isn't that far from Cleveland, and it's not that far from Detroit, and it's not that far from Chicago, which is what we want. Wyatt will have to commute sometimes to Detroit and Chicago for work. Honestly, Lesley, you'd think you didn't want us moving to Michigan. I thought you'd be happy. I thought you'd want me closer so we could spend more time together – me, you, and the baby. We hardly ever get to see each other. I was really hoping this could be something we both would be happy about and could share."

I could hear the tears hiding underneath Addie's voice. I hated it when Addie cried. It reminded me how human she was and how sweet a friend she had always tried to be. It wasn't that I didn't want them near. Well, maybe a little part of me didn't want them near. Okay, maybe a big little part of me. But I had good reason for it. For the last couple of years I had finally found peace in my life. Peace without Addie and Wyatt. My psychiatric practice was doing very well and I had just become a partner in the office I was working in. Plus I was dating again, occasionally. Though lately it seemed I had been racking up the one-night stands, unintentionally, of course. And I had worked hard to no longer harbor deep painful, hurtful, regretful feelings toward Addie and Wyatt. I was in a good place and the thought of the two of them – Wyatt more so than Addie – so close in distance to me made me afraid those old feelings would come back again. I'd worked so long to push the resentment aside. *I'm a psychiatrist, for heaven's sake!* I chided myself. If I couldn't control my own feelings, how could I tell my patients to do the same?

"You know what, Addie, you're right. I'm a terrible friend. Here I am talking nonsense when I should be congratulating you and helping you with the transition. I'm sorry. I guess it was just all too much at once. I don't know where my mind is today."

"Probably still with your pillow," she laughed.

"You're probably right," I chuckled along, even though I had been up since six o'clock and it was now almost eight. "So, have you guys picked a place yet?"

"No. We're coming this weekend to look at houses. I wish we could stop by and say 'hi' but I don't know if we'll even have time. Plus I'm not sure if we're landing in Chicago or Detroit."

"That's okay. Why don't you focus on finding a house and moving first. Then, when you're all settled, maybe we could go baby shopping or furniture shopping, or something."

"Okay! That sounds wonderful! Oh, Lesley, I can't wait to tell Wyatt how excited you are."

I cringed a little. I didn't want Addie to tell Wyatt anything about how I felt. I didn't want her to talk to Wyatt about me at all. But I couldn't control anything Addie did, which made me want to hang up on her. At least I could control that. But I didn't.

"Okay, Addie. You take care of yourself and I'll see you soon."

"Okay. Bye!"

I hung up the phone, walked into my apartment living room, opened the curtains and looked down on the city. I lived on the twenty-sixth floor of a thirty-story building. I found it amazing what clarity was given to the city being so high up, and yet on a clear day I could really only see the tops of a few buildings and the goings on of my own street. In this morning's cloud cover I could discern the Sears Tower's ever-blinking beacon in the distance, its peak slicing clouds as they passed around it. Somewhere to the left, I knew lay Lake Michigan and the erratic morning traffic which followed its coastline. It was days like this I was glad I moved to the city. Traffic would be worse and more dangerous. Lucky for me, my office was only fourteen stories below on the twelfth floor. The morning commute would consist of putting on sneakers for a light jog downstairs.

When I walked into my office at nine-thirty, my secretary was already there making coffee and filing in order the day's appointments.

"Good morning, Jane."

"Good morning, Dr. Trilmon. Did you have a nice walk to work this morning?"

"Yes, it was quite nice. Better than anyone who had to commute in today."

"Tell me about it! I spent the night at my boyfriend's last night and you know he lives in Michigan City, which would normally take about an hour to drive in, but today in the fog it took, like, two hours to drive in, and you know how nervous I get when I drive and how paranoid I am about people getting mad at me if I'm driving too slow, or what if I wouldn't see someone, and God forbid I hit someone because you never know – "

"Did I have any cancellations in my appointments today?" I had to interrupt her. I had a job, after all.

"Your ten o'clock, Mr. Caldwell, called in and rescheduled. Big crisis at work, or something like that. Said he'd tell you all about it at his next session."

"Goody," I said under my breath.

"You know, Dr. Trilmon, I'm sorry about my babbling a moment ago. I just get so hyper, you know?"

"I know, and it's okay. I'll have my morning coffee in my office. Was there anything else for me this morning?"

"Dr. Burk was in briefly." Jane smiled when she said his name. "He left something on your desk and said he would be back in the office around noon. Something personal he had to take care of, I think."

"Alright, then. I'll be in my office."

I sat down at my desk and skimmed over its contents to find whatever Dr. Burk had left for me. My eyes fell to a note on the back of a folded piece of paper.

Lesley,

A colleague of mine gave this test to me. Try it out on yourself. I found my own results surprising. It's designed to calm and give focus to patients in stressful situations. I tried it on a few of my patients and it has revealed for them interesting perceptions of themselves they never knew. Let me know what you think.

Gable

P.S. Maybe we should compare our notes on this sometime, say, over dinner this weekend? I'll be waiting for your answer.

A smile crept over my face as I read the note. For the past year there had begun a slight and ever-growing flirtation between myself and Gable, one I thought someday I may succumb to. How near in the future that day would come would have to be left up to fate, for now. I wasn't looking for anything serious at the moment and I thought that if I ever did start something up with Gable, it would be something I would want to last longer than one night. And according to my present track record, that didn't seem likely. Gable even pressed me weekly for confirmation of a rendezvous, but I wanted to see how the flirtation would grow and what it might blossom into, watching as every Friday a different girl took my place.

Still warm from my thoughts, I picked up the test and unfolded it, beginning at the first question:

1. You are walking in the woods. Who are you walking with?
Wyatt

The answer shocked me. I wanted to say Gable or Addie or my mother or Jane even, but not Wyatt. All I could picture was myself and Wyatt walking in the woods that bordered Point Caneissa, like we did when we were growing up. Strange, I thought. Must be because we did that as children. No big deal. I continued.

2. You are walking in the woods. You see an animal. What kind of animal is it?
A bear.
3. What interaction takes place between you and the animal?

Nothing. I keep walking.

4. You enter a clearing, and in the center of the clearing is a house. Does it have a fence around it?

Yes

5. You pass the house and beyond the fence is a goblet lying in the grass. What is the goblet made of?

Silver

6. What do you do with the goblet?

I take it with me.

7. You continue walking and find yourself at the edge of a body of water. What type of body of water is it?

Lake Michigan

8. How will you cross it?

I will swim.

I skimmed over the professional jargon explaining what the test was, how it was to be administered, and what type of patient it was for. What I really wanted to know was what my answers meant. I thought perhaps it was a test about stability in one's own life, but the questions left so much room for interpretation, my answers could have meant anything. Finally, I got to the analysis.

The person who you are walking with is the most important person in your life.

"What!" I shouted.

Jane opened the door to my office and peeked her head in.

"Is everything all right, Dr. Trilmon?"

"Yes, everything's fine. I was reading a research article I didn't agree with," I said nervously. "You know how passionate I am about research."

"Yes, Dr. Trilmon. I'm sorry to have bothered you."

"No, it's okay, really. I didn't realize how loud I was being."

Jane closed the door slowly, looking very confused, while I looked at the test again for my results.

The size of the animal you encountered is reflective of your perception of the size of your problems with the person you are walking with. Your interaction with the animal is representative of how you deal with the problems you have with the person you're walking with. If you chose a fence around the house in the clearing, you tend to have a closed personality. If you chose no fence, you tend to have an open personality. The durability of the material of the goblet is reflective of your perceived durability of your relationship with the person whom you are walking with. What you do with the goblet is representative of your attitude towards the person you're walking with. The size of the body of water you come to is representative of your sexual desire for the person you are walking with and how wet you get in crossing that body of water is signifying the relative importance of your sexual relationship with that person.

"This is insane," I said out loud. "According to this I love Wyatt." *Apparently more than anything.* And I want to be with him? That's just not true. "This test is ridiculous."

I picked up Gable's note again and re-read it, trying to pinpoint if there was something about the test that was a trick or if I had misread it somehow. Surely this test didn't prove I still loved Wyatt. It couldn't, right? These tests were never like that. There had to be room for some interpretation. It couldn't be so cookie-cutter, hey-you-fit-into-this-category, perfect. I read the note over and over again, letting the words sink deeper into my brain.

What does it mean? What is it saying? Does Gable suspect something? How could he? There's absolutely nothing to suspect.

I read over it one last time, honing in on one phrase – *designed to calm and give focus to patients in stressful situations.* I thought back on my morning and the phone call that broke my breakfast solitude. That had to be it. I had Addie and Wyatt on my mind. It was the phone call. But just to be sure, I picked up the phone and dialed Gable's number to schedule a date for this Saturday. Maybe I had strung him on long enough.

The note fidgeted along my fingertips until it fell from my pinky, landing on its backside, revealing writing I had previously missed.

Just so you know, my lovely Lesley, the person I was walking with was you.

Time to push bad thoughts out and let new, stimulating ones rush in.

Saturday evening came and as the night went on I grew excited at the idea of starting a new relationship, letting myself give in to my emotional desires. But when the sun rose on Sunday, waking me through my bedroom curtains, I was alone – the space beside me having been quietly emptied earlier that morning – the whole tryst lasting one night, and nothing more.

So life goes on, racing, pulsing haphazardly forward until another brief moment stops it suddenly, catapulting it another direction, shifting it away on another path.

It was Wyatt who called me and told me Addie had lost the baby. Addie didn't have the strength to tell anyone, including me, her closest friend. Wyatt waited a week, though, Addie's behavior urging him to pick up the phone and dial his ex-wife.

"Lesley, it's Wyatt," he said, the tension in his voice reaching into my ears.

"Wyatt, what is it? You sound perplexed." I didn't know yet if I should care about what he had to say, but I wanted to seem concerned.

"It's Addie. She lost the baby."

My heart jumped unexpectedly.

"Wyatt, I'm so sorry. When did it happen?"

"A week ago."

"A week ago! Why didn't you call me then? You don't just let something like this go for – "

"Lesley, I think I may need your help."

Wyatt's tone was forceful, more than usual, and I stopped scolding him, waiting for his reproach, but none came. Instead he began speaking calmly to me again, wanting my help more than a fight.

"Addie's behavior," Wyatt continued, "has been very unusual. I'm starting to get worried about her."

"I'm sure you have nothing to worry about. It's common for most women after losing a baby to have feelings of depression, insomnia, panic attacks, anxiety, etcetera. It would be helpful for her to talk to someone, though. You should try to find someone locally."

The psychiatrist in me was coming out, pushing away feelings of friendship and empathy.

"Where am I going to find a shrink in Point Caneissa?" he said bitterly, trying to veil his worry with sarcasm. "Besides, I don't think Addie will talk to anyone local. She really doesn't know the people here like we do. I think she'd feel uncomfortable." Wyatt paused for a moment, seemingly choosing his words wisely. "That's why I called you, Lesley. You're Addie's best friend. You're like family." He paused again. "You're *my* family," he whispered. "Isn't there something you can do?"

I was annoyed. I hated it when Wyatt referred to me as family. He gave up that right when he left me ten years ago. Unfortunately you can't get away from your past, as I've come to learn, since over the years Wyatt has continually been placed in my life without my consent. And then there was the issue of Addie. I cared about Addie, regardless of all the countless times I tried to cut her out of my life. Addie was the constant reminder that where I had failed in my marriage to Wyatt, she succeeded effortlessly. But whatever I tried to do, I could not fill that tiny spot in my heart where Addie's friendship was. Naturally I had mixed feelings when I heard Addie had lost the baby. It didn't seem fair for Addie to be able to keep Wyatt's baby. I hadn't even been given the choice. But ultimately I felt saddened at Addie's loss. I could imagine what it felt like, remembered.

My annoyance soon turned to genuine concern as I responded to Wyatt.

"I'll tell you what. Keep watching Addie for the next couple of weeks. She may just need time to grieve. I don't think it's anything serious yet, but Wyatt, you're right in being concerned. If you want, you could take some time away from work and stay with her, see how she progresses. If you're still worried after that, then call me. I'll come up and talk with her, see if I can't help her."

"Thanks, Lesley. This means a lot to us."

"It's okay. You're both family. I'd do anything for Addie." At the moment I said it, the words felt good rolling off of my tongue. I began to persuade myself that this would be a turning point in my life. No more grudges, no more hard feelings, no more jealousy, no more paranoia. I began to look forward to helping Addie cope with her loss. "Tell Addie she can call me anytime if she needs to talk."

"I will. I guess I'll talk to you later then," Wyatt said, sounding optimistic.

"Yeah." I paused. "Wyatt, you know everything's going to be fine, don't you?" I said finally.

"I know. It's just so hard watching her like this."

"You know, Wyatt, you can call me, too, if you need someone to talk to. I can't imagine how all of this is making you feel. Addie isn't the only one suffering." My heart began to beat faster at the thought of helping him. It never entered my mind before that Wyatt might need me also.

"That's really good to know," he trailed, "but I think it's best we focus on Addie right now."

"Whatever you need, just let me know."

"Okay."

"I'll talk to you later then."

"Okay."

"Bye."

Warmth raged through me as I hung up the phone. I jogged down to my office contemplating this new feeling I had. I didn't know what it was. Was it love, pity, friendship? I couldn't figure it out. I tried to analyze it, find the source, but I couldn't. I didn't want to admit I still had some feelings for Wyatt, and part of me would always resent Addie for marrying him. So many times since our divorce I had forgiven Wyatt in my mind; forgiven him for leaving me, forgiven him for breaking my heart, forgiven him for marrying my friend, forgiven him for being happy with his new wife, forgiven him for trying to have children with someone else. Addie I could not help but befriend, regardless of anything she ever did. She was impossibly simple, yet sweet, and I, though believing myself tough enough to conquer any obstacle, could never seem to discard Addie the way I did with everyone else who I felt betrayed me, hurt me, or made me question my own feelings. Perhaps fate had been playing a part in this relationship also. Whatever this new feeling was, I sat with it all day and through the evening, examining it, trying to figure out my own feelings towards the couple. I grew tired of the investigation, and whatever the feeling was, it slipped away in the night, released in one of my dreams.

Three weeks went by without a call from Wyatt and I pushed the thought of counseling Addie out of my mind, until a knock interrupted one of my sessions.

"I'm sorry to bother you, Dr. Trilmon, but there is a man on line two who says he needs to speak with you." Jane was sticking her head around the door trying not to look at the patient on the couch. It seemed she didn't want to invade his privacy.

"Jane, I'm in the middle of a session. Please take a message and let him know I will call him back in half an hour."

"I told him that but he insists he has to speak with you. I'm so sorry." She looked over at the man on the couch and smiled her apology. "He says his name is Wyatt and that it's urgent."

My heart fluttered. A thousand scenarios were flooding my mind.

"Okay, I'll take the call in here." Jane closed the door quietly and went back to her desk. "I'm sorry David. This will just take a minute." The man on the couch sat up, grabbed a magazine from the coffee table, and relaxed again into the cushions, reading a *Sports Illustrated*.

I picked up the receiver and cautiously pressed line two, preparing myself for the worst. I hoped my advice to him had not been wrong.

"Hello?" a panicked voice answered on the other line.

"Wyatt?"

"Lesley, thank God! I didn't think they were going to let me talk to you. I need you to come home right now."

His wording threw me a little.

"Okay, slow down. What's wrong?"

"I think Addie tried to kill herself."

"What do you mean she tried to kill herself? What happened?" I was becoming more worried. I glanced at my patient still reading the *Sports Illustrated*, relieved he didn't seem to be eavesdropping.

"I don't know. I went to town to get some groceries and when I came back I couldn't find Addie. I looked all over the house, so finally I went outside, down to the beach, and I saw her crawling back in over the ice, soaking wet! I don't know what she was doing out there. I ran out to get her. She was crying and mumbling words I didn't understand. So I carried her back inside. I'm scared, Lesley. I don't know what to do. Lesley, tell me what to do!"

"Okay, calm down. Everything's is going to be all right."

"I don't want to calm down! You said everything was going to be all right last time and look what's happened! Addie's tried to kill herself!"

I was speechless. I didn't know how to console him. Wyatt was right. I had told him everything was going to be okay and I was wrong. Franticly I looked around the room for a book or magazine or paper I could read from that would give me some credibility in my reasoning to him. What did I say to him the last time? Had I diagnosed Addie or just given helpful advice? Had my resentment clouded my judgment? But I was past that. I had felt for Addie, right? My eyes continued to scan the room. I needed something to help me, something to make me a psychiatrist and not a friend or ex-lover. My eyes fell to my desk and the test I had taken from Dr. Burk. It lay in the same spot it did two months ago.

... to calm and give focus to patients in stressful situations...

It was worth a try.

"Okay, Wyatt, I need you to listen to me. We need to focus, all right?"

"Okay."

"Now, picture you are walking in the woods. Someone is walking with you. I need you to focus in on that person. Don't let go of that person. Can you see them?"

"Yes."

"Okay. Keep that person in your mind. Now you come across an animal..."

I continued the questions, asking his answer for each one except for who he was walking with. I assumed it was Addie, pointing my questions more and more towards Addie so Wyatt would focus on what was happening to her. With the last question of the test answered, I thought Wyatt well enough to ask about his wife.

"Okay. Let's think about Addie now. Let's focus on Addie. Where is she now?"

"Upstairs sleeping. What should I do?"

"Just watch her. I'll be there as soon as I can."

"When will that be?" His voice began to break with fear.

"Three, four hours. Look. Don't panic. Everything is going to be all right. We're not even sure what happened yet, right?"

"Right, but – "

"Wyatt, you'll make things worse if you don't calm down. Let's see, it's two o'clock now. I will be there no later than six, okay?"

"Okay. Hurry."

"I promise I will."

"I'm glad I have you, Lesley."

His words caught me off guard again. Wyatt hadn't said those exact words to me since we were married. He used to whisper them in my ear when he thought I was asleep. It was one of the things I loved and missed most about him. My heart fluttered again, new reasoning pumping my adrenaline.

"Wyatt, when you were picturing yourself in the woods, who were you walking with?"

"I was walking with you."

I almost dropped the phone.

"Why? Does it mean something? Should it have been Addie?"

I heard the panic in his voice again.

"No. It means nothing. It's a calming exercise. I was just curious."

"I think it worked, if that helps you. I feel much better now. I'll feel even better when you're here. What time did you say again?"

"I'll be there by six o'clock. I promise."

I hung up the phone and excused myself, telling my current patient that his session would have to end now but that it would be free. Happy at not having to pay, and sticking the *Sports Illustrated* in his coat as compensation for his time, he left. I called Jane in, giving her instructions and a list of patients to call and inform I would not be in the office for the next two days due to a personal emergency. Then I packed up my briefcase and left.

As I walked to my car the same excited feeling came over me again that affected me three weeks earlier. This time I sat with it, let it roll around me and go through my body like a mist. I didn't want to analyze it for fear it would go away. Instead I just let it be, and in doing so, I figured out what it was: it was the joy of finally being in control of Wyatt's life, Addie's life, and my own life all meshed together. This time life wasn't happening *to* me. *I* was deciding what actions would be taken in each individual's life and how to react and deal with those actions. *I* was finally in control. *I* was the counselor now. *I* was the guide of what was about to take place. And then there were Wyatt's answers to the test. I found them fascinating. His were similar to my own. *He* picked *me*. How interesting! And when faced with the body of water he chose Lake Michigan, and he swam across it, the same as me. *Could it actually mean something?* I tried to put the thoughts out of my mind, but I couldn't help but smile as I turned off the Red Arrow Highway and made my way back to my small, quiet hometown.

CHAPTER 4: HEAVY BAGGAGE

Saturday, May 25th, 1974

As Wyatt drove away, the sheriff's last words echoed in his head: "Addie needed help, Wyatt! She was crazy! That's the only explanation." He wondered if it was that easy. From what Wyatt knew of the subject, suicide was supposed to be complicated, not the simplistic act voiced in the sheriff's excuse. There were always reasons; reasons laced with more reasons buried beneath explanations that benefited no one except for a paid investigator. Reasons never soothe the grieving of a suicide victim. Reasons just poke at them, tear and rip away at what little is left of the bereaved. *Cause of Death: Suicide.* It would have been better to tell Wyatt that Addie had died from a heart attack while taking a midnight swim. That was a reason not needing anymore looking into. It was a cause without any choice, without any freewill. But crazy? No, that would have been too easy. There's limited freewill in that explanation, too. No. Wyatt knew enough about Addie to differentiate that she made a choice that night, and he spent most of his nights trying to push the knowledge of that out of his own mind.

So, that was their answer. The police had come up with nothing better than Addie was crazy and that was the reason she killed herself. Wyatt was a good man, as Sheriff Roberts said. There was no reason why Addie did what she did and Sheriff Roberts never understood why Wyatt seemed to believe he had something to do with her choice. It was all so easily accepted, by Sheriff Roberts and the residents of Point Caneissa, that Addie had been driven mad by the loss of her pregnancy. There seemed to be no other reason.

But Wyatt knew the reason behind the choice – no investigation needed. And so did Lesley.

Wyatt pulled into the driveway, got out and pushed the front seat forward. "Addie wasn't crazy," Wyatt shouted as he punched the back of his seat. He pulled his hand back quickly and cradled it, sucking in air as his body braced the stinging. "Maybe *I'm* crazy," he laughed, shaking his hand up and down in an attempt to whip out the pain. He flexed his fingers open and closed, then grabbed the first two bags and headed inside.

On his way back to the car, Wyatt suddenly remembered why he went in to town today. Sheriff Roberts's remark had seeped into Wyatt's fragile conscience more than he had expected. He'd thought too long about it. It was time to think about Prue. She would be here soon, anytime now, actually. *Everyone else seemed to be excited about Prue's visit,* Wyatt thought. *Maybe I should be too.* Perhaps things wouldn't be as bad as he expected.

After he put away the groceries, Wyatt sat down to his now cold, day-old, reheated cup of coffee and crossword puzzle and waited for his sister to arrive. It was quiet in the house. It was always quiet during the day. The night, however, was a different story. It was loud – the sounds of the woods echoing against the stillness and the sound of the water rushing onto shore, hitting the rocks, gravel, and sand. It was like the house was a giant canyon; every noise that reached the house resonated inside its walls. But it was a locked safe as well, hiding Wyatt's secrets from the world. He wondered if the secrets of the house, Persephone's house, would reveal themselves to Prue that night. Would they slip into her dreams and expose his guilt, his anguish? Or would they unveil for Prue the secret of *Addie's* anguish, the reason for *her* suffering? What about *his* suffering night after night?

*****

Wyatt couldn't sleep at night, the pictures in his dreams keeping him awake. He would work into the early morning, reading Addie's writings – her "suicide note" as Sheriff Roberts called it – and drawing out his nightmares of her; the movements, the sound, the detailed vision of watching her die, slowly sinking into the waves outside. Wyatt relied on the memory of his dreams. In his sleep the vision of that night was so clear, but when awake, when trying to remember what exactly happened that night, nothing but the darkness of the water and the faint reverberation of his own screams could be taken from his memory. And so Wyatt would draw until it all came back to him in a flowing canvas of images, signaling he had drifted off to sleep. Addie's incoherent writings would slip from his fingertips as he laid back, his head bobbing across the top of the padded chair as his body swiveled in the nursery, the desk light flickering in the dark of midnight.

I awoke, my heart racing as cold beads of sweat fell from the strands of hair hanging in front of my face. I jolted myself awake and now sat straight up, looking around the room, unable to speak. I pressed my hands firmly into the chair's arms as I looked at the walls in the nursery. The pale moonlight cast black shadows that moved quickly over the walls, around the desk, the crib, and then they stopped, hovering around the door. The shapes seem pasted to the wall as if unable to move from it. I feel as if the shadows are watching me, waiting for something. I am frozen. I can't gather the strength to move. The shadows begin to move faster around the room, circle after circle around me until they are above me, swirling frantically like a black whirlwind on a mid-west summer night. There is electricity in the air. Feelings of remorse, anguish, and panic surge through me. My body shakes. Suddenly, like a flash, the shadows seem to move through the door and down the hallway. I look to my right and there she is, hunched over, kneeling on the ground in her dark red satin nightgown, sobbing, her arms covering her face. I collect my balance and move toward her to hold her, comfort her. She looks at me with hate and disgust in her eyes. She runs to the door, following the shadows through the hallway, down the stairway and through the front door. All this time she's screaming, "Why don't you love me!", sobbing more and more the faster she runs. I run after her with tears in my eyes, which causes me to fall down the stairs, slowing me. I pick myself up and run through the front door. I slide down the bank onto the sand and follow her footsteps to the shore. Through the fog I can see her fighting the waves as she walks through them, her body getting shorter and shorter as she succeeds. "Addie!" I cry. I fall to my knees, the waves foaming around me and retracting into the night. I watch as her life drifts away in the receding waters...

The water. The sound of it hitting the rocks kept Wyatt up at night. Just another specific element forcing him to remember. Exhaustion was his only friend. Maybe that was Wyatt's problem. Exhaustion. He wasn't crazy. No. The secrets in the house played on his weakness. Sometimes, in the darkest hours of morning, Wyatt would see the vision of his wife, screaming and crying, running out to the beach. She was always faint, but he would follow her, always too far behind to catch her, always caught off guard by her sudden appearance. But then, at the edge of Lake Michigan, she would disappear. Wyatt would call to her, but nothing. And then the exhaustion. On these nights fatigue would set in and he would fall to the sand or the rocks and sleep, waking in the morning to find himself cold and wet. Wyatt was sure the cause of these supernatural occurrences was the house, the tales of its haunted past coming back to him from childhood ghost stories. It *had* to be the house. Persephone's house.

*****

Wyatt placed his head in his hands on the edge of the table.
"What am I going to do?"
A tear fell down his nose and dropped to the floor.

Murderer

The word slipped into Wyatt's ear canal, wrapped itself around his eardrum and echoed. The windows began to shake lightly. Wyatt jumped up, knocking his chair to the floor, and walked slowly over to the open kitchen window. He stuck his hand out. No wind. Not even a breeze.

"Why is this happening?"

Murderer

He started to panic.

"I have to get out of here."

Wyatt looked around the room, trying to decide what to take, plotting and planning his escape, but his thoughts were disturbed by a knock at the door.

"Wyatt, I'm here."

The door opened slightly and a suitcase was pushed in.

"Wyatt, I know you're here. I saw you're car in the driveway and I think it's very rude not to help your sister with her luggage."

Luggage?

Wyatt heard the thunk of another suitcase hitting the floor. He closed the window in the kitchen and walked to the front of the house.

"Wyatt, you're not being a good host…"

Down came another suitcase.

"I'm right here," Wyatt said shortly.

"Just in time to carry my make-up bag." Prue handed him a small cosmetics bag.

"Funny."

"Well, I did have to carry it all in myself," Prue sighed. "I don't know what I would have done if the door was locked, which, by the way, isn't safe to keep unlocked. Anybody could just walk in here."

"Anybody did."

"Ha, ha."

"Besides, what would they do once inside the house?" asked Wyatt. "Bake brownies? It's a small town, Prue."

"Oh, I don't know," Prue said slightly flustered. "It's just so remote out here. I never remembered it feeling so remote. Anything could happen to you and no one would know about it."

Wyatt could tell she was hinting of Addie.

"Prue, we grew up in this town. It's home. It's safe."

"I know. It just seems creepy now compared to the city. No neighbors, no noise, no one there to hear you scream if some psycho tries to kill you – "

Her voice trailed off. The words hung in the air and Prue now regretted saying them, fearing she may have insinuated something about Wyatt or Addie she didn't mean. Wyatt could tell she felt uncomfortable.

"Give me a break," responded Wyatt quickly, with somewhat of a chuckle. "It's quiet and peaceful here. That's why I came back, why we came back. Anyway, if something happened to me the whole town would know in a matter of minutes." Wyatt smiled and gave his sister a nudge. "That's how it's always worked around here." He knew all too well how true that statement was.

"I guess you're right."

Prue smiled and started picking up her luggage, suggesting with her body language that her brother do the same.

"Prue, what is all this? 'A couple days', that's what you said."

"Well, I decided to make a vacation of it," Prue answered, pretending to be able to carry only one of her suitcases. "It's been so long since I spent some real time at home. Why? Do you have something better to attend to?"

"Maybe."

Wyatt grabbed two suitcases and walked toward the stairs. She took his arm and stopped him before he started up to the guest room. He looked at her, puzzled.

"I hope that's true. I was in town earlier this morning. I didn't like what I heard. Wyatt, what's wrong?"

Wyatt turned and started walking up the stairs.

"Nothing is wrong," he asserted, gritting his teeth. "Why does everyone ask me that?"

"Perhaps you give them reason to," Prue answered in a matter-of-fact kind of way.

"You know," Wyatt started, "I actually thought that maybe you coming here was a good thing, that it would be fun. But as usual, you go snooping around in my life. We're not twelve anymore!" he shouted down at her. "I don't need your protection."

Wyatt stopped at the top of the stairs to turn and look at his sister.

"You can stay here, Prue, but stay out of things you know nothing about."

Wyatt walked down the hallway, threw Prue's suitcases in the guest room and then turned to walk back to his own room, locking himself in. Prue picked up her remaining suitcases, letting water gather in her eyes and slowly fall down her cheeks as she blinked to get a clear view of the steps leading to her room. Wyatt sat on the edge of the bed, listening to the muffled sniffles of his baby sister. He looked over at the nightstand, finding his favorite picture –

the one of him and Lesley, the first time they found each other at college – realizing it contained yet another woman he had caused significant heartache to.

"Maybe I am twelve," he whispered.

Wyatt sank back into his pillows and tried to remember if his life, at any time, had ever been simple.

CHAPTER 5: ETHICS

Wyatt

"Wyatt, I haven't seen you in a while."

I had walked across the lawn, avoiding paved pathways and sidestepping barren trees and ran into Professor Harrington, my academic advisor, in addition to being one of my political science and ethics professors. I had skipped his classes fifteen times this semester, including his ethics class, which I skipped this afternoon.

I had been on my way home. I needed to make sure I got there before Lesley. I was expecting a letter from the School of the Art Institute of Chicago; a letter she knew nothing about. I hated keeping secrets from Lesley, but I felt like this could be my one exception.

Lesley and I had been married two months when I started tossing around the idea of leaving Notre Dame and pursuing a degree in art. The only problem was I kept this thought to myself, living my life with Lesley as though I was content with the direction our lives were going – graduation in May, summer internship in Indianapolis, graduate school in New York at Columbia University in the fall – but every classroom I went into was just a reminder that I was pursuing something I didn't love and didn't believe in. Lesley didn't know it, but I had been skipping most of my classes this last year, failing tests and missing essays in order to practice a growing craft: drawing.

I always had a talent for sketching scenes and caricatures. I spent my spare time drawing freelance cartoons for different area newspapers, including political cartoons for *The Daily Spectator*, a campus paper. That was the one instance where my major came in handy. Unfortunately I found drawing political cartoons more invigorating than studying for my political science tests – as should most people. So I missed my classes to walk; to walk past classrooms full of wanderers and dreamers, the hopefuls and hopeless, overachievers and the misguided. I walked parallel to walls, following corridors, passing open doors, closed doors, until I came to the exit doors. I never saw the exit doors as exit doors, but rather as entrance doors. You never really exit anything. An exit is just an entrance to something else, and if you trace yourself back, you'd be entering your exit again. Therefore, you're never exiting, but always entering. So I took my leaving Notre Dame not as an exit from politics and law, but as an entrance to drawing in Chicago. Unfortunately, the Academic Probation Board at the University of Notre Dame didn't feel the same way.

I stopped by campus mail on my way home and found only one letter, which was addressed to me. I needed to read only the first line to know what it was: *We regret to inform you....* I was being expelled. I folded the paper and put it back into the envelope, moving it between my fingers as if I were slicing bread. I came to the front of the building and stopped when I reached the doors. *Entering or exiting.* I smiled as I pushed the door open and entered the campus green.

Two months prior to this day, back in September during the second week of classes, I had sent in my application and portfolio for consideration to the art school at the Art Institute of Chicago. I knew it was in the middle of the '63/'64 school year, but I hoped they would make an exception, letting me at least get a jumpstart for summer classes. I called the school every week to see if my application was under review and when I could be expecting a letter. At my last phone call they told me a month, which was thirty days ago. I received one letter of good news today. I hoped for another.

But now Professor Harrington was standing in my path, causing me to stop three feet in front of him. This was the man responsible for my academic probation, and now, expulsion. He was waiting for me to give a response.

"I know," I said finally, not having any real excuse for him. "I've had a lot to do lately. A lot of important things." I began shuffling my expulsion letter through my fingers again. The professor was becoming a real buzz kill.

"More important things than school? I find that hard to believe."

The professor paused for a moment. I hoped my lack of response would signal to him that I didn't want to talk and that I was in a hurry. Instead, Professor Harrington set his briefcase down in the fresh dusting of snow that had covered the campus overnight and leaned against the tree we were under. I hadn't even noticed the tree. I wondered how I missed seeing it. But against Professor Harrington, it was hard to see anything else. Physically the professor was an interesting man; soft face, kind eyes, and a beard that would rival Santa Claus. He would remind you of your grandfather with the warmness of his face, until he would stand, and there in front of you towered a six-foot, seven-inch well-built man in a tweed suit with suede patches over the elbows. It was striking, the difference in perception once this giant of a man stood in front of you. You almost couldn't help but tell the truth to him, which Professor Harrington knew, and he used this to his advantage.

I tried desperately to focus on getting home, but I couldn't help but see how the professor blended into the tree, his tweed and patch suit mixing with the color of the bark and the professor's head just reaching the bottom of the first branch. If Treebeard were real, I imagined him as Professor Harrington, only taller, if that were possible. I smiled and laughed under my breath at the thought.

"Do you find my questions funny, Mr. Trilmon?" The professor stood straight now, accentuating his authority.

"No," I replied. "I was just thinking about something else. Something that just kind of popped into my mind. I take your questions very seriously, Professor Harrington."

"I'm glad. Perhaps you would like to answer them." The professor shifted, agitated.

"I would really rather not, sir. Nothing against you, but it's personal."

"I see. Keeping secrets, are you? What can't you tell your advisor?"

I pulled the letter from my fingers.

"That's just it. You're not my advisor anymore. It's not necessary for you to counsel me." I felt relief. I handed the letter to him.

"I wondered when you would receive this." He examined the letter as he spoke. "I recommended you for expulsion two weeks ago. You may find that harsh, but I felt it was a necessity. I will tell you truly, that if you had come to me with whatever problem you are facing currently, I may have hesitated in my decision." The professor handed the letter back to me. "Secrets are an awful thing to keep to oneself."

"I don't see it that way."

"I'm sorry you don't. You've just had a tremendous door of opportunity close on you."

I crumpled the letter in my fist and let it drop to the ground.

"All I see are open doors, sir, but thank you for your opinion." I started walking away.

"I hope the newly Mrs. Trilmon sees these open doors as well."

I stopped, frozen in my tracks.

Lesley. Why did he have to bring up Lesley?

*****

It was about a month in to the second semester of my freshman year when I saw a girl walking down the center of the quad in a hurry. It always caught me a little off guard to see a girl on campus, but this girl seemed to draw more attention to herself than usual. Her black, curly hair was tied up into a ponytail and she wasn't wearing a hat, even though it had snowed almost a foot the night before. Her high heels clicked against the pavement almost in the rhythm of a heartbeat, her unbuttoned coat flowing open to the left or the right with each step she took, revealing a slender-fitting navy skirt with a tight, low-scooped white sweater. She wore a black choker around her neck with some kind of pendant attached in the middle. It made her neck look long and sleek, and very attractive.

She continued walking down the quad, picking up her pace a little so that she skipped almost every-other step, but then her left heel slipped and she fell to the ground awkwardly, her books splayed out in front of her. I looked around at the other guys near enough to help her. We all had the same idea, so I ran.

I was the first to reach her.

"Are you okay?" I asked as I helped her to her feet. I didn't even look at her face before I bent down to retrieve some of her books. Suddenly there was a second pair of hands grabbing frantically at the remaining books. Luckily they were gloved in white, and very feminine. I took the books out of her hands and looked into her face for the first time.

"Lesley?" I gasped.

"Wyatt! What a surprise," she laughed.

"What are you doing here?" I asked as I helped her to her feet again.

"I have a literature course here with Professor Sherwood."

"Old Sherwood Forest, eh?"

"Yeah," she laughed again. "I hate the way he reads Shakespeare. So melodramatic and loud."

"I know. I had him last semester. I thought I was going to go into hysterics every time I pulled out Hamlet and Macbeth. He's really something."

"Yeah."

I just stared at her as we talked. I couldn't believe how much Lesley had changed from the time I'd last seen her, which was probably just after graduation, to this moment. It hadn't even been a year and somehow, this girl that I had known my entire life, had grown up down the street from, this girl that trudged through the woods and skipped rocks by the lake with me, had turned into a beautiful woman. Gorgeous even. Her dark blue eyes met mine and I noticed for the first time they had little gold specs swimming in the ocean of blue. Lesley was truly breathtaking.

"Wyatt?" Lesley looked at me for a moment, forming a V between her eyebrows. I realized I was staring at her. "Are you okay?" she asked.

"Oh, no, I'm fine. Just a little shocked to see you. What are you doing here?"

"I told you. I'm taking a literature class."

"No, I mean, what are you doing *here*? In Indiana? I thought you were going to go to Wellesley or Barnard or some place like that out east. Why are you here?"

She smiled at me. My heart began to beat a little faster.

"I was going to go to Barnard, only because there would be an easier possibility of me getting into Columbia for my graduate work." Graduate work. She had already started planning her post-graduate studies and we weren't even out of our freshman year. It was so *Lesley*. "But I got a better scholarship to Saint Mary's at the last minute. I guess someone dropped out and I was next on the list, or something like that." She smiled and laughed as she finished her explanation. "Small world, I guess."

"I guess," I agreed. But not small enough.

Tension began to set in as I realized that Lesley had known where I was going to college. I told her I'd gotten accepted to Notre Dame the fall of our senior year of high school. She knew I was here and didn't come to find me, not even to say hello. Maybe she didn't want to find me. That was a whole other feeling of anguish I didn't want to go through. But I had to know, so I asked.

"Why haven't you come by?" I asked. "If nothing else, just to at least let me know you were here."

Lesley looked down to the ground and began twisting her fingers into knots.

"I didn't know if you would even want to see me," she answered quietly. I didn't know why, but all of a sudden her body language shifted, and she was no longer the confident, graceful woman I had seen walking down the quad. She was a nervous girl, in a very womanly body.

"Of course I want to see you. Why would you think I wouldn't?"

"Because you didn't say good-bye before you left." Lesley paused. She said the words so faint and sweetly. I knew I must have hurt her, and I hated myself for it. "When I came back after summer break," she continued, still quiet and reserved, "I came looking for you but you were gone. Your mother said you had left early so you could get settled in. No good-bye. Not even a note."

"I'm sorry," I said slowly, touching her arm and holding it gently. "Really...sorry. I guess I just...well, I just...I didn't know how to say good-bye to you. I mean, you were like my best friend. How do you say good-bye to your best friend? I couldn't."

We stood there for a moment, silent. Lesley looked away from me, searching the quad for nothing, giving her eyes an excuse to look somewhere other than me. I didn't know what else to say. I had never been this flustered around her before, or attracted to her. Lesley had always been pretty, and I'll admit, when other boys from our high school would take her out on a date, I would feel little pangs of jealousy. But I never thought of dating her myself. Right now, I couldn't help but want to do more with her than just date.

"I guess I can understand that," she said suddenly. "It was really hard leaving home, all our friends, family. I can see why you did what you did."

"It's not an excuse, Lesley."

"I didn't ask you to give me one." She looked back at me again, smiling, all her confidence seemingly restored. "It doesn't matter now, anyway. We're here, we've seen each other. No getting around it."

"I guess not," I laughed.

"Say cheese!"

A bright light flashed and I heard a click, then the wrenching of a dial winding forward.

"Ah, Jimmy! What the hell are you doing?" I let go of Lesley's arm so I would have a free hand to punch Jimmy Leherty, but he ducked quickly and took a few steps back.

"Too slow!" he chuckled. He locked his eyes on Lesley. "Who's your friend?"

"Lesley Lindaugh, this is James Leherty."

"Jimmy," he offered, holding out his hand. Lesley took it politely, shaking it twice and then dropping it.

"Jimmy's one of my fraternity brothers," I explained. "And he has this annoying habit of interrupting perfectly good conversations with his presence."

Lesley giggled.

"Oh, was I interrupting something? I'm so sorry, miss." He took Lesley's hand and kissed it. "But I don't think I'd get involved with this guy. A bit of a ladies' man, this one." He continued to hold her hand. "Now me, on the other hand – "

"Okay, that's enough," I asserted, pushing Jimmy's hand away from Lesley's. "What's with the camera, anyway?" I wanted to change the subject quickly. I had to get the mental image of Jimmy and Lesley together out of my head.

"It's for my photography class…which starts in ten minutes," Jimmy said looking down at his watch. He put the camera in his bag. "If I'm late, I'll lose my time slot for the dark room."

"You better go, then," Lesley interjected.

"Yeah." Jimmy paused before he turned and started jogging to class. He turned again about twenty feet away from us and jogged backwards awkwardly. "Hey, Lesley. You coming to the Valentine's Dance? If you don't have anyone to take you, I could – "

"Go to class, Jimmy!" I yelled through my teeth.

"Okay, okay!" Jimmy turned again and disappeared down another walkway.

"What was he talking about?" Lesley asked.

"Oh, it's just a dance they're having at the dance hall downtown."

"The Palace?"

"Yeah. Have you been there?"

"A couple times," she answered. I wondered with who, picturing her with Jimmy and getting angry again. "Some of my girlfriends took me there." Girlfriends. I was relieved.

"There's a dance there a week from Friday. A Valentine's Day dance. Some of the guys are taking their girlfriends." I stopped to take a breath, gaining courage. "Would you like to go? I mean, if you're not doing anything else."

"Sure," she said with a coy smile. "Might be fun."

"Okay." I didn't know what else to say. I was elated that this beautiful creature was going to be on my arm for everyone to see. It was hard holding all that excitement in.

"Shoot!" Lesley said suddenly. "I've got to get back to campus. I have another class in an hour and I have to stop by my dorm room and pick up a paper."

"I'll walk you back," I said quickly, not wanting our time together to end quite yet.

"You don't have to do that. I don't want you to miss any classes on my account."

"I don't have another class for two hours. I'll walk you back and still have plenty of time to make my next class."

"Okay."

Lesley smiled at me as I held out my arm for her to take. She wrapped her hand around my elbow and we began walking down the rest of the quad, turning onto another walkway headed toward Saint Mary's.

"I'm really glad you're here, Lesley," I said as we turned a corner.

"I'm glad, too." She rested her head on my shoulder as we walked. My body tingled with excitement.

"So, are you still going for a psychology major?"

"Yep. You still poly-sci?"

"I guess. My dad kind of pushed me into it, hoping I'll join his firm someday, or something like that. That's all he talked about last summer. Plus I don't really know what else to do."

"But isn't that what college is for? Trying to find out who you are and what you want to do?"

"If you say so, mom."

She jabbed me lightly in the ribs, causing us both to laugh as we continued walking towards Saint Mary's, slowing a little as if to make the walk last a little longer.

"So, how was your summer?" I asked, trying to find something we could talk about.

"It was...educational."

I looked down at Lesley to find a sly smile creeping over her face.

"Did you meet any boys?" I asked, jealousy beginning to race through my body.

"Just one."

A week and a half went by and it was finally Friday. Boys were not allowed on Saint Mary's campus after seven and the dance didn't start until eight, so I parked my car outside the gate and waited for Lesley. I leaned against the hood of the car and smoked a cigarette. Normally I didn't smoke, but I felt so flustered around Lesley that I needed something to calm me down, something to take up the time while I waited for this beautiful woman I was suddenly, involuntarily attracted to. I didn't know why, but I had to be with her. I was drawn to her. And the idea of someone else walking her home from class, taking her to a movie, or kissing her good-night made my stomach go sour.

I flicked the cigarette to the ground, letting it role to my shoe before I put it out. When I looked up, Lesley was walking toward the entrance gate. I couldn't tell exactly what her dress looked like under her coat, but her dark hair was twisted up, the curls lying softly on the top of her head. She was wearing another choker; rhinestones this time. Again they made her neck look slender and dainty. I instantly wanted to kiss it, but I didn't.

Lesley walked through the gate and to the car, stopping in front of me.

"You look beautiful."

"You haven't even seen my dress."

"I don't need to see your dress."

She blushed.

"Shall we?" I held out my hand and motioned to the car.

"Yes, we shall," she said, smiling as she took my hand. I opened the door, helped her into my car, then quickly ran around the front to the driver's side and headed to the dance.

I walked Lesley to the coatroom, removing her coat and checking it in for her. When I returned, I stopped, stunned when I saw her waiting by the stairs. It was her dress. It fit her so well. The dark blue silk hung at her feet, but as it ascended up her body, it became lighter in color and clung closer to her figure until all shades faded to white and the garment wrapped tightly around her breasts, one shoulder exposed while the other held the thin silk dress in place. It took my breath away, and made me even more nervous.

I began my walk over to her, increasing my speed as I noticed more and more of the eyes that were looking at her were other men's. When I finally reached her, I paused, taking in everything about her: the brightness in her eyes, the glow of her cheeks, the curve of her neck and how it followed the other curves of her body.

"Shall we?" Lesley asked as she placed her hand around my arm. I couldn't say anything. I cupped my hand over hers and led her up the stairs. When we reached the top she placed her head on my shoulder for a moment, then lifted it as we walked inside the ballroom.

I don't remember what songs they played that night or who we saw or talked to. I do, however, remember dancing with Lesley, placing my hand in the small of her back and pulling her closer into me. My hand slid gently over her back and I remember being able to feel the warmth of her body through the silk. She laid her head against my shoulder and I could feel her breath quicken against my neck. I pulled her even closer, resting my hand on her bare shoulder. I bent down and kissed her neck, the scent of white lilac filling my nostrils. I held her there, swaying her with the music, afraid to let her go. I wanted everything about her.

I was falling in love with her.

*****

I hope the newly Mrs. Trilmon sees these open doors as well. The professor's words hung in the air, echoing in my ears. I had no answer for him.

"It would be a shame for you to walk through these open doors without her," Professor Harrington continued. "But I'm sure there are no secrets between you." The professor picked up his briefcase, reached for the wadded paper, and stepped forward. "Good-day, Mr. Trilmon." Professor Harrington put the crumpled mass in my hand. "I hope you are successful at whatever avenue you are about to pursue."

With that, Professor Harrington made his way to his office for afternoon student appointments. I turned and watched him walk away. It was odd that, as he moved farther away, the professor grew taller. I imagined branches and leaves growing out of his head into the sky, swaying back and forth with his Treebeard swagger until the friction of movement and sunlight caught the lingering dead leaves of the top branches on fire, the flames slowly moving to the roots of the mighty leader. The picture made me smile. If I got accepted into the Art Institute today, I would draw this image in celebration. I threw my expulsion paper into the air, hoping the wind would catch it and somehow morph it into the flaming fantasy in my head.

Looking down at my watch I realized I had forty minutes to get home before Lesley, so I ran the rest of the way. For the first fifty feet I sprinted, gradually slowing down until I hit the front door, literally. Dropping my book bag, I fell beside it, my back against the door to brace me as I searched for my keys. Finding the ring I looked for the smallest key, the mailbox key, and inserted it into the tiny locked box. Inside, roughly shoved and bent, was a thick beige envelope. I ripped it open and focused on the first page: *Congratulations! You have been accepted....*

"Hey." Lesley called from the living room as she flopped her books down on the coffee table. She began to search for me. "You home?"

"Yeah, I'm in here."

My voice echoed from the dining room. Lesley walked in a circle until she found me sitting at the dining room table. She stood over me, kissed my head, then looked down at what I was drawing. It looked like a tree with a Santa Claus face that had caught fire.

"What are you drawing?" she asked.

"Oh, nothing. It's just something I thought of today. I think it's funny." I had just drawn the last flame.

"I think it's a little disturbing." Lesley picked up the paper and looked at it closer. "It kind of looks like Professor Harrington."

"You think so?" I took the paper from her, trying to hide my pleased expression. "I don't see it."

I rolled it into a cylinder and used it like a cattle prod to shuffle her into the living room. I saw the clock for the first time since I started drawing. It was four o'clock.

"I thought you'd be home two hours ago. I was getting worried."

"I was at the library studying. I have midterms next week and so do you." Lesley took the drawing from me again, looking at it nonchalantly before tossing it onto the coffee table next to the pile of her books. "Don't you think you should be studying instead of spending your afternoons doodling? What did you do all day, since you obviously didn't go to class?"

"I have the greatest surprise for you."

"Really?"

"Yes. We're going out for dinner tonight, anywhere you want to go."

"Why?"

"Because I have a surprise for you."

"But what is it?" She asked suspiciously.

"If I tell you, it won't be a surprise. Now go get dressed. Wear something nice."

"As opposed to what? All my raunchy clothes?"

"Yeah. I mean no. You always look nice."

"Nice save Wyatt."

Lesley walked to our bedroom and started to change.

We decided on *Angelo's*, a little Italian restaurant on the edge of campus. I brought the packet from Chicago. I kept going over in my head what I was going to say to Lesley. Every once in a while Professor Harrington's voice would invade my thoughts; *It would be a shame for you to walk through these open doors without her.* But every time that happened, I shoved a bread stick in my mouth, so that by the time our main course came, I had eaten seven and a half bread sticks. I sat and stared at the chicken marsala, my stomach bloated with expanding carbohydrates. I felt now was the time to tell Lesley my surprise.

"Here." I handed Lesley the packet from the Art Institute.

"What's this?"

"It's my surprise."

Lesley opened it up and started reading.

"Wyatt, what is this? I don't understand."

"I got accepted into the art school at the Art Institute of Chicago. Isn't that great?"

"Why did you even apply? Did you just want to see if you'd get in?"

"No." I hesitated. "I want to go there. I want to get a degree in art. It's what I've decided I want to do with my life. I want to draw. I want to be an artist."

"You're kidding, right?" she snickered.

"I'm being serious. This isn't a joke."

"It better be a joke." Lesley slightly backed herself away from the table. "Wyatt, you're a political science major, not some starving artist with dreams and aspirations of unobtainable greatness."

"Maybe I am."

"No you're not!"

People looked up from their plates to see what the problem was at table three. The owner sent a waiter over to see if he could be of some assistance.

"Is everything all right?" the waiter asked.

"Everything is fine," responded Lesley. "Thank you."

The waiter stayed for a moment, then went back to the bussing station to answer curious wait-staff inquiries.

"I can't believe you would do this in public," she whispered angrily. Lesley leaned over the table and slammed the packet of papers onto my chicken marsala. "Have a wonderful dinner."

Lesley grabbed her purse and quickly walked out of the building.

I looked around and noticed almost everyone in the restaurant was looking at me. Some turned their heads when I looked at them, but others just stared. I pulled all the money out of my wallet and left it on the table. I didn't have time for change. I picked up the acceptance papers, wiped them off best I could, and left *Angelo's* in pursuit of Lesley. Outside the restaurant I could see Lesley about 100 feet away. I started to jog.

The coldness of early winter began to squeeze my lungs with every small leap I took. It was painful. I began to slow down and call my wife's name.

"Lesley!"

"I don't want to talk to you, Wyatt."

When I finally reached her, I grabbed her arm and pulled her to a stop.

"Please. Let's talk." I was trying to catch my breath, the breadsticks and the moistness of the air weighing heavy in my stomach.

"Why talk about it now? You didn't talk to me before you applied to that ridiculous school."

"It's not ridiculous," I snapped. "You know, I thought you'd be happy for me."

"Happy for you? What about us? I want to be happy for us. Did you ever stop to think about us?"

"What about us? Where is *our* life going? Please tell me, because from where I'm standing, my life is not heading anywhere I want to be."

"Wyatt, how can you say that?" I could hear the tears forming in her voice. "You have such a bright future. You're going to be an amazing political advisor or lawyer or senator. Wyatt, you could be whatever you want." It was like she was grasping at air, pulling, reaching for the sense of truth and normalcy she believed she had been living. "You have that internship with Representative Meyers this summer. It's going to open up so many opportunities for you. Plus you're graduating in the top of our class."

"No, I'm not," I whispered.

"What?"

"I'm not graduating at the top of our class. I'm not graduating. I got kicked out today."

"I don't understand?"

"I got expelled from school today, all right! I was put on academic probation last semester, before we got married, and because my grades haven't gone up, they expelled me."

"I can't believe this."

Lesley walked to the side of the road and sat on the curb, brushing away the slush that had formed throughout the day. I followed her, sitting next to her and crossing my arms on my knees. I wanted to look dejected. I thought it might help.

"What's going on with you?" Lesley said finally. "None of this is like you at all. You're always so straightforward and dependable. I just don't understand."

"I don't know that I do either."

I laid back against the sidewalk and looked up into the November sky. I watched as Lesley swiveled her body over me, as if more intent on hearing what I was saying. I wondered if she was really listening or going through remedies in her head to fix everything she perceived I had screwed up. Lesley was always calculating, always planning out things in her head. She never wanted anything in life to come as a surprise. It was the one thing about her I found annoying. As straightforward and dependable as I was, I also had a want for the unexpected. Not all the time, but occasionally I enjoyed the slight thrill of getting lost while driving through the woods, making plans with friends at the very last minute, or dreaming what my life could be if I had chosen a different path. It was this latter one that I sought pleasure from lately. There were too many "what ifs" in my life right now and I couldn't stand the thought of making the wrong decision. Politics and law, I decided, was something I was willing to throw away. Lesley, however, was not. She wasn't a "what if". No matter what I'd pictured, Lesley was in every scenario. She was the reason, the only reason, I hadn't thought of leaving Notre Dame sooner.

"I guess I'm not happy," I said finally.

"Are you not happy with me?"

Lesley looked panicked. I could tell a whole new train of thought had entered her mind. Her eyes began to tear. I grabbed her hand, pulled her down to my chest and kissed her head.

"It's not you." I sat up, still holding her head to my chest, and brushed the hair away from her face. "I love you. It could never be you."

"Then why all of a sudden are you changing everything? Everything was perfect."

"Everything was *not* perfect." I pulled her away from me and looked into her face. "This school, this life we planned out for me is not what I want to do. Lesley, I'll never be happy in politics, or law, or anything here. It's just not satisfying enough for me. It's not enough."

"And *drawing* is?"

"It's not just drawing. But, yes, if that's all I ever did the rest of my life was draw, I think I'd be very happy."

"I don't believe that."

"No, you don't *want* to believe it, but it's true."

"I can't believe I'm having this conversation. My husband wants to quit *Notre Dame* and a promising, stable career in law or politics to pursue drawing. That's insane."

"To you, maybe, but to me it makes perfect sense. Besides, when has any career in law or politics been stable?" I paused, hoping for a smile, but nothing came. "Please, all I'm asking is for you to have a little faith in me."

"No, you're asking for me to have *a lot* of faith in you, and frankly, I'm not sure I do."

"What?"

"Baby, I know you can draw, okay, but changing our whole lives so you can pursue what was only a hobby until today is not a stable decision."

"So, you don't believe in me? You don't think I'm good enough?"

"That's not what I'm saying. I know you're good, but – "

"If you loved me, you'd let me do this."

Anger flashed in her eyes.

"And if *you* loved *me*, you'd understand what you're asking me to do! Do you even realize that I'm going to be the first woman in my family to graduate from college? To go to school because I wanted to, not just so I could find a husband who'd take care of me? I'm just not that girl, Wyatt." She paused, trying to get a grasp on her words. "You're asking me to give up everything I've worked for. You're asking me to start over! I can't do that."

"We're twenty-two! We can do whatever we want! We have our whole lives ahead of us. Don't you remember that first day we saw each other on campus? I was unsure about what I was even doing here and you said that college was about finding out who we are and what we want to do. I finally know what that is." She looked away from me and said nothing. "But that's not the point," I continued, not knowing if I was making progress or fueling a fire. "I'm not asking you to start over. Why can't this be something we do together? Just something along the journey…something we experience together? Why does it have to be just you or just me?"

"Because you made it about 'just you' when you applied to that school!" Lesley pushed herself away from me and quickly stood up. "Please, Wyatt. Just think about what you're doing." She began to cry.

I stood up and grabbed my wife and held her. I felt terrible. I hated seeing her cry. The worst thing in the world is a woman crying. If a woman was crying, it meant I couldn't protect her from whatever made her cry in the first place. I hated that. And now, feeling Lesley's tears begin to soak the front of my dress shirt and her body shake against mine, I wondered how I could combat myself.

"Please don't cry." I held her tighter. I kissed the top of her head and wiped the tears away from her face.

"Why are you doing this?" she sobbed.

"I don't know." I shifted her body and pulled her with me as I made our way back to the restaurant and the car. "Let's just go home."

When we arrived home we flopped on the couch facing opposite directions, still quiet from the fight. I threw my admissions packet on the coffee table. Lesley stared at the small stack of papers which threatened her happiness.

"I don't want you to go," she said softly. "I don't want you to leave me."

"I'm not going to leave you."

"You did before."

I could hear the breaking tears in her voice. I felt cruel, like a villain who had left the damsel alone on the train tracks. I had abandoned Lesley once because of my selfishness, not wanting to see the pain in her face when I told her I was leaving; not wanting to face the pain of my new life without her. I just wanted to touch her now, to feel the warmth of her skin under my fingers and know that she was mine. I slid over to her and put my arms around her waist, then kissed the side of her neck.

"I'm not going to leave you. I love you," I whispered in her ear. I could feel the rhythm of her heart pulse faster. "I love you." I kissed the side of her neck again and she leaned her head forward, letting me follow the curve of the back of her neck. "I love you," I whispered again.

I lifted her to the floor and placed her body on the overgrown shag carpeting. I repeated "I love you" as I removed pieces of her clothing, kissing the parts of her body now naked and responsive to my touch. My breath on her skin caused goose bumps, small ripples that warmed when my fingers and hands went over them.

I can't leave you.

I kissed her lips.

"Don't ever leave me," she gasped.

"I won't ever leave you."

I made love to her believing what I said was true.

I held Lesley as she slept next to me on the living room floor. We enfolded ourselves with blankets, staying close to one another, almost afraid to let go. I listened to the pattern of her breathing, slow and steady, almost inaudible. I laid there thinking, wondering what I was going to do, questioning what I truly wanted. Sometimes I felt I spent too much time thinking. Why couldn't I be spontaneous? It was a question I asked myself often. I turned my head and looked at the small stack of admission papers on the coffee table. *That would be spontaneous,* I thought. I stretched to reach the top letter, grabbing it with two fingers and bringing it closer to read. *Congratulations....* I turned back and looked at Lesley. The sunrise was starting to come through the living room window. I watched as the light slowly crept over Lesley's face. She shifted and turned so that she was on her back, the blankets partially exposing her naked body. I stared at her. She was beautiful. I placed my fingers at the base of her neck and ran them down the center of her body, feeling her breathe and move with the rhythms of her sleep.

I can't leave you.

I kissed her gently on the lips.

"Good morning," she said, eyes still closed.

"Good morning."

"You know, it tickles when you do that."

"When I do what?"

"When you do this."

Lesley took her fingers and slid them down the front of my body.

"I'm sorry," I said, kissing her cheek.

"No you're not."

"You're right, I'm not."

Lesley got up, tied a blanket around herself, and went into the kitchen.

"What are you doing?" I asked.

"I'm making you a celebratory breakfast."

"For what?"

"For deciding to stay."

"What?"

Lesley walked into the living room.

"For deciding to stay and finish out your degree here. I was so scared you were going to leave me and go to Chicago, until we got home." She kissed my forehead. "Last night was just wonderful. I know you'll never leave me now. Oh, I think the eggs are burning." Lesley jumped up and ran back into the kitchen. She continued her conversation from there. "Today you'll go back and talk to Professor Harrington, see if they can't get you back in. You might have to do some kissing-up. Tell them you had some jitters about graduation, or something like that, but now you've figured out what you want and you want to be re-admitted into the program. With summer school, I think you'll still be able to graduate on time."

Lesley walked into the living room holding a plate full of eggs, buttered toast and a glass of orange juice. She set them on the coffee table, then sat next to me. There were two forks, so she began eating.

"You know, I think that this little sidestep was good for us," she said, her mouth half full of scrambled eggs. "Don't you think so?"

"I don't know, I, um – "

"Oh, my gosh! I'm going to be late for my seven-thirty." Lesley jumped up and ran to our bedroom. "I love you, Wyatt!"

I heard the bathroom door slam and the shower start. I sat there looking at the plate of eggs and toast. I didn't know if I wanted to eat them. I thought if I took a bite, that would mean I had caved in, I gave up on my dream. But if they just sat there, undisturbed, I would still have a chance at what I wanted. I debated until I heard the shower stop and Lesley come out of the bathroom. I picked up the plate and threw the eggs and toast in the garbage, grabbing a bowl and some cereal, and sitting at the kitchen table. I still had the acceptance letter. I placed it in front of me as I ate my raisin bran. Lesley came down to kiss me goodbye.

"You didn't like the eggs?"

"No, I ate them," I lied. "I was still hungry."

"What's this?" She picked up the letter. "You don't need this anymore."

"I thought I might keep it as a reminder."

"A reminder of what? A fight that almost broke us up? I don't think so. Better to leave things in the past." Lesley took the letter and ripped it in halves. "Having this would only make you wonder about it and you don't need to wonder about it anymore. You've made your decision to stay." She opened the lid to the wastebasket and tossed the pieces in. "I was thinking that maybe I could go with you today to Professor Harrington's. Sometime in-between my classes. Maybe I could help."

"Maybe. I don't know."

"Oh, I gotta go. We'll meet for lunch in the commons, okay?"

Lesley slammed the front door before I could answer.

It was hard to grasp what just happened. I went over to the wastebasket and fished out the pieces of my letter. As I sat at the table piecing it back together I envisioned my life painted over with all the goals and wants of Lesley's life, the outlines of my dreams barely visible from the surface. It would always be this way, I felt; me caving in every time Lesley shed a tear in disbelief or selfishness. I cupped the pieces of torn paper in my hands and laid them on the stack of admissions papers. Lesley would always have to have a plan. She was strong-willed, something I always found attractive about her. Maybe it was because I had had no direction for my life. It was easy to let her steer. I had never wanted anything more than Lesley, until now. Now I was faced with a decision. And I made my choice before I could think about it.

I went to our bedroom and began taking clothes out of the closet and drawers. I left hangers and dirty laundry on the floor. I turned over wedding pictures and dance pictures and Christmases spent with family together. I went to the bathroom and opened all the drawers and cabinets, finding that only my toothbrush was mine. I brought the small pile of my belongings into the living room. In the front pocket of my suitcase I put the acceptance letter and admission papers. I looked around the apartment one last time, gaining the courage to leave, until I saw a picture on the end table. It was the picture of Lesley and me that Jimmy had taken of us the first day we saw each other on campus. I walked over and picked it up. I loved that picture. We weren't looking at the camera, just at each other, smiling; a private moment caught on film. When looking back on our relationship it was that day I knew there was something about her I wanted. That day had changed my life.

And so would this day.

Politics, law...and Lesley. I walked back to my suitcase, put the picture in the front pocket with my acceptance letter, and then left the house, walking to the bus station, buying a one-way ticket to Chicago.

I knew when Lesley arrived home from her afternoon classes, slightly concerned I had not met her for lunch in the commons, I would be wandering the streets of Chicago, my thoughts getting lost in squares of mortar and glass as I came closer to my dream with every row of skyscrapers passed. I hoped the image of her face would fade among the towering buildings as well. I soon learned the impossibility of that ever happening.

CHAPTER 6: LOSING GRACE

Lesley

Wyatt left me November 22, 1963.

Classes were canceled after one o'clock and as the other girls ran to their dorm rooms or to the rec room to listen to the radio or watch the television, I ran home to Wyatt, only he wasn't there.

I turned the TV on, slightly distracted that Wyatt wasn't home. *Maybe he went to see Professor Harrington,* I wondered. It was possible that he wanted to take care of his re-admittance himself, perhaps slightly embarrassed by his recent behavior. If that were the case, though, he would have been back by now, surely. Office hours would have been canceled along with the classes. An hour went by and Wyatt was nowhere in sight.

I walked around the living room, the kitchen, the dining room, pausing every once in a while to look at the television, trying to ground myself in what was going on in the world. But I couldn't. I was distracted. Hour after hour went by and no Wyatt. Not even a phone call to tell me that he was at a friend's or stuck on campus or that he was alone somewhere, needing time to himself.

Five o'clock hit and I decided to lie down. My day had started early and was preceded by the roughest, most emotionally exhausting night of my young adult life. I was tired and I thought perhaps I could make time go by faster with sleep. Waking up to Wyatt coming home would be the most wonderful thing, so I walked to our bedroom and stood at the end of our bed, removing my plaid wool skirt and navy sweater, kicking them to the side of the clothes hamper. I sat on the edge of our bed, debating on whether or not to take off my slip, when I noticed half of the drawers in the dresser where sitting open. I got up and walked over to them. They were empty. I looked around the room and saw the closet door open. I ran to it and found only my clothes were hanging in it. I fell to the floor, backing myself into the corner of the closet. One of Wyatt's dirty sweatshirts was lying on the floor. I picked it up and cradled it, burying my face deep into the scent of Wyatt's body, the fabric absorbing my tears. I prayed that this piece of clothing, this remnant left on the floor, wouldn't be the last of his presence in my life.

When Wyatt didn't come home that night I knew he had left me. One week later I received a letter from Chicago, no return address. Just a simple note telling me he had made it there all right.

Lesley,

I'm in Chicago, but you probably already guessed that. I'm okay. I've told my parents where I am, so you don't need to worry about telling them. I told them not to mention anything to your parents. I thought I'd give you time to do that on your own. Chicago is a lot bigger than I expected, but I'm doing okay. I wanted you to know that. I hope you're doing okay. I know you will be. You always are.

I'm so sorry.

He couldn't even sign his name.

Two months later I received divorce papers, still no address, no hint of his whereabouts in the windy city. Nothing written on the envelope but our address…my address. I knew he didn't want me to find him.

The morning after Wyatt left, I woke up with an incessant want to go after him. Chicago wasn't far, a two, maybe three-hour drive. But if I went, where would I go? I didn't know where he was, and the more I thought about it, the more it made me angry. Where did he think he was going? Where was he going to stay? Who was going to pay for it? *WHAT THE HELL DOES HE THINK HE'S DOING?*

That was the big mystery. I didn't know what happened. I didn't know if it was something I said or did that made him change his mind but it gnawed at me and I hated that I couldn't figure it out. Over and over again I played those last two days in my mind, analyzing everything Wyatt had said and my response to him – my body language, the tone of my voice, the inflection I used, the actual words coming out of my mouth and whether or not he could have taken what I said a different way than what I meant. I examined every minute detail, mouthing the words as our fight ran through my head. I even watched my face in the mirror as I re-enacted certain parts of the fight, seeing if my face had deceived me in some way, making Wyatt think I didn't love him.

But Wyatt had chosen me, didn't he? He made love to me. He said he'd never leave me. He said he loved me. I believed him. What made Wyatt change his mind?

I spent that first week at home, mostly in bed, waiting for Wyatt to come to his senses and walk through the front door, a bouquet of roses in tow. When I received his first letter, I began to lose hope that he loved me and would come back. Each day pricked at my heart more, tearing pieces of him away from it, until the morning I received the packet of divorce papers, freshly printed and neatly signed by Wyatt's father. That morning I wondered if he had ever loved me at all. *Was it all meaningless?*

I followed Wyatt to the University of Notre Dame. I wasn't stalking him, as my friends' teasing would suggest, but I just felt I needed to go, to be with him. I was accepted into Barnard, Radcliffe, Wellesley, and Saint Mary's. I'd only applied to Saint Mary's because Wyatt had told me he'd gotten into Notre Dame. I didn't even really want to go there. I wanted to go to Barnard and then Columbia. That was my plan. It had all been arranged. But everything changed when Wyatt left for school before school even started – before summer had even ended. I came back from our family vacation home in Mackinaw City to find that Wyatt was gone. I couldn't believe it. He had just left with no warning, no goodbye. We'd spent our whole life together and he didn't even leave a note or call me. I should have realized then that he would always leave me, but I didn't.

I'd spent my whole summer trying to forget about Wyatt, trying to grow up. I knew that Wyatt didn't love me. Hell, he didn't even have a crush on me. But I so wanted him to love me. Sure, I dated other guys in high school, but that was only because I knew Wyatt didn't like me that way and "a girl's got to keep her options open", as my mother always said. So I went away that summer determined to spread my wings fully, knowing that come the fall I would be heading out east, heading away from my home, my friends, my family, my Wyatt. And I did.

I met a boy. A very cute boy, actually, and I focused all my attention on him. And it worked. I think I kinda, sorta fell in love with him. And he taught me…a lot. Enough to know that when I left for college, I would be all right without Wyatt. So I went back home completely ready to say goodbye to Wyatt, only he wasn't there. That was a crushing pain I wasn't ready for. So I changed my itinerary and followed him, sacrificing the first part of my college plan so my heart could go trailing after something it wasn't sure it could even have.

When I got to school, I realized I didn't know if I even wanted to see Wyatt. Obviously he didn't want to see me. If he had, he would have waited until I returned home from summer vacation. And I began to realize how pathetic I was, chasing after someone who didn't love me. All I could think about was Debbie Reynolds falling helplessly in love with Leslie Nielsen in *Tammy and the Bachelor*. Poor stupid, pathetic Tammy, pining after a man who didn't love her – *Tammy! Tammy! Tammy's in love* – or at least he didn't know he was in love with her. Maybe that was the same case here. Maybe Wyatt didn't know he was in love with me! But that was a different kind of sad and pathetic idea all on its own. Besides, crazy, wonderful stories like were only real in movies.

I decided a week after I arrived at Saint Mary's that it was ridiculous that I was there. I wasn't going to hunt down Wyatt. I wasn't even going to try. I was going to finish out my freshman year and then transfer to Barnard where I was supposed to be. I didn't need Wyatt to be happy. I had a plan, after all, and I didn't exactly account for Wyatt in that plan. And I was okay with that. I truly was beginning to believe I didn't want him, so confident in that belief that I walked to and from the Notre Dame campus twice a week, not caring if he saw me or never saw me. My life was on track again. Everything was going perfectly, until I slipped.

The look on Wyatt's face was priceless as he helped me up from the ground that early February afternoon. He looked like he had seen a ghost. Wyatt looked at me differently, too. Something changed in his eyes as we stood there and talked. It was a look I recognized. Not in Wyatt's eyes, of course, but in other's I had been to the movies or out to dinner with. Wyatt thought I was pretty and he liked me. This was my chance.

I did everything I could to keep Wyatt attracted to me. I only wore colors that brought out the features of my face and accentuated the curves of my body. I tried to wear my hair up as much as possible so that my neck was exposed – a part of my anatomy he frequently liked to touch. I wore a white lilac perfume so that it would remind him of summers at home, a place we were both connected to. But most of all I let him talk. I would sit and listen to him talk about his day or his friends or a memory from our childhood. Soon our conversations became easy and natural, and we talked about anything and everything. Our hopes and dreams, our future plans, our fears. And then one day Wyatt showed up at my dorm, unexpected.

*****

"Hey, Lesley!"

The pounding on my door interrupted my reading.

"Hey, Lesley! You in there?"

I could tell it was Sarah-Marie Moore.

"What do you want, Sarah-Marie," I barked as I opened the door.

"Some guy's downstairs asking for you. Sister Catherine won't let him in," Sarah-Marie laughed.

"Who is it?" I asked, trying to figure out what guy would want to come see me, no warning at all.

"I don't know. Some guy. I think I've seen you walking with him back from Notre Dame."

"Is it Wyatt?" Butterflies started fluttering around in my stomach.

"I don't know. Who's Wyatt?" She knew very well who Wyatt was. Wyatt and I had doubled with Sarah-Marie and her boyfriend, and we'd been their alibi more than once, the both of them always sneaking back on campus after curfew.

"You know, Sarah-Marie, you're a real pain in my ass."

"Right back at ya," she laughed as she turned and sauntered down the hall. It made me want to tell Sister Catherine that Sarah-Marie was one of those naughty, lost souls the church was always talking about.

I walked downstairs to find Sister Catherine guarding the door.

"There's a boy out there asking for you, Miss Lindaugh," said Sister Catherine before I even reached the last step. "I don't have to remind you that it's fifteen minutes before curfew."

"No, sister," I responded.

"Good. I'll be waiting right here."

"Yes, sister."

Sister Catherine opened the door, gave Wyatt a disapproving look, and let me pass. Wyatt stood at the doorway looking nervous, hands twisted behind his back, swaying.

"What are you doing here?" I asked, listening as Sister Catherine closed the door, careful not to shut it all the way.

"I don't know," he answered, still nervous but happy to see me. "I just had to see you. Would you like to take a walk?"

"It'll have to be a short walk," I said, motioning to where Sister Catherine was hiding. "I'm being watched," I smiled.

"Oh, right. I forgot about curfew. We could just stay here. It doesn't really matter, I guess." Wyatt started to relax a little, shifting his hands to his pockets. "Just as long as you're here with me." He smiled.

"So, what do you want to talk about?"

"I don't know." He answered.

"What do you want to do? We only have fourteen minutes and counting."

"I don't know," he answered again.

"Wyatt, why'd you come over here if you didn't have anything to say and nothing to do?"

"I don't know," he answered again, only this time he removed his hands from his pockets and placed them on my hips. "I just wanted to see you. I wanted to be near you." He bent down and gently kissed my lips. "I didn't know I had to have a reason."

"You don't," I said, my heart starting to beat faster. I could feel the flush rushing to my cheeks.

"Good." He bent down and kissed my lips again, staying longer this time, his hands forced away from my hips so they could touch my face. One fell from my cheek, tracing the lines of my neck.

"Miss Lindaugh," Sister Catherine called calmly. "I don't think that's very becoming behavior to be showcasing on campus. Do you?"

I pulled away from Wyatt, a slight smile on my face.

"No, Sister Catherine."

"And don't you think it's about time to come in, with it being so close to curfew and all?"

"Yes, Sister Catherine."

"Tell your friend goodnight."

Without hesitation Wyatt pulled me into him, his hand at the back of my neck, his other arm wrapped around my waist, kissing me harder this time, more passionately.

"Goodnight," he whispered, his forehead leaning against mine, his lips finally letting go.

"Goodnight," I said breathless. He took my hand as I started to walk away, letting his arm stretch as the distance between us grew, his fingers sliding against mine until we were no longer touching. I looked back at him before I reached Sister Catherine. Wyatt was standing in the same spot, smiling slyly, happy with this evening's accomplishment. I was smiling too, and I was sure Sister Catherine could see the flush on my cheeks as I walked inside the lighted hallway, Sister Catherine pulling the door closed behind me.

"I'm going to keep my eye on that one," said Sister Catherine, locking the door then tucking the ring of keys under her habit. She crossed her arms. "I have a feeling he's going to be trouble."

"I agree," I said as I bounced up the stairs, smiling and relishing the lingering tingly sensation in my lips.

*****

Wyatt showed up that night with no explanation other than he just wanted to be near me. That's when I knew he loved me. But now things were different. I had spent my whole life following Wyatt – from childhood until now – and he left me. There wasn't any path I could follow now; no trail of bread crumbs to find that would navigate me back to save him from himself. He didn't want to be found. He didn't want to be saved. It was over.

Where did this all go wrong?

It didn't matter anymore what went wrong. I grew tired of asking myself that question. The answer was always the same: I didn't know. I didn't want to blame Wyatt and I didn't want to blame myself. So that left no one. No one was to blame. I stared at the divorce papers in front of me. *Divorce. What does this mean? Separation forever? A new life? A new life without Wyatt.*

I jumped up from the table, ran to the bathroom and threw myself over the toilet, heaving stomach acid into the water. I had barely eaten anything in days, weeks maybe, but the compulsion to vomit was too great to ignore. I sat there for fifteen minutes, praying for the pain to end. When it did, I leaned against the wall and laid my head back. I couldn't figure out why I was sick. Did I eat something bad? I wasn't overexerting myself. What was I doing that made me sick? Then I remembered the divorce papers. That had to be it. They sat on the table looming at me. They taunted me, knowing I would never sign them. "See what you know," I said as I picked myself up off the bathroom floor.

I walked over to the table and looked at the papers. Each page was marked with a yellow arrow where I needed to sign. The lines above my name were unsigned by Wyatt. I wondered if his father would do Wyatt the courtesy of marking his lines with arrows also. Over and over I read them, for two hours since the mailman dropped them off that morning. The words were a blur to me now. I couldn't even remember what the agreements said. I didn't care. If Wyatt wanted a new life, so did I. I turned the pages, searching for yellow arrows, and signed next to each one. I signed them out of spite. On my last signature, I smiled.

"So much for getting sick over *you*."

I put the papers in a return envelope and sent them back to Point Caneissa, confident my heartache and sudden nausea would subside.

I was wrong.

I went three weeks before seeing a doctor. My nausea would hit me at all times of the day: breakfast, lunch, the middle of a night class; it didn't matter. It was as if my body was waging war on itself for something it wasn't responsible for. Nervous and scared I sat waiting in exam room five, going through the symptoms of my illness, trying to remember my anatomy terms.

"Well, Lesley, I think we've solved the big mystery for you."

Dr. Manning walked in the room and sat down in front of me, breaking me from the reverie of my thoughts.

"It's quite an easy explanation, not as bad as I believe you imagined. Actually, I'm surprised you didn't figure it out yourself."

I sat silently, growing angry at his insinuation of my incompetence. If I'd known what was making me sick, I wouldn't have come or I would have at least told him my diagnosis when I got there, to better speed up the prescription process. His chiding me was not accomplishing anything. If nothing else, it was just making me queasier.

"Dr. Manning, if I wanted to be scolded, I would have called my mother, and if I knew what was wrong with me, I would have told you when I got here. So please, just tell me what's wrong with me before I throw-up all over your shoes."

Dr. Manning rolled his chair back a bit, wrapping his feet around the back of its legs.

"Lesley, when was your last menstrual period?"

"I don't know. I've been under a lot of stress lately and I haven't been eating very much. I haven't even thought about it. Why?"

"Well, my dear, it seems as though you're pregnant. The blood test will confirm it, but I'm pretty confident with my diagnosis. You have morning sickness. That's why you've been vomiting."

"But I'm not always sick in the morning. I get sick all times of the day, so I can't be pregnant." I was almost pleading with him.

"Morning sickness is a bad term. It can hit you at any time, not just the morning. Some women feel sick all day long. Some women don't get sick at all. It's different for everyone."

"But I can't be pregnant."

"When was the last time you had sexual intercourse?"

I knew exactly. The night before Wyatt left. The night before my whole world shattered. The night I felt more loved by him than any other moment of my life. The night Wyatt decided to leave me.

"Maybe two and a half, three months. I'm not sure."

"Well, that's how far along I would guess you are. I'd say more like two-and-a-half months. But like I said, we're still waiting on your blood test to confirm it. We should know later today, tomorrow at the latest." Dr. Manning could see that I was panicking. "Lesley, look. I know you're scared. I know this is a lot to take in all at once, but it isn't the end of the world. You're healthy. So far there is nothing to worry about. I'm sure everything will be fine. And you're not going through this alone. You need to tell your husband soon. I know it can be scary, but I'm sure he'll be very supportive."

"I don't have a husband."

Dr. Manning looked puzzled.

"You're file says you're married."

"He left me two months ago. I don't know where he is. I'm all alone."

I laid back on the exam table and covered my eyes, my fingers trying to grasp at tears I didn't want Dr. Manning to see. I wondered if Dr. Manning felt any remorse now, seeing how I was all alone and he treated me as if I hadn't a thought in my head. What did he know about my life? Nothing. He read my file and made assumptions that weren't true. A know-it-all doctor who saw too many pregnant college girls to care about any of them anymore than he had to. He knew nothing.

I raised myself back up and wiped the wetness away from my face. This was just another man who didn't care about me. Why let him make me upset? I wasn't incompetent. I was bright, intelligent, and capable of handling anything. I repeated the words in my mind as I spoke.

"Thank you for your time, Dr. Manning. I don't think I will be needing your services anymore."

"Mrs. Trilmon, I'm sorry if I – "

"I don't need your sympathy, and quite frankly, I don't want it." I began putting my clothes back on, shedding the cotton gown first and standing naked in front of him while searching for my underwear. "I will be seeing my doctor back home from now on. Don't bother calling me with the blood test results. I want a second opinion." I turned around to look for my purse.

"Lesley, I don't think – "

"That's precisely it, Dr. Manning! You don't think! I may be just some college kid to you who made a mistake, but you're the one who made the mistake. You know nothing about me and you presume too much. I hope you don't treat all your patients this way. You'll be a very poor man if you do." I grabbed my file sitting on the table next to him. "Goodbye Dr. Manning."

I walked out of Dr. Manning's office holding my file close to my chest. The nurses stared as I walked past. No one tried to stop me. Dr. Manning still sat paralyzed in exam room five. No one knew what to do. When I got in my car I screamed, letting out all my rage and anxiety, then I started laughing. I turned on the car and looked in the rearview mirror at myself, smiling. It was the first time in almost three months that I felt like myself again.

I didn't go to my family doctor in Point Caneissa like I challenged. Instead, I went to another doctor off-campus who confirmed Dr. Manning's diagnosis. Feeling the weight of my solitude, I called my mother and asked her to come visit, explaining I had news I wanted to tell her in person, praying the outcome wouldn't be as bad as I knew it could be.

"I hope nothing is wrong, Lesley-Ann. You'd tell me if there was something wrong, wouldn't you?"

"Yes, mother. I don't really want to talk about it over the phone. Just please come this weekend. If you can come down sooner, I think I'd prefer that. But whenever is fine."

"Lesley, you're scaring me. What's wrong?"

"Nothing's wrong. There's nothing to be scared about. I'm fine. I just want to see you."

"I'll trust that you're telling me the truth." My mother paused, seemingly contemplating what the problem could be. Then she asked the question I was dreading. "How's Wyatt? Is everything okay with him? How are his classes going?"

I hadn't told my parents Wyatt left. I hadn't told my parents he wanted a divorce. Frankly, I was shocked word hadn't gotten around town yet about the whole ordeal, but it gave me hope that perhaps Wyatt's leaving wasn't as awful as I believed it to be. If his family was being discreet about it, maybe he was unsure of his decision. After all, he hadn't signed the divorce papers when I received them. Maybe he was coming back. Maybe he'd changed his mind.

"Lesley, are you there?"

Maybe I was kidding myself.

"Yeah, I'm here."

"I thought maybe I lost you."

"No, I'm here."

"So how's Wyatt? You haven't said a word about him since you called."

"That's one thing I need to talk to you about. But not on the phone. I've got to go. I'll see you this weekend, okay mom?"

"Okay, but this is all very – "

"Love you. Bye."

I hung up the phone before she could say anything else.

My mother showed up on Thursday, waiting outside our apartment…my apartment door until I arrived from my afternoon classes.

"Mother! I didn't expect you until tomorrow or Saturday. What are you doing here?"

"You said to come as soon as I could. So here I am, half crazed out of my mind, waiting for someone to tell me what the hell is going on. Where's Wyatt? Why isn't he here? I didn't think he had classes on Thursdays."

"He doesn't. I mean, I don't know. Let's just go inside, alright?"

"Fine. But you better have some answers young lady. This better not be some kind of 'I miss mommy' game."

I opened the front door to the apartment, my mother barging in before me and dropping her suitcase on the living room floor.

"If you and Wyatt are having some little fight, I don't want to hear about it. I told you when you married him you were on your own, as far as that's concerned. I don't want to be one of those mother-in-laws who's always trying to solve their children's problems, always prying into their lives. You're twenty-two and I'm perfectly fine accepting you as a capable adult. There better be a legitimate problem here, Lesley, or

I – "

"Wyatt left me mother!"

I shouted the words as I slammed the front door. I couldn't take the non-directional scolding anymore. My mother was just talking to hear herself talk. She did that when she wasn't in control of a situation. It was a trait I tried desperately to hide in myself. I looked over at my mother and found her sitting on the couch, mouth slightly open, in shock. I walked over and sat beside her, taking her hand.

"Mom, are you okay?" I rubbed her hand as I spoke.

"I'm fine, I'm fine. It's just a little shocking, that's all. When did he leave?"

"About three months ago."

"Why didn't you tell me sooner?"

"I thought he would come back."

"And what makes you think he won't now?"

"I've already signed the divorce papers. It's over."

"You signed divorce papers without showing your father and me? How could you do that? What did they say? What were the terms and agreements? Did he leave you anything?" A look of horror flashed across my mother's face and she quickly changed her line of questioning. "But that doesn't even matter now. What about the church? You can't get a divorce. You have to get an annulment. Please tell me you got an annulment!"

"Mother, that's not the point."

"Like hell it isn't! Lesley, you have to be smart about this. I know you love him, but he left you. You deserve something for that!"

"It's not important. I don't care about that."

"I'll see to it that his parents hear from our lawyer."

"His father *is* your lawyer," I said, trying not to laugh.

"Well, we'll get a new lawyer. We're not going to lie down and play nice. He deceived you, deceived us."

"No he didn't! Besides, it doesn't matter. I already signed the papers. It's done and over with, and that's how I'd like it to stay."

"How can you say that? Where is he? I want to talk to Wyatt. Is he at a friend's? I want to see him now!"

"I don't know where he is."

"Well, what's his class schedule? We'll wait for him after class."

"He's not on campus. He's gone."

"Gone? Gone where?"

"Somewhere in Chicago."

"Chicago! What's he doing in Chicago?"

"He's going to school there. That's why he left."

"He left you to go to school in Chicago? That doesn't make any sense. What's in Chicago that he couldn't do here?"

"He's going to some art school. I guess he wants to draw or paint, I'm not sure."

My mother started laughing.

"You've got to be kidding me! This is ridiculous. Wyatt left you to go to art school? That just doesn't make any sense. None of this makes sense! Are you sure you're telling me everything? You didn't have a fight, or anything?"

"Of course we had a fight, but you're missing the point."

"Maybe it was something you said that made him leave."

"Why does it have to be my fault?" She was making me angry. My mother always made me feel as though everything was my fault. I hated that. "He chose to leave on his own. I didn't do anything. Wyatt didn't do anything. It's nobody's fault. Now please, can we get past this?"

"I'm just trying to understand what happened. None of this makes any sense to me."

"It doesn't matter if it makes sense. The fact is that Wyatt left me. That's all you need to know about it right now."

"I think I need to know a little more."

I felt I was going around in circles.

"Mother, you're missing the point. I didn't ask you down here to talk about Wyatt leaving. I have something to tell you. Something big."

"Bigger than your husband leaving you?" She said snidely.

"Yes!" I got up from the couch and started pacing the room. "For crying out loud mother, just shut up and let me talk for once."

"Lesley!"

"No! I just want you to sit there and listen. No comments, no remarks. Just listen. I'm not asking you to fix anything. I just want you to be supportive for once, okay? I just want you to be a mother!"

I could tell she was hurt. Seeing the tears well up in my mother's eyes made me feel ten again. I hated yelling at her, fighting with her. I'd become such a pro at it over the years, but I still felt sick after every fight with her. That was the kid in me who wanted nothing more than loving approval. That was something I feared I'd never grow out of. My mother's distress caused me to move forward, kneeling at her lap, taking both hands in mine.

"I'm not trying to be mean," I spoke softly, "I'm just scared."

"Why are you scared, sweetheart?"

"I've made a huge mistake, and there's nothing I can do about it. I can't change it. I didn't mean for it to happen, and now I don't know what to do."

"Just tell me what it is and I'll help you. I promise."

"Really?"

"Of course."

I laid my head down on my mother's lap and reached my arms around her legs, hugging them tightly. Feeling the stress of her daughter's embrace, my mother stroked my head and spoke to me calmly.

"Tell me what's wrong."

I took a deep breath and sighed.

"I'm pregnant."

"Oh Lesley!" She leaned down and kissed my head. "Everything will be all right. This isn't the worst thing in the world that could have happened."

"It is to me." I started to cry. "I don't know why this is happening. It's not fair."

"I know sweetie. Life isn't fair sometimes, but we have to keep going. We have to keep living and figuring out what is meant for us."

"Why was this meant for me? I didn't do anything to deserve this."

"I don't know. But you know what we have to do, right?"

"I know. I'm going to have to raise the baby on my own."

"What?"

By the tone of her voice, I knew I had picked the wrong answer.

"You don't want me to keep it?"

I pulled myself off my mother's lap to see more clearly the expression of her face. I wasn't sure what was about to happen, but whatever it was, I could feel another fight coming.

"Of course not. How can you think of keeping it? It'd be different if you had Wyatt, but you'd be a single mother. Everything you've worked hard for would be for nothing. Graduate school would be out of the picture because you'd have to get a job to support yourself and your child. How can you think of keeping it?"

"I don't know. I just thought I'd get through it somehow. I thought you and dad would help me."

She stood up abruptly, knocking me to the side of the couch. She started pacing the room franticly.

"Lesley-Ann Lindaugh, grow some sense! You can't keep this baby."

"How can you be so cruel?" I shouted.

"I'm not being cruel! I'm being practical!"

"I'm not doing it! I'm not having an abortion by some fly-by-night carnival doctor just so you can keep up appearances!"

"Who's asking you to?"

"Wait, what are you saying?" I asked. I was genuinely confused.

"I'm not asking you to get an abortion. I would never even consider such a thing. I'm not a monster." She paused, collecting herself. "There are other options. In fact, I know a really nice well-to-do couple in St. Joseph who've been trying to adopt for years. I'll give them a call when I get home. Let's just pray they say yes."

"Are you asking me to give my baby away? How can you do that? I can't give my baby to strangers."

"But they won't be strangers once you get to know them. Their names are Jim and Cheryl Lynn. He owns a few factories up north I think. They're really more acquaintances of your father's, but I've met them numerous times. The Lynns seem like really nice people."

"Mother stop. I can't do what you're asking me to."

"You certainly will. There is no other option."

"And if I don't?"

"You will."

"No I won't! This is barbaric. I won't give this baby up, no matter what you say!"

We paused for a moment, catching our breath and our thoughts. I looked at my mother, a woman who had given birth to three children, a woman who nurtured them and raised them practically by herself, and here she was, asking me, her own daughter, to give up the chance to do the same. Why? On some womanly level I had hoped she would sympathize with me, but I was getting no remorse. Did she truly have no feeling, no heart? Why was she doing this?

She didn't give me time to contemplate very long. Calm and collected, she began to cross-examine me again.

"Why are you so determined to keep this baby? There's nothing but heartache ahead of you if you do."

I took a deep breath before answering.

"Because it's the only piece of Wyatt I have left." I began to cry again. My mother knelt down, picked up my face and looked into my eyes.

"I know you love him. I know you want him to come back, but it doesn't look like he is. You said so yourself. Don't keep this baby just because of *him*. Don't let this man ruin your life. Don't let him ruin your baby's life."

I knew she was being genuine. She was right. What did I know about raising a baby?

"Okay," I whispered softly.

"Good."

It was now the end of March, almost four months since Wyatt left me. I was trying very hard to focus on my classes. I still wanted to graduate in May with the rest of my class. Plus I needed to keep my GPA above a 3.24 in order to remain admitted into Columbia. My current GPA was a 3.82, but if I failed all my classes this semester, my GPA would plunge to a 2.8. But that didn't matter. If I failed, I received no credit and I wouldn't have enough credit requirements to graduate. So I tried to focus, ignoring the increased activity in my abdomen, trying very hard to seem normal. I looked normal, thanks to my mother and her obsession with keeping up appearances. She forced me to wear a girdle, hoping the tight, unyielding garment would hold me in, making me look like I always had, except for maybe a pound or two heavier. I hated wearing it. It was painful and unnatural to push something inward that obviously needed to protrude out. But I wore it out of fear – fear the other girls would find out I was pregnant, fear the sisters would look down on me, fear I wouldn't be taken seriously as an intelligent woman who wanted a successful career in a man's field. But mostly I wore it because my mother had threatened that if I didn't, she would make me wear a corset, which meant she would have to come and live with me in order to lace it up every morning, and my mother living with me was a fear I didn't want to come true. So, I was good and focused, and come May, I graduated at the top of my class.

I tried to go home after graduation but my mother convinced me to stay with my grandmother in Holland until the baby was born. I knew it was because it would be harder to hide my condition in Point Caneissa. Everyone knew me. And everyone would talk. My mother didn't want anyone to wonder anything about me. It was bad enough that the whispers had already started in town about the dissolution of my marriage. My mother didn't need me home adding fodder to the fire. And even though Holland wasn't that far from Point Caneissa, no one really knew me there, so the fear of any secrets being revealed was minimal. I would be just another girl walking down the street or shopping at the store. I was anonymous.

Originally I had an internship in Indianapolis at one of the local hospitals, but thanks to my grandmother, the widow of a former hospital board member, I was able to get an internship in the psychiatric ward at Grandview Memorial Hospital. It also helped that my grandmother still volunteered her time there, and money. That was one of the things I admired most about my grandmother: she had all the money in the world, it seemed like sometimes, but she never flaunted it, forgoing extravagant vacations with friends to spend her time helping the sick and dying for no money at all. It amazed me that my mother shared the same genes. I wondered sometimes if my grandmother actually gave birth to my mother, they were so different, and I smiled at the thought of two baby girls switched at birth. But if that were true, then she wouldn't be my Gran, and I definitely wanted to be connected to her in some physical way.

It hurt not telling my grandmother what I was going through, how scared I was. But I was ordered to make sure my life went on as normal, and it did, except for my inward expanding abdomen. My "predicament" as my mother called it, was kept a secret from everyone, including my father. My mother made all the arrangements, from doctor's appointments to adoption papers. Everything was discreet. Once a decision was made, it wasn't talked about again. It was better that way. Days went by faster, all rushing toward that second week in August. It would be a quick move, but by September all this would be over and I would begin graduate school at Columbia University in New York. In September I would be able to breathe again – mostly because I would be out of this girdle.

It was hard keeping up this charade, walking slowly during the day at the hospital and taking small breaths because breathing normally was impossible under the restriction around my ribs, forcing the tiny body up and inward under my lungs. And I was always starving, my mother insisting that I eat like a normal girl my age and not some farm animal at a trough. My bites were painfully calculated at the breakfast and dinner table, and I wondered how my grandmother never noticed this change in me, but she never said anything and continued about her days as she always did.

During this short span of time in my life, night was my favorite time of day. It was the only time I got to relax, throwing the girdle to the floor and covering myself in a nice, roomy, white cotton nightgown. I could breathe normal and I could eat normal. After dinner I would always sneak leftovers up to my room and devour them right before I drifted off to sleep. I couldn't sleep when my stomach was angry at me so I tried to appease it, night after night bringing up leftover chicken or beef or mashed potatoes, throwing what I couldn't eat out the window for the cats to delight in. I was sure my grandmother noticed *this* behavior, asking where the leftovers were those first couple days I was there, but again she never said anything, letting the mystery of the missing food go after that first week. But she would figure it out soon enough.

It was June. I was seven months pregnant. I just finished the rest of the leftover ham we had had for dinner when my stomach turned and growled at me, again. *How can I still be hungry?* Lately it seemed like I needed more and more food to quiet my appetite. I didn't know what to do. I'd brought up everything that was leftover at dinner and it was all gone. My stomach growled again, then again, and again. It was almost painful, but I felt this compulsion to eat. I had to have something. I tried to think if there was something in the house I could just grab or if there was something I could fix myself that wouldn't make any noise in the process. There was nothing. But then I remembered seeing something in the fridge; something wonderful – a chocolate frosted chocolate cake.

I tried not to think about it. The cake was for a party for one of the nurses at the hospital tomorrow. My grandmother had spent half the afternoon making it. But I couldn't stop thinking about it. Gran made the best chocolate cakes I'd ever tasted, and her frosting was so creamy and thick. I had to have it!

Before I knew it I was downstairs in the kitchen, kneeling on the floor, eating the chocolate cake with my hands, the refrigerator door still open. It was perfect. My stomach quieted as I ate it, my body happy – no, elated – with the moist, chocolate confection and the fullness being achieved from it. Lost in my binge, I never heard my grandmother coming down the stairs or notice when she turned the corner into the kitchen.

"Lesley?"

My grandmother stood ten feet away from me, staring down at me on the floor, cake spread all around me.

"Gran? What are you doing down here?" I asked, my voice muffled by a mouth full of cake.

"I was about to ask you the same thing." Her face was in shock. "Lesley, honey, what are you doing?"

I looked down at the obliterated cake in front of me, smeared icing mixed with crumbs spread across the front of my nightgown and around the cake plate on the floor. I'd almost eaten the whole cake. I didn't know what to say or how to explain it.

"Gran, I saw the cake in the fridge earlier. I was hungry and...oh, Gran! I'm so sorry!" I started sobbing.

I couldn't control it any more. All those emotions rampant underneath my tightly confined body came raging out, inhibition left somewhere with the decimated cake. My grandmother rushed over, falling on her knees in front of me.

"Oh, Lesley. It's alright."

She leaned in to put her arms around me. I pushed away, terrified of her touching me. I didn't have anything on underneath my nightgown and I knew if she hugged me, she would feel the bump of my abdomen and the movement behind it. Gran pulled away and I could see the fear on my face reflected in her eyes.

"It's okay, Lesley," she spoke softly. "Sometimes," she paused, holding her hand about six inches away from my belly, moving it in a slight circle. "Sometimes we just *need* chocolate cake." She smiled, then laughed lightly. I leaned over and let my head fall in her lap.

"Gran, what am I going to do?" I whispered.

She leaned down and kissed my head, then took my hand and motioned for me to get up, helping me off the floor.

"We're going to get you cleaned up," she answered. She tried to lead me out of the kitchen but I was glued to my spot, the same fear creeping over my face again. Gran dropped my hand, then cupped my face gently, but quickly, and started walking away from me. "I'll go get you another night gown and leave it in the bathroom. You go take a shower and leave that one outside the door. I'll see if I can't get those stains out before your mother can see it. No reason she has to know." Her words trailed down the hallway softly and it sounded like she almost sang the last part. I was very glad to have my Gran, even if I had to have my mother to get her.

The next month went by smoothly, and again my grandmother said nothing to me about what happened in the kitchen or showed signs of wondering what the cause was of that particular incident. The only difference was that I noticed she now made enough food at dinner for three instead of two. Other than that, everything went on as it normally did, but not for long.

July 14th. My mother and I were just getting back from a routine doctor's appointment in the neighboring town when we heard the phone ringing inside the house.

"Do you have my keys?" I asked.

"No, I thought you had them."

"But you drove."

"*My* car. Why would I need your keys to drive my car?"

"I don't know, just look in your purse."

"You look in your purse."

"Fine."

We started searching the compartments of our handbags, the phone ringing, unanswered, and then silence.

"I can't believe this. I know I gave them to you, and now, I've missed the phone call."

"Please," my mother retorted. "No one's *that* important."

"Whatever," I sighed. "Wait, here they are!" I pulled the keys out of the side pocket of my skirt.

"Told you so."

"Don't gloat."

Pleased with herself, my mother took the keys and unlocked the door. I flopped myself on the couch as she walked into the kitchen.

"Would you like some water, dear?"

"Yes, please." Pulling my shirt up under my breasts, I began to wipe away the moisture collecting on my sweat-soaked girdle hiding my small, growing belly. "I hate July!"

"You'll hate August even more," she said, handing me a glass of ice water. I rolled the glass over my stomach.

"Yeah, yeah. I'm going to go change into a nightgown. I can't take the heat anymore."

My mother laughed as I walked up the stairs. I changed as quickly as I could, peeling the girdle off my sweat covered body. I took my shirt and tried to soak up all the perspiration, then placed the nightgown over my head, letting it fall over my frame. The cotton felt cool against my warm body. I headed downstairs again, hearing the phone ringing in the living room. I hit the last step and jogged to the table at the end of the couch, picking up the receiver just in time to hear my mother answer the phone in the kitchen.

"Hello?" I heard my mother's voice answer.

"Lesley?" My heart almost stopped beating.

"Who is this?" my mother asked.

"Lesley, it's Wyatt."

I didn't need him to tell me who it was. I recognized his clear, warm voice immediately. I opened my mouth to talk to him but I couldn't force anything out, not even a squeak.

"What do you want?" my mother said sharply. I hated that she was speaking to him this way, speaking to him at all, but I couldn't do anything. I was frozen in my spot, unable to pull the phone away from my ear.

"I know you're mad at me, Lesley. You have every right to be."

I started to panic. Wyatt thought he was talking to *me*. And my mother would never correct his assumption. She'd rather talk for me anyway, and there was nothing I could do about it. Couldn't he tell it wasn't me? I never wanted to admit how similar my mother's voice and mine sounded. But I never wanted to admit that I was similar to my mother in *any* way. If he could just realize it wasn't me talking.

"I know it's kind of out of the blue. Your dad said you were staying with your grandma." He paused. "I wanted to talk to you."

"So talk," answered my mother.

Wyatt sounded reserved, like he was holding something back. What, I didn't know. My heart beat faster as I waited for each word he said.

"I have something to tell you, and I don't know how to say it. Um…oh, God…uh…my parents are dead."

"Oh, no," my mother gasped.

"They were in a car accident in Saugatuck. They were on their way back from visiting me…trying to talk some sense into me." I could hear the tears in his voice. My mother said nothing. "The funeral is Saturday," he started again. "I'd really like to see you before then. I really need someone to talk to. I really need you, Lesley. I miss you. I know what I did was stupid, but it's not unforgivable, right? I haven't even signed the divorce papers. Please say it's not unforgivable." He paused again, waiting for an answer.

"No," my mother said softly.

"What?" Wyatt's voice was filled with shock.

"No," my mother whispered, almost inaudible.

"But Prue can't make it until Friday," he pleaded, "So I'm up here all alone until then. I hate being alone. I really miss you. I want to see you. I need to see you. I don't know what else to say. Please come. I'm falling apart without you."

"No," she said again. "I'm really sorry, Wyatt." She hung up the phone before he could say anything else.

I stood there in the living room, still frozen with the phone in my hand, listening to Wyatt begin to panic.

"Lesley? Lesley?" He started to cry. "Lesley?"

I desperately tried to say his name, focusing all my attention into forming the letters with my mouth, but nothing came out. My mother walked into the living room and saw me standing there, phone in hand. She pulled the phone out of my grip and placed it back on the cradle. I stood there a moment, tears gathering in my eyes.

"How could you do that?" I asked finally.

"I did what I needed to do," she answered, almost as if she was trying to convince herself. "It doesn't matter now. It's over and done with."

I turned and started walking toward the stairs to my bedroom.

"What are you doing?" she asked.

"I have to pack. I need to leave as soon as possible."

"Where do you think you're going?" She grabbed my arm.

"I'm going to see Wyatt. He needs me."

"I don't think so."

"Why not? He *needs* me." I pleaded.

"You think you can show up eight months *very* pregnant and everything will be all right? That everything will go back to normal?"

"Yes!"

"NO!" she countered. "You're living in a fantasy world if you think that boy will overlook this. He doesn't love you."

"He said he needs me!"

"He's in pain! He'll say anything!"

"That's not true," I argued. "I know he still loves me! I could hear it in his voice."

"He's a grieving child. Let him be. He needs time to deal with that first. He doesn't need the sudden responsibility of you showing up on his doorstep."

I knew she was trying to rationalize Wyatt's actions, but I wasn't listening. I didn't want to hear her. I couldn't. All I could hear was Wyatt saying my name.

"I don't care what you say!" I shouted. "I'm going."

"No you're not." She ran to the stairway to stop me. "Think about what you're doing. Just stop and think about it for one minute. You can't ask him to deal with this also. It's too much."

"Who are you to make that decision?"

"I'm your mother!" She grabbed my shoulders. "You listen to me and you listen good. Everything will continue as scheduled. You will not go to Point Caneissa, you will not go to the funeral, and you will not talk to that boy! Do you understand?"

I shook my head no as tears began to stream down my face.

"Lesley-Ann Lindaugh you open your eyes and look at me!"

She forced my chin up and I stared into her eyes. She wasn't angry. She was scared.

"Please," she started again, calmer. "Just think about what you're asking of him. His parents have just died, no warning, no goodbye. Think about that. He's alone and has been for the better part of a year. Of course he misses you. But this," she placed her hand on my stomach, "this is too much to ask of him. You can't ask him to be a father when he just lost his. You can't ask him to be responsible for someone else when he's barely able to be responsible for himself. You know I'm right about this."

I didn't want to admit she was right but I couldn't fight her logic. I was too overwhelmed to think of a way to get what I wanted, so I shook my head in agreement.

"Good. Now, I'll go back home and do a little damage control, say that you wanted to come but couldn't because it'd be too hard seeing him or something like that." She wiped some tears away from my cheek. "Everything's going to be fine. I know this is hard, really I do, but you have to believe I have your best interest in mind. Look, if he really loves you, he'll reach out to you again. Let him get past this period in his life, then see what happens."

"Sure."

She kissed my forehead.

"I'll get my bag and start on my way home. I'll call you later, alright?"

"Alright."

"Remember what I said, now."

"I know."

She ran upstairs, grabbed her bag, got in her car and headed home. I watched as my mother pulled away, then sat on the couch and stared at the phone.

Nine-thirty that night I got up enough courage to dial Wyatt's parents' house. My face was swollen and red from tears, and my voice had begun to become hoarse from sobbing. When Wyatt answered the phone, he heard only one forced, barely audible sentence: "Wyatt, I'm so sorry." And then a busy tone.

The day of the funeral I continued my rounds at the hospital like I normally would have, trying desperately not to think about Wyatt and his phone call. I'd spent the last three nights crying over it, but today was the hardest. Today was the day I knew he needed me most of all and I couldn't muster up the courage to get in my car and drive to Point Caneissa. What prevented me was the look I imagined on his face when he saw me. I didn't look that different than when he'd seen me last, the ever-tightening girdle doing its job excruciatingly brilliantly, but I knew Wyatt would notice. My breasts were larger and my hips were slightly wider. And if he didn't notice by just looking at me, he would definitely notice once he hugged me, placing his arms tightly around my waist only to feel my abdomen hardened and slightly bulging. And if the baby kicked, that would be it. His face would be full of shock and anger and fear.

I couldn't take it. I leaned against the wall across from the nurses' station. My thoughts had made me exhausted and a little dizzy. I stood there taking little breaths, trying to calm myself without drawing attention.

"Lesley, are you all right?" one of the nurses asked. I tried to see which nurse was speaking to me, but I couldn't make out her face. It was blurry.

"Why?" I asked, trying to focus.

"Because you're bleeding," she answered, slightly anxious.

"I am?"

I tried to look down at myself, but everything went black.

When I woke up, I was in a hospital room. I didn't know what was going on, but I felt different. Very different. I looked around the room. A nurse was checking tubes that were attached to my arms, fluid being pushed through them.

"The doctor will be in in just a minute," she said politely. And she was right. Dr. Stotch walked in just as she finished writing down the measurement of the liquid being pumped into my arm.

"Hello, Ms. Trilmon," said Dr. Stotch, his greeting a little cold.

"What's going on, Dr. Stotch? Where am I?"

"You're in the heart ward," he answered plainly.

"The heart ward?" I began to panic. "Is there something wrong with my heart?"

"No," he said stiffly. "But I couldn't very well put you in the maternity ward, now could I, seeing how you've hidden your pregnancy so well from all of us. Plus your grandmother never mentioned anything about it, so I assume she doesn't know either." I shook my head no. "I didn't think so," he answered. Then Dr. Stotch turned his body rigidly, looking down on me with anger in his eyes. "How could you do this, Lesley? How could you be this irresponsible, this careless with yourself? Malnourished, bound so tight you could barely breathe, blood pressure through the roof. You could have died!"

"I...my mother – "

"Oh, yes, I've talked to your mother," he said snidely. "I had a few words for her as well. She informed me of the adoption that is supposed to take place, if it ever does."

"What does that mean?" I asked, frightened by everything he said and how he said it.

"I had to deliver you, Lesley. By caesarian. I had no other choice. I couldn't just let you die from your own ill-conceived actions. I couldn't just let the baby – "

"The baby!" I shrieked. "Is the baby okay?" I wasn't sure if I wanted to know the true answer. Maybe he would lie to me to make me feel better. Doubtful.

"The baby, for now, is alive. She can't breathe on her own – "

"She?" I interrupted.

"Yes, she," he answered, the anger rising in his voice again. "She can't breathe on her own and we're monitoring her heart. We think she might have some kind of murmur. It's hard to get a good reading on her because she's so tiny."

"Tiny?"

"She's very small. She barely weighs three pounds. She's the smallest baby ever born alive at this hospital, no thanks to you."

She was alive. That was all that mattered. My baby was alive.

"You can stop berating me, Dr. Stotch. I think I've had enough for today, thank you." I was trying to hold back my tears.

"I don't think you fully understand what you've done, Ms. Trilmon."

It was his tone that set me off. I was tired of being judged. This man knew nothing about me.

"No, Dr. Stotch, I don't think you understand. I've put myself through my own personal hell these last eight months, knowing full well what I was doing and feeling every consequence to my actions. And for what? To almost die? To live only to give my baby away? But that's only *if* she lives! But I guess I'll never really know that either, will I? She's not even mine anymore!" I pushed myself up a little, away from the bed, trying to see Dr. Stotch on the same level as he was looking at me from. "Trust me Dr. Stotch when I say I would have rather died on that operating table than have to live with the knowledge and the pain of what I've done."

Dr. Stotch stepped back, not knowing how to respond to what I said. There was nothing he could say to make me feel worse than I had made myself feel. He went into doctor mode again.

"The baby is being transferred to the children's unit at Detroit Lutheran. It's the closest hospital with the ability to possibly help her survive. Mr. and Mrs. Lynn have been informed of the arrangement and are on their way."

"And my mother?" I asked, not really wanting to know if she was coming, just involuntarily wanting her there for some bizarre, sadistic, childish reason.

"She didn't say. I assume she's on her way, but I don't really know." Dr. Stotch turned to walk out of the room, then paused. "I did, however, tell your grandmother you were here. I had to. Word started to spread around the hospital and she was volunteering in pediatrics today. I told her you had an emergency appendectomy. It was the only logical way to explain the incision on your stomach. It's in the wrong place, but I doubt she'll know that." He traced his finger over the lower-right side of my abdomen where an appendectomy incision would have been. "And I told her you were in this ward because I had nowhere else to put you, which there is truth in. Probably the only truth in this whole situation." He turned again and walked to the door, not looking back as he spoke. "Would you like me to send in your grandmother?"

"Yes, please," I answered softly.

"Fine."

Dr. Stotch opened the door and left the room. I never saw him again.

I bent down awkwardly – pain surging through my abdomen, my body only allowing me to move and bend certain ways – and grabbed the extra blankets at the end of the bed, heaving them over my stomach. I didn't want my grandmother to touch me for fear she would suspect what I was positive she already knew. She walked in just as I placed the last cover over myself.

"Oh, let me help you," she offered as she started to rush toward me.

"No, I got it," I interrupted quickly. "I've got it, Gran."

She walked over and placed one hand on the side rail of my bed and brushed the hair away from my face with the other.

"How do you feel?" she asked.

"Different. Very different."

"I know exactly how you feel, sweetheart," she responded, placing her hand on my cheek.

"You've had an appendectomy?" I asked.

"No." Her eyes moved away from me, almost unable, it seemed, to look at me.

"Gran?"

"The smallest baby ever born in this hospital was born today," she announced, still not bringing her eyes to mine. "Did you know that?"

"No," I lied.

"I went to see her."

"You did?" Shock and surprise filled my voice.

"Yes I did. She's the tiniest thing I've ever seen, but very pretty…almost like you were when you were born." She paused, but I didn't say anything. "And there was the strangest thing about her eyes."

"What about them?" I was starting to panic. Was there something Dr. Stotch had left out? Was there something wrong with my baby?

"I just couldn't believe it," she began. "Most babies' eyes are blue, sometimes brown, but this little girl's eyes were green. The greenest, brightest green you could imagine." She stopped and looked at me. "I've only ever seen eyes like that once in my life."

She knew.

A tear rolled down my cheek. I tried to push the image of Wyatt's face out of my mind, but I couldn't, his unique, beautiful green eyes staring down at me, smiling. At least in this image he was happy. My heart began to break all over again, something I didn't even know it was capable of doing, convinced it had been completely shattered. My grandmother leaned over to look me in the face, her eyes gentle and understanding.

"Sometimes in life we don't get what we want."

She held a locket out in front of me. I took it and opened it. Inside there was a small picture of my grandmother, very young and very pregnant, standing next to a man I didn't recognize – a man who was holding her very affectionately around her bulging waist.

"Gran, who is this? What are you trying to tell me?"

"Just that I understand how cruel the world can be sometimes, how it feels to be left alone, your choices taken away from you." She took the locket back from me and closed it without looking inside. "I know what it feels like." She placed her hand on top of the mound of blankets over my stomach.

"And what does it feel like, Gran?" I asked as I placed my hands over hers, not wanting to push them away, only to hold them.

"Empty." A tear fell from her cheek and landed on my hand.

"No," I argued, trying to hold the welling tears in my own eyes. "I feel hollow. There is a distinct difference."

*****

Dear Mrs. Lynn,

My mother has informed me that you intend to name your daughter after me. I am truly honored, but I was hoping that I might convince you of an alternate name – one that would mean the world to me. I've been told that the baby has my husband's eyes, and he had his mother's eyes. She just recently passed away and it would mean a lot to me, to us, if you would consider naming your daughter Grace. That was my husband's mother's name. I would prefer this to my name, seeing how she was such a great lady and I've yet to live long enough to achieve great things. I know it's asking a lot, but please consider it...for me.

Lesley

Dear Lesley,

There is nothing that I wouldn't consider doing for you, my dear. You've given me the greatest gift one can give. Mr. Lynn and I have discussed it and are proud to announce the birth of our daughter, Grace Lesley-Ann Lynn.

Yours, forever grateful,
Cheryl Lynn

*****

And so, on July 18th, 1964, Grace Lesley-Ann Lynn was born.

September came and I walked around my new college campus trying to breathe again. It wasn't any easier than it had been the last nine months. I prayed, though, that it would get better.

The day Grace was born I half-expected Wyatt to show up in my room, smiling and endearing, never wavering from my side. He didn't. Still, I had hope that he would find me. After all, my mother had said if he loved me, he would find me again. But he never called, and September left as quickly as it arrived – with no word from Wyatt.

Then, a packet arrived; forwarded to my new address, full signatures at every arrow, finalized.

Wyatt never did call, he never wrote, and so I believed my mother was right. Wyatt didn't love me after all.

Addie

"Addie?"

I heard a knock at the door and a woman's voice calling my name. Wyatt had called Lesley.

I sat curled up in the rocking chair with a blanket surrounding my entire wet body. Everything was damp now – my hair, my clothes, the blanket – it had all dried to a dampness, the warm blanket soaking in the dripping water from my extremities to make everything even. There was no feeling, no hot or cold, just numbness now. I had sat like this for the last four hours, Wyatt never coming in to check on me or to try and remove my frigid clothes. I was sure he had been pacing downstairs, nervous, not knowing what to do. That's why he was avoiding me. He didn't know how to help me. I wondered if anyone did.

"Addie, can I come in?"

Lesley's voice pierced the silence in the room again. I didn't answer her. Not that I didn't want her to come in, I just didn't care whether or not she did.

"Addie?" Lesley said again as she slowly pushed the door open. "I have some dry clothes here, Addie. Would you like me to help you put them on?"

"No," I answered flatly.

"Why not?" She sounded surprised.

"I'm fine with what I have on."

"You're not cold?" she asked.

"No."

I heard Lesley step into the room further. I didn't look at her as she walked across the room, my body curled and facing the window above Wyatt's desk. Lesley walked in front of me, I was sure, so I could see her place the clothes on top of Wyatt's drawing table.

"Just in case you change your mind."

"I doubt I will."

I listened as Lesley walked back to the door, moving it closed but not shutting it all the way. I kept my eyes on the window as she walked back across the room, taking a spot along the opposite wall, leaning against it.

"How are you feeling?" she asked.

"Fine," I responded, my automatic response to everything these days. "A little tired, maybe."

"That's not what I meant."

"I know what you meant," I retorted. Lesley shifted her weight.

"Do you want to tell me what happened today?"

"Did something happen today?" I asked, a small smile creeping over my face.

"I'm glad to see your sense of humor is still intact," Lesley answered, annoyed. "You want to tell me why you tried to kill yourself today?" The smile left my face.

I wondered if it was that obvious, if my actions screamed suicidal. I thought, perhaps, it looked like an accident, like I'd gone for a short, curious walk on the ice and I slipped or it cracked. Not that I tried to commit suicide. I wasn't sure if I was that far gone yet. After all, I had changed my mind.

"I wasn't trying to kill myself," I said softly, wanting to believe the words as I said them.

"What were you trying to do?" asked Lesley.

"I don't know. I just wanted to walk."

"And you thought the ice shifts of Lake Michigan a good place to go walking?"

"As good as any other," I lied.

"I don't believe you."

"You don't have to," I responded. "I know what you're trying to do. Don't try to psycho-analyze me, Lesley," I said, still not looking at her. "You can't fix me."

"I don't want to fix you," she answered, her voice unwavering.

"Why not?" I asked, a little taken aback by her comment.

"I can't fix someone who doesn't want to be fixed." She paused. "Especially someone who seems to be relishing in her own depression."

I didn't respond. I didn't want to give anything away. Lesley already knew me too well. I didn't need her in my head any more than she already was.

"Did you change your mind when you got out there on the ice?" she asked. "Was it colder than you thought? Did it make you feel alive, all those tiny little freezing pins of water pricking your body relentlessly until you couldn't take it anymore and climbed out? Did it scare you?"

I said nothing.

"It doesn't really matter," she continued. "Killing yourself is hard business. You have to really want it. Not just entertain the idea, but focus on it, pushing out all emotion, all physical pain, until you feel nothing, until you're completely numb, no feeling."

"How do you know how I feel?" I snapped.

"I know exactly how you feel," she answered.

"Oh, no. Don't you dare. Don't you stand there and tell me you understand how I feel. How I feel empty insi – "

"You feel hollow," she interrupted. I whipped my head up to look at her, to see if she was playing some kind of game with me. Her eyes were dark and focused, free of any scheming or thought except for her own pain. "You feel as though someone has ripped the inside of you out, scraping everything clean until a hollow space appeared where once it was full. No one asked you. No one gave you a choice. They just hollowed you out." She paused. "Empty can be filled again. Hollow is hollow forever."

Grace. She was talking about Grace. Lesley knew exactly how I felt.

"I changed my mind," I said slowly, quietly, "when I reached the melting ice. I didn't think it would feel like that. I thought it would be easy." I paused, looking at Lesley intently. "Don't tell Wyatt."

"I won't if you won't."

I knew she wasn't talking about my secret.

"Does this feeling ever go away?" I asked.

"No."

CHAPTER 7: THE HOUSE

Saturday, May 25th, 1974

While waiting for Wyatt to end his tantrum upstairs, Prue walked around the first floor of the house trying to pinpoint the differences in its appearance since her childhood. It was rumored that the house was haunted or possessed, whichever version of the story you chose to believe in, and it made Prue feel uncomfortable every time she came to visit Wyatt there. And seeing how it was the scene of Addie's suicide, which couldn't have helped the tainted aura surrounding the house, it took Prue a year to come back, despite her guilt-ridden sisterly concerns.

When Prue was a child she always felt the house was filled with something supernatural. Urban legends and ghost stories trickled down through the town over the years and fell upon the ears of its children, the energy of folklore thriving on young minds, keeping it alive. The house was historic, confirmed as part of the Underground Railroad at the height of its use, so the stories that surrounded it were vivid and wild. It didn't help that for most of Prue's childhood the house was owned by Persephone, a woman who did psychic readings and hypnotism. Persephone's family had owned the house for at least four generations, and it was rumored that she was a practicing witch. When Persephone left her house for weekly errands into town there were always whispers and glares, words said behind cupped hands, and small children hiding behind their mothers in supermarket lines as Persephone paid for her vegetables and meat.

Prue was eight the first time she heard any of the stories about the house. Wyatt was having a campout in his tree fort and Prue wanted to see what he was doing, so she convinced her parents to go into town and buy the ingredients for smores because that's what the boys wanted, or so she had told them. When her parents' left, Prue made her way through the wheat field next to their house until she reached the willow tree that stood in the middle of her grandfather's fields, pausing and taking a deep breath before she climbed up the ladder her father had built as a child and peeked her head through the door.

"What do you want, peanut?" asked Wyatt, peeved.

"Mom and dad went into town and told me I had to stay up here with you until they come back."

"What? No way," said Bobby, Wyatt's best friend. "No little sisters allowed."

"But they said – "

"No," interrupted Tommy. "You just stay outside and keep the Boogeyman company." They all laughed.

"Tommy, that's not very funny," pouted Prue. Wyatt could hear tears forming in her voice.

"Okay, guys, that's enough. We can let her in until my parents get back." Wyatt moved over to make room. "Come here, Prue."

Prue sat next to Wyatt, held her legs and leaned against the side of the tree house.

"Fine," said Richie.

"But if she's gonna stay," added Bobby, "she has to sit through ghost stories."

"I'm not afraid of you or any ghost story you can tell!" Prue hated ghost stories, but she didn't want the boys to know. She would just suffer through the two or three days of nightmares. She wanted to stay.

Bobby began to tell the story.

"There's an urban legend about the old Wynter house in the old part of town, near the abandoned shipyard right on the lake. Have you heard it?"

"No," answered Prue.

"Good. You know how that house was a part of the Underground Railroad?"

"Yeah."

"Well, the story goes that the house is haunted."

"Haunted by what?" asked Prue.

"Evil spirits of the voodoo witchcraft the slaves brought with them."

"You're lying." Prue's voice trembled.

"Am not. See for yourself. At night, if you're real quiet you can sneak up to the house, and if you look in the basement windows you'll see words written in blood on the walls, glowing."

"You're a liar, Bobby!"

"Go see for yourself. Persephone's a witch and she talks to all those evil spirits."

"No, she isn't! You're making things up!"

"Okay, Bobby, that's enough," yelled Wyatt.

"Hey man, she's the one that wanted to stay. I was just telling a story."

"I don't believe you," cried Prue under her breath.

"Go look it up in the records. That house is cursed, I swear. Every fifteen years something bad happens in or around that house."

"I don't believe you, Bobby Williams! You just wait! I'm gonna tell my mama on you and she's gonna tell your mama and you're going to be in big trouble!"

Prue jumped over the boys and stumbled down the ladder just in time to see the headlights of her parents' car coming up the driveway. She could hear the boys laughing behind her. They made her feel like a stupid, silly little girl who believed anything and was scared of everything. She didn't want to believe the story, but what if Bobby was telling the truth?

The story couldn't be true. Prue knew that nothing bad ever happened in Point Caneissa. Bobby had to be lying. He was always like that, trying to scare Prue or make her believe unbelievable things so she would look foolish. But regardless of how much she wanted to believe the story wasn't true, Prue couldn't help but wonder, and the story stuck with her throughout her childhood, keeping her up late some nights, her eyes seeing shadows of strange forms that weren't there.

It wasn't long after this story was implanted into Prue's mind that her mother decided to stop smoking. Her cure was Persephone's hypnotism. On Tuesdays, Mrs. Trilmon would pick up Prue from ballet and on their way home, they would stop at Persephone's house for that week's hypnotism. And every week, Prue would sit in the car or, if the wind wasn't coming off the lake, she would sit on the bottom steps of the back porch and watch the waves of Lake Michigan hit against the weathered rocks and sinking sand. Her mind would wander during these hour-long sessions and Prue tried to deny her fear of the validity that the house was haunted, or that Persephone was really a witch, but her brain struggled to tell her imagination that the story couldn't be true. Determined to prove herself right either way, she periodically spent Saturdays at the public library researching old newspapers and town records. She didn't really look for anything in particular, just read every article as if casually thumbing through a magazine. If something caught her as strange, she wrote it down in her notebook. In two months, she had four notebooks full of strange happenings, tragic accidents, marriage announcements, and land titles with lists of who they belonged to since 1829. But there was nothing clear-cut that proved what Bobby said: no murders in the house, no historically detailed accounts of what went on in the house during the Underground Railroad years, no names of slaves, no accidental deaths, no articles of paranormal happenings, nothing. So once there was nothing left to research, Prue took her notebooks and hid them in the farthest corner of her parents' attic, hoping the shadows would disappear with them. But they always seemed to find a way to creep back in.

One Tuesday afternoon while walking along the water, jumping from rock to rock in an imaginary game of hopscotch, Prue heard something coming up behind her. She froze in mid-hop, one foot landing in a pool of water while the other stayed bent in the air. The hairs on the back of her neck began to rise.

"You should be careful out here on the rocks," a voice said from behind her right shoulder. "You might slip out here all by yourself and no one could save you."

Prue just stood motionless, foot still in the air, wavering.

"Are you all right, Prue?"

Prue stood straight at the sound of her name. "I'm fine," she said quietly.

"You don't act fine." The voice was getting closer. Finally a whole person appeared before her. "Are you sure you're okay?" The woman put her hand on Prue's arm.

"I'm okay." Prue's posture softened. "I was just playing hop-scotch. No big deal." The woman looked genuinely concerned. Her eyes were kind and deep and they made Prue feel safe, whoever she was. "Do I know you?" asked Prue.

"I don't think so. But *I* know *you*. My name's Persephone. I'm helping you're mother."

Prue slightly stiffened again.

"*You're* Persephone?"

"Expecting something different?"

"But you're…you're not…you're – "

"I'm not old and wrinkled with warts and a broomstick?" Persephone smiled.

"I wasn't going to say that!" Prue scrunched her face as she always did when she was losing an argument or in an embarrassing situation. She hated both feelings and right now she felt she'd made a fool of herself, so she switched to other questioning. "Where's my mom?"

"She's had a hard session. She's sleeping right now. She'll probably be asleep for about an hour."

"Oh."

"Do you want to come inside? It might get cold out here waiting for her."

"No, that's okay."

"Well, maybe we could go up to the porch, get you off of these rocks. That would make me feel better at least."

Prue looked up at the house and the porch that surrounded it. She focused on the space she could place between herself and Persephone.

Deciding it was adequate, she agreed and followed Persephone up to the house.

Prue sat on the top step as Persephone leaned against the banister and stared at the lake. The sound of water surrounded them which made Prue suddenly have to pee. Afraid of going into the house, Prue crossed her legs and looked at the hydrangea bushes lining the walkway.

"What are you afraid of?" asked Persephone, now staring at Prue, her eyes not as kind as before.

"I'm not afraid of anything." Prue's voice cracked and she began to feel even more uncomfortable.

"You're afraid of *something*. I'm just not sure what it is yet." Persephone walked closer to Prue.

"Well, I'm not afraid of you!" Prue pushed herself against the post. Persephone came and sat beside her.

"I know you're not afraid of me. You wouldn't talk to me if you were." Persephone leaned against the opposite post, looked around at the house and the land, then focused her eyes back on Prue. "You're afraid of this house."

Prue was shocked, and her mouth fell open like a caught bass.

"How do you know that?"

"I can see it in your face. Plus you've never been inside. I thought maybe it was because you've never been invited in, but today when I asked you to come in, I knew something wasn't right." Persephone paused. "So what about this house scares you?"

"Nothing." Prue turned her head away and pretended to look at something intently.

"Do you think that it's haunted?"

"Why would it be haunted?" Prue tried to ask calmly.

"That's what people think in this town. I'd be surprised if the children here didn't think that also."

"Is it?"

"Is it haunted? What do *you* think?"

"I don't know what to think." Prue put her chin on her knees, frustrated at the indirectness of their conversation. In her head she thought her questions could be easily answered, but Persephone seemed to be holding back, circling.

"What makes you think this house is haunted?" asked Persephone.

"The stories. All the stories."

"Ah, *the stories*? What stories exactly?"

"About the Underground Railroad and the things that happened here." She paused. "And other things," Prue said under her breath.

"It sounds to me like you were misinformed. Would you like to hear a little bit of history about the house? Maybe then you'd be okay to come inside."

"Sure!" Prue sat upright, eager to hear all the answers to her nightmares.

"Okay then," Persephone began. "The house was originally built by a man from Detroit. Beauregard Wynter."

"Beauregard?" interrupted Prue, giggling.

"Yes, Beauregard," smiled Persephone. "He was a prominent shipyard owner. In fact, he used to own the shipping yard right over there." Persephone pointed down the side of the beach to where the remnants of the old shipping yard laid in ruin. "He was also my great-grandfather down the line; too many great-greats to count."

Prue laughed.

"Beauregard built this house as a summer villa, a getaway for his family and a place he could watch his ships as they passed by on their way to and from Chicago, carrying iron, brick, and limestone from New York and Pennsylvania – supplies for the great westward expansion. But he also built the house as a "station", a safe place for runaway slaves to stay. You see, Prue, when my great-grandfather was young, he grew up on a plantation his family owned in Tennessee and his daddy owned slaves, just like his daddy before him and his daddy before him."

Persephone's eyes shifted and she stared out into the lake. Prue noticed her tone changed as well.

"Unfortunately for Beauregard," Persephone continued, "he fell in love with one of those slaves, a young girl named Moriah. His father discovered them one night and was more than furious. He took Beauregard, put a whip in his hand and ordered him to whip Moriah until she was dead, but Beauregard couldn't do it. So his father did, making Beauregard watch every lash rip into her skin, having Beauregard held down so he couldn't try and save her." Prue watched as a tear rolled down Persephone's cheek. "His father whipped her until she didn't cry anymore, until she just laid there, motionless. His father thought she was dead, so he left, smiling and laughing at his son. But she wasn't dead. My great-grandfather heard her soft, muffled breathing and could see the faint rise and fall of her chest. He picked her up and he ran. He hid her in barn lofts and abandoned farmsteads, tending to her wounds, speaking to her softly, saying he would never leave her. Eventually, after her body had healed, Beauregard married her, and they ran to Detroit and started a new life."

"Beauregard married a slave?" Prue asked in shock.

"Yes, he did," answered Persephone, not knowing yet how to take Prue's reaction.

"That must have been very hard for him," Prue replied softly, her face full of thought.

"Yes, it was," responded Persephone. "But he worked hard, made lots of money, and built this house. Beauregard's intentions were good, and his family only visited the house during the summer, the busiest time for escapee movement. The rest of the year he left the house open for those fleeing to Canada; a gardener was left in charge of their transportation. It was the times my great-grandfather wasn't here that conjured up the stories you've heard."

Persephone leaned closer, her body language rigid and her face cold as she painted a wild picture of the past.

"It was believed by some folks that in the basement of this house there were performed certain rituals of voodoo – bloody sacrifices and mind possession with pinpricked dolls in clutched hands – the chants and ritualistic words written on the walls in inaudible languages for the spirits of the dead to awaken and hear. No one knew for what purpose they chanted, for safe passage or to curse the owners who pursued them, but it was said the house would moan at night and gleam like a beacon onto the lake. It was too much spiritual turbulence, and it made a rift in the energy around the house, causing spirits to stay, trapped by the words on the walls. It was thought by the travelers of this house that the energy of the lake would cleanse the evilness around them, the evilness that followed them from their plantation prisons. But they didn't take into account the darkness of the woods. And though the lake is clear and serene, the Michigan woods around here echo the fear and voices of the past, carrying it along the wind and against the bedroom windows of the small, frightened children of Point Caneissa."

Persephone looked at Prue and saw her eyes widen as she ended the story. Persephone's eyes became kind again as she continued.

"Or so they say. That's the story I hear around town."

"Is it true?" Prue's voice cracked as she spoke.

"The voodoo story? I wouldn't think so. I've never seen any words painted in blood on the basement walls. I go down there all the time. It's where I keep my winter canning." Persephone was trying not to laugh, but Prue didn't notice.

"So the story about the Underground Railroad isn't true? It's all made up?"

"No, that part's true. It's my family's history. But a story or a rumor is only as real as you make it to be."

"What do you mean?"

"Well, look at the story I just told you. If no one believed that slaves actually traveled through this house, even though we have proof they did, it would be as though it never happened. Without belief, it would be forgotten, and then non-existent. Things are only true because we choose to believe they are."

"But what about the evil spirits? You said they're caught here by the woods, so they must be real." Prue could no longer hide the fear in her voice and she wondered if Persephone could detect that, possibly catering her answers to comfort Prue. She secretly wished Persephone would.

"Spirits are just like anything else, good or evil, and I never said there were any here," answered Persephone, tone unchanging. "But if there were, it wouldn't matter. For me, they're not. I don't believe they dwell here. They're only here for those who believe they are. They only haunt those who think about them." Persephone looked Prue square in the face. "My advice to you is not to worry about them. They're only as real as you make them."

"But what if that stuff really did happen?" squeaked Prue.

"What does it matter?"

"I don't want them to hurt me! What if they follow me home? What if they try to hurt me when I'm sleeping, or something worse?"

"I've lived here my whole life and they've never hurt me, if they even exist."

"Maybe there's a reason why they don't hurt you."

"And what reason would that be?"

Prue paused and considered what she wanted to say. The question burned inside of her and it tossed about in her mind with the possibilities of the answer. After all, Persephone had already joked with Prue about the idea of her being a witch, so maybe she wouldn't be mad if Prue said it. There was only one way to find out. And so Prue answered Persephone, quiet and reserved, but dying to know the truth.

"Maybe you're a witch," Prue said slowly.

"What makes you think I'm a witch?"

"People in town. I've heard them talking about you."

"Do they say good or bad things?"

"I don't know."

Prue was lying. She had heard nothing but bad things about Persephone from the people in town. Persephone picked up from Prue's body language that her reputation in town was not a good one. It didn't surprise her that people thought that she was a witch, and most of the time Persephone didn't care what other people thought of her or what she did in her house, but the uncertainty of a child made her feel uncomfortable and she began to actually wonder what, exactly, people were saying about her.

"I want to know what *you* think. If I was a witch, would that make me evil?"

"I don't know," answered Prue. "I guess it would depend on if you really *were* a witch."

"Are witches evil?"

"Well, yeah."

"Then I'm not a witch," stated Persephone clearly. "And since I'm not a witch and no evil things dwell here, I think it's safe for you to come inside. What do you think?"

Prue looked at the door to the house. The screen door hovered lightly in the breeze from the lake. There was something calming about that door; it looked more inviting now. The sound of it creaking in the wind was comforting and it reminded Prue of summer vacations at her grandmother's house in Frankfort. She looked at Persephone. Persephone wasn't what she expected. She seemed warm and interesting, and her eyes looked at Prue with kindness and feeling. Prue felt she could always tell how someone was by looking into their eyes. Persephone's eyes reminded Prue of Wyatt and the way he would look at her when she would cry and need him. That feeling of protection that shone from his eyes now came through in Persephone's. She took one last look around the porch and then looked at Persephone.

"Sure," said Prue. They both got up and Prue followed Persephone into the house. As they walked in, Prue looked at Persephone and asked, "What's your real name?"

"You don't believe Persephone is my real name?"

"It just seems like an odd name for a parent to name their child, unless you're Demeter."

"You know Greek mythology?" Persephone asked, surprised. "That's unusual for an eight-year-old."

"I find history fascinating," replied Prue, "and Greek mythology is a very interesting part of history."

"Hmm. Perhaps we can have a conversation on *that* someday."

"I would love to!" Persephone held the door open and Prue stopped before going in, looking up at her, still waiting for an answer. "So?"

"Francine," answered Persephone.

"I would have gone with Persephone, too," laughed Prue, seeing Persephone crack a thin, sly smile. They stepped into the house and waited for Prue's mother to wake.

From then on Prue looked forward to her mother's visits to Persephone and continued her friendship with Persephone even after her mother was cured of her smoking addiction. Persephone was Prue's one reassurance that good always triumphed over evil, no matter how strong the evil was. When Prue went to college Persephone gave her a bracelet with a slender blue crystal dangling from the center. "It will protect you from anything you think is evil," said Persephone. "Just in case you don't feel strong enough to combat your fears." Persephone hugged and kissed Prue that day. It was the last time Prue ever saw her.

Prue never realized how much of an impact Persephone had made on her. Their conversations always revolved around the weird, the interesting, the abnormal, and the explanation of those things. Prue always wanted an explanation. But mostly they talked about history, facts and findings of the past, and Prue always found herself coming away from Persephone's invigorated and interested in the world and people around her. It's what made Prue study anthropology and archaeology in college, focusing on ancient cultures and their mysticisms. She had been on digs, researched ancient cultures, and worked in museums, making sure each historical project she worked on was handled properly and historically accurate. Every once in a while she would study certain myths, legends, and folklores, curious if any of them would actually be true. On her downtime from work she would research them, figuring out the mysteries of these tales, finding their answers to be everyday occurrences; nothing uncommon, nothing supernatural, no phenomena, nothing to be afraid of. But there could always be the possibility.

Could there be spirits here?

Now Prue stood in Wyatt's living room wondering if there really were any lingering spirits in the house, watching her, watching Wyatt. She played with the blue crystal dangling from her wrist. Prue never took the bracelet off, hoping that in some way it did protect her.

Prue walked around the living room and went to the window. She watched the small waves of the lake roll in and she suddenly felt the urge to go swimming. She went upstairs, grabbed a towel, and left the house, stripping her clothes as she went. When she got to the shore's edge Prue paused and looked at her bracelet. Always afraid of losing it in the water, she took it off and placed it in the towel, then stepped into the water.

The lake was still chilled, the winter cold not completely shaken out of it yet. It would not begin to warm up until the first week of June, but Prue continued walking, every step further plunging her into the bitter water. Soon she couldn't feel the pins running across her skin, pricking the numbness into flesh and muscles. She now began to feel warm. The wind against her wet skin made her cold so she swam further out until she could no longer touch the sandy bottom. The waves weren't very high today and Prue liked the way they gently rolled her around in the water. She leaned her head back into the water and pointed her toes down, arching and whirling her arms in a circle, twisting her around in the water. It was a wonderfully free feeling.

After awhile Prue began to notice the shoreline further away than she remembered. It didn't worry her; the distance wouldn't be hard to swim. She was more surprised at how relaxed she'd become. She wondered if Wyatt noticed she was gone; if he had come out of his room and was perhaps worried about her. She hoped he was.

Prue grew eager to see his concerned face and turned her body to start swimming toward the house. She went to kick her legs but couldn't, the feeling of something pulling on them prevented their movement. Suddenly she was being forced under the water, a suction dragging her toward the sandy floor. Prue hit the bottom abruptly, her fingers sinking into the tiny pebbles of lakebed as she tried pushing herself up, but she found her legs tangled in something. Prue opened her eyes but the water was filled with mud and sand. She pulled and pulled, kicking as her arms hopelessly tried to aid in the fight. Finally one of her legs broke free and Prue pushed herself toward the surface, her left leg still struggling with the coiled object around it. When she reached the surface she laid on her back and choked in the fresh air, gasping and coughing until her lungs calmed and breathed normally again. Only after that did she reach for the object still attached to her leg. When she finally unwound it she laid it on the surface of the water, spreading it out so she could fully see it, then held a part of it out of the water for a better look. At first it looked like just a piece of cloth, its dark red color now distorted by the settled mud in its fibers, but when Prue looked at it closer, it was familiar, something she'd seen before. And then it hit her.

Prue dropped the fabric and franticly started swimming to shore. The waves seemed bigger now, her body rapidly giving into exhaustion. Finally her feet touched sand and she walked herself onto the beach. Anxiously she grabbed her towel, searching for her bracelet, trying to force it onto her wrist. She wrapped herself in the towel and laid on the beach, breathing in the cool air above her as she tried to figure out what happened. Prue could only think of an undertow and that somehow, as she hit the bottom, she got tangled in the cloth. It was eerie, that cloth. It looked like a satin nightgown she gave Addie at their last Christmas together. *But that's insane,* she thought. *My mind must be playing tricks on me.* A large wave hit the shore and the foamy water reached Prue's feet and she felt something slide over them. When she sat up to see what it was, Prue saw the hem of the nightgown covering her toes and what looked like red finger marks on her left calf. Prue screamed, pushing herself away from the dark red cloth until she gained balance and traction, enabling her to run, losing her towel on the beach, the clasp on the bracelet coming undone in the process. She ran toward the house, afraid to look back.

When Prue reached the house the finger marks on her leg were gone. From the porch she followed her footsteps to the water's edge, looking for any sign of the nightgown or anything else strange and out of place. But she saw nothing, not even her towel. She examined her half naked body for more finger marks but found nothing. *Did I do that to myself? Did I imagine it all?* She didn't know. Prue watched the waves grow small again, slow and meticulous, and gathered her clothes before going in the house to search for Wyatt, her childhood fears creeping in behind her as she entered.

Addie

I couldn't sleep. I was now past the point of exhaustion where your mind pains with thought and it is all your body can do to just sit or lie down and stare into the night without sleep, without the gentle release of the hindered world around you. It felt like I hadn't slept in months. For so many nights now I had gone without sleep, my body only giving into my fatigue in the morning, when the sun hit the windows of our bedroom and I could see the light from the bed. My eyes would close and I would sleep briefly, until Wyatt would wake up and our day would begin.

Tonight, like many nights, I was in the nursery waiting for the sun to rise. That's when I planned to sneak back into our bedroom as if I never left. I didn't know what time it was now, but it was still dark and the moonlight on the lake only reached my eyes when I rocked forward, my hands resting on the book in my lap while my fingers grasped hold of its edges. It was my grandfather's book – a re-telling of folklores that had been passed down for generations in our family – that he put together and bound himself. *Tales from the Old Country*, he titled it, and when I was little and couldn't sleep, he would get it from the top shelf in his bedroom closet and read it to me while I lay next to the fireplace. He gave it to me when I left for college, saying he never wanted me to forget where I came from, or go without a good night's sleep.

Not long after I'd lost Ean I pulled my grandfather's book out, desperate to leave behind my sorrow and wakeful nights for dream-filled sleep. But it had the opposite effect on me now. Instead of causing sleep it charged my mind, the stories and images vividly coming alive for me as I waited for the sun to rise. For this reason I didn't read it often, only pulling it out when my mind seemed fully awake and I wanted to pass the time quickly.

The first story touched me the most. It told of two lovers broken apart on their wedding night and I tried not to read it because it made me cry. But tonight I had reached that point where my body begged my mind to shut off, but it wouldn't, so I took the book from the nursery closet where I hid it, for Ean, and began to read from the beginning, praying I would see the sun begin to light the room before I reached the end.

There is a legend in my village, a moral fable told by all. It is a simple tale, and one all aspire to. It is a common virtue that connects us and keeps us grounded. I thought, once, I had achieved it. I have since then found I have not.

It takes place long ago, between the marshland bogs and the greenest hills to the west, in the fallen valley where the grass only grows so high and abandoned trees weep dewy tears of isolation as the sun rises. It was before the two great houses merged to form our village; when the air was still wild and fairies guarded the night. Diarie still speaks of the end of the wild time, the only one of us old enough to remember it. She tells the tale of the lovers, the one Doerian, her grandmother, told her as a child. It was Doerian who showed Diarie the last of the wild wind of Aedammair, carried on the wings of the last fairy of Éadaoin. She is now the only one still living that can bring the magic ones back, through Doerian's spirit.

There were two lovers, Fionna, daughter of the House of Aedan, and Brennan, son of the House of Conehar; the children of the great two lords whose land met in the middle of the fallen valley. As a symbol of friendship, the two lords arranged a marriage between their oldest children, bringing their lands together and strengthening their power. So it was set, upon Fionna's seventeenth moon, she would wed Brennan under the blessings of the night fairies of Éadaoin. Until that moon Fionna was forbidden to see Brennan, but her desire to see the man she was betrothed to was greater than her respect to obligation and duty, as were Brennan's own curiosities. And so they would meet in the middle of the fallen valley under the Tree of Eden, hidden by the vale of night, given the right to fall in love and find a life together.

Now, when in love the heart blinds the eyes and mind to observance, and though our lovers felt and thought they were alone in the night, they were closely being watched by Tarloch, gatekeeper of the marshland bogs which lead into the underworld of Awyn, where revenge and terror are conjured by those willing to bargain their soul. And so, night after night Tarloch watched them, growing jealous of their love, until Fionna's seventeenth moon began to rise over the fallen valley. In the middle, under the Tree of Eden, above the parted grass stood a newly built platform ready for the night ceremony. And as the moon reached its peak ascent, Fionna and Brennan were wed, becoming one in the eyes of their people, the beginning of a new village.

The people turned to melodies on tambourines and stringed lutes, dancing in circles and pairs, breathing in the night and the mist and the untamed wind. No one saw the lovers leave, slipping away from the dancers, running beyond the Tree of Eden into the field, laying among the grass. But Tarloch was watching, and when Brennan took Fionna, her seventeenth moon flowing across her uncovered skin, Tarloch screamed, the echoes loosening him from the marshland bog.

His eyes still on them, Tarloch ran.

The earth trembled as his feet came down on it, but no one noticed except Doerian, who had retired from dancing to sit under the Tree of Eden and stare up into the moon, dreaming of when she would be old enough for her own marriage ceremony. She was a servant in the House of Aedan, assigned to leave with Fionna after the marriage night. Doerian felt the earth move underneath her. It was not the dancers, she had discerned, but something coming towards them from far away. She looked into the distant darkness and saw the large figure of Tarloch coming from the marshland bog. When Doerian saw what he was running towards, she began to scream.

"Fionna! Fionna!"

The wind carried her shrieks across the grass of the fallen valley to Brennan's ears, and when he looked to see who was watching them, he saw Tarloch running towards them.

Brennan lifted Fionna to her feet, grabbed her small hand and began to run. The people ceased dancing as Doerian's screams became louder. They came to the tree and watched as Brennan pulled Fionna through the fallen valley, trying to escape Tarloch. The people ran to protect them, circling them as the lovers made it to the platform under the Tree of Eden. But the village was not enough to protect the lovers, and Tarloch threw them, making his way to Fionna, ripping her from Brennan's arms.

"She is mine!" roared Tarloch, standing ten-feet above the tallest villager, holding Fionna above them.

"No, she is mine!" yelled Brennan, trying to fight his people to get to his beloved wife.

"If she is yours, you will die. If she is mine, you will live," bellowed Tarloch.

"Don't hurt him," screamed Fionna. "I will go with you if you leave Brennan and my people under no harm."

"No!" cried Brennan.

"Brennan, please!"

Brennan came closer, fighting through the mass of villagers trying to save him, fighting his own father who tried to pin him down to the fallen valley, calling fairies and spirits to keep him there. But nothing would keep Brennan bound, and finally, he stood in front of Tarloch.

"Fionna is mine." Brennan's voice resonated through the air. His words were deep and firm, and he stood there, unmoved.

"Then you shall die!"

Tarloch unsheathed the Sword of Wrath from his back and in one thrust, Brennan was dead. The villagers gasped and fell to their knees. Tarloch secured his sword and moved to leave, Fionna still in his grasp.

"Leave me," she cried.

"But you are mine," answered Tarloch.

"No," said Fionna. "Brennan is dead, and therefore, I am his. Leave me, and never return as long as I or any of my descendants are still living."

Tarloch placed Fionna next to her lover's body, and vanished.

Fionna kissed the still warm lips of Brennan. And when she did, Fionna felt a movement deep inside of her. She smiled. But soon the warmth left her lover's body and she wept; she wept for Brennan, and she wept for her life without him.

As the days went on, the movement inside Fionna grew stronger, and before her eighteenth moon she bore a son who she named Breandan, inflicting the strength of his father. But she only looked upon his face once, to see it's brightness before choosing to meet Brennan in the upper world, living that life as they were entitled to on earth. Before she left this world for the next she called Doerian, her maid-servant, and made Doerian promise to look after Breandan, to teach him their ways and to tell him the story of his parents. Doerian agreed, then watched the life of her princess fade away.

Doerian kept her promise, taking Breandan every eve of his birth to the middle of the fallen valley, between the marshland bogs and the highest green hills, where the grass only grows so high and the abandoned trees weep dewy tears of isolation as the sun rises, and she would tell him the story of his parents. As he grew older, he yearned for a love like the one which created him. When he found it, he continued the tradition with Doerian, having her speak of love to his children. And this continued for generations, until Doerian passed her knowledge down to Diarie, her granddaughter, after out-living the great-great grandchildren of Fionna and Brennan.

That is where I find my way into this story. I am Brogan, descendant of Fionna, ward of Diarie. I fell in love, like Fionna, as we all aspire to do, but something is not right; something has gone wrong. My love is Ciaran, a descendant of the House of Conehar, and like Fionna, I met with Ciaran in the middle of the fallen valley, underneath the Tree of Eden, on the platform built for Fionna and Brennan's wedding, until the eve of my seventeenth moon. Our marriage ceremony took place on the platform and Ciaran loved me just as Brennan had loved Fionna. And we lived like this for many years' moons. I gave him everything he wanted. And when he wanted a son, I bore him one, and named him Ean; God is gracious. I could not love Ean, though. I loved Ciaran too much. Nothing came near my love for him. So, when Ean cried, I held him, but I did not love him. When he was hungry, I gave him my breast, but I did not love him. When he was hurt, I healed him, but I did not love him. My eyes were always on Ciaran, and because he loved Ean, I cared for the child, but I did not love him.

I watched Ean grow and how his father loved him, and I grew angry at moments, but I knew Ciaran loved me more, as I did him. Diarie watched me with my son and with my husband. She saw the trueness of my heart.

"You will face grave pain," she warned me, "If you do not open your heart to your son."

"I have achieved the love we all aspire to and yearn for, the love which binds us all together, the love of Fionna and Brennan," I told her.

"You are nowhere near that love, my child," Diarie said to me, but I did not believe her. And time passed with no grave pain.

On the eve of our wedding year the Faolian village threatened the fallen valley and we prepared for war. It is the duty of the women in our village to choose one man or boy from our household to fight. When Lord Darrah, my brother and ruler of our village, came for my choice, I told him Ean, and gave him my son.

"No," cried Ciaran. "He is just a child. I will go."

"No," I said. "He will become a man on the battlefield. Let him go. It is my choice, not yours. I cannot lose you."

"I will not let him go."

"I cannot let you go," I told him. "I love you too much. Please, brother, take Ean."

"I will not let you take him, Darrah."

"It is not your choice, Ciaran. My sister has spoken."

"But he is just a child!"

"I will give you another," I begged.

"I do not want another," Ciaran yelled. "Please, Darrah, do not take him! He is my only child. He has only just passed his sixth moon."

"He will be a man soon enough. Brogan has spoken. I must take him."

The other men that had been chosen held Ciaran as Lord Darrah took Ean from our house. Ciaran cried for them to bring Ean back, but they never did.

Not long after the scrolls of fallen men began to appear on the walls of the great castle. And in among the names of the dead lay written, "Ean, son of the House of Ciaran". After that, Ciaran would not speak to me.

"Addie," Lesley said as she put her hand on my shoulder and shook me lightly. "Addie it's morning," she said softly. "It's time to wake up."

I turned my head and yawned, eyes closed, hands still holding the book in my lap.

"What?"

"It's morning," said Lesley. "I wouldn't have wakened you but Wyatt insists you get up. He says he has work to do."

"Lesley?" I yawned as the mumbled name came out of my mouth. "I forgot you were here." I opened my eyes and focused on my best friend.

"I thought you might have, especially when you came into this room last night. Normally you try to avoid it while I'm here."

"You noticed that?"

"I notice everything," she smiled.

"I wonder what I'm still doing in here." I was genuinely puzzled. "Normally I go back to our bedroom before Wyatt wakes up." I looked up at Lesley, pleading. "I don't want Wyatt to know I spend a lot of time in here."

Lesley leaned down in front of me.

"Well, between you and me, I think he already has a pretty good idea that you do."

I quickly looked away from her gaze.

"I just don't know what happened last night," I said, trying to direct the conversation away from Wyatt. "I don't know what kept me in here last night, or what put me to sleep."

"Maybe it was this." Lesley picked the book up out of my lap. "*Tales from the Old Country.* That sounds like it'd put anyone to sleep." Lesley laughed and placed the book back in my hands.

"It's my grandfather's," I said slowly.

"Oh, I'm sorry. I didn't mean to make fun of it." Lesley was clearly embarrassed.

"No, it's okay." I paused, trying to figure out what had happened last night. Usually I could remember everything leading up to morning, but this morning was different somehow. Someway, I had fallen asleep last night – the first night since I'd lost Ean – and I couldn't remember how or why.

"I remember now," I said, interrupting my own thought. "I think I had a dream last night. I must have. Otherwise, why didn't I go back to my own room to sleep? I fell asleep in here reading."

"That's great, Addie," answered Lesley in a happy, positive tone.

"Yeah, but something isn't right. Something is different. If I could just remember."

"Who knows why we do the things we do while we sleep," interjected Lesley. "Look, I'll take this and you go take a shower and get ready. We can talk about it over breakfast."

"Okay."

Lesley lifted the book from my lap and walked out of the room, just in time to bump into Wyatt in the hallway. I watched through the partly opened door as Wyatt caught Lesley in the awkward collision, her satin robe falling open as he grabbed her, revealing her negligee underneath. I couldn't help but notice the closeness of their bodies during the whole incident. I felt something very wrong in the manner of their laugh, the way Wyatt held Lesley as he balanced her again, and the way Lesley looked at Wyatt as he re-tied her robe. I watched as they bent down to gather papers and the book, each handing the other their belongings, their hands lingering too long with the other. The moment was brief, but for me it lasted indefinitely, the images burned now into my subconscious with the other memories my heart wanted to forget but my mind would not let go.

Wyatt walked into the room and kissed me on the forehead, almost instantly causing me to forget the scene I had just witnessed.

"Did you sleep well?" he asked as he set some papers down on his desk.

"I guess I did. I didn't even know I had fallen asleep until Lesley woke me."

"I was a little surprised when I woke up this morning, and a little worried I might add." Wyatt smiled as he spoke with a slight scolding tone. He reached for my hand and pulled me up, grasping the curve of my lower back. "But no matter now. I've found you and I'm very pleased to see you." He leaned down and began kissing the side of my neck.

"Wyatt, cut it out," I giggled. "Lesley's just downstairs."

"Oh, who cares? Lesley doesn't care. Can't a man kiss his wife?"

He continued his advances.

"Wyatt, I mean it. Stop. I'm not ready."

"I bet I could change your mind."

Wyatt reached for the back of my nightgown and began pulling it up.

"Wyatt, I said stop!"

I thrust my arms down, forcing Wyatt's arms to let go, and pushed him away. He tripped and fell to the floor.

"I don't want to do this!" I cried as I watched him fall, then left the room for a long, tearful shower.

After I toweled off I put on my robe and walked over to the window to find Lesley walking a plate of eggs to Wyatt who was now sitting on the beach next to a shifting of rocks. Lesley sat on the closest rock to him and cradled her legs, resting her head on her knees. They were talking about something – the earlier fight, no doubt – but something didn't seem right. I got a feeling, a strange pit-of-the-stomach feeling, that caused the hairs on the back of my neck to rise. I watched as Wyatt placed his hand on Lesley's foot, then on her calf, slowly letting it fall to her ankle, then back to her calf, patting it a couple of times as if to say "Good Job!". The air in the room shifted and I felt a cold chill run across my body, the feeling in my stomach worsening, deepening, as if someone or something were there with me, watching me. I turned my head sharply around the room, but there was nothing there. It was a strange feeling, this bitter shudder; one that had been with me since we moved into the house. I took a deep breath and looked back outside, realizing Wyatt and Lesley were staring at me.

Did they know I was watching them?

There was no way to tell. I felt foolish, like an embarrassed child whose parents kept laughing even though the disastrous scene ended hours ago. I thought I read the words, "Does she not trust us?" coming from Lesley's mouth. Did I trust them? There was no time to explore that question. Wyatt and Lesley were headed up to the house. I quickly threw on some sweats and greeted them as I bounced down the stairs.

"Hey," I said as I reached the final step.

"Well, aren't you all dressed up," Wyatt said snidely.

"Wyatt, that doesn't help the situation here," scolded Lesley.

"It doesn't hurt it either," he said as he began walking up the stairs. "Let her stay depressed. I don't care anymore. I'm beginning to think she doesn't even have feelings anymore." The words came abruptly as Wyatt slammed the door to his office. Lesley and I could hear him ripping the nursery wallpaper off the wall, then silence.

"It was just a tiny rage," I said suddenly. "Nothing to be worried about."

"Addie, how can you say that? Wyatt is very upset."

I left Lesley standing by the stairs. I walked to the living room, grabbing a book from the bookshelf, then headed to the kitchen and poured myself a cup of coffee, setting the book on the counter. Lesley soon followed, dumbfounded.

"Addie, go up there and talk to him. He said some hurtful things to you."

"It's okay. Really. I deserve it."

"Why?"

"Because of what happened this morning. Didn't Wyatt tell you?"

"Yes, but Addie, he had no right to hurt you like that just now. You both need to talk this out, get to the bottom of whatever it is that's bothering you two. You need to release your pent up anger."

"They're just words, Lesley," I laughed.

"Words with deep feelings and meanings behind them."

"They're just words."

"Addie, I don't think –"

"Besides," I interrupted, "You were the one, were you not, that told me I needed to take my feelings at my own pace? Only reveal and talk about what I am ready to talk about?"

"Yes, but –"

"Well, I'm not ready to talk about what happened upstairs just yet. Wyatt and I both know what the problem is. I don't know about him, but I'm just not ready to face that battle. You understand, don't you?"

I had that ring of pleading in my voice, that sound that makes your heart and mind soften slightly, enabling a conversation change, leaving the conversee at the whims of the converser, forgetting everything that happened previously. At least I hope I did.

"I understand," said Lesley, unwillingly. "Are you sure you don't want to talk about it? Any of it?"

"You know what I want to talk about? Dreams."

I grabbed the book on the counter and brought it over to the table.

"Addie," said Lesley, rolling her eyes as she saw the title of the book, "it's ten in the morning. I don't even think I could handle Freud at ten in the morning. Besides, what's this sudden obsession with dream interpretation?"

"I think I had one last night."

"A dream or a dream interpretation?"

I looked up at Lesley. Lesley had a smirk on her face.

"Aren't we the witty one this morning."

"Thank you, thank you," said Lesley. "But in all seriousness, it's great that you're dreaming. It means your mind is breaking down some of its own strongholds. It's good. It's healthy activity. But why the Freud? The *Interpretation of Dreams* is some heavy stuff."

"Well, I remember something from college, something Professor Talcott said. I remember him saying Freud said you could interpret dreams based on what was in them, what was taking place in the dream."

"Yeess."

"So I thought I would read up on it so when I dream again, I'll be able to interpret what it means."

I opened the book and began to skim the pages.

"Addie, I think you're misunderstanding what Professor Talcott was saying. Freud doesn't give you some secret code that magically tells you what your dreams mean."

"I know that," I replied, slightly insulted. "It says right here that we have 'dream-thoughts' and 'dream-content' and that they both will be immediately comprehensible, once I've learned to read them. That doesn't sound so hard. Once I've learned what one means, I'll know what the other is."

I continued to read intently.

"But Addie, you're over-generalizing it. It's much more complicated than that. Imagine you were watching a foreign film with no subtitles. You would understand, for the most part, what was going on in the film by the motions and actions of the actors. But until you get those subtitles, you don't know entirely what the movie's about."

"So what you're saying is that the movie is the dream-content and the sub-titles are the dream-thoughts?"

"In a sense, yes."

"See, I'm already getting the hang of this dream interpretation thing!"

"Addie," Lesley sighed, "I wouldn't get your hopes up about all this. Dreams, for the most part, are unreliable. Your mind is a very intricate instrument. We can't always determine why it remembers one thing and not another, or why you dream of things from twenty years ago or of something ridiculous like chewing grape bubblegum while running a marathon over the Mackinac Bridge. You just never know. Sometimes dreams don't mean anything."

"I don't believe that," I whispered.

"I'm sorry if I ruined your excitement. I think it's good that you're dreaming. It's terrific. It means these emotional walls that you've put up are finally starting to crumble. Your mind wants to work through whatever it is you're feeling, so why not give it a chance?"

I continued to stare down at the paper. Lesley couldn't tell if I was reading or trying to avoid our conversation.

"Look, if this is really important to you, I might have a solution."

"What?" I responded, unenthused.

"I have been known to do a little dream-interpretation with my own patients from time to time. Why don't you keep a journal, a log of your dreams. Write down everything you can remember from them and we'll see if we can't get to the bottom of them together."

"You really think it will help?"

"It can't hurt."

I stood up and hugged Lesley.

"Thanks, Lesley. I really think this is going to work."

I started walking to the door.

"What are you doing now?" Lesley asked.

"I think I'm going to take a walk along the lake. Get some fresh air and clear my mind, maybe remember what I dreamt last night. I know there's something wrong with it." I looked over at the kitchen table and saw my grandfather's book sitting on it. I went over to it, brushing my fingers along the cover. "I distinctly remember reading the beginning of this book last night." I stared at the leather cover as I spoke, almost in a trance. "But I feel like the end was different somehow, that it ended a way I'd never read before. But it seemed familiar." I began to remember seeing a little boy named Ean. I quickly pushed the thought aside. I would deal with it later, when Lesley wasn't here. "Besides," I said, suddenly full of artificial happiness. "Wyatt needs time to cool down."

"Do you mind if I go with you?" Lesley asked.

"Actually, I'd kind of like to go by myself, if that's okay."

"No, that's fine," she answered. "I understand. Maybe I'll try to talk to Wyatt, see how he's doing."

"I wouldn't bother. You know Wyatt. When he's ready, he'll come down and act like nothing ever happened. Let him fester in his room up there."

"Still, maybe I should talk to him. It can't be good for him to 'fester'."

"Lesley, just leave him alone. It's not your job to fix everyone." I finished putting on my jogging shoes. "I'll probably be back in about an hour." I turned from the open door to see Lesley standing at the bottom of the stairs. "Lesley, just leave him alone. Everyone needs time to breathe."

"I heard you, okay?"

"Good."

Before I shut the door I heard Lesley's footsteps jogging up the stairs. Had Lesley always gone after Wyatt? Had they always had secret conversations without me? Would they? I didn't know anymore.

CHAPTER 8: ON BROADWAY

Wyatt

It was a coincidence that I ran into Lesley four years after our divorce. She was sitting with a friend at a table away from me in a coffee shop on Broadway. I was working on my latest magazine cover assignment and had only noticed her nervous giggling, an annoying, yet familiar sound I never bothered to acknowledge by looking up and seeing where it was coming from. Though I had a brief conversation with her shortly after our separation (one I wished I could forget), I hadn't thought of Lesley in a long time, which is why I never took a second glance at Lesley across the coffee shop. Not even after I passed her for the second time on my way to the counter did I notice her. Instead I focused on my next hot chocolate, the cure for my ever-increasing distaste for coffee, having already drunk five cups of the bitter java drink too fast.

I wanted to jolt myself up with caffeine. My pre-layout deadline was in two days and I had only drawn crap for the last week: stick figures, clouds, my apartment, my dog – endless crap. I felt I couldn't get into a groove, so I decided to go to Joe's Diner and hopefully rejuvenate myself into drawing something worthwhile. My solution was the five cups of coffee, drunken as fast as possible, and a nice corner table. I was warming my stunted thoughts with the second hot chocolate when Lesley seemingly forced her way over, only slightly propelled by her adjacent friend.

"Wyatt?"

I looked up and found my ex-wife standing in front of me, painfully smiling while her friend stood hiding behind her as some kind of girlfriend moral support. I was a little shocked. It wasn't that I was angry or upset at seeing Lesley again, I was just a little apprehensive at what our meeting might mean. After all, our last conversation didn't work out well for me, on any level. Plus I didn't know the etiquette required in such situations. Should I hug her, kiss her cheek, shake her hand? Or should I do nothing, as if she wasn't standing right in front of me waiting for a response? Then there was the more pressing question: Would I feel a spark if I touched her? A lingering repressed bit of electricity between us I didn't even realize existed or secretly wanted? I didn't know. All I knew was that I had become content with my current life, and this surprise meeting made me somewhat uneasy. But my interest quickly shifted from why Lesley was there, to who she was with. And though Lesley was still attractive after four years, – very attractive – I chose to be more attracted to her younger, prettier companion. So I indulged the meeting, if only to be introduced to Lesley's enchanting friend.

"Lesley?" I stood up and hugged her awkwardly, hoping this was the right move. "I can't believe you're really in New York? I'd almost forgotten you were going to go to Columbia. That was the plan, wasn't it?" As if I couldn't remember.

"Yes," she answered sharply, a nervous tone in her voice. It almost sounded as if she were shaking. "I'm getting my PhD there right now."

I grabbed an extra chair and we all sat down.

"I always figured you for an Ivy Leaguer. I never understood why you gave up Barnard. I think it would have suited you better."

"Better than Saint Mary's? Perhaps." Lesley forced a sweet smile, grasping for words. "But, for some childish reason, I thought I had a purpose in going there. It took a long time, but I realize now I was wrong. There wasn't anything for me there."

Lesley stared straight into my eyes as she spoke, quickly moving her gaze to her friend as soon as her thought was finished. I knew she didn't say the words to be hurtful, but spoke them out of hurt.

"Anyway," Lesley interrupted the silence, "What are you doing here?"

"Uh, well, things didn't quite work out the way I thought they would in Chicago. The art scene wasn't happening enough for me there." Actually, the art scene was fine in Chicago. It was just too close to home, to memories I wanted to forget, and I didn't need Lesley to know that. "But here in New York, it's explosive! So I moved here and transferred to NYU. I'm actually doing quite well," I said as I placed my sketchbook on my lap, under the table away from possible curious eyes.

"NYU? What are you doing all the way over here?" asked Lesley. "There's got to be dozens of coffee shops between here and NYU."

"I like the scenery over here better." I looked at Lesley's friend, causing the pink in her cheeks to rise even more. "Helps me to imagine more clearly."

"Oh," Lesley responded, rubbing the bridge of her nose with her middle finger, then gliding it across her right eyebrow. I knew she felt awkward. Lesley always touched her nose when she felt uncomfortable or didn't know what to say. But in this incidence, she recovered quickly. "I wonder if I've ever seen any of your work. I'm sure you're – "

"Ah-hem."

Lesley was interrupted by the noise of her friend clearing her throat, who, at that moment, was looking somewhat apprehensive about suddenly involving herself in our conversation. It took Lesley a moment to figure out that what her companion wanted was just an introduction.

"I'm sorry," Lesley said slowly. "I seem to have no manners. Wyatt Trilmon this is Addison Daugherty. She's an undergraduate at Barnard. I'm mentoring her this semester."

I stood up slightly, reaching my hand over the table, trying to balance myself and my sketchbook.

"Hello, Addison."

"It's Addie," she replied, taking my hand and blushing slightly. "Hi. I pick up the *Campus Talk* newsletter all the time. I think I saw some of your artwork in it."

"Yeah, you probably did. I do work for them every couple of months. It's just a side thing though."

"You do the little cartoons, right?"

"Yeah."

"They're really cute."

"Thanks. Although 'cute' isn't really the word an aspiring artist wants to hear." I smiled at Addie, trying to show I wasn't offended by flirting with her. "But the work's not much different than this comic my buddy and I do."

"Really? What's it about?" asked Addie sweetly.

"Well, it's about this kid who lives in this small Michigan town. One night during a bad thunderstorm, lightning strikes his house, shocking him and causing a power outage. Afterwards, he begins to see all these paranormal happenings and then ends up solving mysteries with his new ability."

"*The Night the Lights Went Out?*" Addie interrupted, excited.

"Yeah. How did you know?"

"When I'm home on break I always pick one up. I like to scare my little brother with them. He won't go outside in the rain anymore because he's afraid he's going to start seeing ghosts and stuff. Keeps him up at night. It's great," Addie said laughing. "But I don't remember seeing your name on the cover. I know I would have recognized it because Lesley – "

A sharp jab interrupted Addie's sentence from under the table.

"I use a pseudo-name," I intervened, trying to breeze over any awkwardness. "We put it on ourselves, with our own money. It doesn't make us that much. I guess I'm a little embarrassed by it."

"You shouldn't be. It's a great comic."

I was a little enamored. Addie was the first girl I met who actually knew my work, or a piece of it at least. It relaxed me knowing I didn't have to try and impress her with my starving artist routine. *That* I saved for gallery openings and magazine queries. I put my sketchbook back on the table and began an inquisitive conversation with Addie.

"So, I take it you're a psychology major?" I asked, slightly opening my sketchpad to an empty page. I took my pencil and began tracing the outlines of Addie's face.

"How did you know?"

"Lesley was a psych major at Saint Mary's, so I just figured that's what she was mentoring you for." I was now penciling her large, almond shaped eyes. As I looked at them I lost myself a little, drawing stray lines I soon erased.

"Lesley's a great mentor," Addie replied, looking over at her friend. "I've learned so much from her this year."

"So where are you from?" I asked, desperately wanting to change the subject off of Lesley in order to find out more about my current enchantress.

"I grew up on Long Island. My father's an architect in the city." I began to focus on her words now, letting my pencil slacken and fall from my hand.

Halfway through our interaction Lesley excused herself to use the ladies room. Until that point I forgot she was even there, positioning myself so that Lesley was now outside my peripheral vision. Addie excused herself with Lesley. I used their absence as time to finish my sketch of her. Addie was beautiful. Her sandy blond hair accentuated her skin tone perfectly, giving her the slightest hint of pink in her cheeks and causing her golden brown eyes to pop from her black lashes and perfectly curved eyebrows. Her face was soft, no blemishes peeking through to the surface, and her cheeks were round but structured. I regretted not bringing my oil pastels.

"I don't think it would be all that bad." I heard Addie's voice getting louder.

"What?" I responded, putting my finishing touches on her sketch and raising my head to meet her eyes.

Lesley and Addie reached the table and quickly stopped their conversation, Addie sitting down across from me, shyly smiling. Lesley continued to stand, causing Addie to get up from her chair, which she had positioned closer to mine on her return. Lesley smiled flirtatiously at me as she locked arms with Addie.

"Wyatt, I am so sorry but we have to go now. Addie has a midterm paper I have to help her with."

"I do?" Addie squeaked.

"Yes, you do. Professor Clarkson's class, remember?"

"I thought that wasn't due for another two weeks." Addie seemed genuinely confused.

"Well, it doesn't hurt to start early and we have time right now."

"But – "

"Addie!" Lesley pinched Addie's arm to make her quiet. "Wyatt, I'm sure we'll see each other again soon. Look me up sometime, okay?"

"Sure." I focused all of my attention on Addie now, tearing the sketch from my notepad and folding it. "It was really nice meeting you."

"It was nice meeting you, too." Addie shyly looked down at her free hand which I had just grabbed, slowly moving my fingers over the top of it and placing the sketch in the palm of her hand.

"Maybe we could get together sometime," I offered.

"Okay."

"We have to go now," Lesley interjected.

I dropped Addie's hand and watched them walk away from me.

"I'll see you later then," I yelled as they reached the door.

"Sure," Lesley said from outside. "Maybe next week." I could hardly make out what she was saying through the window but I watched them intently as they made their way up Broadway and out of my sight.

Two weeks went by before I gathered up enough courage to call Addie for a date. I found her number in the college registry and it'd been sitting on my nightstand for eight days. Each night I would pick it up, contemplate the call, then set it back down and fall into a restless sleep, dreaming of horrible first dates with Addie's face on the bodies of all my ex-girlfriends. Finally I mustered up the guts to call her and she, of course, accepted.

Things were going well. Three dates went by and I found my new relationship with Addie progressing nicely. Fortunately none of my previous nightmares had come true. Each date was alluring and seductive. With every encounter I became more intrigued and resolved to see and learn more of Miss Addison Daugherty – until the fourth date.

I decided to invite Addie to my place for a home-cooked romantic dinner. Candles lit the apartment and there were fresh flowers on the table. The ambiance it created was perfect. But when Addie arrived, I could tell something was wrong. After seating her across from me, I sat down, waiting to hear what so obviously was perplexing her mind.

"What's the matter?" I asked finally, after watching Addie twirl her tuna casserole noodles for the last five minutes.

"I don't know what to do," she responded, zoned in on her own thoughts.

"You're going to have to fill me in a little here."

"I think we have a problem."

"Already? We've only been on four dates."

"Technically, three-and-a-half."

"Okay, three-and-a-half." I smiled at her. "What problems could we possibly have already?"

"I think we should tell Lesley."

Seductiveness and intrigue came to a screeching halt.

"Lesley," I grumbled under my breath. "I thought we decided to wait on that little thought until we knew where this was going." I got up from my chair and walked over to Addie, kneeling and picking up her small, smooth hand. "I feel I'm still just getting to know you. I don't think we need to tell Lesley just yet, or at all."

"But I do," Addie said quietly.

I dropped her hand and stood up.

"What business is it of hers anyway? I haven't seen or talked to her in four years. I have no ties to her."

"But *I* do, Wyatt," she pleaded. Addie paused for a moment, collecting her thoughts. "She's my friend, my best friend. You just don't go dating your best friend's ex-husband without telling her. It's just not kosher."

"This is ridiculous."

"No it's not!"

"Yes it is! Lesley's not your keeper and she certainly isn't mine! I don't need her permission to date you or anyone else."

"Anyone else? Are you dating other people?"

"No! You're getting off the point." I walked away from the table and started pacing the apartment. "I can't believe we're fighting about this."

"We're not fighting," Addie answered, following me into the living room. "We're just having a heated debate over a difference of opinion."

I looked over at Addie. I could tell she was trying desperately to make me smile. She was cute that way. It was one of the things I found charming about her. I walked over to her, grabbed one of her hands and pulled her into me, putting one arm after the other around her.

"A heated debate, huh? I've never heard it called that before."

She pulled herself away from me, still loosely in my embrace.

"I don't have fights, Wyatt. Just the occasional disagreement."

"That's good to know."

"So, where does this current debate leave us?"

I could tell Addie was trying to read my thoughts by my facial expressions. The more I looked at her the more I wondered if telling Lesley was really that bad of an idea. How much trouble could she really cause? I'd known Lesley my whole life and not once did she ever get excessively angry over anything – except for when I left her, but I figured that was a natural reaction for any normal person. So, with caution thrown slightly to the wind, I agreed Addie could tell Lesley.

"You won't regret it, I promise."

"We'll see."

Two days later, Lesley showed up at my door a little breathless and disheveled.

"I wondered when you would come here," I said as I opened the door.

"I found myself walking in your neighborhood, so I thought I'd look you up."

"I'm guessing you talked to Addie."

"Last night," she replied as she forced herself into my apartment. I could tell Lesley didn't want to be there, her middle finger in overdrive, stroking the bridge of her nose and eyebrow.

"It probably came as a little shock to you."

Lesley sat down on the couch, not waiting for me to join her.

"Well, am I shocked you went after a pretty girl like Addie, no. Am I shocked that you went after one of my friends, a little. A good friend at that. And one I'm mentoring. Plus she's so much younger than – "

"Okay, I get it. You're shocked." I sat down in a chair across from Lesley, legs hung over the side. "Is that why you're here?"

"No, maybe. I don't know," she said a little exasperated. "I guess I'm here because if we're telling each other truths about ourselves, I have something to tell you. Or maybe it's Addie that's telling the truth. Would you like me to tell her, and then maybe she could tell you, and then you could tell her how you feel about it, and then she could tell me, and we could all continue living in the seventh grade."

"Cut the crap, Lesley, I don't want to hear it. Just tell me what you came here to tell me."

"I'm engaged," she blurted out.

I just stared at her. For the first time in four years the thought of Lesley with another man made me want to vomit. I couldn't move. Motion made the emotional blow to my stomach even worse.

"Wyatt, are you okay?"

Lesley's words made me realize I was staring.

"I'm fine. I'm a little shocked."

"Then we're even."

"I don't see how."

"We've both 'shocked' each other with a little secret."

"Yours is not a little secret."

"Oh, really? Had we never seen each other again, would you really have cared if I ever re-married?"

"I don't know."

"You don't know. You never did know anything. I don't know why I even came. I don't know why I even care."

"Lesley that's not fair."

"Life isn't fair, Wyatt. I learned that four years ago."

Lesley got up and headed for the door. I caught her halfway.

"Lesley, please. For what it's worth, I'm really, really sorry."

"That's not enough."

"I'm not asking for it to be. Look, can we talk about this?"

"Do you love her?"

I felt like I'd been hit again, only this time in the face. *What kind of question was that?* Did I love her? I'd just met Addie not that long ago, who just so happened to be with Lesley, of all people. I still didn't know how I felt about *that*. How was I supposed to answer her question? My head started to tingle a little and I knew I didn't have a real answer for Lesley, so I exaggerated, slightly.

"I think I might. I think I could."

"But you don't know?"

"Of course I don't, but don't tell her that."

"Addie's a kind person."

"I know."

"I don't know if I can do this."

I could hear the tears welling up inside of Lesley as she spoke. I hated that sound. My stance loosened.

"If you don't want me to, I won't see Addie anymore. I don't want to hurt you again. I don't know if I have the stomach for it."

I noticed Lesley took a step back, and then another.

"You would do that for me?"

"Sure."

"Alright then. I guess we could talk about it. Maybe set out some ground rules or something. I think I could handle it better if I knew what to expect."

Lesley turned around and made her way back to the couch. For the first time since our meeting in New York, I noticed her – *really* noticed her. I noticed everything about her – her legs, her body, her lips, her eyes, her cheeks, her hair – everything. I smiled as I walked back to my chair, watching Lesley make herself comfortable on my couch, her skirt creeping up slightly as she sat and crossed her legs. She wore her dark hair down, the curls softly flowing over her shoulders hiding her neck, my favorite part. I almost wished she had worn her hair up so that slender curve wouldn't be hidden, but I had never seen Lesley this way before, and I liked it. I forgot how attractive she could be, all flushed and eyes bright with tears. I always loved her most when she cried. It gave me great joy having to protect her from the world and the harshness of it. I hated it and relished it at the same time. But then I noticed the ring on her left hand and a pang shot straight into my stomach again. *Why am I feeling this?*

"So what's your fiancé's name?" I asked, the question dauntingly hanging over me in the air.

"Sam."

It was the middle of January. Addie and I were supposed to meet Lesley and Sam for a movie in Midtown. I had just left Addie's apartment. She'd come down with the stomach flu and wasn't going to be able to go out tonight. I'd tried calling Lesley to cancel the double date, but no one answered, so I found myself walking in the slush to cancel in person.

I turned the corner to find Lesley huddled under the marquee, alone.

"Hey, where's Sam," I called as I walked toward her.

"He's got to work late. I tried calling you but no one answered."

"That's funny," I said as I caught up to her. "I tried calling you because Addie's sick and couldn't make it, but you weren't home."

Lesley laughed a little. "So much for our double date." She wrapped her arms around her body trying to stay warm. "Now I have nothing to do tonight."

"Me neither," I echoed. I hated being still, not doing anything, no plans. It leaves the mind open to wander. Plus I wasn't ready to go back and listen to Addie throw-up all night. "Hey, you want to see the movie anyway?"

"Just the two of us?"

"It's not a date, if that's what you're worried about," I assured.

"I know that!" she snapped. Her eyebrows softened as she realized her overreaction. Lesley looked around at the crowd of people filing into the theater. "I guess that'd be okay. There's no harm in the two of us seeing a movie together. We're friends."

Lesley didn't sound wholly convinced.

"Exactly," I reassured. "Nothing weird about it at all. Just two friends seeing a movie." I stepped forward, motioning to the ticket counter. "Shall we?"

"Sure. Why not?"

We stood in line for five minutes, bought our tickets, separately of course, then made our way into the theater. I noticed Lesley was chuckling under her breath.

"What is it?" I asked.

"This." She moved her hands slightly above us. "Sam and I were just talking about this exact situation."

"What situation?" I still didn't know what she was getting at. Apparently, *Sam* did, which made me a little annoyed.

"Me being alone with you."

"What?"

"Sam has this fear of what I might do with you if we were all alone in a dark, concealed spot."

"Why?"

"Because he thinks I might still be in love with you." Lesley started laughing. It wasn't a nervous laugh, like I expected, but a natural laugh. She truly thought Sam's concerns were funny. It kind of hurt.

"That's ridiculous," I played along, not wanting Lesley to know I semi-wished she still loved me, if only for selfish, childish reasons. "Why does he even think that?"

"He says I'm enthralled by the 'simplistic and trivial' conversations we have. And he says he caught me staring at you and Addie when we all go to the movies. Says he thinks since I think he can't see me, I let my guard down so my true feelings come out."

"Do you?"

"Stare? Sometimes," she answered honestly. "But only because the two of you amaze me. Each of you is so different from the other, and somehow you both make it work. It amazes me."

I never knew Lesley viewed us this way. I wondered if other people had noticed how different Addie and I were from each other. I'd never thought about it before. I tried to let my physical attraction for Addie guide our relationship. I didn't want any heavy emotional baggage to get in the way of something that could be good. So far, it was working.

"But," continued Lesley, not letting me expand my thoughts on my current relationship, "that isn't Sam's biggest fear in this whole nightmare."

"What is, then?"

"You," she answered plainly. "More than anything Sam fears what you would do if left alone with me in a dark, concealed place."

Just then the lights went down and the reel clicked to play the concession stand advertisement. I looked around at the seats in front of us, to the sides, and to the back. Sam was right. It was dark in here, easy to conceal lovemaking on all levels. I couldn't tell if the couples up front were holding hands or if there was a couple in the back kissing or if the couple down the row from us were exploring those sexual boundaries even further. I started to picture what I would do to Lesley, how I would ease into making my move and then what it might progress into from there. I moved my hand slowly on top of hers.

"Oh," she squeaked quietly. "Did you want the armrest?"

"No, that's okay," I replied quickly. "You can have it."

"Don't be silly."

Lesley turned her body slightly and crossed her legs, leaning a portion of her back against the armrest. It was almost like she was leaning into me. If the armrest wasn't there, we would be touching – I would be holding her. I put my arm across the back of her seat. She didn't protest, so I left it there, letting my mind wander into Sam's fear again, the dancing popcorn on the screen being the last thing I remember.

I graduated from NYU that spring and by chance was offered a job in late June. An assistant producer at a children's cartoon network in San Francisco picked up my comic book while visiting New York and sent a small portfolio of my pictures to his office. Within a week the offer was handed to me in a brief phone call with a plane ticket reserved for me at the airport. After three very long meetings over a two-day span, my mind was almost made up. It was a great offer, but accepting it meant I would have to move to San Francisco. Plus the work I would be doing was a little off from what I truly wanted to do, but I convinced myself it wouldn't be that much different than drawing my comic, and it would be more stable than freelance work, which is really all I had going for me at the moment. The salary was more than I expected at this stage in my career. But money wasn't the issue. My parents had left Prue and I a substantial amount of money, more than either of us imagined they'd had. And though I wasn't necessarily deprived financially, only playing the starving artist to gain sympathy and work, the offer was still more than I had anticipated. The last piece of the puzzle was Addie. Our relationship had gotten quite serious over the last seven months and I wasn't sure what step I should take next. I didn't want to leave her, but I wasn't sure she would go with me. And I definitely wasn't sure I was ready for marriage again. I had three days to make my decision, so I went for a walk, ending up at Joe's Diner on Broadway, where Lesley was once again sitting at a corner table, only this time alone.

"Hey." I walked over to her and pulled out a chair to sit down.

When Lesley looked up I could tell she was annoyed at being interrupted from her reading, her eyebrows forming a V into her forehead and her eyes glossy with a tinge of rage that her mind was trying to keep suppressed. But then she saw me and her eyes instantly cooled, meaning it was safe to sit down next to her.

"What are you doing here?" she asked.

"I just needed a little air to clear my mind."

"And what, pray tell, could be worrying your pretty little mind?"

I laughed. She said it like Scarlett O'Hara, in a sinewy southern accent, which reminded me of when we were younger, when we would joke around with each other, when we told each other everything. I liked that feeling. It comforted me. It made me want more.

Lesley cocked her head to the side, letting her long, dark, wavy hair fall over her shoulder and around her face. This was beginning to be my favorite look.

"Well?" she asked.

I knew that face. I'd loved that face once and now found it hard not to feel towards it again. I reached over and grabbed her hand.

"Let's go for a walk."

"Okay," she replied, puzzled at my gesture. "Is something wrong?" Lesley lifted her hand out of mine, moving it to her book as an excuse.

"No. Just thought it would be a nice evening for a walk. We can watch the sunset over the skyscrapers. That'll be fun."

"Tons, I'm sure."

My hand found its home at the small of her back while I led her out of the coffee shop.

"I have to return this book in an hour. Do you mind if we make a stop by campus?"

"Not at all."

"Maybe we could watch your sunset from the library steps."

"Sure. Why not?"

Lesley looked at me and shook her head, but said nothing. We remained in silence until Lesley handed her book back to the Reserve's librarian. She turned to leave but I grabbed her.

"Let's talk. How about over by the window."

I started pulling her toward a couple of chairs by the nearest window.

"I thought you wanted to watch the sunset," she protested.

"We can watch it from the window."

I plopped her down in a chair, then sat in one directly across from her.

"Wyatt, what's going on?"

"Nothing," I answered quickly. "I just thought we could spend some time together."

"Oh, really? That sounds *sooo* like you."

The comment hurt. I did want to spend time with Lesley. I missed spending time with her. But the weight of my job offer dilemma was bearing too much on me. I wanted to share it with someone and when I saw Lesley, I knew she was the one I wanted to share it with. I just didn't know how to share it with her. So, awkwardly, I tried to steer the conversation.

"Don't be like that," I tried again. "I really want to talk to you."

"Alright," Lesley replied with a sigh and a thrust back into her chair, a sign she was giving up. "Let's talk."

"Great. How's Sam?"

"You brought me here to talk about Sam? I don't buy it. What's really wrong?"

I paused, debating for the last time whether to share my dilemma with her. Realizing I had nothing to lose in telling Lesley my feelings and concerns regarding Addie, I laid my feelings out in front of her.

"Did Addie tell you about my offer in San Francisco?"

"Finally," Lesley exhaled as she leaned forward. "Yeah, she did. And when were you going to tell me, by the way?"

"I don't know. Soon."

"Hmm." She squinted at me, trying to sum me up. "Well, it sounds like a great opportunity. I'm really happy for you."

Lesley smiled sweetly as she spoke to me. She seemed truly happy for me. I knew that part of her happiness was due to the fact that, if I left, a sense of normalcy would be brought back to her life. I couldn't help but feel a little pain in that. I knew I created the awkwardness, the uncomfortableness every time I mentioned Addie's name. But now I wanted Lesley's help, so I pushed my questioning on.

"How did Addie sound when she told you?" I asked.

"Well, she seemed to be okay. She did do a little of her normal pouting, but I think she realizes this is a great opportunity for you. Anyone who loves you can see that..." Lesley paused and took a breath, closing her eyes as she finished her sentence. "And she definitely loves you."

I wondered, as she sat there, silent, if Lesley was really talking about Addie. For the moment, I tried to believe she was, not wanting to admit there could be another possibility.

"Do you really think so?" I asked, trying to sound optimistic.

"Wyatt, if you can't see that that girl is completely and totally in love with you, you're dumber than I give you credit for."

"Very funny." Lesley could tell I was vexed, so she tried to calm my thoughts.

"Look, you know Addie loves you. She follows you around like a lost puppy. Even Sam sees it. He thinks it's cute."

"Do you think I should marry her?"

"What?" Lesley lost her breath for a second and her eyes widened as she fell back into her chair, trying to regain a normal breathing pattern. "I didn't mean...I don't understand. What in the hell kind of question is that?"

People looked up from their newspapers and reference books to see what the elevated conversation in the corner was about. I moved closer to Lesley to calm her down and reassure onlookers that this wasn't a fight.

"Lesley, I'm sorry. It just popped out. I can't get the thought out of my head and it's driving me crazy. I need someone to talk to and you're the closest friend I have right now. Please let me talk to you about it. I need your help."

"I don't know if I can do this," Lesley stuttered.

"Please Lesley. Just think of me as a patient. Someone you don't know personally who's come to you for help."

She paused, thinking about my offer.

"Okay, Wyatt. Talk to me. Tell me what's wrong."

I proceeded to tell her my dilemma.

"I love Addie, Lesley, I really do, but I don't know if I'm ready to marry her. This job offer is a huge opportunity, though, and I don't know if I want to give it up so I can stay here in New York with her. If I ask her to come with me...what if I ruin her life? What if I mess things up like I did with us?" I paused and sat back in my chair, taking deep breaths to help gather my thoughts. I rested my arms on my knees, then leaned forward to look Lesley straight in her eyes. "I blame myself for everything bad that happened between us. I want you to know that. You loved me so much and I threw it all away. I don't know if I'll ever get over that. You were my best friend, and if I couldn't make *our* marriage work, what chance do I have with someone else?"

Tears began to form in my eyes. I was determined not to cry in front of Lesley. As long as I'd known her I never cried in front of her, not even when we were married. That was a touchy subject for me now. Since the day I left her, I always saw Lesley as standing in my way when it came to my own life, but recently my view of her had begun to change. Lesley handled life with more maturity now; her decisions were all well thought out. She had grown, I thought, into a beautiful woman. Or had she always been this way, my eyes blinded by my own selfish needs. I couldn't tell anymore. But as I sat across from her confessing my fears, I saw the hurt and pain I once caused plaguing the muscles of her face, the way her eyes seemed to tremble as I spoke of our past. And the small space of skin above her suprasternal notch, that little space nestled above her collar bone, pulsed quicker as her mind reflected back.

"It's okay, Wyatt." Lesley spoke quietly, trying to hide the moisture forming in the back of her throat. "You shouldn't dwell on us. I don't." I could tell she was lying, her raspy, congested voice becoming elevated, but the words sounded sincere. "Besides, it's not good for your psyche. You need to move past this. If I didn't, I would never have met Sam, and look at me now." She looked down at her engagement ring, a teardrop falling from her eyes and hitting her hand. Lesley then placed her left hand on top of mine, letting the teardrop glide down the side of her hand onto mine. I removed my hand to rub my eyes, pressing my own composed tears to the sides of my face.

"How did you know Sam was the one?" I asked. "I mean, did you feel any hesitation in saying yes, or am I just a freak?"

"I asked myself the same questions you did. Everyone does. Everyone has bad relationships. It's getting past those bad relationships that lets you feel love again." She paused. I could tell she was searching her mind for technical jargon that would help her through this – something that would make it not so personal – but she was drawing a blank. "What it came down to," she started again, slightly flustered, "was whether I could see myself spending the rest of my life with Sam, and I answered myself with a yes. Can you see yourself spending the rest of your life with Addie?"

I knew that question was painful for her. I watched as she squirmed in her chair, waiting for an answer she didn't really want to hear, an answer I didn't want to say. It's hard not to fall in love again with someone you never really fell out of love with. I reached over and held Lesley's face, wiping away the stray tears she couldn't control.

"I saw myself spending the rest of my life with *you*."

"Wyatt," Lesley grabbed my hands and placed them on her knees, "that's not the question I asked you."

"I don't want to answer your question."

"Wyatt, you're not being honest with yourself. You're the one who wants answers, remember? You're the one who wanted to talk."

"Well, let me ask you a question, and be honest with yourself. You said that anyone who loves me can see that this is a great opportunity for me and that I should go, correct?"

"Yeah."

"Do you think I should go?"

"Yes," Lesley responded, without hesitation.

I studied Lesley's face. I saw honesty and love in it. I moved my fingers to her cheek again and wiped the falling tears into the crevices of my hand.

"How could I have ever done this to you?"

I moved closer to her, holding her face in both hands, her eyes closed as I leaned in.

"Wyatt, please." I stopped. "Go love Addie," she whispered. I could feel her body shaking.

"I don't know that I want to." I breathed the words into the air, audible only enough for Lesley to hear. I leaned in a little further, enough that our lips touched, and I lost my self-control. I began to kiss her, gentle at first, afraid she would pull away, but she didn't. Lesley leaned into me and I pulled her face into mine, slipping one of my hands behind her head. She loved me. I knew she did. And though I should have been, I wasn't surprised that I loved her too. I always had. After I left her, my life consisted of just going through the motions, wandering aimlessly. But this moment – this was real. Lesley moved her hand to my wrist and gradually pulled away from me, her face still in my hand.

"Please. Go love Addie," she muttered, her head dropping, causing me to let go.

"What if I don't want to?" I asked, a little shaken myself.

"Wyatt – "

"What if I want to stay here and love you?" Lesley didn't say anything. "What if I told you that I secretly came to New York to find you?" She looked up at me, puzzled. I was a little puzzled, too, but I couldn't stop the words coming out of my mouth. "I came to New York knowing you would be here, wanting to find you and hoping I wouldn't all at the same time. I just didn't want to admit it until now. Isn't it possible that I still love you?"

"No," she whispered.

"You still love me."

"No," she whimpered. "I love Sam."

I felt like I'd been hit again, only this time it was sharp as the heat surged through by body.

"No," I affirmed.

"Yes. None of this matters." Lesley looked down at her hands fidgeting on her knees. "I'm going to marry Sam."

Anger shot through my body. I looked past Lesley and out the window only to see Addie walking carelessly down the walkway opposite of the library. She was smiling. I watched her bouncing step until I couldn't see her anymore. I looked back at Lesley, wanting, temporarily, to lose our past.

"I can see myself with Addie," I forced. "She's the one."

Lesley didn't raise her head.

"That's great. You should – "

"I have to go. Thank you, Lesley, for…talking to me. It really helped." I got up to leave. She finally looked up at me.

"Where are you going?"

"I have to go catch someone before they get too far."

"Okay?"

"I'll see you later." I started walking for the door.

"Wyatt?"

I stopped. If she told me she loved me, I would stay. I would forget about Addie, forget about San Francisco. I would stay just to be with her, if she told me she loved me.

"I hope that you're happy, I mean, in whatever you decide."

I said nothing. No response. I began walking away again, leaving the library without saying goodbye. Once outside I looked up the library walls to see if Lesley was watching me from the window. She wasn't there.

I started running to catch up with Addie, trying to forget about what just happened. When I was about twenty feet away from her, I slowed to a fast paced walk, not wanting to pounce on her and startle her.

"Hey, beautiful," I said, placing my hands over her eyes. She stopped. "Guess who?"

"I would have to say my gorgeous boyfriend Wyatt, or my sexy Latin lover Alejandro." Addie pulled my hands down and began to turn around. "Either way, it's going to be a good night." She kissed me and we proceeded to walk toward her apartment holding hands. "So what are you doing here?"

"Oh, I was, uh, asking Lesley about something. We were over at the library. I saw you through the window and I just had to see you. You were too irresistible to pass up." I leaned over and kissed her neck.

"Thank you," she giggled. She began counting burnt out streetlamps as we walked in silence, counting to seven before indulging her true curiosity. "So what were you two talking about?"

"What I should do about San Francisco. You know I have to make a decision by Monday, right?"

"Yeah." She paused. "Have you made a decision yet? Not that I'm trying to rush you or anything."

"Not yet. At least I think not yet. I have so many things to consider."

"Like what?"

"Well, for starters, it's San Francisco. That's three thousand miles away from friends. I mean, I've kind of made this place home. Plus the cost of living – "

"New York's not any better," she interrupted.

"That's true." I was a little caught off guard. Usually Addie would cutely weave her questions and concerns into conversations in a roundabout way, tricking you slightly into telling her what she wanted to know, but tonight she was direct. She wasn't giving me any room to wriggle out from. But I tried, nonetheless, to avoid her ever-sharpening inquiries. "It's also not the kind of drawing I wanted to focus on either."

"You said yourself it wasn't that much different than your comic and some of the freelance work you've done. Plus you took some cartooning classes. I remember you said that. So it's not as if you don't have the training. They wouldn't have picked you if you didn't." Addie's points were becoming stronger.

"I guess I did say that. Actually, I think I really might enjoy it."

Addie stopped walking and faced me, pulling the sides of my shirt and turning my body toward her so I would have to look at her.

"So what's stopping you?" she asked bluntly.

"It's a big decision, and to only have three more days to decide – "

"What's stopping you?" she asked again.

"I don't know," I replied quietly. I knew I was lying but the fleeting braveness I experienced in the library was gone and I just wasn't ready to face my feelings for Addie yet. Pouring my heart out to one woman a night was enough.

"Oh," she said dejected. We began walking again. "I think you should go," she said suddenly.

"What?"

"I think you should go to San Francisco and take that job." Addie looked straight ahead as she talked. "I think it's too big of an opportunity to pass up. Anyone that loves you can see that."

I stopped her and stood in front of her. She just looked at me.

"Did you talk to Lesley today?" I asked, stunned at her words.

"No. Why?"

"No reason," I quickly answered.

"Look. Everyone will understand if you go, Wyatt. They just want the best for you."

"What about you? What will you do if I go?"

"I'll still love you, wherever you are."

Addie's face was serious as I smiled and leaned down to kiss her. She let me hold her, her body falling into mine as it always did, as her mind soaked up the romantic thought of how we currently looked to passersby. She had made up my mind.

"Come on," I said as I let her go and grabbed her hand, beginning to drag her across the street.

"Where are we going?" she yelled.

"It's a surprise!"

It was after ten-thirty and I frantically began to scan the street. I was looking for a store that sold jewelry, and since most were closed now, I grabbed Addie and dragged her, running about three and half blocks before stopping.

"Stay right here," I said, slightly out of breath and sitting her down in a chair outside a café.

Addie watched as I walked about thirty feet away to a street vendor closing up for the night. I made sure she could see we were talking but that she couldn't see what I was looking at and what the vendor was trying to sell me. After ten minutes I walked back and kneeled in front of her. I took her hands and brushed my thumb across the tops of her fingers while clasping something in my right hand. She sat and waited impatiently for me to explain.

"This may be the most impetuous thing I've ever done."

I stopped and looked up at Addie. She had the strangest look on her face. She looked excited but also like she was in some sort of pain, or bracing herself for a punch in the face. It made me more nervous, so I placed my gaze on her hand again and continued.

"I feel that there are two really great opportunities in front of me and I've spent the last few days trying to decide which opportunity meant more to me...which one would help me accomplish what I want from life." I paused and took a long breath. "And after agonizing over them both, I've decided that I want both."

"Wyatt, I don't understand. What are you talking about?"

I let go of her right hand and held her left, freeing up the newly bought trinket in my hand.

"Addison Daugherty, will you marry me?" I held out a sterling silver ring with a small, turquoise stone in it.

Addie sat motionless, staring at the ring I held in front of her. After a minute of silence I thought perhaps I had made a mistake, so I began making excuses for myself.

"I know it's a little sudden and we won't have that much time to plan." She continued to stare at the ring. "And this would be just a starter ring. I didn't have time to pick something else out, but when we get to San Francisco – "

"Yes!" she said, snatching the ring out of my hand and placing it on her ring finger. Addie clasped her hand against her heart.

"Really? You want to get married?" I was a little overcome.

"Of course I do, silly. Why do you think I asked you all those questions?" She leaned down to hug me, then placed a kiss on my cheek. "This is so wonderful! We don't have much time to plan. When do you think they'll expect you in San Francisco?" Addie pulled me to my feet and we began walking back to her apartment.

"I don't know. Maybe a week from Monday, maybe two. I didn't discuss it that far."

"We definitely should get married before we move. Where can we get married that quickly?"

I could tell her mind was wandering through the millions of wedding ceremonial options New York had to offer, each one taking months of planning, which she didn't have, and the resolution of sadness in her eyes as she had to move on to the next one, getting no further than where she had started. I stopped walking.

"I didn't mean we had to get married this week. Why do we have to get married before we go to San Francisco? We could get married whenever. It doesn't have to be right now."

"You don't want to get married?" Addie looked like she was about to cry.

"That's not what I said. I just don't understand why we can't plan all this once we're in California. It seems like a lot to figure out in one week."

"Maybe you should have thought of that before you asked the question."

Addie turned her back to me, arms folded, facing the storefronts as people walked around us on the sidewalk. They stared at her stance, solid and frigid, some smiling or laughing, others irritated at the roadblock. I grabbed her elbow and tried to turn her around.

"Why is this so important to you? Why does it have to be this week?"

"Because," she replied, slightly whining and crying at the same time. I put my arms around her and said the only thing I knew of that could make her feel better.

"Okay."

Addie threw her arms around me and jumped up and down.

"Thank you! Thank you! Thank you!" She stopped, grabbed my hand, and we proceeded walking.

"So, where can we get married? Where do you want to get married?" she asked.

"There's the courthouse," I said as I watched her face for a reaction. "We could get married by the justice of the peace."

"Uggh! I'm not getting married at the courthouse. I want a wedding, Wyatt," she whined. "Every girl deserves a wedding, even if it isn't going to be the wedding of her dreams."

"There has to be something or somewhere in this city we can get married in or by with no reservations. Hey, how about the Statue of Liberty?" I laughed under my breath, bending over slightly to cushion the quick jab Addie gave me.

"Wyatt be serious. This is important to me. This is the biggest thing that's going to happen to me in my whole life. I want it to be special. I want it to be beautiful."

Addie rested her head on my shoulder as we walked along in the stale, heated streets lit with fluorescent and incandescent bulbs. I searched the sky as we walked, trying to think of something that would make Addie happy. I found nothing but bricks, glass, and a starless sky.

"Well, there's always Las Vegas," I said finally, sighing as the sentence escaped from my mouth.

"What did you say?" Addie stopped and stared at me.

"I was only joking. I'm sure we'll find something here."

"No, no, no! Las Vegas has possibilities. I never thought about Vegas."

"I wasn't serious," I said, imagining myself standing next to Addie in front of Elvis singing *Today, Tomorrow, and Forever* as we exchanged our wedding vows. "I was just trying to lighten the mood."

"No, it's perfect. Vegas is open twenty-four hours a day, seven days a week. There are a thousand possibilities."

"You're serious?"

"Aren't you?"

"Yeah, but Vegas? Don't you want something more? Something a little less clandestine?"

"No, I don't. I want you. I want to get out of New York. I want to start a new life, the life I've always wanted. And I don't want to get married by some crummy judge in a courthouse. Las Vegas is exotic."

I laughed, trying to imagine Las Vegas as anything but corny; that showgirls were really paying their way through med school and bouncers went home every weekend to check on their aging, naïve grandmothers as the mob counted their mounting stacks of money in the back.

"Stop laughing," Addie snapped. "I'm being serious. I want to get married in Vegas, and if you love me and really want to be with me, you'll want to get married there too." She waited for me to answer.

"Let's go to Vegas," I said finally. "But no singing Elvises."

"I promise," she squealed, jumping up and down, trying to kiss me as she jumped. I put my arms around her shoulders, then pulled her closer to me to stop her jumping.

"So when do you want to get married?" I asked.

"Tonight!"

"Tonight?" The reality of my proposal began to sink in.

"Well, not actually tonight, but we'll book a flight tonight and be there in the morning, early afternoon at the latest, then we'll get married, have a short but wonderful honeymoon and still have time to plan for San Francisco. It all works out!" Addie kissed me and started to walk away. I grabbed her hand.

"Where are you going," I demanded.

"I'm going to get Lesley."

"Why?"

"Because she's my maid of honor. You have to go get Sam. He's your best man. Plus they double as witnesses. I thought you'd know all that. Didn't you have attendants when you married Lesley?"

"Yeah, but – "

"Oh, and you have to get the airplane tickets. We have to hurry." She kissed me again, slightly jerking her hand out of mine, and began to walk toward the edge of the street. "We'll meet you at your apartment at four. That gives us what, five hours?"

"I guess – "

"Oh, and I did talk to Lesley today."

"What?" I was confused.

"You asked me earlier if I'd talked to Lesley today and I told you no, but I lied."

"What did you talk to her about?" I asked, not really caring what they discussed.

"About you and San Francisco. See, I wanted you to stay and I asked her how I could get you to stay. But she told me that if I really loved you, I should let you go, and if I told you that, you would make the right decision. And you did! Now we get to spend the rest of our lives together! Isn't Lesley wonderful?"

"Wait, so she told you to tell me all that so I would ask you to marry me?" I was beginning to get angry. I wondered if I'd been played for a fool.

"No, no, no, silly! She just told me what she would do if she were in my shoes. So I put myself in hers, hoping things would work out the way I wanted them to, and they did!"

Did Addie trick me? I began to go back through the evening's events and sort out what Lesley said, what Addie said, and what I said. Things had become too jumbled.

"We don't have time for this," Addie said as she moved to the curb. She hailed a taxi and it stopped across the street. "I love you!" she yelled as she ran across the street. I watched as she got in, its taillights eventually meshing together with all the other city lights, undistinguished from anything else. I finally did the same thing, only catching a cab uptown toward Sam's apartment.

Sam took the news of my newly established engagement better than I expected. I always saw Sam as a man of reason; someone who definitely thought things through clearly. He was kind of perfect for Lesley in that way. I was shocked when Sam congratulated me with a firm, open arm hug and a large, cheerful smile.

"That's great," Sam said. "I was wondering when you'd pop the question. I'm surprised you waited so long."

"Why do you say that?" I asked.

"Well, if it had been me and I was dating someone like Addie, I would have grabbed a hold of her so quick her head would still be spinning. I'd want the whole world to know she was mine. But that's me. I'm a fast mover. I asked Lesley to marry me, oh, two, three months after we started dating."

"Really?"

"Yeah," continued Sam. "But we had known each other for a while before we dated. Actually, we were quite good friends before we started dating, so it just seemed natural when I asked her to marry me. I'm sure it's the same with you. Am I right?"

Sam put his arm around my shoulders, smiling that sneaky guy smile, shaking me a little as if some unspeakable thought was traveling between our brains with unknown sexual undertones each didn't want the other to know he wasn't understanding. I just smiled back, ignoring my own uncomfortable thoughts about my ex-wife marrying this man. It bothered me, being around Sam, knowing he was with Lesley and the probability their relationship was an intimate one. It bothered me since I first heard this man's name escape the lips of my former wife. But that was beside the point now. Lesley had made that abundantly clear. There was a long pause and I forced myself to think of something else to say.

"I guess when two people are meant to be, they always find each other," I replied finally, not believing a word I said. "That's how I'd describe me and Addie…and you and Lesley of course." I felt I had to add the last part.

"Yep, we sure are two lucky sons of bitches." Sam walked over to his kitchen, took a bottle of scotch out of his cabinet and poured two glasses. "Let's have a toast to our women and our lives."

"Actually, I was hoping you'd come with me to my apartment," I said, taking the glass.

"Your apartment? Why?"

"Well, Addie and I have decided not to wait to get married. We're going to Las Vegas tonight and we were kind of hoping you and Lesley would come with us. Addie's over at Lesley's right now."

"Tonight?"

I shook my head in confirmation.

"Wow. You guys must really want to get married." Sam winked at me. "But that's cool. Lesley and I had been talking of taking a vacation in Las Vegas. It'll be fun."

"You don't think this is all moving too fast?" My voice was somewhat shaky.

There was a noticeable uneasiness between us now. To this point our friendship had been casual. It was our girlfriends that brought us together, and it was our girlfriends we mostly talked about when alone. Never before had either of us asked for advice or gone in depth into our personal relationship. Mostly our conversations consisted of what we had done that week or our petty annoyances about women that all real men moan about to each other from time to time. I had put Sam in an awkward position.

"Wyatt, what do you want me to tell you?" Sam snapped, his uneasiness floating to the surface. "That you're making a mistake? That Addie isn't the one for you?"

"No, that's not what I meant. I just feel…." My voice trailed off.

"Perhaps you think Lesley's still the one for you?"

I looked up, shocked. I wondered if it had been that plain on my face for everyone to see. I certainly hadn't noticed it. Or at the very least I had tried to avoid noticing it.

"Now, whoa, whoa…wait. That's not it. That's not it at all," I said, my voice shaking even more as I spoke.

"Really? A man senses things, Wyatt, and I'm sensing you're a little unsure about that statement."

"No, I'm not," I replied, slightly panicked. "I swear I'm not. I love Addie. I want to be with her. Lesley's just in my past. It's hard not to let the past get the best of you sometimes, but that's it. I love Addie, Sam."

"I'm sure you do. What I'm not sure about is your relationship with Lesley."

I had to stop this – all of it – now.

"There's nothing there. I swear," I said finally.

"Okay, then."

We both picked up our glasses and finished our scotch.

"You know," Sam began calmer, "I think the idea of marriage and everything that goes along with that image is a lot harder on men than it is on women." Sam went to his bedroom, got out his suitcase, and started rummaging through his closet and dresser for underwear and shirts.

"Yeah," I answered, following him into the bedroom.

"I mean, women wait their whole lives for one day, planning every detail since the time they're, like, three. So jumping feet first into the romantic illusion is much easier for them." Sam closed the suitcase and searched the room for his keys.

"I guess."

I found the keys on the nightstand. I picked them up, jiggled them in front of his face, then dropped them into his hand. I headed downstairs with Sam close behind. Reaching the lobby, I waited. Sam pushed the lobby door open and we both stepped out onto the lighted city sidewalk, the low hum of electricity flowing around our ears.

"To tell you the truth," Sam said finally, "the thought of marriage gives me small panic attacks sometimes."

"Really?" I was genuinely surprised. "I never would have thought you felt like that. Does Lesley know?"

"What man in his right mind would tell their fiancé that marriage scares him? I'd be branded an idiot. Besides, I don't want to deal with all the repercussions that would go along with that statement. Lesley would think I didn't love her enough and that's not the truth. Marriage is just a difficult thought sometimes, that's all."

"What scares you the most?"

"I'm not exactly comfortable talking to you about this."

"I'm sorry," I retracted quickly. "I don't know why I'm acting this way. Let's talk about something else."

"I'm thirty-six," Sam divulged. "It's an age thing. Lesley's ten years younger than me. It's a big difference. Sometimes I think maybe I fell for Lesley so quickly because I'm getting older and there wouldn't be that many more opportunities for me to find someone. Especially someone like Lesley. She's young, beautiful, smart, terrific body – "

"Yeah, Lesley did always have those great legs," I blurted. Sam seemed a little threatened.

"Besides the superficial reasons," Sam continued, with more authority in his voice, "I wonder sometimes if I'm truly ready for the commitment."

"What makes you sure you are?" I turned to hail a taxi.

"What made you so sure you were? What makes you sure now?" Sam opened the taxi door, then slid in next to me.

"109th and Amsterdam, please," I told the cabdriver.

"Who ever really knows if they're ready for marriage? I guess you just follow your feelings and hope they're right. Sounds a little sappy, doesn't it?"

"A little?" I laughed. "It sounds like something out of a romance."

"Thanks a lot." Sam jabbed me in the shoulder. "Let me ask you this. If you're so afraid to marry this girl, why did you ask her?"

"I didn't say I didn't want to marry her. I love her." I began to tense up in my defense.

"Then why all the personal questions about marriage? I've never been married before. You're already one step ahead of me in that department."

"That's not funny."

"I wasn't making a joke."

Silence fell in the backseat of the cab. I leaned my head back and watched the reflections of buildings and stoplights in the rear window. Sam edged himself into the corner of the cab and sat quietly, watching his tortured companion. He tried to never let it show, but there was a part of Sam that was jealous of me. How could he not be? It's instinctual to be jealous of the ex-boyfriend or the ex-husband. They've had something you'll never experience with the girl you love. Plus, I knew Sam was never really sure Lesley was over me and it bothered him sometimes. The thought of me still being in love with Lesley bothered him even more. Lesley and I laughed together about the idea, trying to find the humor in lingering emotions for each other the other wasn't sure existed. But Sam, he couldn't let the idea go. He tried not to let the thought creep into his brain, but every once in a while it would slip past the protective shield of his ego into his subconscious, causing nightmares he'd wake up screaming from. As any normal man he told himself it was nothing, and went back to bed. Tonight he couldn't force the thoughts away. It turns out he had good reason to be concerned, Lesley and I acting out his greatest fear earlier this evening. But in all this there was the bright, shimmering thought of Addie. In a way, she was Sam's salvation from this jealous torture, and if he could just get me past my cold feet and into a wedding chapel, his life would go back to normal, he hoped.

"I think you're making a really good decision." Sam's voice broke the silence in the car.

"What?"

"I think this is a good decision, if you still want to know my opinion."

"Thanks," I replied. "I just don't know if I'm making the right one."

"Life isn't about knowing whether or not you're making the right decision. Life is about living and taking chances, and then learning from those chances, results good or bad. Despite what may happen in the future, don't you want to take a chance on Addie?"

Sam's words sounded sincere. I felt my escort was trying to be a real friend now, taking in the advice and letting it bounce around in my head. *Addie's worth the chance, isn't she?* I felt the cab stop and watched as Sam handed money to the cab driver.

"You didn't have to do that," I protested as I stepped out of the cab.

"Consider it the first stepping stone towards an exciting new endeavor."

"I guess this is sort of exciting," I said, trying to hide a smile.

"Most definitely."

CHAPTER 9: THE FLAMINGO

Lesley

Pound, pound, pound!

"Lesley!"

Pound, pound, pound!

"Lesley!"

It was one a.m. Someone was pounding on my door. And apparently I knew them, which meant now I was going to have to get out of bed so I could kill them for waking me up at one-freaking-a.m. in the morning!

"Lesley! Come on. Wake up!"

As I got closer to the door I recognized Addie's voice on the other side.

"Somebody better have died, Addie. Otherwise, that somebody's going to be you." As soon as I opened the door I was bum-rushed with a bear hug. She almost knocked me to the floor. "What's all this about?" I was extremely annoyed.

"Lesley, I've had the most wonderful night!"

Here we go. Addie must have talked to Wyatt. He must have told her he loved her. I wondered if he asked her to come to California with him. I wasn't sure that I really cared. After our little interaction earlier this evening, which I was sure he left out of his professions of love to her, I really didn't care what Wyatt told Addie. I didn't really care what they did together, just as long as it was away from me. Let him take her to California. See if I care. I bet you it won't even last.

"And then he asked me to marry him!"

"What?"

Everything stopped.

Eight months. That's how long it had been since I first saw Wyatt in that coffee shop on Broadway. It seemed shorter some days, longer others, but there it was – eight months come and gone and a chance meeting now had turned into an abrupt engagement.

It was impossible not to see the chemistry between Wyatt and Addie. I prepared myself for their relationship before there was a relationship. I could feel their attraction the first time I introduced them, something I tried very hard not to do. But Addie just couldn't help herself. Seeing it right there in front of me is what hurt the most.

I replayed that first encounter in my head. I had seen Wyatt walk into the coffee shop, order his drink, and sit down at a table across from ours without even seeing I was there. I watched him intently, trying to figure out if it was really him. After the second time he passed our table, I confirmed to my "friend" that it definitely was my ex-husband, maybe. And so I studied him again, knowing that the human body naturally doesn't change much in four years, but that if it was Wyatt, he had seemingly changed enough to make me wonder if it was truly him. His hair was lighter, his body more toned than I remembered, and he seemed a little taller. He was also wearing glasses, a look I hadn't seen him in since he was thirteen. Addie thought he was very good looking. I stared at him, smiling, trying to see the boy I once married in this man across from me, intently scribbling on the piece of paper in front of him. After awhile the man took his glasses off and rubbed his eyes. There he was, the boy I once loved – the boy who broke my heart and abandoned me – sitting fifteen feet away from me. I got up, walked over, and took the chance.

How different things would be now if I'd just stayed seated.

It was about halfway through that first interaction at Joe's Diner that I excused myself to use the ladies room. I could tell Wyatt had forgotten I was even there. Addie excused herself with me, excited to discuss Wyatt while using the facilities. I, on the other hand, was somewhat annoyed that my pupil was attracting more attention than I was. It'd been four years since Wyatt last saw me, and in my opinion, I was prettier than ever. Why I couldn't find some lost attraction between us was beyond me. I listened to Addie rattle off about how cute Wyatt was and why didn't I introduce them before. I faked peeing, flushing the toilet for effect, then came out and washed my hands.

"I didn't even know Wyatt was in New York." I interrupted Addie's rambling on about Wyatt's comic book. "Besides, he's my ex-husband. I would have never imagined introducing him to any of my friends. I never really expected to see him again."

"How can you say that?" Addie exclaimed. "He seems wonderful. And so interesting, too. Why did you ever leave him?"

"*He* left *me*," I said, just as the toilet stopped flushing, my voice elevated to be heard over the noise. The words echoed through the bathroom and the three other women in the room stared at me, two giggling and one looking extremely uncomfortable. "It doesn't matter anyway," I said, trying to regain my dignity. "If I'd stayed married to him, I'd probably be working at this diner instead of getting my PhD. He wasn't that good of a lover either."

"Oh," sighed Addie.

"He's a taker, not a giver," I continued as we walked out of the bathroom. "Who wants that?"

"I don't think it would be all that bad," Addie replied quietly.

I felt the awfulness of that remark now. It was a lie, what I said about Wyatt's lovemaking. Addie undoubtedly knew that by now. That was a different kind of image that made my stomach turn, Addie and Wyatt together in some passionate, contortioned position left mostly depicted on romance novel covers. Perhaps that's why Addie waited so long to tell me about Wyatt. They were having too good of a time. But I knew that wasn't true. It was guilt that kept Addie from telling me about Wyatt at first. It wasn't everyday Addie dated her best friend's ex-husband. Addie looked up to me immensely, which is one reason she found Wyatt attractive. If he was good enough for me, he was good enough for her – probably too good. But that didn't stop her. He was too intoxicating to resist: handsome, well built, an artist from the Village, and he was an older man by six years. To a twenty year old beginning her sophomore year in a major she didn't want, studying at a college she hated being at, he was her ultimate choice in a MRS degree. That was really the only reason Addie left home, hoping college would produce for her the love of her life. Where else do you find a well-educated, career-oriented man who will, undoubtedly, take care of you into your golden years? It wasn't until their fourth date that Addie knew for sure she was going to marry Wyatt and realizing it, she decided to tell me who the new man in her life was.

I was internally livid as my pupil sat in my cramped living room and told me she was dating my ex-husband. Outwardly, I was composed and cool, not wanting to let this *child* see my inward rage. Addie waited for a scolding, but none came. We sat in silence staring at the apartment's stained carpet. I lulled my response around in my head until I actually believed the words coming out of my mouth; "I think that's great, Addie. Wyatt would be a good choice for you. He wasn't for me, of course, but for you, he just might be perfect." The speech left a sour taste on my tongue and I rubbed my taste buds across the ridges of my mouth trying to get rid of it. Addie plowed me over onto the couch with hugs and ecstatic thank-yous. So, life went on.

I continually told myself that I was fine with the arrangement and that Sam, the man I would love and who would protect me for the rest of my life, was better than any man I'd ever been with. He would be the last and I could finally prove that someone loved me, infinitely. I had hoped, however, that Sam and I would be married before Wyatt could have even thought of asking Addie to marry him. Now I sat regretting my second chance meeting with Wyatt at the coffee shop on Broadway.

"Let's go for a walk."

That was the phrase that did it. When he said it, my mind drifted back to our childhood. Whenever Wyatt had a problem I would find him in his tree house waiting for me. Usually Prue was at the base of the tree trying to get Wyatt to let her in, but it was me who successfully got Wyatt to lower the ladder. I would climb up to him, look at his troubled face and say, "Let's go for a walk". It was our code word for spilling our guts. And now Wyatt was waiting for me again and I couldn't refuse the gentle feeling of past love creeping over me. Perhaps that's why I told him Addie loved him. And now that's why Addie was pounding on my door at one a.m., why all this was happening. I felt that I helped push Wyatt into a decision I wasn't quite ready to deal with myself. But it was better than dealing with the alternate possibility.

I could still feel Wyatt's touch holding my face. *He* leaned in, didn't he? *He* kissed me, right? Did I fall into him? Did I kiss him back? I could feel Wyatt's hands on me, on my cheek and at the base of my neck, pulling me in. I could feel myself falling into him, my lips moving perfectly with his. I remember wanting more. *STOP!* I didn't want to think about our conversation at the library anymore. I made a mental note never to go back to Joe's Diner, convinced it was cursed, destined to cause people to make bad decisions and say things they didn't really mean.

Addie noticed I hadn't said a word since her arrival and confused my pensiveness for annoyance, which she figured she was causing with her drawn out story, so she got straight to the point.

"We have to get ready to leave now." Addie walked into my bedroom and started throwing clothes on the bed to be packed. I followed, confused.

"What are you doing with my clothes?"

"We have to get ready. We only have a few hours before the plane leaves."

"What plane? Did I miss something?" I had only been half listening to her, so it was possible I had missed something big. What could be bigger than her engagement, I hadn't the faintest idea. "Please tell me why my clothes are now all over my bed."

"Okay, don't freak out or anything but, Wyatt and I are getting married in Las Vegas! You're coming with, so let's get you packed!"

"Wait, can you run that by me again?" I definitely had missed something during my introspection. I plopped down beside the pile of my clothes. "You're getting married in Vegas?"

"Yep."

"Tonight?"

"Yep, well, not tonight, but definitely when we get there. Our plane leaves in four hours. Let's see. You'll need a bikini for the pool and a sun dress – "

"Addie focus!"

Addie dropped her handfuls of clothes and hangers, turned around and quickly sat in the chair across from me. I got up and kneeled in front of her, holding her hands for stability and nervously ran my thumb back and forth over her newly placed engagement ring.

"What's going on? Please calm down and explain to me why all my clothes are now splattered across this room and why, in God's name, are you leaving on a plane to get married in Las Vegas?"

Addie smiled and kissed my cheek.

"You're coming with us, silly! You've been married before. I thought you'd be better at this." Addie began to slightly swing my hand as she spoke. "You of all people should know you need a maid of honor to get married, and you're mine! Wyatt went over to get Sam. He's coming too. Wyatt said he was so excited!" Addie got up and continued her clothing search.

"Wait. Sam's coming too?"

"Yeah. Isn't that wonderful? I'm so happy we've all become such great friends." Addie stopped her search, joined me on the floor and hugged me. "I wouldn't want anyone else there but you. You're the whole reason this happened. I can't thank you enough. You're the best friend I ever had."

I went limp in her arms. I couldn't believe it. I didn't know what to feel. But I couldn't *not* go to Vegas, so I hugged Addie back, then joined her in packing a suitcase.

Twelve hours later Sam and I were at the Flamingo in the Garden Suite getting ready for a night out on the town with the newly married Mr. and Mrs. Trilmon.

The ceremony took ten minutes. Though not terribly romantic, the scene was, in its own way, lovely. Slightly jetlagged, Sam and I stood in The Little Lovers Wedding Chapel watching Addie and Wyatt getting married by one of the many on-hand ministers.

Again, chance played a starring role in Wyatt and Addie's relationship, enabling them to have a ceremony quickly. It came to be that some nosey, fairly jealous groom called off his ceremony after he found his fiancé and best-friend skinny-dipping in the hotel pool after two o'clock in the morning. Though not there for the spectacle that occurred in the lobby as all parties of the torrid love triangle were leaving, the Trilmon party did however meet a honeymooning couple who witnessed the scene, who then informed Addie and Wyatt of the possible opening of a ceremony spot. So the six of us, newly befriended honeymooners included, went down to The Little Chapel and began picking out floral arrangements from the onsite wedding coordinator. With a few hours until the nuptials, we separated for preparation and promised to be at The Little Lovers Wedding Chapel at four o'clock. Excited, Addie and Wyatt invited the maid, who had just finished cleaning their room when they got there, and, of course, the couple they met in the lobby who were on their honeymoon. The couple, John and Katie, just finished a night of blackjack, winning a thousand dollars and giving a hundred of it to Addie and Wyatt as a gift.

After the clapping ended and the small party of guests left, the newly wedded couple decided to drag their best friends up and down the strip. Though tired, Sam and I felt obliged to follow our travel companions.

"It was a nice ceremony," Sam said after fifteen minutes of silence. I had been in the bathroom staring at myself in the mirror, trying to figure out which dress that Addie packed for me would make me look the most ravishing and irresistible. When I didn't respond, Sam walked into the bathroom and watched as I held three dresses in front of me, trying to make a decision. "You will look beautiful in anything you put on."

"I don't want to look beautiful. I want to look irresistible. Why should Addie be the only pretty one today?" I singled out a deep red, low cut cocktail dress and hung it around my neck.

"Isn't it bad to be jealous of the bride on her wedding day?" Sam asked, smiling.

"I'm not jealous!" I snapped. My mood changed quickly with the realization of my hasty retort. "I just want to be seen, too. What's so wrong with that?" I smiled devilishly and kissed the side of his mouth.

"Exactly whose eyes are you trying to attract?"

Sam said it with a laugh but I heard the seriousness in his voice and it caught me off guard. I stepped back a little and tried to think of something clever to come back with. Why *did* I want to be the center of attention? After all, it was Addie's day, not mine. I didn't even want it to be my own wedding day; I just didn't want it to be Addie's either.

Why is that, I wondered. Since I'd found out Wyatt and Addie were dating, I hadn't slept well, the image of Wyatt seducing Addie – of him touching her the way he used to touch me – would wake me up at night and leave me in a cold sweat. It didn't happen every night. Only nights I would observe their closeness while on a double date at the movies, or the way Wyatt would reach and stroke the back of Addie's neck at dinner. Every time he touched her I would feel the caress of his hand from my past, a sensory memory eking its way to the surface. Sometimes I would immerse myself in it, enjoying the feeling it would bring. Sam had confronted me about it before I even realized I did it. It made me question everything, and I hated it.

I pushed the negative thoughts out of my mind, walked over to Sam and tried to look deep into his eyes.

"I only have eyes for you, baby," slowly biting his lip and pulling away from him to finish getting ready.

"Cute. Very cute."

"I thought so," I answered, a smile creeping to my face.

"We have to meet Wyatt and Addie in ten minutes. You might want to hurry up and choose something to wear."

"Don't worry. I'll be ready to celebrate in seven."

It took me another twenty minutes before I felt I was seductive enough to hit the bright lights of Las Vegas. If I had wanted attention, I succeeded. Although proud to have me on his arm, Sam couldn't help but feel a little territorial. After all, several men seemed to be coveting his property. At every available chance, he slightly lifted my left hand to make more prominent my engagement ring to male onlookers. I noticed his over protectiveness and flaunted my own arm candy a little, until I could no longer stand a drunken Wyatt and his nauseatingly happy wife. For the last six and a half hours we had been traveling up and down the Strip, having a glass of champagne at every casino we came to in order to toast new beginnings, growing exceedingly louder and happier as we made our way through the lighted city. Around midnight, out of pure exhaustion, Sam stopped our group.

"Guys, we have to stop," Sam said finally. "Lesley's getting tired."

"Com'on," Wyatt slurred. "Celbrate wit us."

"No, I think you've had enough celebrating."

"No." Wyatt tried to slap Sam on the back but missed. Sam caught him, then awkwardly hailed a taxi.

"You two go enjoy your wedding night," Sam said as he opened the taxi door and slid Wyatt into the back seat. Addie followed, giggling at the thought of her wedding night. She fell into Wyatt as the taxi drove away, a little light-headed and content with the day's events. I knew that Addie had finally achieved her life goal: getting married.

Sam and I began slowly walking back to the Flamingo. I closed my eyes and let him lead me to the hotel, our room and eventually back to New York; back to some sense of normalcy. I felt him stop and I opened my eyes to a night sky. Confused, I lifted my head from his shoulder and found we were standing across the street from The Little Lovers Wedding Chapel.

"What are we doing here?" I asked.

"I don't know," Sam answered. "I just can't believe all the people who've gotten married there. Celebrities too. And now our friends. It's just amazing, don't you think?"

"Fascinating," I said with a yawn. I closed my eyes again and placed my head on Sam's shoulder. Just then his body jerked.

"Just look at that! Look at those stars!"

I opened my eyes and saw tiny pinpricks of light fighting the night sky.

"It's not like New York," he continued. "You can't see stars in New York. Too many lights filling up the sky. But here it's different. It's beautiful, isn't it?"

"I've seen better," I responded.

"Better than this?" Sam put his arms up in the air, as if to hold the entire night sky, then flapped them down at his sides. "Where?"

"Michigan," I sighed, putting my head back down on his shoulder.

"Michigan," he laughed.

Usually Sam wasn't this sentimental, but I convinced myself it was the jetlag getting to him and too much champagne. A normal remark would have been that there was too much money being pumped into a town just for entertainment, causing the night sky to dim and the real beauty of nature being masked. I mean, you could barely make out the Big Dipper, the lights were so bright. And I would have agreed with him if he'd said that, but instead I stayed silent. He mistook my silence for agreement with his thoughts.

"Let's get married," he said quickly.

"We are getting married." I held up my engagement ring. "See, you've already asked me," I laughed. I leaned against him, putting my head underneath his chin and my arms in front of me, forcing him to hold me like a large ball. I closed my eyes again and began listening to the pace of his heart beating faster. It was soothing to the point I could have fallen asleep right then.

"No, I mean let's get married tonight, right here."

"What?" I jerked away from him and saw by his face he was serious. "But…I don't…Why?"

"Because I love you and I want to be with you and I don't want to wait any longer. Wyatt and Addie had the right idea. If you want something, take it."

"Wyatt is impulsive and Addie is an idiot," I said sharply. "I can't believe you want to get married. Here! Of all Godforsaken places. What about our families, Sam?"

"We don't need them. It's just about you and me, no one else. We'll have a party or something when we get back."

I was running out of excuses.

"What about school? I have one more year and then internships. We decided to wait until I at least finished my doctorate. What about all that?"

"We'll work around it. I have classes to teach and you have classes to take, big deal. We can work through it. All that matters is that we're together."

"But I've already started booking things for the wedding. We've got the Plaza ballroom and the church and the photographer – Sam be serious! We can't possibly get married here. Too many things have been put into motion. My parents took out a loan and there's the – "

"Marry me. Now. Tonight."

"But I – "

"Lesley, if you're not ready to marry me now, you won't be ready to marry me ever. Step out on a limb with me. Marry me."

"No…." I stepped away from him and he stared at me, stunned. "I can't marry you. I'm not ready." I slipped the diamond ring off my finger.

"I don't understand?"

"I can't marry you." I walked up to him and placed the ring in his front shirt pocket. "I won't make another mistake. I can't."

"Lesley, please – "

"No."

"Why? Can you at least answer me that?" He asked the question as if we were playing some sort of childish game, he the grown up and I the child.

"Because I don't love you." I answered him honestly. The words came out so easily, I almost didn't believe I'd said them.

"How can you not love me?" he asked, seriousness entering his tone. We were no longer playing a game. He began to plead to me. "All the time we've spent together; the first time we kissed; the long weekends in Vermont…How can you say you don't love me?

"Because I don't." Again, it was easy to answer him so matter-of-factly. I was kind of proud of myself, but I didn't know why.

"Yes you do. I know you do. You're just scared. You're afraid to make another commitment – "

"I don't love you, Sam."

He was begging me now.

"Yes you do. Don't say you don't because I know you do."

"I love Wyatt!"

I quickly placed my hands over my mouth in shock. I couldn't believe what I said, but I knew it was true. All this time Addie and Wyatt had been dating I truly had been jealous of them. Sam had been right after all: I still loved Wyatt. It wasn't fair that the man I once loved so much never took a second look at me; that he lost all his feeling for me. It wasn't fair I never got a second chance with him. He loved me once, why didn't he love me still? I thought maybe he did, last night in the library. It felt like he did, the way Wyatt held me, the way he wanted me, kissed me the same as he did four years ago. But he married Addie anyway. I couldn't explain it.

I saw the shock and hurt in Sam's eyes and tried to think of something to explain myself, but nothing came.

"I'm so sorry, Sam. I didn't mean for this to happen." My voice choked and trailed off.

I turned and ran away from him towards the hotel in order to pack my things before he could catch me.

When I reached our room, horrible thoughts began to enter my mind as I threw my suitcase on the bed and began throwing my clothes and toiletries into it. A high-pitched giggling and then a loud moan interrupted my rushed packing. It seemed to be coming through the walls. I paused a moment to pinpoint where the noise was coming from. It was drifting in through the vent above the headboard. I moved closer and put my ear against the wall. I heard the slow, muffled rocking motion of a bed and remembered it was Addie and Wyatt's room that was next to mine. It was their wedding night. It was really happening. Wyatt and Addie's life was actually beginning. A marriage, a house, kids...*Grace*. Addie knew about Grace. I didn't tell many people about her, but for some reason I felt I could trust Addie with Grace, a decision I now grew sicker about the more I thought of it. They were married now. *Would she tell Wyatt?* I pulled the covers off the bed, wrapped myself in them and walked over to the window, sliding down the glass and wall until I hit the floor and fell into the corner, sobbing.

I sat there crying until the shadows shifted in the room. The sky would be light soon and Sam, inevitably, would be coming back to the suite. I had stayed too long. I got up, finished packing, and quickly left the hotel, running out of the lobby just as Sam was checking for messages at the front desk.

Not until the plane touched ground in New York did I cry over the loss of Sam. Just one teardrop fell as my eyes watered at the jolt of the landing. I wiped it away quickly, as if it never fell, and with it went any significant feeling I ever had for Sam. It was that easy. I wondered, briefly, if I truly had loved Sam or if I was using him as a stepping-stone to achieve some idea of a traditional, solid relationship. *But who does that?* I asked myself. Narcissistic, crazy people. People I would one day treat. People I would make my career on. People unlike me. I was truly searching for love, obviously in the wrong place, but I was searching. Perhaps it was time to take a break. A calming warmth fell over me. I grabbed my carry-on and stepped into the single-file departing line on the plane. Now only twenty-three people were between me and my normal New York life outside the plane. Twenty-two, Twenty-one, Twenty…

AN INTERLUDE: FRIDAY, MAY 25TH, 1973

Addie

I woke up in a cold sweat. The room was dark and I could feel Wyatt breathing next to me. Seven days. This had happened every night now for seven days and as I rose from my bed I wondered if this dream would ever stop. I was not accustomed to my dreaming, especially one so vivid that seemed to stay the same yet change slightly at the same time. It woke me every night, the places and people coldly etched into my memory.

I left my room with Wyatt and walked down the hallway to the nursery and sat down at Wyatt's drawing table. It hurt me that he put his work here, in our child's room, turning it into his office. I could never get him to understand why it hurt me so much. There were other rooms in the house he could have chosen to work in. Why this room? Why not the guest bedroom? It's not like anyone visited us – except for Lesley. And why couldn't Lesley sleep on the couch? *Why this room?*

I had spent most of my time in the nursery this last week, taking Lesley's suggestion of writing my dreams down. I only had the one, so I vigorously wrote it down each night after I woke – several times – each time remembering something I'd forgotten in the previous translation. I didn't even try to hide from Wyatt the amount of time I was spending in the nursery, only leaving when he needed to work. He would lock me out and I would sit by the door or lean against it, waiting to hear his footsteps, signaling he was done. I would remain in the nursery between meals and naps, forced walks and trips to town, all under the guise that I was working through my problems as Lesley instructed and my mind worked best while in this particular room. Part of this was true – I was working through my dream like Lesley wanted me too, writing every detail down as she encouraged. And I did feel more at ease when in the nursery, more able to think clearly. But I had no intention of showing my work to Lesley, stashing the *Interpretation of Dreams* in the closet next to a hamper full of written pages. That's where I kept my dream-thoughts and my interpretations of them. I prayed Wyatt would never find them.

After I turned the desk lamp on, I pulled a blank tablet of paper from the desk drawer and began to write this evening's tale.

When my pen finally stopped, I looked around the room to find it beginning to fill with the dim light of morning. I had written out my dream ten times, the pictures always fading at the death of Ean. That's where it always ended, but that's where it also differed from my grandfather's story. I was dreaming my grandfather's fairy tale, that much I had deciphered on my own, but there were aspects of it every night that changed, that differed from the story in some way. And then there was the ending. The story ends with the birth of Fionna's son, her legacy living on, with Brogan only the narrator. The second part of the story was completely of my own subconscious making, and I every night I dreamed it, the battle in which young Ean dies became clearer, his lifeless body crumpled under his blood-strewn face. I always cried at that part, writing down in detail what I saw in my sleep, the tears blurring the ink. I looked around the unfinished nursery, forced to relive the pain of never even being given a chance to love my own child. How could anyone ever give their child away? That was a part of the dream I could never understand.

I felt I could spend all day deciphering this latest installment and as the room began to fill with more of the coming morning's light, that's what I decided to do. I went to the door and locked it, realizing Wyatt would be up soon. I didn't want to be disturbed. I laid my current writings on the floor, then went to the closet and retrieved Freud's *Interpretation of Dreams*, placing it on the seat of the rocking chair. I went back to the closet and gathered the hamper full of a week's worth of writings. I spread them out in front of me, in order, and stared at them. I looked at the rocking chair and saw the book lying on the seat. Lesley didn't have faith in my interpretation skills. I wonder why?

I leaned over to the rocking chair and picked up the book, turning to a random page, and started to read. Already drowsy from a night filled with agitated thoughts and writing, I edged my way back to the center of the room, the center of my thoughts, the center of my dream, and laid next to my writings. I placed the book on the floor in the middle of this chaotic mess, my head resting on one side of the open pages, and fell asleep.

Bang, Bang, Bang!

I awoke suddenly to a loud pounding. The sun hadn't completely filled the room yet but it was enough for me to realize that I was in the nursery. Looking around I found my papers strewn about the floor and the *Interpretation of Dreams* was still opened to the page I had first opened it to.

"Addie, open this door!" screamed Wyatt as he hammered his fist against the nursery door. "Addie, are you in there? Open this door!"

"Wyatt, I'm okay."

"Well, isn't that just terrific. Why don't you unlock the door and prove it?"

"Wyatt, I'm kind of in the middle of something in here. I'd like to be alone."

"Addie, you're scaring me." His tone quieted as he tried to reason with me. "Just open the door and we'll talk about whatever it is you're doing in there."

"No, Wyatt. I need to figure this out on my own. It's personal. I'm not ready to talk to anyone about it. I'm not even sure what it is yet."

"Damn it, Addie! What the hell is wrong with you? You open this damn door right now! There are other people in this house besides you."

I got up and moved to the door, keeping it locked.

"Who? Like you?"

"Yes, me! And Lesley."

"Oh, your precious Lesley! What would we ever do without your precious Lesley?" I was beginning to hate the sound of her name.

"Addie, you're sick." I could hear the rage building in Wyatt's voice as he spoke. His caring words were laced with disdain. There was no love in his tone. I knew I was losing him. "Let us help you."

"I don't want your help!" I screamed.

"When Lesley gets here tonight she's going to hear all about this!"

"Just leave me alone!"

"Fine! You can die in there for all I care!"

I heard Wyatt move away from the nursery and run downstairs, slamming the front door as he left the house. I couldn't hear or see where he went, just the sound of the car starting up and gravel hitting the side of the house as he left.

I braced myself against the door as I slid to the floor, looking at the room around me. I remembered coming here in the middle of the night. I remembered writing franticly the pieces of my dream. And I remembered having the same dream again, this time the image of Ean was a picture of my genetic make-up. The features of this boy were striking – eyes the shape of Wyatt's but colored in shades of brown like mine, the same sadness coming from his pupils as I saw in myself. His nose was Wyatt's, his mouth mine, and the shape of his face was my father's. I thought he was beautiful. It was painful to imagine his face. But I never saw him as my own; never made the connection my subconscious was trying to tell me. Maybe it was too much for me. Perhaps I needed Lesley's help like Wyatt had suggested. Or maybe it was the exhausting events of the early and mid-morning that was blocking what seemed to be so obvious to my inner-mind. Either way, I found my way again to the middle of the nursery, surrounded by papers, my head cushioned by one side of the open pages of Freud.

I woke up, startled. Not by anything around me, but by my own dream. It was the same dream I always dreamt, but something was different. It was longer. There was more to it. And something was very wrong. The hair on my arms was standing on end and the feeling of pins and needles had started at the back of my neck and extended down my shoulders and spine. I reached for more paper and a pen and through hazy eyes wrote what I could remember.

It had been two moon cycles since the death of Ean and still Ciaran would not speak to me. I begged him, tried to give myself to him to bear him another son, but he would not speak, he would not touch me. I was not the only one to give my son away to battle, but I am from the House of Aedan, and so I was looked upon and spoken about and the eyes of the people would not reach mine when I walked past. So I found new places to walk, valleys and hills where I would be unseen, and this is where I spent my days.

On the eve of my wedding year, twelve moon cycles being passed since the first, I found myself walking in the middle of the fallen valley towards the Tree of Eden. I don't know why or how I came upon that path, but something guided my thoughtless mind to that place. In the distance I saw Diarie, her arms outstretched and a golden light flowing down around her. I thought it strange, so I walked closer, the Tree of Eden getting nearer and the platform around it becoming clearer. As I came upon the platform I saw two figures, unclothed and engaged in marital rites. It was passionate and savage, their want and desire rising into the air and mingling among the leaves of the Tree of Eden. I moved closer to see these lovers, trying to discover who carried the passions I once had. I could not see their faces, but then the man lifted his lover, his craving for her mounting, and I saw her face. It was Lysaerie, the last fairy of Éadaoin, only in human form. She was more than beautiful – magnificent and heavenly. No one had seen her in many cycles, since the fairies left the fallen valley. Only Diarie could bring her back, which is why Diarie was there. I had seen drawings and paintings of Lysaerie, but none of them compared with her real beauty. What man had been chosen for such a great honor?

I should have left them alone, but curiosity overcame me.

I moved to the steps of the platform and before I reached the top the man turned his face and I saw him. It was Ciaran.

I said his name softly in disbelief and he looked at me, continuing to move with his lover, taking in every part of her. "Why don't you love me, Ciaran?" I cried to him. He did not answer. He did not care.

I stopped writing. For a moment my thoughts went blank and an image quickly flashed against my mind. It was of Wyatt and Lesley entangled together in the same sexual embrace of my dream. I suddenly stood up, dropping my papers to the floor. They scattered everywhere and when I looked down at them I realized this short-term obsession now covered every inch of the nursery room floor. I laughed. "This is insane," I said out loud. "It's just a dream." I turned to the door, opened it, and headed downstairs.

When I got to the kitchen I realized Wyatt was still gone. It didn't matter. I wasn't ready to deal with him yet anyway.

I sat down at the kitchen table and wondered what it was I wanted to do. Did I want to eat, have a drink, go for a walk, a drive…no, none those would work. Instead I felt exhausted, as if my mind and body had been through a war. So, I decided on sleep, but not in the nursery. In my bedroom, in my bed with Wyatt. Perhaps he would find me there when he came home and kiss my forehead like he'd always done. *That would be nice.*

I got up and went to the stairs, making my way to our bedroom. A chill hit me mid-way up. It seemed like an odd day…

CHAPTER 10: HIDING PLACES

Saturday, May 25th, 1974

It had been an hour since Prue came in from the lake – running into the house, scrambling to put her clothes on as she threw herself onto the couch, crying – and she realized that her brother wasn't coming out of his room to console her. *Figures*, she thought. In actuality, for the last half hour Prue had been fake crying, making whines and air sucking noises in an attempt to break Wyatt from his boys-only "Fortress of Solitude". She used to do the same thing when they were younger, faking a skinned knee so he would leave his friends and walk her home or to the Tasty Freeze if she had a dollar. Sometimes Prue would even lie and say one of the older girls from school was picking on her, just so Wyatt would let her climb into his tree-house and spend an afternoon with him.

Prue had always been somewhat of an annoyance to Wyatt – what little sister isn't? But when it came right down to it, Wyatt couldn't resist those tears, real or fake. Whenever he saw them falling down her checks, his big brother instinct would kick in and Prue always suckered him into spending the rest of the day with her. Wyatt caught on right before middle school and spent the years between then and now deciphering which was a real cry and which was a fake. Wyatt felt himself a master now and knew that for the last thirty or forty minutes his sister had just been forcing noises up the stairs and through the crack under his door. Wyatt assumed all the noise was caused by their argument earlier, and Prue, now away from the lake and her panic, wondered if what she thought she felt and thought she saw in the water even truly happened. Was she still scared or was there something else driving her sniffles and choked crying through the house? In their childhood it was always worth the effort to see if Wyatt would react, but Prue knew now that he was on to her.

Feeling silly about her overexcited imagination, Prue threw off the blanket she had pulled over her head, wiped the tears away from her cheeks and decided to snoop around the house. If there was something supernatural going on, she was going to find it, or avoid it – Prue hadn't decided. Besides, if she just so happened to find something else, a clue as to the cause of

Wyatt's strange behavior, that would be a bonus. And her experience in the water would be her excuse for all her snooping.

"Something *is* wrong," Prue said to herself, "and if Wyatt won't tell me what's wrong, I'll just find it myself."

It's interesting where people hide their secrets. Most people pick an out-of-guest-range location like a place in their bedroom, unless they have a spouse or significant other who they're hiding the secret from. Maybe a chimney or the attic, the tank of the toilet, or, if you want to get really creative, the empty space inside the wheel well of your car. Ultimately the place you choose is an intimate spot where no one goes, where you feel safe. Unfortunately for Prue, Wyatt was in his bedroom, which would have been her first choice, looking under his bed to see what he kept next to his dirty magazines, just like he did in high school. She started eliminating rooms in the house as she walked around downstairs. *Let's see. Not the kitchen because I'll be cooking in it, not the living room because I have to clean it,* fingering dust off the mantle while continuing her thoughts, *...you can't hide anything in the bathroom; you couldn't pay me enough to go in the basement; no cellar, and he wouldn't be dumb enough to hide something in the guest room.* Prue started walking up the stairs. *Whatever he's hiding must be in that room with him.*

When Prue got to the top of the stairs, she turned and crept toward Wyatt's door. She placed her ear against it to see if she could hear anything sounding like pain or remorse, hopefully resulting from hurting her feelings earlier. Instead she heard light snoring and a slight squeak caused by the force of Wyatt's exhaling against a loose bedspring.

Maybe he cried himself to sleep.

It was wishful thinking at most. The reality was Wyatt had heard her coming up the stairs and didn't want to be bothered yet. He could fake sleeping as well as Prue could fake crying.

There was nothing left for Prue to do but go to her room, unpack, and wait for Wyatt to re-emerge into the world of the vibrant and living. *Let him sleep. I hope he has bad dreams.*

The guest room was at the other end of the hallway. Prue turned around quietly and began to slowly walk that direction; in case Wyatt was awake, she didn't want him to know she was checking on him. When she got halfway down she noticed the door to the nursery was cracked open. Prue had completely forgotten the nursery was even there. It seemed like only a fragment of time she was able to be anxious about becoming an aunt. Prue had never even seen it but remembered talking to Addie about it one night in a worried telephone call. It was Prue who convinced Addie not to change the nursery theme to baby jungle animals, since Wyatt had already started on it and since, Prue reminded Addie, she seemed so excited about the Winnie-the-Pooh theme earlier. Two weeks later Addie had her miscarriage and the thought of the nursery had slipped out of Prue's mind until now.

The idea of walking into a dead child's room bothered Prue. It was an unpleasant thought, like a pyramid scheme of the mind where all the feelings surrounding it doubled the more you thought about it, until they were so big it was unbearable, and they collapsed around you. So Prue stopped thinking about it and just pushed the door open.

The walls were painted in a mixture of pastels with a wallpaper border at the top, half of it peeling off, slowly dragging to the floor. The crib was on the far side of the room, in-between the closet and changing table. On the other side was a rocker with a large stuffed Winnie-the-Pooh bear sitting in it. A matching mobile hung over the crib and slightly turned with the air from the vent opposite the crib. Colorful plush animals lay strewn across the floor next to unopened baby gifts. In the corner a baby swing with a bow on top sat collecting dust. In the center of the room, in front of the double window, sat Wyatt's artist's desk.

Prue walked around and touched everything. Wyatt's desk was the only thing in the room that seemed out of place. No dust gathered on the wooden surface and the sun seemed to shine only on this one piece of furniture, never extending beyond its shadow and creeping to some other object in the room. It was alive when the rest of the room felt dead and cold; a ruin. She stood in front of it and watched the sun recede into evening.

Once the glow from the window left, Prue turned the desk lamp on. Under it was a sketchbook. Prue picked it up and flipped through the pictures. She didn't pay much attention to it until she realized the pictures were repeating themselves in the same order every ten pages. She sat down and studied the pictures more closely under the light. It wasn't like anything Wyatt had drawn before. It was a comic book, that she was certain of, but what it depicted she had no idea. As Prue turned the pages again she tried to piece together the story they were telling.

The first page showed a moonlit place in the middle of a field, two people meeting in the center with a strange dark creature in the distance watching them. The second page seemed to be a marriage ceremony, the same two lovers atop a platform surrounded by people. The third was the couple again, naked and making love, with the dark creature from the first page running towards them. The fourth showed the young man stabbed, the girl at his side crying, the dark creature receding into the night. The fifth page was in four parts, each corner having its own depiction. The first was again in the moonlit place in the middle of a field, but this time two different people meeting. The second image was the same two people in a marriage ceremony on the platform. The third involved a small child being torn away from who Prue perceived to be his father, and the fourth was of that same child being killed horrifically in battle. The sixth page was of two lovers, explicitly intertwined but only the woman's face could be seen. Prue thought it eerie how the woman so much resembled Lesley. She found the depictions in the scene strange also, but continued to flip through the book anyway. The seventh page was a drawing of the living room downstairs, the image of Wyatt passionately holding Lesley on the floor with a glimpse of what seemed to be Addie off in the distance. The eighth page was a drawing of Addie, running along the beach in the middle of the night into the water, with nothing but a dark red nightgown on. The site of the red nightgown sent shivers down Prue's spine, the impression of the red marks on her legs still vivid in her mind. The ninth was a funeral. Among the people drawn Prue recognized herself, along with Lesley and Addie's mother. But Wyatt had left himself out. And on the tenth page Prue found it divided in four, each corner again having its own picture. The first was of Wyatt, lying on the nursery room floor surrounded by pages with words and drawings, above him jagged black figures with yellow eyes, circling. The second image was of Addie, standing in the doorway wearing her red colored gown. The third showed Wyatt running after her, Addie already in the water. The fourth and final image was of Wyatt crying on the sand, tiny words printed at the bottom of the page saying "Addie, forgive me!"

"Oh, God," Prue dropped the book on the desk. She looked around the room at all the baby things. "It must be torture for you."

Prue looked down at Wyatt's desk and noticed something she didn't see before. Neatly stacked around his desk were small piles of paper, some crumpled, some torn. She picked a few up and recognized the handwriting to be Addie's. She read through a couple and found that some of the pictures Wyatt had drawn resembled some of the pages of writing. Prue had heard rumors that Addie had left a suicide note, but nothing like this. She picked up more pages and read them, realizing even more now how disturbed Addie truly must have been. The pages seemed more like ramblings than a suicide note; disjointed thoughts of a depressed woman. Prue picked up the sketchpad again and began to slowly flip it page by page, the same pictures over and over again telling the same story, each sequence seeming darker than the last. She flipped to the last page with the man by the lake. "Wyatt, why are you doing this to yourself?"

"What are you doing in here?" Wyatt had just pushed the door open.

"I was just looking around. I didn't have anything to do. I was waiting for you to come out but – "

"You can't be in here."

"I didn't mean to upset anything, I was just – "

"What are you looking at?" Wyatt saw the sketchpad open, hidden behind her. "Give me that. You can't look at that. It's private."

Prue lifted the sketchpad and held it firmly while Wyatt walked over and tried to take it from her. She wouldn't let it go.

"Wyatt, what exactly is this? Is it some new comic you're working on? I'd really like to know. There's something about it that doesn't feel right." Prue pulled him down to her level so he would have to look at her.

"It's a project I'm working on, and there's nothing wrong with it, so just give it to me. It's none of your business anyway."

Wyatt reached again for the pad of paper but missed as Prue pulled it away from him and moved to the other side of the room.

"I find the drawings in it a little disturbing, especially the ones with Addie in them. I mean, come on Wyatt, you can't think these are okay. They depict your wife's suicide for God's sake."

"How would *you* know?" Wyatt walked over to Prue and grabbed the book, her hands still firmly around it. "You weren't even here."

"Neither were you." Wyatt didn't respond. He just stared at the floor. "You weren't here that night, Wyatt, were you?"

Prue let go of the sketchpad and watched as Wyatt tried to regain his balance. He stood up, ignored her question, and began to walk out of the room. Prue was a little faster to the door and she slammed it, almost catching his fingers in the frame.

"Answer my question."

Wyatt stood there attempting to control his anger. He swayed back and forth a little, trying to get a sense of depth perception. He had lost control of the situation and it was throwing his awareness of things off-kilter. He found the doorknob with his hand and began to turn it, but Prue put herself against the door to keep it shut.

"Wyatt, I'm tired of wondering if you're okay. I'm tired of wondering what's going on with you and what you're hiding in here. Don't run away from me. Please, Wyatt. We only have each other. Don't close me off." She put her hand on top of his, grabbing the sketchpad and holding it in front of his face. "Answer me. Why did you draw this?"

"Why are you doing this, Prue?"

"Because I'm worried about you. Wyatt, those drawings are disturbing. Over and over again you've drawn them. The whole book is full of them. What are you trying to say?"

Wyatt laid his head against the door, then turned to look Prue in the eyes, grabbing the sketch pad and holding it in front of her.

"These are pictures of the night Addie died. I'm the reason she killed herself."

Wyatt didn't blink or flinch or react in anyway. He just stood there and stared at her, waiting for a response. Prue slowly let go of his hand and Wyatt slid his body down the door until the floor abruptly stopped him. Prue followed. Wyatt placed his head in his sister's lap, Prue cradling it while she searched for answers somewhere in the room, in the glow of the desk lamp.

CHAPTER 11: COUCH CONFESSIONS

Wyatt

"Eight o'clock, right on the dot," I said as I opened the door.

"You know me, never late for an appointment," answered Lesley as I took her suitcase and walked with her into the living room. "Where's Addie?" she asked.

"She's been locked in the nursery all day." I stopped and leaned against the armchair, holding Lesley's suitcase with both hands, facing her. "At least I think she has. I just got back not too long ago myself. We had a fight this morning."

"A fight? About what?" Lesley tilted her head, letting her hair fall over her right shoulder. The light in the room cast a dim shadow across the bare part of her neck. It looked very exposed and kissable. I tried to avoid looking at it.

"She wouldn't let me in that damn room," I answered nervously, trying to concentrate on my words while pushing my carnal thoughts to the one side of my brain I had been storing them in the last couple of months – make that years.

"I tell Addie I'm worried about her," I continued, "that I'm scared of what she might be doing in there, and she just blows it off like it's nothing." The words flowed smoother now, calmer. I remembered my argument with Addie this morning. The words had bounced around in my head all day. I could hear her voice crystal clear, echoing in my ears. "Addie says she's okay, that she's working out something personal. What's so personal she can't tell me?"

"I don't know, Wyatt. I really don't."

"I just wish she'd talk to me."

"I know."

I was sincere in my plea and as much as I tried to hide it, I knew Lesley could see the emotion coming to the surface of my face. I had resigned to the fact that over the last several months my feelings for Addie were in a constant state of change, but that didn't make her actions any less painful. It was something I knew I could conceal from others, but not from Lesley. Lesley would always be able to find the truth, which scared and excited me.

"But we can talk about all that later," I said suddenly. "It's kind of a mood killer anyway. Sit down on the sofa. I just got the fire started." I walked over to the stairs and set Lesley's suitcase down. "How about a glass of wine?"

"That would be lovely," she replied.

I noticed a change in Lesley's voice as I walked over to the kitchen and retrieved two wine glasses from the cupboard and a bottle of Cabernet Sauvignon. It reminded me of when we were together and Lesley would persuade me into doing whatever she wanted, with just the change in her voice. I wondered as I walked back to the living room what she might be up to in that pretty little head of hers.

"So how was the drive up from Chicago?" I poured as I talked.

"The usual. Boring. Long. Seen everything twice type of feel."

"Or three hundred."

"Exactly," she laughed.

"Yeah. I used to hate driving up here from school to visit my parents." I set the wine bottle on the coffee table and handed Lesley her glass, then sat facing her on the other end of the couch.

"Well, at least when you were in Chicago the trips must have become a little more bearable, getting to drive along the lakeshore. I'm sure your parents were happy that you didn't move too far away from home."

I could feel the sorrow tighten on my face instantly. Lesley must have noticed because her body language changed completely. She was no longer relaxed but sat upright and angled in what seemed like an uncomfortable position. We'd never actually talked about my parents' death. I could see her mind trying to grasp at something to transition to, but nothing came.

"You know, Wyatt," Lesley said very slowly, "we never talk about you when I come up here. We're always so focused on Addie. Not that we shouldn't be." I could tell Lesley seemed a little nervous as she spoke, moving our conversation into uncharted territory. "But sometimes I wonder how you're handling all this. I've been coming here for almost three months and we've never once talked about you."

"Are you trying to psychoanalyze me?" I laughed, attempting to lighten the mood.

"Maybe a little," she smiled – God, how I loved that smile! I wondered how I'd lived without it for so long. "I used to know what you were thinking," Lesley continued. "I've lost that somehow. I miss it."

"Yeah. I never knew how you got into my head, but you did." I moved to the floor in front of the fire and stared at it. I tried to think about Addie. That, after all, was the reason Lesley was here – the only reason. "Sometimes I wish

I could see into Addie's head, to know what she's thinking, how she's feeling. And sometimes I think I wouldn't be able to handle it if I could."

Lesley moved off the couch and sat next to me.

"I ask myself if it was maybe something I did to cause all this, for her to lose the baby and everything that's followed."

"Oh, Wyatt."

"But I know that's crazy, right?" I took a sip of wine. "I mean, I've moved my whole life for her, you know?" I paused for a moment, contemplating my next question. "Do you think it's weird that my studio is in the baby's room?"

"No," Lesley answered plainly. "Why?"

"Addie does. She says it's as if I wanted our baby to die so that I would have a place to work, when in actuality the only reason I work at home is because of her."

"I know."

"That stupid room. We've had so many fights about *that* room. I want to get rid of all that stuff in there, all the baby toys and furniture. It's depressing. I want to move on. But Addie, she just wants it to stay the same. She'd spend all day, every day in there if I'd let her." I stopped and breathed in another sip of wine. "That's what we fought about this morning. Addie locked herself in there before I ever had a chance to stop her. It's not healthy, Lesley. It's not right. It's not a baby's room anymore."

I lowered my head and closed my eyes. Lesley placed her hand on my arm, squeezing it firmly, then slowly rubbed her fingertips along my forearm until their comforting touch made its way back to the side of her face, holding her head up as she looked at me.

"I know, Wyatt," she said softly. "I'm trying to work with her on it, but it's taking more time than I thought."

"I just feel alone sometimes, you know? It drives me nuts, that feeling." I looked at her now – straight into her dark blue eyes. In the firelight they were the color of indigo dye, the flames drowning in their watery depths. They drew me in. "Do you ever get that feeling, even if you're with people, that you're alone and no one can see or hear you or help you?"

"All the time," she replied. "Everyone does."

"Really?"

"Yeah."

"It sucks."

I set my glass down on the floor. Lesley got up and began walking around the room. She paused at the mantle, looking at the pictures Addie had collected and framed over the years. She stopped at one in particular, recognizing it from our past.

"This is the day we found each other at Notre Dame," she said, a little taken off guard.

"Yes it is."

"Where did you get it?"

"I took it, the day that I left."

Lesley turned around and looked at me, holding the picture in her hands.

"I thought I had lost it." She looked down at the picture, then again up at me. "Why did you take it?"

"It was always my favorite picture. That day changed my life. I always wanted to remember that."

Lesley looked down at the picture and just stared, not saying anything. When she moved to place the picture back on the mantle, the fire caught the welling tears in her eyes, an emotion I thought she would try to hide from me, but she didn't. She moved slowly around the living room again and reclaimed her spot next to me, quiet and pensive. I leaned my head back on the couch, ashamed that my actions – past and present – had made her cry.

"Do you ever wish we were still married?" Lesley whispered. I turned my head towards her in shock. She quickly corrected herself. "I mean, do you wonder what it would have been like if we had stayed together?"

I could feel my expression soften as I entertained the idea of Lesley and what it had been like to wake up to her every morning; her young, glowing face dreaming as the morning sunlight slipped through the curtains of our cramped, University Village apartment. The glow of the firelight cast the same blush across her face now.

It was hard for me to tell exactly when I fell in love with Lesley. Until recently, I had perceived our relationship as consisting of many coincidences that finally brought us together. But when, exactly, did I fall in love with her? To ask people around Point Caneissa they would have told you we had been together since childhood, but the truth was that Lesley was the first to fall and spent most of her life watching me from a distance, waiting to be the one I would ultimately choose. I saw that now. What a whirlwind of events our lives had been...to have to pinpoint the precise moment. But I knew. That picture; the first day I saw her on campus. I kept it on the mantle, taking it in my hands every once-in-a-while when I wanted to remember the curves of Lesley's face. It had only been a couple days since I picked it up, looking at it more often now since I had moved back home, since the loss of the baby. And lately, the more I looked at it the more I realized my total and utter abandonment of Lesley all those years ago. How I loved her then. But it was a good decision though, right?

Once enrolled in art school my creativity burst from my mind and hands to paper and canvas and I found I was more talented than I had ever imagined. In addition to my classes, I worked outside the studio drawing cartoons for newsletters and designing small press magazine covers and advertisements. Plus I had my small quarterly comic book which I had funded and produced myself under a pseudonym. That had been my real passion since I was nine. But not wanting to be branded a nerd or geek, I kept my secret from everyone, except Prue. Now, I had made it. Now, I was successful. My dreams had come true. It never occurred to me until now, looking at my ex-wife in the firelight through slightly inebriated eyes, that I could have made a mistake. *How many chances had I given up to be with her?*

I remember the night I married Addie, or rather the morning after. The night we got married was still fuzzy, even all these years later, having listened to Addie's retelling of it to new friends or neighbors numerous times. The morning after, though, is extremely clear in my mind. I woke up, groggy and hung-over, with an overwhelming feeling of, well, not panic but something a little shy of panic – I don't know if there's a word for it – but just this overwhelming feeling. I could feel Addie next to me. It wasn't a bad feeling or a warm feeling, but I could sense her lying there. I moved to touch her but it hurt to move. My head throbbed with the nights' festivities. I had never drunk so much in my life and have never since. I tried to remember what we did, bits of the ceremony coming into view, casino hoping, and drinking – lots of drinking – but then an image of Lesley in red popped up. Lesley. I tried not to think about her. Less than thirty-six hours ago I had kissed her, passionately, and I had enjoyed it, yearned for it even. Less than thirty-six hours ago I would have followed her anywhere, if she had asked me. If she had said she'd loved me...I would have done anything she asked of me. I did. Lesley told me to love Addie and now Addie lay beside me, naked, asleep, and married. I was married. Sharp stabs of pain coursed through my brain. I tried to concentrate on something in the room. I couldn't open my eyes yet so I tried to focus on a sound, a humming or street noise – anything but a ticking. What I heard were noises coming through the wall above our bed from the room next door. It was the sound of a bed creaking, maybe someone rolling over, but then I remembered who was in the room next to ours: Sam and Lesley. Lesley was lying in bed next to Sam, naked, asleep – or not – but not married. She would be soon, though, and then she would never be *mine*. But then she could never be mine. I guess I made sure of that last night. *Thirty-six hours.* If I'd known that was going to be the last time I ever kissed Lesley, I would have kissed her longer, deeper. I would have held her closer, taken in the scent of her hair and the softness of her curls as they brushed against my fingers or the touch of her skin, lightly dewy from nervousness and surprise. I heard the bedsprings squeak again through the wall. I pulled my pillow over my head and tried to go back to sleep, deciding now that I hated Sam.

Addie and I made our way to the front desk and waited for Sam and Lesley to meet us. We had plans to meet for a late breakfast. I grew concerned when only Sam met us in the lobby, but that soon turned to relief. Lesley had left him.

I loved Addie. She was my wife – is my wife – after all. I did choose to marry her, spontaneous as it might have been. But I did love her. I just loved Lesley, too. That day I had resigned myself to the fact that I would always love Lesley, in varying degrees of course, but love nonetheless.

Realizing Lesley was still waiting for an answer, I thought back to my old excuses of why I left her, trying to word them in my head so they wouldn't hurt her feelings. I regretted ever thinking them.

"I used to ask myself what happened to us, why we didn't work out," I said finally.

"What was your answer?"

"I told myself we were too young to know what we were doing, but I was just lying to myself. We wanted different things and were too bullheaded to give in to one another."

"Isn't that a part of being too young?" Lesley asked, optimistically.

"I suppose. But look at us. We did all right. We got what we wanted in the end, didn't we?"

"Did we, Wyatt?"

I turned away from her and stared into the fireplace. I could see the flickering light reflecting against my water-glassed eyes.

"But I did love you, more than anything," I said softly. "I should've given in." I took another sip of wine, then just stared into my glass, watching tiny bubbles aerate the fermented red liquid.

"Do you really mean that?" asked Lesley, her voice cracking and slightly airy from holding her breath in anticipation.

I looked at her face and found the young girl I fell in love with once. She was so different from Addie. *Why did I leave you?*

"Yes, I do." I meant it. At that moment I felt I could fall in love with Lesley all over again, that I had fallen in love with her again, that I'd never stopped. I felt alive, more so than when I first met Addie; more so than I had felt in months, which was more important. I wanted her. I wanted someone, anyone, to love me.

Lesley placed her hand on mine and I looked down at it, seeing small new creases and feeling the softness of a touch I remembered and believed I had longed for. She moved in to kiss me and when I looked up, our lips met. The exhilarating rush of warmth flowed through my body. I craved it and feared it all at once. Scared I would lose this feeling of closeness, of being touched by another human being who loved me, I placed one arm around her waist and my hand on the back of her head, pulling her closer to me, devouring her mouth. Lesley moved her lips to my neck and I gasped in relief as I laid her gently on the floor, whispering into her ear, "I love you." As I unbuttoned her blouse, my fingers moved down her body, remembering her curves and the softness of her skin.

"Don't leave me, Wyatt," she sighed.

I hovered above her face, drawn into the heat of the fire radiating from her partially exposed body. I moved closer.

"I'll never leave you."

I kissed her again, wrapping my arm around her body and rolling her on top of me. Lesley pushed herself up, straddling me, throwing her head back and opened her eyes to find Addie paralyzed at the end of the staircase, just watching us, her jaw slightly dropped, trying to make the faintest whimper.

"Addie!"

I let go of Lesley and looked at her to see what was the matter, fearing that thoughts of Addie had slipped into her mind and perhaps she felt guilty. When I saw her face, I lifted myself slightly and turned around to see my wife staring at us.

"Oh, my god! Addie."

Lesley jumped off the floor and backed away from me, holding one hand in front of her mouth to hide her smeared lipstick and the other holding her blouse shut.

"Addie."

Lesley's voice was faint and almost unheard. She kept walking backward until the wall stopped her. It had felt like a dream, but the abruptness of the wall brought Lesley into the realness of the situation. She grabbed the wall with both hands and closed her eyes. "Oh, God forgive me! Hail Mary, full of Grace. The Lord is with thee. Blessed art thou among women…"

I slowly stood up. I tried to speak but nothing came out except for closed squeaks of trapped air. I began to take painful, calculated steps towards my wife.

What am I going to do?

I didn't know what to say or how to act, or even if I could bring myself to hold her.

Did she really see what happened?

I was kidding myself, really, but Addie's silence gave me more confidence that perhaps she had not witnessed my lustful act; that perhaps she was lapsing back into her depression from earlier in the day. Finally I was close enough to reach out for her and spoke her name.

"Addie."

"No!" she screamed as she ran to the nursery. I tried to follow her but she reached the room before I was even halfway up the stairs. The slamming door shook the house and all of the objects in it.

"I have to leave," I heard Lesley say quietly. She had felt the wall shake with Addie's anger and it woke her from her Hail Marys. I stumbled slightly down the stairs to find Lesley mumbling to herself as she picked up her bags.

"Lesley wait – "

"No. I have to go." Lesley didn't look at me while she spoke. "I'm ashamed of myself. I'm so sorry. I didn't mean to hurt her, Wyatt. Please tell her that," she begged. "I have to go."

"Lesley don't go. Wait! I don't know what to do. Don't go." I tried to grab her hand but she jerked away from me.

"I have to go. I'm so sorry, Wyatt. I'm so sorry…." The words stumbled out of Lesley's mouth slowly as she walked away from me, staring at the floor trying to find the baseboard of the door. "I'm so sorry. Tell her I'm sorry." She felt the doorknob, turned it and pushed herself outside, then ran to her car.

I heard the motor start and the echo of her car driving away. I never went to the window to watch her leave or stand in the open doorway to beg her to stay. Instead I listened to the sounds of the crickets outside and the noises of the house settling in the night, then slowly made my way to the staircase and walked up it. I curled myself against the wall of the hallway attached to the nursery and placed my hand on the door, then quietly listened to the sobs of my wife on the other side.

CHAPTER 12: PAST LIVES

Lesley

I walked through the door and handed my coat to Wyatt. It had become our weekly Friday night routine. Wyatt would meet me at the door at eight o'clock after my three-hour drive up from Chicago. I began looking forward to my weekends with Wyatt and Addie. Wyatt decreed me his "in-house psychiatrist" and praised me every visit for coming to help his wife. But it wasn't his praises that made me return every week or the small progress I was making with Addie and the struggles with the loss of her baby. It was the hope that a spark would ignite between Wyatt and I again that made these long weekends bearable.

A spark.

That's all I needed in order to tell Wyatt how I felt, how my flame for him had rekindled a month or so ago and now all I was waiting for was the perfect moment to show him how I felt. I wanted to tell him that I loved him, that I'd always loved him. I wanted to tell him I had cried so often for him: the day he left, the day he called about his parents, the first day I saw him in New York, the day he married Addie. I wanted to tell him about Grace. I wanted that perfect moment, when he would look at me and I would feel whole again, like I used to when he would hold me all night or when he would randomly grab my hand while walking me to my next class or across campus. *The perfect moment.* What would that be like? Not this. This was a different kind of feeling; a sickening, all-consuming self-loathing.

But would I have done it all differently?

I asked myself that question as I sped away from Wyatt and Addie's house, not knowing if I wanted a true answer. After all, I leaned in, I wanted to kiss him. I felt his wanting, his longing. Wyatt said he loved me. *He said he loved me, right?* But *I* leaned in. *I* initiated it, physically at least. But he wanted it; he wanted me. Would I have gone all the way with it?

"Yeeesss!" I screamed as I slammed on the brakes and swerved off the road. "Yes."

I sat in my car, hunched over the passenger seat, sobbing. I lifted myself up, took a deep breath, then began beating my hands and wrists against the steering wheel screaming, "No! No! NO!" Exhausted, with tears streaming down my face, I laid my head on the seat and fell into myself. I didn't know what to do.

"I just wanted…I just wanted him to know…I loved him. I just wanted him to know."

Was that it? Was that all I wanted? For Wyatt just to know?

"Yes…I just wanted him to know. I'm not an adulteress. Never would I ever under normal circumstances behave like I did." I pulled down the visor mirror and began wiping the tears away from my face. "We had been drinking, and the fire. I would never do that to Addie. Wyatt would never do that to Addie. It was a mistake, a misunderstanding." I paused as I caught a real glimpse of myself; my face was red and puffy, and my eyes were swollen and glistened in the dark. "I just wanted him to know."

I slammed the visor up and put the car in drive, making my way back onto the road. Where would I go? I didn't know. I just wanted to drive. For a moment I thought maybe I should go back to Point Caneissa, back to Wyatt. After all, he had begged me to stay, to help Addie. Would that be the right thing? I didn't care. I never wanted to go back, never wanted to see Point Caneissa again. I would give up Wyatt.

The perfect moment.

"I can't believe I'm doing this. I can't believe what I did, what I was about to do. Stupid Lesley! You're so stupid! I'm so stupid. Idiot. You always do this. He's not yours. He never was. He doesn't love you! Move on with your life! Please, God, move on with your life!"

I accelerated, yelling at myself as I followed the coastline anywhere but Point Caneissa, wiping a stream of tears away as I drove.

I drove in zigzags north, then back southeast and finally northeast driving along the Michigan coast before deciding to go to my family's vacation house in Mackinaw City. The summer season hadn't started yet so the house would be empty, and since no one would know where I was, no one could call and bother me. Patient emergencies would just have to wait until Tuesday.

It was just after four in the morning when I got out of my car to open the garage door. It creaked loudly over the sound of the running motor and I looked around to see if anyone noticed, forgetting that most people, if any were there, were in bed. I pulled my car into the garage and placed the garage door back into its worn groove in the ground. When I reached the house I found the hidden key between the soil and edge of the flowerpot by the front door. Once inside the house I followed the moonlit windows until I came to the kitchen, searching for candles to light the house instead of electricity. My reflection in candlelight would be easier to cope with.

My mother always kept scented candles in the kitchen so that even if she wasn't baking, it smelled as though she was, giving the neighbors the homey impression of herself she wanted. I picked a match from the box on the counter and struck it, lighting the candle on the windowsill and listening to the spark and crackle of carbon lain dormant for a year. The instant smell of smoke entered my nostrils and calmed my senses as I picked the candle up, retracing my steps through the house until I found the stairs, making my way to my small, cramped, dusty room, the scent of hot apple pie lingering in the trail I had made. My room was at the end of the hallway and as I walked down it I avoided my reflection in the mirror, which was fifteen feet in front of me. It was an optical illusion to make the house seem bigger than it was, but tonight it was just a painful reminder of what a whore I was, or had become. The closer I got to it the more I felt the impressions of Wyatt's lips and fingers on my body; the warmth of his breath on my neck and against my cheek as I released for him part of his sexual tension. It was exhilarating, that feeling. I remembered the first time I felt it.

It was our sophomore year in college, the first time Wyatt made love to me, under an oak tree outside of the college green, off campus so no one would see us. In the mirror I saw myself, young, naïve, and in love, waiting for Wyatt to make his move. Wyatt's mind was adrift that night also, and I could feel the nervousness and tension as he kissed me in the moonlight. I placed my hand on the side of his face and ran my fingers through his hair. His body relaxed and he laid me on the ground, looking deep into my eyes, and told me he loved me. There was something about my touch that calmed him, and that night I realized it, keeping it as my own little secret and pleasure. Tonight I manipulated it, knowing his weakness, his loneliness, and satisfied my own lustful wants and needs.

My degradation beat down on me and I turned away from the mirror, running the opposite direction into my parent's room, slamming the door behind me as wax spilled onto the floor and my bare feet. I set the candle on the dresser, blew out the flame, and tucked myself under the covers of my parents' bed, praying I would fall asleep. Luckily my mind was exhausted, and instead of conjuring up malevolent images of my earlier actions, my thoughts ceased once my eyes were closed, and my breathing picked up a steady, rhythmic murmur.

The bed was on the opposite side of the room from the window so it was nine o'clock before the sun hit my face and woke me. For a serene moment I forgot where I was, and the comfort of total relaxation crept into my muscles, causing me to stretch and smile. When I opened my eyes and saw my grandmother's dresser and my father and mother's wedding picture sitting on top of it, I realized what house I was in – and why – and began to cry. My chest heaved with the force of my tears. It was an hour before I left the bedroom and made my way downstairs.

I walked around the living room and looked at the different childhood memories my mother showcased to all their summer friends. In the center of the mantle sat mine and Wyatt's engagement picture. I was a little surprised. At their own home my mother had neatly tucked away all pictures of Wyatt, telling her friends it was a shame the marriage had ended, but that I was most likely better off for it. I had become successful and independent, and that's all that really mattered. I never would have guessed my mother secretly kept pictures of Wyatt and I on display. Perhaps she missed Wyatt, too. My fingers followed the outline of our young faces.

How different we look now.

Feeling another tear forming in my eyes I turned the picture over and went to the kitchen to make myself breakfast, finding only bare cupboard space and moldy cheese in the refrigerator. I grabbed my purse and left the house, deciding a walk into town would produce some kind of sustenance.

I decided on Riley Mills. I turned a corner and walked into the small diner.

"Lesley Lindaugh! My goodness, it seems like it's been years since I've seen you," Mrs. Mills said as she gave me a hug and proceeded to follow me to a corner booth.

"It has been years," I replied, slightly irritated.

Riley Mills was a local restaurant my family frequented during our summer vacations. The Mills had owned the restaurant for three generations and now Riley Mills III was owner and operator, since his father passed away. Mrs. Mills, his mother, started out as the pastry cook before she married her boss, but as she got older, and nosier, she chose waitressing as her full time profession, not wanting the restaurant help to be in any other hands than her own family's.

I sat down in the booth, and without missing a step, Mrs. Mills quickly walked past me and sat across from me, more curious than genuine in her questions concerning my current life.

"Little Lesley Lindaugh! I just can't believe it."

"It's Dr. Trilmon now. I thought my parents would have told you."

"You know, they did. I just plum forgot all about that. I heard you're living in New York now. What's that like?"

"I was living in New York, but I live in Chicago now."

"Wow! A real world traveler! How's that like? Must be nice."

"I wouldn't call it that. I don't travel the world or anything, but my life is busy. I keep myself really busy. Do you think I could get a cup of coffee, Sue? I really need something to wake me up this morning."

"Long night?"

"You could say that." I put my head in my hands and began to rub and squish my face.

"You stay right here." Mrs. Mills patted me on the head. "I'll be right back with that coffee."

I pushed myself up against the wall and swung my legs along the seat, making myself comfortable for the long interrogation I knew was about to come underway. Mrs. Mills was the town gossip, and as she was away retrieving my coffee, I was playing a believable story out in my head to tell her.

"Here you go." The aroma of coffee broke my thoughts as Mrs. Mills poured the long stream of liquid in front of me. Mrs. Mills sat the pot of coffee on the edge of the table and reclaimed her position across from me. "I drove by your parents place on my way home last night and it still looked locked up for the winter. No lights or cars, didn't know anyone was there. That's why I was so surprised to see you. Did you get in late last night?"

"Yeah. A little too late, I guess."

"Well, that drive up from Chicago will do it to you. So, what brings you to town so early? I'm not expecting to see your parents here for another two, three weeks at least."

"I just needed to get away from my office," I said quickly, picking up my cup and slowly slurping the hot, caffeinated beverage.

"That busy? I just can't believe little Lesley Lindaugh is a big city psychiatrist!"

"It's Dr. Trilmon," I mumbled through my coffee.

"I'm sorry. I always forget you married that Trilmon boy. I never liked him. Then again, I didn't know him very well, only meeting him the two or three times you brought him up here. Your parents sure love him though."

"What?" I was sincerely surprised. "My parents talk about him? What do they say?"

"Oh, lots of stuff. They say he's an artist or something like that, out in San Francisco. Mostly they talk about how he should've never left you. Good riddance, I say. They don't like his new wife that much either."

"They talk about Addie?"

"Is that her name? Strange name. Anyway, it's mostly your mom that does the talking, but your dad never disagrees with her. That Addie doesn't sound very nice."

"Addie's my best friend."

"Your best friend married your ex-husband?" Mrs. Mills laughed under her breath. "*That*, your mother left out. Doesn't sound like a very good friend to me."

"She's a good woman." There was a shortness to my tone.

"I didn't mean to offend – "

"You didn't," I interrupted. "I'm just telling you she's a good person, and she's my friend, despite what my parents might say. Wyatt loves her very much," I said softly. "I'm really happy for both of them."

"That's nice. I'm glad to see you're all friends. I suppose that makes life easier. Do you get to see them often?"

"No," I said quickly. "Not really. I see them more since they moved to Point Caneissa, but not in at least two or three months. Not since Addie lost the baby."

"Oh. I'm sorry to hear that. Your mother never said anything about that."

"It happened about four months ago, and I doubt you've even talked to my mother since it happened."

"That's true. So you stayed with her, Addie I mean?"

I shook my head yes.

"She's lucky to have a friend like you, so close and all."

"I don't know if I'd agree with that." My stomach went sour and I felt like vomiting, keeping my composure through the pain.

"Sure you are," Mrs. Mills replied encouragingly. "She's lucky to have a friend like you, considering she stole your husband and all."

"That's not what happened."

"It's okay," Mrs. Mills interrupted. "You don't have to explain it to me. I hear about that kind of thing all the time." She got up and lifted a pad of paper from her apron. "So, now, what can I get you?"

I grabbed my purse and began to slide out of the booth.

"I'm not feeling that hungry anymore," I said, walking past Mrs. Mills to the door.

"Did I say something wrong?" she yelled.

"No. I just don't feel well," I yelled back, leaving a dollar bill on the counter by the register. "That's for the coffee."

I left the restaurant and walked to the nearest ferryboat dock. It was Memorial Day weekend and the crowds had begun to come to the city, gathering in droves around the docks, waiting to cross the straights into a by-gone world: The Island.

The ferry ride was about twenty minutes, and when I stepped off the dock I felt miles away from my problems. There was an entire lake, a freshwater sea, between me and my life. I felt light and happy as I walked up the dock to the center of town. I turned left onto Main Street, following it to the Boardwalk, making my way to the first empty bench I found. And there I stayed, all day, watching the ferryboats, cargo ships, and sailboats pass each other, the lake waters churning in their wake.

No one spoke to me until sunset, the sky still partially lit from the horizon. A man approached me from behind.

"Excuse me, are you okay?"

What an odd question, I thought. *Do I not look okay?*

"I'm fine," I responded.

"Are you sure? I could help you back to your hotel if you want."

"I'm not staying here."

"Well, if you were looking for the last ferry, that's it right there."

I looked over and saw the man pointing to a ferryboat already halfway to the city.

"That's okay. I'll just stay here tonight."

"On the boardwalk?" The man laughed.

"Yeah. On the boardwalk."

"I'm afraid you can't do that."

"Why not?" I was getting angry by this new annoyance.

"Well, for one, it's going to get cold tonight. Somewhere between thirty and forty degrees I think. And two, they'll arrest you. You can't sleep on the boardwalk. Sort of uglies up the place. We're going for a certain kind of ambiance around here, if you hadn't noticed."

I smiled and laughed.

"At least you have a sense of humor," the man responded. "I was kind of hoping I was dealing with a crazy person."

"You never know," I said. "I could be waiting for the right moment to spring it on you."

"I doubt it."

The man walked around and stood in front of me, blocking the setting sun from my face. When he saw me, his face wrinkled and he paused.

"Do we know each other?" he asked.

"I doubt it. I don't know anyone here. I haven't been here since I was sixteen or seventeen years old."

"And that would make you…"

"It's not polite to ask a woman's age."

"No, it's just that you look so familiar. I've lived here all my life, and we look about the same age."

"I don't know whether to be flattered or offended."

Coyly, I smiled at him, pushing the loose strands of my hair behind one ear. The man sat down next to me.

"I know we know each other. My name's Travis Grover."

"We do know each other," I answered. "Lesley Lindaugh."

I reached out my hand to shake his. Travis grabbed it and pulled me in for a hug.

"Wow! Lesley Lindaugh. I knew I knew you. It's been years! How are you?"

I was thrown a little by Travis's excitement.

"I'm fine. I didn't realize you'd be so excited to see me."

"Come on, really? After our little affair?"

"We were seventeen, Travis. At that age, nothing counts as an affair. Just raging hormones."

"How romantically put," responded Travis.

"Not that it wasn't special or anything." Hearing Travis's reaction made me feel embarrassed by my comment.

"I'm just teasing you," he laughed. "I think the way you described it was very eloquently put."

"Thank you." I smiled and put my hand over my face. "I don't feel as much of my foot in my mouth as before."

"You're welcome." He paused. "So what are you doing here on Mackinac?"

"Well, currently I'm trying to figure out how I'm going to get across the lake, back to my parent's cottage."

"Oh, will your parents be worried? I could fly you back over if you'd like."

"Fly me back over? How?"

"I own a little plane. I take tourists for scenic rides over the lake. It wouldn't be any trouble. I'd hate for your family to be worried about you."

"I'm alone. I mean, I came by myself. I'm staying by myself. There isn't anyone to be worried."

"Oh. I could still take you over, if you wanted. I wouldn't even charge you. We'll call it an old friend's discount." He smiled at me.

"That's sweet, but I couldn't do that. It's too much trouble. I would never ask that of you. I guess I'll just stay at one of the hotels."

"No can do," said Travis.

"Why not?"

"You do know what weekend it is, don't you?"

"Right. I forgot."

"People have been coming to the island all day. There isn't a room left. Not even at the Grand Hotel."

"I guess that poses a problem."

"You could always stay with me," offered Travis.

"What?"

"Why not?

"I couldn't. I wouldn't want to impose."

"No imposition. I'm offering."

"I don't know."

"I promise you'll still be alive in the morning," he said with a smile.

"Well, that's reassuring. I guess I really have no other option, do I?"

"Not unless you want to spend a night in jail. I'm sure they'll be just as accommodating."

"No, that's okay. I think I'll take my chances with you."

"Good. I hope you're up for a walk because we have a little ways to go."

Travis grabbed my hand and began leading me to the north side of the island.

"Travis, this is beautiful!" I gasped as we walked up the narrow path to his cabin in the woods. In the distance behind us the lake reflected tiny specs of light from the sky, swishing back and forth in the wind. "It's breathtaking, really."

"Thank you. To me, it's just home, but what you said is nice too."

"Humble as ever, I see."

"One has to be when you live in such a breathtaking place as this." Travis smiled at me and put his arm around my waist. "Come on. Wait until you see the cabin. You might faint."

"You know, I don't remember you being this funny when we were teenagers."

"It was the raging hormones. They blocked it."

We both laughed and entered the house.

The downstairs of the cabin was completely open; no walls dividing the living room to the kitchen to the dining room. Just very open, airy, and warm. I walked to the middle of the room and turned in a circle, taking in the large open space.

"I don't know," I said. "I'm thinking I liked the view outside better," smiling as I looked over at him.

"Just sit down on the couch and make yourself comfortable."

I plopped myself down on the leather sofa and chuckled a little. I felt young again, and nervous, and excited, and flirtatious all at once. The cushions and pillows came up around me and I leaned my head back, eyes closed, waiting for Travis. Travis walked to a closet, pulling extra blankets and pillows out.

"I hope the couch is okay for tonight. Unfortunately I don't have an extra bedroom, unless you want to take my room and I could sleep on the couch."

Travis dropped the pillows and blankets on the couch, startling me from my languid position.

"Oh, no. The couch is fine. I wouldn't want to disrupt your bedroom routine or anything."

"I think it's safe to say that's already happened."

"Oh." I felt flushed.

"Well, if you're going to sleep out here tonight I'd better get a fire started. Like I said before, it's supposed to get cold tonight. I wouldn't want you freezing to death out here."

Travis walked over and opened the back door, bringing in large pieces of firewood. As he carried in the weathered logs, I couldn't help but wonder what his body would look like carrying them in with his shirt off, his muscles flexing and straining under the weight. The thought made me smile, remembering the summer he spent with me, entirely shirtless. That was a good summer.

Travis started the fire and walked back to the couch, picking up blankets and pillows and laying them down on the floor next to the fireplace.

"Here. You might want to sleep closer to the fire. It will keep you warmer."

I moved down to the floor and made my way to the fireplace.

"Kind of like camping."

"I guess." Travis got up and walked to the kitchen. "Would you like something to drink? Scotch, wine. I have some soda – "

"Wine is fine."

"Wine it is."

Travis opened a bottle, poured two glasses, and walked back to the living room.

"I hope white is okay."

"White is fine." I took a glass as he sat down next to me, putting a blanket around my shoulders.

"So, what brings you here," asked Travis. "You seemed a little lost earlier."

"I just needed to get away. That's all. My life was a little too hectic. Too erratic. "

"How so?"

"Well, I have all these patients to deal with, and this friend. It's all very complicated."

"Patients?"

"Yeah. I'm a psychiatrist."

"Say no more." He took a sip of wine.

"What about you? What about your life? Any kids, girlfriends, wives?"

"No, no, and no," replied Travis. "None of those have I had."

"No girlfriends, ever?"

"Well, yeah, but not presently. It's kind of hard dating on an island. You know everyone and their business, and they all know yours. It gets weird after a while."

"But don't you ever want to get married?" I asked with a little whimper in my throat. Gazing at him I felt it would be a shame if he never got married. Travis would have beautiful babies, even if his future wife ended up being unattractive – as highly unlikely as that would be. There'd be no holding back the genes in his gene pool.

"Sure. I'm just waiting for the right unsuspecting tourist to come along. Someone I can get back to my cabin, who's all alone and no one will miss, who will like the view outside of the cabin better than inside, and who will sleep next to my fireplace instead of in my bed."

"That's very charming. Am I to assume, then, I could be a victim in this scheme of yours?"

"Ask me in the morning. I'll know more by then."

"Okay."

We both smiled and turned our heads away, sipping our wine, waiting for the other to start another conversation. After a few minutes, the silence was too unbearable, so Travis started his questioning again.

"So, Dr. Lindaugh, what's that like?"

"Actually, it's Dr. Trilmon."

"You're married?"

"*Was* married. It didn't last very long. I was in college…it was a long time ago."

"Trilmon. That name sounds familiar. Wasn't that the boy you claimed was your boyfriend the summer we, you know, 'went steady'?"

"I don't remember saying he was my boyfriend. I might of told you I liked him, but –"

"No, I remember the first time I tried to kiss you, you pulled away, saying something about this boy from home, blah, blah, blah. You don't remember that?"

"Vaguely," I answered with a smirk. "But I was young then and I didn't know what I was doing."

"What about now? Are you fully in control of your actions?"

"I like to think so."

"Good. Unfortunately, I'm not."

Travis leaned in and kissed me, pulling me closer to him. I jumped at first, but then fell into him, dropping my glass of wine and placing my hands on his chest.

"Wait," I gasped, pushing him slightly away from me. "We can't do this."

"Why not?" asked Travis, moving in again and kissing my neck.

"Because – "

Travis kissed my mouth, then pulled away, holding my face.

"Because is not a reason," he whispered.

"It's all I've got."

"Then you have no reason."

"Okay. Sounds good to me."

I pulled him in, kissing his mouth and reaching for his sweater, pulling it off as he tried to unbutton my shirt. Clothes half off, Travis gently laid me on the floor and began removing more of my clothing, kissing the parts of my body he remembered were sensitive to his touch. I lay there, arching my back and curling my fingers, my body recognizing a touch it had long forgotten. I smiled when he kissed the crevice behind my left knee. It had taken him almost all summer to find that spot, but when he did, he found me very responsive to it. I laid there enjoying my memories, his touch, my passion. No one else had ever found this spot, except for Wyatt. Wyatt, who knew everything about me. Wyatt…Wyatt. I opened my eyes and saw Wyatt's face. I felt his touch on my body, his fingers running along my skin and his lips caressing the sensitive parts of my body. I turned my head and saw Addie, standing there staring at us while I felt Wyatt begin to make love to me.

"No! No! Stop! I can't do this!"

"What?" gasped Travis. "What's wrong?"

"I can't do this!" I pulled away and covered myself with blankets.

"Why? Did I do something wrong?"

"No. I just can't do this."

I got up and started pacing the room. Travis grabbed a blanket and wrapped it around his waist. He followed me.

"Something is wrong. What is it?" he asked.

"I don't know, I don't know."

"I don't believe you."

"I had a fight, all right? Are you happy?"

"What are you talking about?"

"I didn't tell you when I got here, but the reason I'm here is because I had a fight with my ex-husband. I had a fight with Wyatt."

"All this because you had a fight?"

"Yes, no, I don't know. I mean, I'm upset. I'm not thinking clearly. I just wanted to get away, you know? But I can't do this. I'm vulnerable. I know that. I'm always vulnerable when I fight with Wyatt, or when I talk to him, or when I think about him."

"It sounds like you're not over him."

"You think?" I snapped, flaring my eyes at Travis, but then I quickly focused down at the floor, ashamed. "Look, I can't explain it. My relationship with Wyatt is different. Not that I want it to be, but it is, and I can't do this knowing I'll regret it in the morning. I couldn't lead you on that way."

"I'm sorry," said Travis.

"Why should you be sorry?"

"If I'd known, I would have done a better job of keeping myself…to myself, I guess."

"How could you have known? That's my fault."

"True. What do we do now?"

"I just want to sleep," I said.

"Okay, then. Goodnight."

Travis turned and began walking toward the stairs.

"Travis," I said softly.

"Yeah?"

"Would you sleep with me tonight?"

"What?"

"I mean, sleep down here with me tonight. I feel silly and old and stupid, and I don't want to be alone tonight."

"Lesley, I don't think – "

"As a friend? As an old, familiar friend. Please sleep with me tonight."

"If that's what you want, okay."

Travis walked back to the fireplace and sat down in front of it, keeping a distance from me. I knelt down and laid on my side, still wrapped in blankets.

"Thank you," I whispered.

I turned over and tried to fall asleep, but sleep was the furthest thing from my mind. After a few minutes Travis heard the muffled sounds of crying. He reached over and rolled me towards him.

"Come here."

Travis wrapped his arms around me.

"I'm so sorry," I cried. "I don't know why I do these things."

"It's okay."

He held me, letting me cry until my steady, calm breathing was the only thing he heard, and fell asleep.

The sun crept through the highest windows in the cabin, shining light down on my face, awakening me. I turned and found myself lying naked in Travis's arms. In the morning light I saw the boy I had spent a summer with. That's how I would remember him. Slowly I moved out of his arms and quietly tiptoed around the room, picking up my clothes and putting them on as I found them. *Seven-thirty.* The clock above the mantle chimed once. I had half-an-hour before the first ferryboat left dock. Quickly I found the rest of my things and carefully made my way out of the cabin without waking Travis.

When Travis woke it was nine o'clock. He searched for me but couldn't find me. Not wanting to leave things the way they had been the night before, he went down to the dock to see if he could find me, but I was already gone. Remembering my family had a house in the city, he took the next ferryboat and found himself on the other side of the lake. After asking a few people in town where the Lindaugh place was, he made his way to my parents' cottage, knocking on the door and waiting, realizing no one was home. I was gone.

When I got back to the city, I decided to leave for Chicago. There was no reason to stay in Mackinaw, and inevitably I would have to face the consequences of my actions. I opened the garage, removed my car and once again began following the coastline. When I hit the Indiana/Michigan border I agonized at the thought of all the patient queries waiting at my answering service. I drove a little slower, trying to prolong the inevitable. An hour and twenty-one minutes later I opened my apartment door to the sound of my telephone ringing. *Maybe they're tired of taking my messages,* I thought as I pictured a frazzled young operator tired of taking messages all weekend from mental patients. I groaned as I answered the phone.

"Hello?"

"Lesley-Ann Lindaugh, where the hell have you been?"

I instantly recognized my mother's voice.

"Hello, mother," I said sarcastically.

"I've been trying to call you since yesterday morning. Where are you?"

"I just left the cottage."

"In Mackinaw?"

"Yes." I could feel the plethora of questions surging her mind.

"What were you doing out there?"

"I just needed a little break from the city. It's not like I – "

"We don't have time for this," she interrupted.

"Mother, is something wrong?" I began to panic as the distress in my mother's voice became more prominent.

"Have you talked to anyone from home since you left?" she asked.

"No. Why?"

"Sweetie, I'm afraid I have some really hard news to tell you. It's Addie." My mother paused. "She's dead, Lesley."

"What?" I screamed into the phone.

"I know, I know. I was shocked too when I found out. The whole town is in shock. They found her body yesterday. I tried to call you, but...it doesn't matter. I think you should get here soon. Wyatt isn't taking it so well. Of course he isn't because his wife – "

"Mother stop it. You're babbling."

"I can't help it. I'm just so...all the things I said about that poor, sweet girl. I was just looking out for you."

"I don't have time for this!" I snapped. I pulled the phone away from my ear and tried to choke down my emotions. Calmer, I began again. "I don't know if I should come. I don't know if Wyatt would even want me there."

"Oh, I think you should," she said between sniffles. "She was your friend, right?"

"Yes, but – "

"And we know what Wyatt meant to you, to all of us. I really think you should be here for him. With his parents gone now and Prue out of state, we're the only family he has." My mother seemed genuine in her concern.

"All right. I should be there in a couple of hours."

"Good. And Lesley?"

"Yes, mother?"

"Check in every hour or so on your way up. I don't need anything happening to you."

"Yes, mother. I'll see you in a little while. I love you." I hung up the phone before she could respond.

I picked up my bag, not having had time to unpack, and went down to the garage and settled into my car, again. I looked at my tired face in the rearview mirror, searching for excuses not to go. I turned around and pulled out of the parking garage onto the streets of the city and eventually the highway, catching faded glimpses of Addie's face in that same rearview mirror as I came closer to Point Caneissa.

CHAPTER 13: A MIRAGE

Saturday, May 25th, 1974

Prue cradled Wyatt's head for twenty minutes before he shifted and lifted himself from her lap.

"That's enough of this," he said as he pushed himself up off the floor.

Wyatt pivoted and reached for the doorknob, turning and opening it, causing Prue to lean uncomfortably against the floor as Wyatt walked out of the room. Disgust came from her as she sighed, listening to him walk down the hall. She waited to hear where he would go. If he went to his room, she wouldn't follow, but anywhere else was fair game. Prue heard the sound of Wyatt's feet clomping down the stairs and was out of the room before he was halfway down.

What is wrong with him?, she screamed in her thoughts. Prue was playing questions over in her mind; what did he mean "he was the reason Addie killed herself", and what *were* those drawings in that room, and why was he being so damn difficult? She thought her brother had finally snapped – that all his sense of reality was gone and the illusions in his head were becoming real to him. She didn't want to believe he was crazy. *He couldn't have killed Addie. That's ridiculous, isn't it?* Prue allowed the thought to enter her mind, but she refused to accept it.

When she reached the first floor, Prue found Wyatt sitting in the living room on the floor, staring at an empty fireplace. She hesitated before entering. The room seemed bright and cold; no shadows lingering in dark corners, all secrets tucked carelessly away in some unknown, indiscreet place. Prue felt a presence in that room, a sensation, an instinct, and the pressure of it against her body signaling some impending doom. She hadn't felt that way since she was a child. Prue touched her wrist, searching for the bracelet Persephone had given her, but it wasn't there. Panic hit her and she felt like she couldn't move. *This is ridiculous. I am not a child anymore.* Prue convinced herself to move forward, pushing herself every step of the way.

Wyatt had found his spot on the floor between the couch and the coffee table. He didn't even know Prue had entered the room until she plopped down next to him. His body jumped as she secured her spot, placing her arm around his back and pulling him closer to her. It reminded Wyatt of their mother and how she would pull them into her bosom and stroke their hair when she knew something was wrong. It was his mother's way of getting her children to open up their secrets and worries to her. Suddenly, Wyatt felt a hand on his head, stroking his hair and his sister's voice speaking to him softly.

"Wyatt, tell me what's wrong."

"Stop patronizing me, Prue." Her tone irritated him. He shifted away from her and leaned against the couch. "I don't need your sympathy."

"You obviously need something. Valium, marijuana, maybe some kind of anti-depressant, something," she replied, trying to smile to show she was joking. Wyatt knew her well enough to hear the side of her that was serious.

"I don't need anything. I'm fine."

"I was only kidding."

"No you weren't. Part of you was serious. Part of you thinks I'm crazy. You have to think I'm crazy."

"What am I supposed to think?" asked Prue, her voice slightly elevated as she stood up. "I go into town and find you've become some kind of myth, a recluse, only coming to town every couple of weeks, maybe, and you never talk to anyone when you're there. Poor Mrs. Garvey thinks you hate her."

Wyatt internally smiled at the thought of Mrs. Garvey telling Prue he hated her. *That'll teach her for bagging so slow.*

"And then I get here and you're completely closed off to me. You won't talk to me. I go upstairs and find a petrified nursery with disturbing images *you* drew, and the only explanation you give me is that *you're* the reason for Addie's death. Hell, maybe you even killed her. I don't know! What am I supposed to think about that? Huh? When my used-to-be-sane brother tells me he's responsible for his wife's death? You tell me!"

"I know," said Wyatt quietly, almost in retreat. "You're right."

"Oh, no you don't. Don't give me that sad little boy response. I want answers."

"I wouldn't even know where to start."

Wyatt covered his face with his hands and rubbed hard, stretching and defining wrinkles caused by the last year-and-a-half of stress. He rested his head back against the couch cushions.

"Do you think any of the stories about this house are true?" he asked. Prue felt uncomfortable. She didn't know what to say.

"You know how I feel about this house," she replied, naturally searching her wrist for the missing bracelet. "You and your friends used to tease me about it when I was a kid. It doesn't matter anyway. They're not true. Just old wives' tales to scare little children into being good."

"I believe they're true."

Wyatt's voice trailed off. Prue hesitated in her response. She felt like a child again, unguarded and uncertain as to what her brother was trying to get from her. Her inner child was shouting, *Yes! I believe! Finally someone else believes too!,* but the adult in her was cautious, trying to read into what her brother was saying.

"Wyatt, that's ridiculous."

"Is it? You were friends with Persephone. What did she say about this house?"

"We didn't talk about the house."

"You're telling me that in all those years, all that time you spent with her, not once did you talk about the stories surrounding this house?"

Prue thought carefully. Persephone and the way people perceived her was very important to Prue. She always felt that she had to protect Persephone; that the ignorant comments made in town still hurt, no matter who said them. But this was Wyatt, and he seemed genuine in his questioning, his confusing search for answers.

"She said there was nothing to be afraid of. Nothing ever happened here."

"Really?" replied Wyatt sarcastically. "I don't believe that. I think you're hiding something. Perhaps she worked some voodoo on you to make you forget." He laughed a little.

"Persephone was my friend, Wyatt, and that's more than I can say for you right now."

Wyatt saw the hurt in her eyes.

"Look, I'm sorry. But this house, it's just got me turned upside down. I think there is something seriously wrong here. I can't explain it any other way." He paused. "I just want to know what she said about the house."

"I don't see what this has to do with anything. I think you're trying to avoid my questions. Just some sick, twisted game for your amusement, like when we were kids. When are you ever going to grow up?"

"I'm sorry, Prue. I don't know what to say."

Prue felt herself giving in again. That was the thing about Wyatt. He had this irresistible, honest charm about him that no matter what he did to upset you, it didn't matter, because in the end, you believed him when he said he didn't mean to do it, even if he did. Prue believed Lesley fell for this quality, too. How else could Lesley have forgiven him for leaving her, for pursuing a life without her, and for marrying her best friend? It had to be that unstoppable, uncontrollable, irresistible charm. She didn't know if he was truly sorry, but Prue wanted to believe Wyatt. And so she caved in.

"Persephone said that there wasn't any evil here. There was only evil here if you believed there was, and since I didn't, there wasn't. It was that simple. No evil, no ghosts. Just made up stories."

"I believe there is, so there must be," Wyatt said, his voice tapering off slowly.

"Don't be ridiculous. Like I said before, it was just old wives' tales. No truth to any of it."

"If that's true, then why have you been searching your wrist for your bracelet since we started talking about the house?"

Prue looked down at her wrist and found that she had made deep red circles on it from rubbing her hand around it tightly.

"You know," began Wyatt, "this is all starting to make sense now. The stories, the baby, Addie's writings."

"What writings?" asked Prue.

"I don't know where to start," said Wyatt, almost excited. "I guess I would have to start with the night Addie lost the baby. Everything seemed so perfect until that point. We hadn't been here long and Addie had just finished unpacking the last of our boxes that day. I'd been in the nursery all weekend trying to finish it as a surprise. I didn't know something was wrong – how could I – until I heard her screaming from our bedroom." He paused. "And then there was nothing. No joy, no love, no kindness. I'd tried to comfort her, Prue, I really did, but everything I did seemed to push her further away from me. That's when I called Lesley."

Wyatt stopped.

"And?" asked Prue. "What happened?"

"I think I fell in love."

"Wyatt, we all know you loved Addie very much."

"Not Addie," forced Wyatt, breathlessly. "Lesley."

Prue was suddenly very intrigued.

"I didn't mean for it to happen, but I didn't stop it either. My intentions were good, always good, but things just got twisted around. It must have killed Addie to see us together, to know what was coming."

"Wyatt, what are you talking about?"

Wyatt started calmly.

"She came every week. Friday, Saturday, and Sunday, like clockwork. We made the guestroom her own little space. At first, I think Addie was happy she was here, but then it all changed. Everything was different."

"What do you mean? What changed? What was different?"

"I don't know. Addie became distant, and started pushing me away even more. But she was here to help me, console me."

"Who? Lesley?"

"Yes, Lesley. Addie must have known, must have seen. Addie's writings were obsessed with it. Every move we made, every word we said, every moment we were together drove her crazy. Addie saw everything…more than we did, I think."

"I don't understand this whole scene you're painting for me. It doesn't make sense." Prue was getting aggravated at Wyatt's indirectness.

"It doesn't have to," Wyatt said calmly.

Wyatt was more relaxed than he thought he'd be. Talking about Addie's death always made him nervous, his self-loathing creeping up on him the more he would talk about it. But now with Prue, he felt no secret hiding inside of him. He was telling a story, like Addie's writings, of some vivid tale that happened long ago that he couldn't feel anymore; it had become relentless against him, and he fought it no more.

"It all started right here. Lesley was sitting right where you are now. It was all very innocent, I think. I didn't plan it. I don't think Lesley knew it would happen either. But it did."

Prue sat quietly trying to figure out what her brother was saying. He talked in circles trying to get around the main point and while she waited, her curiosity was screaming at him to hurry up. *How unfortunate our brains are not connected,* she thought. *Then I would already know your secret and you wouldn't have to tiptoe around it. It must be good, though, otherwise you would have told someone.* Prue felt significant, a little prestigious, knowing she would be the first person Wyatt had really talked to in a year. Her eagerness became too much.

"Get to the point already!"

The words were out of her mouth before she even completed the sentence in her head. She cupped her lips in shock. Wyatt stopped and stared at her.

"I'm trying to tell you something very important," he said finally.

"I know. I don't know what I was thinking. I'm sorry. Continue, please." She was chiding herself more for possibly ruining her chance to find out this secret than she was for hurting his feelings.

"Well, suddenly all these feelings I had for Lesley came rushing in on me."

"Wait a second," interrupted Prue. "You're going to have to fill me in here a little. Why are you talking about Lesley? I thought we were talking about Addie."

"I'm telling you what happened the night Addie died! Aren't you listening?"

"Why should I apologize for you not making sense?," asked Prue. She could sense that Wyatt was getting mad at her and the feeling was becoming mutual. "Besides," she continued, trying to fight her emotions, "no one knows why Addie killed herself. No one was here. How could you possibly know? Is this for hurting your feelings when I got here? Because if it is – "

"Prue shut up! Just listen for once in your life! The world does not revolve around you and what you do. For God sakes! I was in the house when Addie died. I was here!" Wyatt pushed himself away from Prue and began pacing in front of the fireplace. "I was here."

"But you were at a convention," Prue said quietly. She was half scared of him now. "Sheriff Roberts said – "

"I lied to Sheriff Roberts. I lied to everyone. I was here."

Wyatt stopped pacing and sat next to Prue again. She backed away from him putting a small distance between them. "Now, would you like to know what happened? May I continue?"

Prue shook her head yes, almost afraid to speak.

"Addie and I had a fight that morning. I had just gotten so tired of her erratic behavior. She had locked herself in the nursery sometime during the night. She wouldn't let me in, wouldn't listen to reason. I was afraid for her life, Prue. Really, I was, but she wouldn't let me in. Not just the room, but herself. Addie wouldn't let me help her. Wouldn't let me touch her. Wouldn't let me hold her. I just got angry, you know?"

Wyatt looked at Prue with sincerity, as if his actions to be foretold were the only actions he could have taken – a desperate man looking for confirmation.

Prue shook her head in agreement again, not knowing how else to respond.

"I couldn't take it anymore, so I left. That comic book convention, I had signed up for it before Addie lost the baby and I never canceled. I guess part of me hoped she would be well enough by then for me to leave her alone for a weekend. But I had to get out, so I jumped in the car and drove to Livonia."

"Wyatt, I know you were in Livonia. Sheriff Roberts told me, told everyone. Addie committed suicide because she was depressed, not because you two had a fight."

It was her tone, again, that irked him. That motherly, patronizing tone. *What is she trying to do, anyway?,* Wyatt wondered. Did she want the truth, or did Prue want a glossed over version of the truth, the truth he had incessantly, it seemed, told everyone else? Wyatt didn't like that truth anymore. It was too clean. It fit too perfectly. It made him look like a victim when in his own mind he clearly wasn't.

"I didn't stay there, obviously," he continued, choosing to ignore Prue's interruption. "I knew Lesley would be coming that night. I just needed to get away for a few hours, and then I came back. When I got home, Addie was still in the nursery. I assumed she'd been there all day. This time, though, the door wasn't locked, and so I let myself in and found Addie sleeping in the rocking chair. Papers were strewn all over the floor. She had left the window open and the wind had made a mess of everything, but I didn't care. I barely noticed. All I saw was her sweet face, that young girl I married. Her body shivered in the breeze. I closed the window and grabbed a blanket from the trunk to cover her. I leaned over and kissed her forehead, and her face and body turned away from me, as if it recognized my touch and was repulsed. It hurt. I loved her so much in that moment and her body had cringed at feeling me. I couldn't look at her anymore. I left the room and went downstairs, just in time to meet Lesley at the door."

Wyatt paused. That feeling, that look on Addie's face came back to him. It still hurt. All he had wanted to do was love her, and not even her subconscious would let him. Had Addie's hatred toward him been so great? Was that what it was? Hatred? A tear rolled down his cheek. He let it linger there, rolling to his chin, until it became heavy and dropped to the floor.

"Wyatt, I'm sorry," Prue said quietly. "It must have been awful for you. Why didn't you tell me? I would have been there for you. We were all so focused on Addie, I didn't even think about how you were feeling. I'm sorry."

"What could you have done?" Wyatt asked honestly.

"I could have been here for you. I could have come and visited you, maybe stayed for a little while, until things started getting back to normal."

"That's why I called Lesley."

"I can understand that," responded Prue. "I mean, who better than a trained professional and Addie's best friend to help get things back to normal. But still, I would have come."

"I know."

"Did it help?"

"No."

Prue thought she was beginning to understand Wyatt's weird behavior, his anguish over the loss of his wife. The story seemed so complicated, and yet, he told it very simply, so matter-of-factly that Prue was beginning to doubt all her assumptions of what happened that night. Surely Wyatt didn't drive Addie to kill herself, but perhaps there was more to their relationship and the events leading up to that day than she had led herself to believe. Perhaps Wyatt and Addie's relationship wasn't perfect, like Prue had always let herself think, but instead flawed, like everyone else's. Wyatt and Addie always acted as though they were meant for each other, one always complimenting the other. More so than when Wyatt had been with Lesley, or so it seemed when Wyatt and Addie were out in public, with friends or family. It had never crossed Prue's mind that they might have had problems. It was becoming real to her now, their life together, those last few months, and Prue's perfect perception of them had started to crack and crumble, something she wasn't sure she was ready for. But she listened anyway.

"You're quiet," Wyatt said finally.

"This is all a little hard to take in. I mean, I thought I knew…"

Prue paused again.

"Do you want me to stop?"

"No," answered Prue. "Please, go on."

Wyatt took a deep breath. Wyatt didn't look at Prue as he spoke. He looked straight ahead into the fireplace as he told the rest of his story.

"The night it happened, Lesley was sitting right where you are and I was looking straight ahead. We talked of old times, what happened in the past, what's happened since. She touched my hand and I looked down at it. So familiar, so small, so lovely."

Wyatt paused again, looking down into his lap and blinking violently, as if something was caught in his eye. It was only memory, though.

"When I looked up, we were kissing. It was innocent. But I wanted it so badly – to be touched, to be loved. I wanted Lesley so badly, Prue. I couldn't help it. It felt so natural, so right, like we'd never been apart, almost as if it were meant to be." His voice trailed off a little. "I would have made love to her, Prue. I know I would have," he whispered, clenching his fists. "And I don't know that I would have regretted it. I wouldn't have been sorry if I had gone through with it." He looked at Prue, tears in his eyes. "I loved Lesley. I would have done anything for her."

He stopped, letting the tears again roll down his face, grow heavy and then drop to the floor. Prue put her hand on top of Wyatt's and began rubbing it. It was the only thing she could think of to do. Wyatt barely noticed.

"Oh, Wyatt," she said quietly. "You don't have to finish if you don't want to. I don't need to know."

"I have to finish. It's okay. There isn't that much more to tell anyway." Wyatt paused, regaining his thoughts, then continued. "Lesley had gasped, saying Addie's name. I lifted myself and turned around. There was Addie, standing at the end of the stairs."

He pointed behind Prue and she turned to get a better picture in her mind.

"Addie saw the whole thing, or at least most of it. At first I wasn't sure what she had seen. I thought maybe she had seen nothing. But I was kidding myself. I got up and started walking towards her. When I reached out for her, she screamed and ran up the stairs. Lesley went into some kind of shock, I think. I'm not sure. Everything was happening so fast it's hard to be sure of what happened. I tried to help Addie, console her, but Lesley wouldn't stay and help me explain. Maybe if she'd stayed..." Wyatt trailed off until his breath no longer made audible words. Prue took his hand.

"It's okay," she said.

"No it's not." He began to cry. "After Lesley left I went upstairs to find Addie. She locked herself in that damn nursery. I tried to calm her, to reason with her. I told her it was an accident, that I didn't mean for anything to happen with Lesley, but it did. I told her I was leaving; that we had our problems and I didn't know that I wanted to work through them, didn't know if I *could* work through them. Then I told her I was going after Lesley. That's when it started." Wyatt stopped and wiped the drying tears away from his cheeks, then looked directly at Prue. "All Addie did was scream and cry. She must have known, must have heard it in my voice that I was going to leave her. But all I could think of was, where could Lesley be? All I wanted to do was go after Lesley. I wanted to know if she was okay. In my pleading with Addie I began wondering where my life had turned downward. Do you know what I realized?"

"What?"

"It was when I left Lesley. All this time, all I had done was because I was trying to forget the fact that I loved her. I loved her, Prue. I loved her so much that I pushed her away. It's why I married Addie in the first place. How sick is that?"

Wyatt waited for an answer. Prue wasn't sure what the appropriate answer to all this was.

"I don't know," she said finally. "I've never been in love like that before." *I don't know if that is love,* Prue secretly thought.

"It doesn't matter anyway." Wyatt relaxed into the cushions of the couch, leaning his head back and placing his arms up and to the sides, one resting behind Prue's head. "I stopped pleading with her after awhile. It was pointless. She didn't believe me. *I* didn't believe me. I was kidding myself if I thought our marriage wasn't over. So I accepted it. I just sat and waited for her to calm down. When I couldn't hear her crying anymore, I told her I understood if she wanted me to leave. I understood if she wanted to leave. I wasn't going to make her stay and I wasn't going to stay if she didn't want me to."

He stopped. Prue looked at him, waiting, wanting to know the end, but he didn't begin again.

"So, then what happened?"

"I followed the sound of her screaming."

Wyatt said it so nonchalantly.

"What?" asked Prue, startled.

"Addie had said some things, things I couldn't believe to be true. I told her she was lying, and she unlocked the door."

"What did she say? What was she lying about?"

"It doesn't matter," said Wyatt quickly. "I opened the door and confronted her. Told her I was leaving. She said I never loved her, and it hurt to hear her say that. At some point I *had* loved her, I just couldn't remember it anymore. So I went to her, wanting to console her, but she threw herself away from me. I followed the sound of her screaming out of the house until I reached the beach. I couldn't hear her anymore. I thought I vaguely saw a body fighting the waves on the lake. The waves were too strong. I couldn't go in after her." He paused. "Everything gets a little fuzzy after that. I wasn't even sure Addie went into the lake until I met with Sheriff Roberts in the morning. He said some fisherman found her body. 'No sign of foul play,' he said. Right. He should have looked at her heart."

Wyatt was silent. He wanted Prue to take in every word he said. He waited for her questions, knowing they would cut into him, causing that deeply protected part of his psyche to bleed, hopefully to death. He didn't want to feel this guilt anymore. He wanted someone to reassure him everything was all right. He wanted numbness – no thoughts – the point beyond pain. He wanted to feel normal again.

Prue didn't know what to think. This whole fantastical story was a little hard to digest. It was so melodramatic, and her brother was not one to express excessive emotion at any time. He was always thoughtful of others, but also very calm and collected. He hardly asked for advice, choosing to figure out problems on his own and making decisions quickly and sometimes on a whim. A whim by normal standards, that is. For Wyatt, though, they always worked out, as if he had planned out his actions days or months in advance. Prue could never figure out how it was that everything seemed to work out for Wyatt. She was a little jealous of him in that respect. She was so cautious and calculated. If she were married, she would never leave her husband to pursue a new career path. She would never jump on a plane to Vegas and get married. She would never date an ex's best friend. But all these things seemed to have worked out for Wyatt, until a year ago. Could everything Wyatt said be true?

"I don't know how to respond to all of this, Wyatt," Prue said finally. "It seems a little far-fetched. I mean, if it were true, I would think someone would have seen Lesley. If she were up here every weekend, someone would have seen her. Someone would have told Sheriff Roberts. We would have known about this sooner, I think."

"Maybe," Wyatt said. "But we were careful."

"What does that mean?"

"It doesn't matter."

"Wyatt, you're scaring me. At times you're so forthcoming and others you're just so cryptic. It's not like you. We used to be able to tell each other everything. Now I fear something is wrong with you, something I can't help you with."

"It's this house," he said abruptly.

"What?"

"It's this house. It haunts me."

"Wyatt, that's not funny." Prue began circling her wrist again.

"I'm being serious." He lifted his head from the couch and looked at Prue. "Why do you think I asked you about it in the first place?"

"I don't know. I thought maybe you were making fun of me."

"Prue, we're not children anymore. There are more important things to do than make you feel foolish. Again, this isn't about you."

"I never said it was."

"And yet we keep coming back to it. I tried to tell you everything, to confide in you, but you don't believe me."

"It's a little unbelievable."

"Of course it is! Everything that has happened in this house is unbelievable. You of all people should know that. Why do you think I'm telling *you*? I thought you'd understand."

"Wyatt, you're scaring me."

"I'm scaring myself," he sighed. "I don't know what else to tell you. You wouldn't believe me anyway."

"Believe what?"

Wyatt thought carefully before he spoke.

"Sometimes, late at night, when the mantle clock strikes midnight, I see Addie."

Prue picked up the semi-empty dishes from the coffee table. Wyatt had barely eaten anything. Normally, she would have taken this as an insult, Wyatt always devouring anything she put in front of him, but this evening had revealed so many jumbled, unexplainable feelings that Prue was surprised she was able to eat the full bowl of spaghetti she had dished for herself. Quietly she walked through the large open space adjoining the living room, kitchen, and dining room. Prue tried gently to set the dishes in the sink, only to cause them to come crashing together in the bottom when she let them go. The silverware rang against the stainless steel and porcelain, waking Wyatt from his concentrated, private thoughts.

"Is everything okay?" he yelled from the living room, stretching and turning his neck to the side, but not moving otherwise.

"Yeah. I'm just a little clumsy, I guess. I don't think anything broke, though."

"Good."

Wyatt didn't say another word. It had been like that for two hours. The both of them sat in silence, watching the fireplace, or the clock, or each other as they attempted to eat the quickly thrown together meal. Prue would make a comment, Wyatt would respond, and vice-versa. Neither one of them had brought up the subject of Addie.

After Wyatt confessed he believed he sometimes saw his dead wife roaming the house after midnight, Prue tried her best to divert the conversation to anything else. Wyatt took the hint and said nothing else on the subject. He spoke when spoken to, tried to complement the food, and watched the clock. It was ten-thirty. Wyatt stared at the clock, wondering what would happen in an hour-and-a-half.

Prue walked into the living room, set two double-shot glasses and a bottle of vodka on the coffee table, and then sat next to Wyatt.

"Would you like me to pour you a shot?" she asked, already in mid-pour.

"No thank you. I'd like to have as clear a mind as possible. I would suggest the same for you."

Prue picked up the filled shot glass and drank the whole thing, in one swallow.

"I'm tired of having a clear mind. I just want to relaaaxxx."

She poured herself another shot.

"You might want to take it easy there," said Wyatt.

"Why? I think this is the perfect ending to this impossible day."

Prue giggled a little as she ended the sentence. Wyatt took the glass from her and set it on the table.

"I think you're relaxed enough. Besides, you never could hold your alcohol very well."

Prue leaned over and picked up the vodka bottle.

"I'm doing just fine holding my alcohol, thank you very much."

Wyatt laughed, leaning his head back against the couch and smiling. Prue grew angry at his laughing, only because she knew he was laughing at her, and she hated being made fun of. She hated looking ridiculous. It brought back bad childhood memories of being picked on for no other reason than sport. *Why was he laughing, anyway?* It's not like *she* had concocted some fanciful story about Addie's death. And now she sat waiting, watching for something to happen. It made her feel stupid and childish, as did most of this evening.

"What's all this about, anyway? Is Addie supposed to pop up and scare us or what?"

"That's not funny, Prue, and it's insensitive."

"Oh, really? Well, I wouldn't know anymore. It's hard to tell now what's truth and sincerity opposed to fiction and false empathy."

"What?"

"You know what I'm talking about."

"No, I really don't."

"Wyatt, stop playing dumb. I'm sick of all of this. It's not funny anymore. So I believe in ghosts, blah, blah, blah. You don't have to make fun of me for it."

"Okay. That's enough vodka for you this evening."

Wyatt took the vodka bottle away from Prue, picked up the empty shot glasses on the table and walked to the kitchen to put it away. He walked back to the couch and reclaimed his spot next to his sister.

"So what *are* we doing here, Wyatt?"

"We're going to sit here until midnight."

"And then what?"

"I don't know."

"What do you mean you don't know? I thought you knew what's going on?"

"I don't know what's going to happen. Like I said before, sometimes at midnight, I see Addie. That's why I want to have a clear head. And you should too. So I can show you."

"Why do I feel like I'm in one of those cheesy horror movies? All I need now is a camera and a divining rod."

Prue put her hands up to her eyes and cupped them as if they were a camera, searching the room for varying degrees of shadow and mist.

"Prue!"

"Well, I'm sorry! That's how I feel! I can't help it. Right now I just want to go upstairs, put on my pjs, and crawl into bed. Hell, if the ghost wants to crawl in there with me, so be it."

"Don't be cruel."

"I can't help it! After this whole melodramatic night I'm tired. I don't know what to think and I don't want to talk about anything anymore! I just want it to be tomorrow so we can start over, or yesterday so this hasn't happened yet. I just want my sane, loving, big brother back. Okay? That's what I want. Sleep, and you back to normal."

Prue curled her arm around Wyatt's and leaned her head on his shoulder, closing her eyes. Wyatt felt her sinking into sleep.

"Just stay up for one more hour," he whispered. "Just one more hour. Until midnight, alright?"

"Okay." Prue yawned as she spoke, letting the light in the room drift to darkness until she couldn't hear or see or feel anything surrounding her.

The mantle clock chimed its half-hour chime, causing Prue to open her eyes slightly, squinting to see the time. It was eleven-thirty. She was still curled around Wyatt's arm. He hadn't moved, but she could tell he was still awake. His breathing was steady and his chest lifted his arm every time he inhaled. It was comforting. Prue concentrated on the lifting and falling of her head against her brother's body, and fell into her dreams, again.

The mantle clock was in its fifth chime when Prue finally lifted her head from her brother's shoulder. She rubbed her eyes and stretched, waiting for the loud clanging to stop. Leaning back against the couch she counted them, *eight...nine...ten ...eleven...twelve...*until they stopped. She turned her head to speak to her brother.

"Addie..."

It was barely audible but Prue heard the name escape his lips. She opened her eyes and sat up.

"What?" she whispered.

"Addie."

Quietly, he spoke her name again. Prue watched Wyatt slowly move towards the empty space in front of the stairway. In the darkness, through her sleep-filled and slightly intoxicated mind, Prue watched the space in front of Wyatt move. It was blurry, it could have been nothing but her own mind playing tricks on her, but it moved quickly. The front door came open and the breeze off the lake began to make the curtains sway throughout the downstairs. Then, Wyatt was gone. He ran out of the house and down to the lake. Prue ran after him, slipping on the rug just as Wyatt reached the opened front door and left the house. Prue tried desperately to follow him but she had to stop and nurse the increasing pain of a sprained ankle.

Wyatt kept running.

He made the decision earlier in the day that his exhaustion would not get the best of him this night. Wyatt had played that night over and over in his head, searching for the mistakes he had made in trying to save Addie. He wasn't prepared the night Addie died. Tonight he was. The torture of that night being replayed in front of him – Wyatt figured it was a game the house was playing with him. It trapped his secrets and haunted him, making him experience the agony of that night, not letting him succeed in saving her. Tonight was different though. Wyatt was prepared and wide-awake. He didn't need to follow her screams. She was ten feet in front of him. He ran faster to catch her, his feet sinking in the sand. Just as her feet touched the water Wyatt grabbed her hand and pulled her back. Her dark red nightgown fluttered in the breeze. She looked at him in horror. She stared at his hand holding her wrist, then looked back into his face. He could see the color of her eyes in the moonlight, the gold changing into darkness until there was no reflection of light. The image of Addie tried to pull away from him, but he grabbed her other hand. Her body turned from peach to pale gray as she screamed, the figure of what she was shattering into a thousand different pieces and crumbling in his hands. He looked at the dust as it fell through his fingers onto the sand. Wyatt collapsed, sobbing, his hands dug deep into the remains of his wife.

Prue hobbled slowly out to the embankment to see if she could see Wyatt. Finding him crouched down about twenty feet away, she limped her way out to him. The waves were coming in faster now and when she reached him she tried to pull him out of the three inches of water that surrounded him.

"No!" he screamed as he grasped for the wet clumps of sand his fingers had been clinging to. "Addie is out there. Prue, help me find her!" He crawled back into the water and began digging up wet sand.

"Addie isn't out there, Wyatt!" Prue yelled over the small waves.

"Yes she is." He continued digging.

"No, she's not." Prue slid on her knees across the wet sand, grabbing Wyatt's hands, preventing them from digging anymore. "Addie's dead. She's not out here."

"But I saw her."

"I saw nothing. She's not out here. She's gone."

Wyatt fell limp into Prue and sobbed. She tried to brace his weight but it fell too much on her ankle, so she held him for a minute, then convinced him it was time to go back inside. As they walked up the path to the house, each leaning on the other, Prue looked behind her once more, out into the lake. In the darkness she thought she saw a figure swimming in the water, but then it was gone, hidden by a rushing wave. She looked harder at the shore and saw a red colored cloth receding into the sullen water of the night.

CHAPTER 14: FADING WALLPAPER

Wyatt

A week after Addie lost the baby I packed up my utensils, arranged for my drawing table to be delivered to the house, and locked up my tiny downtown studio indefinitely. I had rented a space in town shortly after Addie and I moved to Point Caneissa. Having a space away from the house, I thought, would help me keep my work routine in check, which is what the studio in San Francisco wanted. They agreed to keep me on as a freelance artist at a pay cut, which was my punishment for leaving. Even with the monthly commute to Detroit or Chicago, I was still happy with my decision. With the revenues from my comic and the small investments I had made after my parents' death, I felt that in my move to Point Caneissa I had secured financial stability for my family. Walking away from my small rented studio, financial stability no longer seemed like enough.

The road home grew familiar to me now, daily passing my parents' house – now Prue's – the small inner-workings of my hometown rooting itself again in my memory. February on the Michigan coast is cold and stark, the lake freezing into mounded white walkways of the unknown. *If you started walking on the ice, could you make it to Wisconsin without it cracking,* I wondered, *without the cold, flowing water underneath swallowing you up?* I questioned if anyone ever tried. Perhaps I would try, stopping my car on the side of the road, leaving it running with the door open, and just walking into that white nothingness. If it did swallow me, the pain wouldn't last long. It would be easier than going home.

Depression. That was a heavy word. Much like the ice and the water flowing underneath it, depression could swallow you unforgivingly, taking you down until you fought no more. Was it painless? I imagined not. I saw the pain in Addie's face every day and felt helpless. I tried for a month to console Addie, trying to break her depression, but I failed.

It was a Wednesday, a normal day, except for finding Addie in the nursery rocking a large Winnie-the-Pooh bear and singing a lullaby gently into the stuffed toy's ear. That was the day Addie tried to kill herself while I was in town shopping. At least that's what I thought had happened. I had found her, soaking wet, crawling along the breaking ice fifteen feet out.

Beyond that, it was hard to tell. Had she gone walking, searching for the water she knew would drown her sorrow? Or had she taken a misstep and cracked the ice by accident? It was March now, and the ice had begun to crack and melt and recede back into the lake. Perhaps it *was* an accident. But I believed the worst; my wife had lost all will to live. Frantically, I called Lesley and she agreed to come up. Once here, I begged her to come every weekend and counsel Addie.

"Please," I pleaded. "There is no one who will treat her like you will. You're a friend, family. You love her. Who better than you, someone who loves her, someone who knows her, to counsel her?"

"I don't know," answered Lesley hesitantly. "I might be *too* close. You should never counsel close friends. What if it turned out badly?"

"It won't. Please, Lesley. For me. I need you."

"Okay."

That was it. Neither of us knew at the beginning of this new arrangement what old feelings would be rekindled, and those feelings would eventually bring us back to the beginning of this whole ordeal – back to Addie and the lake.

Moments; tiny split-second decisions that make up a life. Is that all life was? Good decisions, bad decisions, all weaving the small sections together of the fabric of life? Split-second decisions. I decided that was all my life had been as I sat outside the nursery and waited for my wife to stop crying. Lesley had left me. That was her split-second decision, and now I didn't know what to do. What was next? My wife had found me about to make love to another woman, my ex-wife no less. Where do you go from there?

Downstairs.

I walked downstairs to get a screwdriver to try and unlock the door. It seemed like an endless journey. My mind was full of thoughts I couldn't control. Like my body's passions earlier in the night, I now found my brain traversing my thoughts at breakneck speed, accelerating with every step. I couldn't stop them. I had no control. But one thought outnumbered all the others: Lesley. I couldn't stop thinking about Lesley. I wanted her there with me. Not to console Addie or fix whatever disaster was waiting for me. No. I wanted her there because I wanted to know that she was all right. I wanted her there so that she would be near me. I wanted her there because *I loved her.* I stopped. Once, I had pushed my feelings for her aside and left, trying not to look back for fear I would return to her and lose myself in doing so. But now, tonight, I felt more like myself than I had in years. Who was I, anyway? Who had I become? A man in a cotton-candy marriage gone horribly wrong, who couldn't make decisions for myself for fear they would turn out bad. I looked back on my life with Addie. Had I made any decisions? Or were they all Addie's plans?

I sat down on the bottom step and began to laugh.

How had I not seen it before? Looking back on my life with Addie I realized almost every decision, every change in our life had been decided by Addie before I had even known about it. How could I have been so blind? This last decision, the baby, was the final straw. *Had she planned everything?* I wondered now if Addie knew five years ago I would propose to her. That was ridiculous! How could she? But still, *those words.* What were the words she had said? *"I think you should go to San Francisco...anyone that loves you can see that."* Those words. Those were the words that made me propose. Lesley had said those exact same words. That's why I proposed to Addie. I thought she loved me like Lesley had loved me. *Did Lesley say those words to Addie?*

That one thought changed my whole view on my life.

I got up, walked to the kitchen, opened the utility drawer and grabbed the screwdriver. Walking up the stairs I felt like a new man. I felt in control of the moment. I'd made a decision, without Addie.

At the top of the stairs I turned and stopped at the nursery. I wasn't ready to see Addie yet. I kneeled on the floor and leaned my back against the door, placing the screwdriver next to me. I could hear that Addie had stopped crying. She was sitting in the rocking chair, slightly moving its gliders back and forth, enough for the wooden floor to creak on her down-thrusts. I thought this was the perfect moment.

"Addie," I began quietly, "I've been thinking about some things and I just want to talk to you, okay? I'm not going to try to come in. I just want to talk."

The floor ceased to creak. I knew I had her attention.

"I want you to know that I didn't plan for all this to happen. I didn't know. It just did. Not that I'm making excuses. I take full responsibility. I mean, I don't know what I mean. Look, Addie, we have some problems – obviously we have some problems – and I'm not sure we can work through them."

I heard her walk to the other side of the door, lean against it, and slide down to the floor.

"I don't know that *I* can work through them. I don't know that I want to, and I don't think you want to either. Everything that's happened the last couple of months, you, me. I think we both know we're not the same people. I think we want different things."

212|P A I G E K. P A L M E R

Addie continued to sit silently on the other side of the door.

"Look, after tonight, I'm not going to ask you to stay. I can't. Too much has happened. I wouldn't want to put you through that pain anymore. I hope you won't ask me to stay, either. I don't know that I can."

I paused. I wanted what I was saying to soak in. I didn't know if I had explained myself, but I hoped she understood that I wanted to leave.

And then I said the wrong thing.

"I think I'll leave for tonight. I'll be back tomorrow, hopefully. I'm worried about Lesley. I think I should go look for her."

"What?" Addie screamed.

I jumped away from the door and stood three feet in front of the nursery, waiting to see how Addie would explode.

"How can you say that? How can you even think of going after that *slut*?"

"Addie, calm down – "

"Calm down! Let's see. I catch you about to sleep with my supposed best friend tonight and you want me to calm down? You're such an asshole!"

"Addie, please – "

"Maybe I should have seen this coming. Even when we were dating I could tell you still had a thing for her."

"Addie that's ridiculous."

"Is it Wyatt? Then why, Wyatt, have I spent our entire relationship together trying to get you to love me? I thought if I acted like her you would love me, or if I got you away from her you would love me, or if I were just perfect enough you would love me, or if I had your baby you would love me, but sadly, no! You choose to continue to love a whore! Did she ever tell you how many men she's been with? Has she?"

"Addie, that's enough!"

"No, I don't think it is. Maybe you like whores. Maybe if I was a whore you'd love me."

"Addie stop it!" I yelled as I slammed my fists against the door. She countered back.

"NO! Why shouldn't I feel this way? After what I saw tonight, I have a right to say whatever the hell I want about Lesley, about you, about anyone!"

"Addie, we can talk through this calmly."

"I don't want to be calm! All I ever wanted to do was love you, and to have you love me. I wanted to be happy and raise a family. I thought that would make you happy. But you never wanted *our* baby. I would have given you a beautiful baby. I would have loved you. But instead of loving me and the child I would have given you, you love a woman who gave your child away!"

"Addie, what are you talking about?" I seriously thought that Addie had lost her mind. Nothing she was saying was making sense. I wasn't even sure I wanted to hear what she had to say, but I listened anyway.

"Oh, did Lesley forget to tell you?"

"Tell me what?"

"How cute. Your whore is keeping secrets from you!"

"Addie stop calling her that. She's not a whore."

"What else do you call a woman who steals another woman's husband?"

"Is that what you call yourself?" I shouted.

There was a pause.

"I didn't steal you from her," Addie whispered.

"You might as well have," I answered.

"How can you say that, after all she's done to you?"

"She hasn't done anything to me! You've lost your mind."

"I told you," she said quietly. "The baby. How can you still love her after the baby?"

"Addie, Lesley had nothing to do with the loss of our baby. You had a miscarriage. That's all."

"Not *our* baby. Her baby. Your baby with Lesley."

"You're not making any sense. I'm leaving. I can't take any more of this nonsense."

"When you left Lesley she was pregnant!" Addie shouted.

I stopped and turned back around, facing the nursery.

"What?"

"Lesley was pregnant. She didn't want you to know. She didn't want anyone to know. She told me before I ever met you. It was part of a trust exercise when she was my mentor. I never told anyone. That was the whole point."

"You're lying," I said angrily. "Lesley would have told me."

"I'm not lying," Addie pleaded. "Lesley wanted to tell you. She said she was going to tell you when your parents died but her mother wouldn't let her. She stayed with Lesley until the funeral to make sure she didn't contact you. Man, that woman always was a bitch," giggled Addie

"You're lying," I repeated. I heard the door unlock. I reached for the doorknob, turned it and walked in. Addie stood leaning against my drawing table. "You're lying."

"You're baby lives in St. Joseph. Her name is Grace. Although she's not a baby anymore. She's probably eight or nine by now – "

"You're lying!"

"I'm not lying! Lesley gave your daughter away like she was some old, unwanted toy, and you stand here now pining away for her. How can you do that? I love you, Wyatt! Why can't you see that?

"I don't have to take this. I'm leaving." I turned to walk out of the nursery. Addie grabbed my arm.

"No!" she screamed. "Wyatt, please, listen to me." I jerked my arm from her and backed away.

"No!" I yelled. "I'm not listening to your lies anymore!"

"You're an adulterer," shouted Addie. "An adulterer! Why didn't I see it? You never wanted me. You never wanted the baby. You never loved me!"

The words hit me hard in the chest, as if she'd kicked me in the heart and knocked the wind out of me. Did I love her? Or was I what she said, an adulterer? Nothing sounded right at the moment.

"Addie, I do love you," I answered quietly, "I mean, I did love you. Please listen to me." I walked over to her again and she jerked away from me.

"Stay away from me!" I didn't listen. I felt like this was all my fault and that I had to console Addie until she was calm. Perhaps when she was calm, I could get truthful answers out of her. I tried to hug her as she fought me off.

"No! Stop it!" Finally she broke away from me. "Why can't you love me?" she screamed, running out of the room.

I waited a few seconds, hearing the front door slam against the wall, then sprinted out of the room. I didn't think Addie was going to leave the house. I was midway down the stairs when I slipped and fell to the bottom, her threatening screams echoing against the trees outside and then drifting into the house through the open door in front of me. Crawling to the door, I regained my footing on the doorsill and began running after my wife. I could faintly hear Addie's crying over the sound of rushing waves. As I ran onto the beach my feet became heavy under the sand. Determined, I jogged along the coastline until I saw the frame of a woman fighting the gradually deepening and rushing water about fifty feet out. "Addie," I called. Nothing. "Addie," I called again. Still nothing. I watched her only for seconds and then she was gone.

I continued walking up and down the beach for an hour looking for Addie, but I never found her. Scared, I ran back to the house, got in my car and started driving south.

Things went blurry after that.

It was the smell of frying eggs that woke me up. Then the tempting aroma of bacon sizzling against a cast iron skillet. And fresh baked bread. The scents of a homemade country breakfast mixed with the wind coming off of the lake and beat against my face. It awakened my stomach first, which then woke-up the rest of me. I breathed in the cold air around me and tried to relax my body but I couldn't. I was leaning against something very hard. I pressed my hands against the ground to push myself up but they sunk into the earth, reaching wet sand as the dry sand filled in over them. I opened my eyes and looked around. I was at the beach. Lake Michigan was in front of me and I assumed some type of civilization was behind me. I sat up and leaned against the side of my car. Apparently in the night I had driven to a beach, parked my car in the sand and fallen asleep. I had no idea where I was. But wherever I was, I was not in Point Caneissa.

It was daylight. The sun was desperately trying to reach over the tops of trees and onto the lake. It had not succeeded completely, though, its rays casting scattered bits of orange down the coastline and against the tips of waves as they rolled to shore. Morning. The sweet aroma of morning. I had almost forgotten about it. Again I smelled the eggs and bacon and bread and decided that breakfast was what I needed right now. *After all, it is the most important meal of the day.* I smiled at the thought of eggs, bacon, toast, a glass of orange juice and a cereal box dancing across the TV screen as cartoon characters tried to convince America's youth to eat breakfast. *Well, it worked on me,* I told myself as I walked away from the beach, leaving my car in the sand, and followed my nose up the grass-covered cliffs.

I found a pathway leading up the cliff and at the top was a row of houses mixed with small businesses. I walked down the sidewalk and found myself surrounded by a little village of bed and breakfasts. Only one, though, had a small café on its porch and front courtyard. The Bleaker Inn. I opened the gate and sat at the first empty table, finding a morning newspaper left behind by its previous occupant. *The Herald-Press, Saturday, May 26th, 1973, St. Joseph, Michigan.* So I was in St. Joseph. Suddenly Addie's words crept out of my foggy memory. *Your baby lives in St. Joseph. Her name is Grace....* I wondered if I had ended up here by accident or if my subconscious mind drove me here. I certainly didn't intentionally drive myself here and had no –

"Oh, I'm so sorry!" I heard a young voice shriek as what seemed like a bucket of water came soaring at me, soaking and ripping the newspaper apart before hitting me in the chest. The sound of glass shattering against the brick pavement came swiftly after. "I'm such a klutz!"

I put the soaked newspaper down and found a young girl to my left gathering broken glass off the bricked ground.

"Here, let me help you with that," I offered. "You shouldn't be picking up broken glass like this with your fingers. It's sharp and you could cut yourself." I bent down and started picking up large pieces and placing them on the tray she had been carrying. "Don't you have a broom and dust pan you could clean this up with?"

"I don't know," said the little girl. "I'd have to ask Aunt Sylvie. Oh, Aunt Sylvie is gonna kill me when she finds out about this! I broke a plate earlier this morning and she already yelled at me for that!" She sounded like she was about to cry.

"It's okay," I tried to reassure her. "I'm sure your Aunt Sylvie will understand. A lot of these bricks are uneven. Anyone could trip on them."

"You really think so?" The girl asked in a hopeful voice. She stopped picking up pieces of glass and looked up at me. She was beautiful. Dark, curly black hair, high cheekbones, full little lips and a dimple chin. It was a face I recognized, a face from my past – a face I loved. This little girl was the spitting image of Lesley at the age of ten. Only something was different. Something was a little off. I looked into her face again and found the one thing that wasn't Lesley's – her eyes. This little girl had the strangest color of green eyes, bright and clear – my mother's eyes; my eyes.

I sat back a little and just looked at her. I couldn't believe what I was seeing. She squinted at me and moved back a little.

"Are you okay, mister?" she asked.

"I'm fine," I answered quickly, realizing she noticed I was staring at her. "Just a little wet." I said with a laugh, trying to ease the situation.

"Sorry about that," she apologized again, looking down at the broken glass once more with concern. "When Aunt Sylvie finds out about this she's really gonna let me have it." She started picking up the pieces again with her fingers. I put my hands over them.

"Please don't do that," I said, almost commanding. "It can wait until you get a broom." The girl dropped the glass and pulled her hands away from mine, not concerned or scared in any way, just unsure of what to do next.

"Are you on vacation?" she asked.

"No. Just had to get away from home."

"I feel like that all the time," said the girl. "When I feel like that, I go running, until I can't run anymore. Then I go home. It feels good."

"Yeah, it does," I agreed. "I used to do that when I was a kid, too. Small world."

"I guess," she answered uncertain, trying to maneuver her way through a conversation with an adult.

"Do you live here?" I asked.

"No," she giggled, as if I had suggested something ridiculous. "My Aunt Sylvie lives here. She owns this house. I just help out during the summer. It's Memorial Day weekend, you know."

"Oh, yes. I had forgotten." I hadn't, but it made this beautiful little girl smile and laugh at my unbelievable forgetfulness. "Aren't you a little young to be working the summer scene?" The little girl shook her head from side to side.

"I always come to help during the summer and I always start on Memorial Day weekend. I usually just help out with the cleaning and laundry but my Aunt Sylvie said when I turned nine I could help wait tables, maybe make some extra money. I don't turn nine until August but Aunt Sylvie said she'd go ahead and give me a chance." The little girl looked down at the pile of glass. "But she'll never let me wait tables when she finds out about this."

"It was an honest mistake, ah, what did you say your name was?"

"I didn't," she answered promptly. "But it's Grace. Grace Lynn."

I almost fell over.

"Grace. That's a lovely name. My mother's name was Grace."

"Yeah, it was my grandmother's name, but that's all I know about her."

"You never met your grandmother?"

"No." Grace scrunched her nose as she answered. I wondered if it was a hard subject for her to talk about, not knowing her grandmother.

"Look," I said, trying to brighten her mood. "Why don't you go get a broom and a dust pan and some towels and I'll help you clean this mess up. And Aunt Sylvie doesn't need to know about it."

"Okay," Grace squealed. "I'll be right back." She began to run up the bricked walk.

"Grace," I shouted down the little walkway. She stopped and looked at me. "Are you adopted?" I couldn't stop the words from leaving my mouth, but I needed to know.

Grace's nose scrunched up and she smiled. "How did you know that?"

"I guess I'm psychic," I tried to say with a chuckle.

"Then you should have seen the water coming and ducked."

Grace giggled as she turned and ran up the stairs to fetch the dry towels and broom. I didn't stay and wait for her return. It felt wrong being there with her, knowing a secret she would never be privy to. I left the newspaper on the table along with all the money I had on me. I didn't know what else to leave and I felt I had to leave something. I walked out of the courtyard, the gate swinging in the breeze, and made my way back to my car. When I reached it, I got in, turned the engine on and looked up to the cliffs again. I could see the back of the Bleaker Inn. I imagined Grace standing at the table staring at the empty chair and the small pile of money on top of the table. I imagined her face, confused yet giddy over her unearned tip. I imagined her confessing her morning mishap to her Aunt Sylvie while giving her aunt part of her generous tip to pay for the broken glasses. That's just the kind of girl Grace seemed to be. Honest, concerned, and loving. That was the kind of girl Lesley had been. I imagined the two of them were more alike than either would ever know – and I secretly hoped that somewhere in that lovely little girl lay a small bit of me, however tiny it might be. I imagined her face.

I could have gone my entire life without seeing that face and been happy. But then I would have never met Grace, and that, in some odd and uncontrollable way, seemed unacceptable.

As I imagined Grace in my mind I saw more of myself in her – the way she moved and ran up the stairs, the way she laughed. I saw parts of myself in Grace, what little they were. Maybe Addie was right. *Addie...*

I put the car in drive, followed the road away from the beach and headed back toward Point Caneissa. I debated in my head as I drove if I really witnessed my wife's disappearance under the waves or if the night's events were just an illusion. I was thoughtful as I drove. I thought of Grace, of Lesley, and I thought of Addie, fearing the truth of my actions and hopeful that the entire night was just a bad dream.

I pulled into my driveway around noon and found Sheriff Roberts waiting for me. Sheriff Roberts walked over to the car and opened the door.

"Good mornin', Wyatt."

"I think it's more like afternoon, Richie. What are you doing out here?"

"We have a situation, Wyatt. Now before I go into any details, I have a few questions to ask you."

"Okay." I was becoming more nervous and Sheriff Roberts could see it in my face.

"Where were you last night?"

"I was at a convention in Livonia, for my comic book." I didn't know why I was lying, but I continued as if everything I was saying had actually happened. "I've been there since yesterday morning. I was worried about Addie, so I decided to come home this morning. She hasn't been alone since she lost the baby. Why? Has something happened?"

"Wyatt, I hate to be the one to tell you this," Sheriff Roberts paused. "Old man Kinsey...old man Kinsey, he, uh, found...he found Addie's body this mornin' while he was fishing. She was...she was floating...floating in the water. She's dead, Wyatt. Addie's dead. I'm so sorry."

I fell against his car, stunned. Sheriff Roberts waited for an emotional outburst, but none came.

"At first we thought she had been attacked," he continued, the words coming easier to the sheriff now that he had told his friend his wife was dead. "She didn't have any clothes on when he found her. Upon further inspection by the coroner, though, there doesn't seem to be any signs of foul play. But we'll know more after the autopsy. Wyatt, at this point, we're classifyin' it as a suicide."

Though I knew the words my friend was saying were true, I felt a strange compulsion to defend Addie.

"How can you say that, Richie? You don't know anything. You don't know her."

"Wyatt, we looked in the house. We had to as part of a possible homicide. We found what looks to be like a suicide note – writings, really – strewn all over the nursery."

"Writings?" I echoed back. "What kind of writings?"

"Strange, story-like ramblings. Our psych-guy says they may be repressed emotions about the baby."

"How did he know about the baby?" I asked, wondering nervously which child of mine they had been talking about, since Addie had known about both.

"Everyone knew Addie lost the baby, Wyatt. This is a small town. Everyone knows everything about everyone else." Sheriff Roberts sighed. "It's a shame this had to happen to you here." He took his hat off and wiped the sweat from his head. "Did you want to read some of the pages we found? It might shed some light on the situation for you."

"No."

"I'm sorry, Wyatt. Addie was under a lot of stress. You said so yourself. I guess it was just too much for her."

"I don't know what to do." I covered my face with my hands. Sheriff Roberts thought I was crying.

"I'm sorry for askin' where you were last night. It's standard procedure. You know that, right?"

"It's okay, Richie." I stood up and rubbed my face, stretching and looking into the sky.

"Come on. Let's go inside. I'll make you some coffee."

Sheriff Roberts led me into my own house, cutting the crime scene tape across the still open front door, and navigating me around investigators to the kitchen where the Sheriff began a pot of coffee and ordered some lunch for everyone. He sat next to me and tried to comfort a shocked and grieving husband, who just also happened to be his friend.

CHAPTER 15: STONEWALLS

Lesley

I felt sick as I watched the coffin hoist lower Addie's floral carved oak casket into the ground. I noticed that the sun had shone all morning, until the line of cars drove up along the winding road of Park Cemetery and stopped alongside the large pile of earth covered by blankets of imitation grass nestled behind a line of chairs, all neatly tucked under a makeshift tent. As the mourners found their places, the sky clouded – the Michigan gray settling in for the reverend's send-off. Looking up into the sky I waited for the clouds, heavy with jaded tears, to pour forth on the small party that gathered by the soon-to-be-filled grave. Everyone was crying, except for Wyatt and myself. Wyatt just stared into the distance, as if he was looking at something and nothing all at once. He stood away from the small crowd, all piled in under the tent, never sitting next to his sister, never comforting his mother-in-law. I looked around the cemetery and noticed there weren't any trees nearby. All of the trees were outside of the cemetery, lining the stonewalls. *If it were to start raining,* I thought, *Wyatt would have nowhere to run to for shelter.* I remembered the small umbrella attached to my wrist and wanted to go to Wyatt, to stand by him in case the clouds could contain themselves no longer. But my feet would not move, grounded like the tree I wished would protect him from the earth's sorrow.

The funeral began. It was too uncomfortable to stomach, almost unbearable. But the days preceding this event were even worse.

I arrived in Point Caneissa three days ago and reluctantly made my way to Wyatt's house to join the party of mourners that had gathered in and around the scene of Addie's death. I mingled my way around family and police officers trying to avoid an encounter with Wyatt. I didn't want to see him. I didn't know how to react to the whole thing, mostly because I wasn't sure what had even happened. The weekend seemed a blur, a dream almost, so much so that when I tried to retrace my steps I couldn't put in order the places I had been or the events I had seen. Nothing made sense. I began to panic as I walked around the terrace. I wanted out. I started walking faster, circling the hedges until I saw the shadowy lines of the driveway and the silver shimmer of the front of Prue's Mustang. My car was parked only fifty feet behind Prue's. *One hundred feet to salvation.* I prepared to sprint.

But nothing came of it. I felt my feet become slow and heavy under me. My mind was whirling and the scenery around me began moving in slow motion. I was blacking out. I felt my body lunge to my right, hit something, then fall to the ground.

What I hit was Wyatt, and upon seeing whom he had caught, he dropped me, fearing people would see him holding me. When he realized his stupidity, he picked me up and placed me on the wicker swing on the front porch. When I regained my sight and balance, I got up and saw Wyatt standing ten feet away from me, staring past the corner of the house into the woods.

"What happened?" I asked.

"I'm not sure. I think you blacked out or tripped or something. I didn't actually see you fall. I just accidentally caught you. Right place, right time, I guess."

"Yeah, I guess." My stomach was churning sour juices up my esophagus. I choked down the mixture as I tried to start a conversation. "I don't know what I'm doing here."

Wyatt cocked his head sideways and looked at me.

"What do you mean?"

"I don't know why I'm here. I feel like I just ended up here somehow."

"Are you being serious or are you speaking metaphorically?" He sounded so calm and together, philosophical even, like a switch went off in his brain and turned him into someone completely different. When his parents died, Wyatt was inconsolable, crying sporadically throughout the planning of their funeral. At least that had been what my mother had told me when I arrived that afternoon. I prepared myself for a broken man, one I might have to scrape off a cracked floor and hold until he was whole again. Looking at Wyatt now, I felt he didn't need or want me, and the pain of that made my body flush with rancid warmth. I tried to answer his question.

"A little of both, maybe. I don't know. Things seem so blurred. I feel like I should be waking up from a dream, but can't."

"This isn't your dream to be waking up from," he replied, distant.

"I don't see it that way."

"You should." Wyatt paused and looked away from me, then turned his whole body to face me, leaning against the wooden posts of the covered porch. "Why are you here, Lesley?"

"Well, because of Addie, because she...she.... My mother called this morning and told me Addie was...was...dead. I came because – "

"It doesn't matter," he interrupted. "You look exhausted."

"Wyatt, what happened?" I blurted.

Wyatt shrugged his shoulders.

"I don't know what happened. I wasn't here."

"What do you mean you weren't here?"

"Just what I said. I wasn't here. I don't know what happened."

"But that night – "

"You know, Lesley, I really don't feel like talking about this right now and I really don't feel like being around you, either." He started to walk away, then paused and turned around to look straight at me. "I don't know why I'm here. I feel like I just ended up here somehow, like everything's blurred. I feel like I should be waking up from a dream, but can't."

"Wyatt…"

He ignored me and kept walking around the house until I could no longer hear his footsteps anymore. I knew he was mocking me, repeating my feelings sarcastically, meanly. It was something he always did when I irritated him and he didn't know what else to say. It hurt, but I took some joy in it also, Wyatt acting towards me as he did when we were married, when we were friends.

When she knew Wyatt was gone, Prue came around the other corner and quickly sat next to me.

"I think it's so good that you're here, Lesley."

"Hello, Prue," I answered with an annoyed sigh.

"I just knew as soon as you found out, you'd be here. It's just like you. Wyatt always could open up to you."

"I have no idea what you mean." I hated the way Prue sometimes made me out to be some kind of a saint. I wasn't – in no way, shape or form.

"Well, just now, when you guys were talking. I saw you talking from down by the beach. I thought I'd go walking. Wyatt's been in such a melancholy mood."

"His wife just died."

"Yes, I know, but he hasn't talked to anyone. That is, until you got here. I didn't even know you arrived until I saw the two of you."

"There is no two of us, Prue," I said sharply.

"No, I mean when I saw you talking. It just shocked me, I guess."

"Why?"

"Because, like I said, Wyatt hasn't talked to anyone since he found out about Addie."

"No one?"

"Not a soul. I tried to get him to open up to me, but nothing. I got a hard, cold shoulder. That's why I hurried up here. I was so happy to see him actually talking to someone. I should have known he'd open up to you. You always had a way about you that Wyatt trusted. I wish I had that."

"Oh, I think you have that. I think he'd trust his own sister better than his ex-wife."

"I wouldn't be so sure of that, Lesley. This whole scene has really rocked him. I don't think he's handling it too well."

"I would hope not. His wife just died. That's enough to rock any *normal* human being."

I knew I was being a little condescending, but I couldn't help it.

"I don't want to talk about this anymore," said Prue.

"That's fine with me."

We sat in silence on the wicker swing, gently rocking back and forth. Both of us ignored the water-rusted chains that creaked every time we pushed too far back with our heels. We fell into a rhythm, and when the melodic silence was too much for Prue, she asked the question I knew she was trying to hold in.

"So, what did Wyatt say? What did you guys talk about?"

"I thought we weren't going to talk about this anymore."

"We're not. This is a whole different line of thought."

I shifted my body and looked at Prue, eyes narrowed as if I had caught Prue in some secret lie.

"No it isn't. This is why you came up here in the first place."

"I'm just concerned," Prue responded.

"No you're not," I said smiling. "You're curious."

"For me it's the same thing."

"I know," I replied, rolling my eyes. I paused, leaned back against the swing, and thought about my conversation with Wyatt. "We really didn't talk about anything. Now that I think back on it, he didn't really say anything. It was like a conversation of circles."

"What is that supposed to mean?" asked Prue.

"I don't know. We seemed to be talking around the main point but never got there. Like we were walking in a circle. That's the best way to describe it, I guess."

"That doesn't make any sense."

"I know. I told you we didn't talk about anything."

"Somehow, I don't believe you."

"Why not?" I was getting irritated and offended.

"It doesn't matter. He talked to you. That's what matters. At least he's talking to *someone*."

"Prue, he didn't say anything to me!"

"It doesn't matter. What matters is that he talked to you. Now maybe we can focus on some other people."

"What other people?"

"Addie's mom for one. She's just a wreck."

"Addie's mom is here?"

It felt like a small jolt went through my body, hearing Addie's mom had come to Point Caneissa. It made Addie's death sink in – become a little more real. I didn't like it.

"Why wouldn't she be here?" asked Prue. "That'd be kind of strange."

"No, I just thought they weren't on very good terms. Not since she dropped out of college and married Wyatt, actually," I explained, trying to recover from my absentmindedness. "I don't even think they've spoken to each other since then."

"Well, I'm sure her daughter's suicide came as a shock, especially since she hadn't talked to Addie in such a long time. She didn't even know Addie had been pregnant. She has to feel horrible right now."

"Addie committed suicide?" This was the first time I heard the cause of Addie's death.

"Yeah. I thought you knew. I thought your mother told you."

"She told me Addie died but she didn't say how. Suicide? I can't believe it." Guilt shook through my body as I tried to stabilize myself on the swing.

"I'm sorry, Lesley. I guess I've been a little pushy today. If I'd known you didn't know – "

"It's okay, really. What did Wyatt do when it happened? Did he say how it happened?"

"He doesn't know. He wasn't here."

"What?"

"He was at some comic book or artist convention in Livonia. He didn't find out about it until he got back. Sheriff Roberts told him what happened."

"That doesn't make any sense."

"Why not?"

I stopped myself before I answered Prue's question. No one knew I'd been coming up to counsel Addie. Wyatt was very sensitive about the town's knowledge of Addie's condition. He knew as the days went by his wife was losing her sanity, and the heavy burden of that he wished to carry alone. He persuaded me to take the back way to his house, avoiding the short jog through town, which would have landed me at Wyatt's half an hour sooner. But what's an extra half hour? I never really paid much attention to this particular wish of Wyatt's, but now, so soon after Addie's suicide, I perceived my negligence as a consequence to Addie's death. I thought it odd, now, how adamant Wyatt was about keeping my visits a secret. He hadn't even told his sister, obviously. Knowing Prue, she would have brought the subject up already. *Did he know something would happen? Did he suspect anything?* My thoughts flowed swiftly down the natural line of questions until they stopped suddenly at the last one: *Did he do something bad to Addie?* My face grew pale and I could again taste the bitter juices in my stomach creeping onto my tongue.

"Lesley, are you all right?" Prue took my hand and tried to rub blood flow back into my cold, clammy veins. "You look like you've seen a ghost."

"I'm all right. I'm okay. I think I may have a low blood sugar problem. I keep meaning to get it checked out but something always seems to come up." I felt this an adequate excuse for my reaction to my own thoughts. I tried to focus on them but Prue kept interrupting me.

"Are you sure you feel okay? You look just awful. Maybe we should take you into town to see Dr. Jansen."

"No, that's alright. I have an appointment scheduled next week. I just have to make sure I keep it."

"Still, maybe we should go inside. You should eat something."

"I'm not hungry!" I snapped. "I'm fine. I told you." Prue dropped my hand, sat back away from me, and just stared. "I'm sorry," I began in remorse. "Maybe I should try to eat something or lie down."

"Whatever you want to do is fine."

I could tell Prue's ego was slightly hurt.

"Would you walk with me, Prue? I don't feel like being alone."

Prue smiled and hooked her arm with mine.

"Sure. Do you want me to make you something to eat?"

"I'll decide once we get inside." I stopped Prue as we turned the corner to the backdoor. "So Wyatt wasn't here at all the night Addie died?"

"No. He was in Livonia. I told you that already."

"Did he tell anyone he was going to Livonia?"

"No, but Sheriff Roberts checked it out. He was registered on the list at the convention. Why?"

"Oh, no reason. I'm just trying to put it all together."

Prue tried to continue walking but I interrupted her with more questions.

"So, was there a note, a letter, saying why she did it?"

"Nothing that the police will talk about. But I have a feeling Wyatt knows something. They keep talking to him and showing him all kinds of papers. But they won't say anything to anyone else. It's unbelievably frustrating," Prue whined.

"Then how do they know it was suicide?"

"Well, Sheriff Roberts said all factors at the scene led to suicide. No sign of struggle, no natural cause of death, the way they found the house. She was depressed, Lesley. Everyone saw that. I just wish Wyatt would have called you, reached out, something, so you could have helped her."

Prue forced me to step forward and into the house.

"I didn't know Addie was so far gone," I said quietly.

"How could you? Did he call you at all, let you know what was going on?"

"No." I said the word under my breath, but it was audible. I hoped that if I inhaled the word, it wouldn't be lying. Either way it felt the same. "They're sure Wyatt wasn't here? They're sure it's suicide?"

"Of course. What else would it be? You make it sound like it's Wyatt's fault or something." Prue placed a full teapot on the stove, then turned around and stared at me, eyes narrowed. "You don't think Wyatt had something to do with Addie's death, do you? Because that's just ridiculous."

"No, no." I didn't know what I believed. "It's just that, if Wyatt knew how bad Addie was, why would he leave a suicidal wife to go to a convention? It doesn't make sense. So if he didn't go to the convention, then he was here when it happened, which means he most likely saw something. I just don't understand why he won't tell anyone what he saw."

"Because he wasn't here when it happened!"

Just then, Addie's mother walked into the kitchen, slightly dazed, and sat next to me at the table.

"Hello girls."

"Hello, Mrs. Daugherty," I answered.

"Lesley, it's been so long since I've seen you."

"I know, Mrs. Daugherty."

"Tell me, did you talk to my Addie before she died?"

"No, Mrs. Daugherty, I didn't." My heart hurt as I lied to my friend's mother. I felt the pain stronger and stronger as I thought about the last time I saw Addie. If Addie did kill herself, I felt I could have been the cause of it. Did my jealousy and passion win out, destroying my devoted friend?

"Did you know she was going to have a baby?" Mrs. Daugherty asked.

"Yes, I did," I replied softly. "She called and told me herself."

"You talked to my Addie about the baby?"

"Yes."

"Was she happy?"

"Yes," I mumbled, trying to hide the growing tears. "Very happy."

"I wish she would have told me. Did she come to you when she lost the baby?"

"No," I answered.

"Me either," said Mrs. Daugherty, adding sugar to the cup of tea Prue placed in front of her, stirring the mixture. "Me either."

I sat and listened to Addie's mother ramble, hating myself more and more as the afternoon went on.

This is how the last three days advanced, culminating into this solitary, allusive moment. The hoist made a wrenching shriek, then stopped. Father Halse walked away from the grave, followed soon after by Wyatt, who walked in the opposite direction. Mourners and townspeople slowly walked in small groups towards their cars. Wyatt continued walking away from them, paying no attention to where he was going, but very aware of where everyone else was.

"It's all just so sad," said Prue, hooking arms with me as she walked diagonally between Wyatt and the group of mourners. "I don't understand why he wants to suffer through this by himself. It's just not like him."

"People change, Prue, especially following traumatic situations," I answered. "Everyone grieves in a different way."

"Still, I don't think he should be alone. He needs to talk to someone. Why don't you go over and try talking to him?"

"Me? Why me?" I grew nervous. "You're his sister. You try talking to him."

"He won't talk to me. Besides, he's already opened up to you. Even if you didn't talk about anything, he still talked to you."

"But – "

Just then Addie's mother joined us, halting our argument.

"Prue, do you think you could take me home. I'm not feeling well. I don't want to be alone. I just don't know what I'm going to do!" Mrs. Daugherty began to cry.

"I'll stay with you, Alma." Prue put her arm around Mrs. Daugherty, then turned her head around to whisper to me. "Go talk to Wyatt. I'll take care of things back at the house."

I sighed and began walking the buxom landscape of the cemetery. I could feel the eyes of townspeople follow me as I dared to do the one thing none of them would. I could no longer hear their feet crunching on pebble walkways. No car doors slamming, engines turning on and proceeding out of the sacred hamlet on their way to free food and punch, in hopes of witnessing the dramatics of mourning family members over stale coffee. Instead, they all paused, waiting to witness perhaps something more shocking, more relevant, more entertaining than a reception wake. Two ex-lovers stood in the middle of a cemetery in the distance. It sounded like the beginning of a bad play. *Let the spectacle ensue.*

"Hey." I walked up to Wyatt and quickly joined his pace. "What are you doing all the way over here?"

"I feel like walking," Wyatt replied. "What are *you* doing over here?"

"Seems that I've been chosen as the sacrificial lamb, so to speak."

"What are you talking about?"

"Don't pretend you don't feel all those people watching us. Everyone is curious about you, about us. 'What will they talk about? What will they say?' It's sickening."

"I think it's all in your head," Wyatt said calmly. "No one cares about this. They shouldn't, anyway."

"Whatever, Wyatt. You grew up in this town. You know how it is. Besides, Prue cares. She's why I'm here. She doesn't think you're handling Addie's death very well."

"I'm handling it just fine."

"I've been trying to tell her that. Maybe *you* should tell her that. At least then she might leave me alone."

"I doubt it."

We continued walking, passing sculpted angels, crosses, and private mausoleums. Nearing the cemeteries edge we finally heard car doors slam and the distant reverberation of starters clicking to life the heavy metal pieces of the funeral procession. A stonewall encased the cemetery, and when we approached it, we sat on it and waited to speak until the crushing sound of pebbles ceased to be.

"I've been trying to figure out why this happened," Wyatt said finally.

"I don't know what to tell you." I spoke softly, reserved. I didn't know what we would talk about, but whatever it would be, I feared it.

"So many things have happened these last few months. It's hard to put it all together. I've tried to catalogue it in my mind, but somehow, it all gets jumbled together again." He paused and ran his fingers through his sandy-brown hair. "I don't know what I'm talking about. I'm sorry if I'm rambling."

"That's okay. We can talk about whatever you want."

"Are you trying to psychoanalyze me?" he laughed, as he always did when he asked me that question.

"I don't think I could if I tried."

I smiled at him. There was a lift in tension. I felt more comfortable alone with him now than I had in years. I wondered if he would tell me now what actually happened that night; if he would confess his true feelings about what had transpired. Prue had been right when she said I had a way of getting the truth out of Wyatt better than anyone else. I felt perhaps he might open up to me again. It was at least worth a try.

"I've been talking with Addie's mother."

"How is she?" Wyatt asked, looking unconcerned.

"Terrible. I think she may need some serious therapy. I've referred her to a colleague of mine in New York. With help, I think she'll pull through."

"That's too bad." Wyatt crossed his legs and leaned back, almost putting chin to chest as he spoke. "I always thought Alma was a good person, a good mother, despite their differences. It's a shame she and Addie couldn't have worked things out. Maybe if they had, she could have comforted Addie through all this. Addie wouldn't have been so alone."

"Addie wasn't alone, Wyatt. She had you."

"She had no one."

There was silence.

The wind in the trees picked up, moving and swaying, throwing the breeze around their tops from one to the other as if pitching a ball. May was still in the air, even though hints of June's radiating heat floated through the small openings of shifting leaves. One ray of sunlight landed on Wyatt and stayed, heating his black suit. Feeling uncomfortable, Wyatt took of his suit coat, folded it, and laid it on the stonewall, then slid to the ground, bending his legs and leaning his back against the rocks, his head high enough to lay on top. I followed his motions, sliding down sitting sideways, facing him, my legs bent to my side to accommodate my dress.

I placed my hand on Wyatt's.

"Addie wasn't alone."

"We don't know that," Wyatt sighed. "We'll never know how she really felt or what she really thought. She never really opened up, to you or to me. She was alone, because she wanted to be."

"How can you say that?" I retorted. "You did everything you could. You stayed with her throughout this whole ordeal. You worried about her, took care of her, did everything you thought was best for her. You can't blame yourself for Addie taking her own life, or whatever happened that night."

Wyatt looked over at me somewhat puzzled. I wondered if he knew I was suspicious about what had happened after I left that night. I knew Wyatt had lied to the police, had lied to everyone, but did he know that I knew? Neither one of us said anything. I could feel Wyatt staring at me, searching my body for meaning. I regretted making the comment. I felt silly. I knew Wyatt. He could never hurt anyone. He loved Addie. *He loved Addie.* That was a whole other pain I had forgotten about. Wyatt had loved Addie. No matter what had happened, it didn't change that one, heartbreaking fact. I felt remorse.

"I'm sorry, Wyatt. I didn't mean it."

I looked down to the ground as I spoke, watching some ants crawl around the spaces between Wyatt and I. I noticed one was following the outline of our hands, then I noticed our hands. Wyatt had not removed his hand from under mine. It remained there, relaxed and unmoved. I could feel his blood pulsing against my palm. It was steady and warm, normal. This also made my heart ache.

"I don't know what I'm saying," I said finally. "I'm not taking this all very well. Everything has come as such a shock to me. It's rocked me, Addie's…I don't know what to say."

There was silence again. Wyatt continued to look at me. His eyes had never left me. I could feel him searching my movements, my expressions for clues, for answers. To what, I didn't know. But he kept his eyes on me, reading me, never looking away. Then finally, he spoke.

"I know you, Lesley. I know how you feel. I know how you think. I know your heart."

"Wyatt – "

"I know that you think this is all your fault. I know you, and it isn't."

"Yes it is," I said, tears starting to roll down my face. Wyatt had found the clue, an answer to my secret thoughts. All this time I had focused on what had happened after I left that Friday, not my actions before. For me, it was easier to think that Addie's death had been caused by an event that had nothing to do with me being there that evening. It had nothing to do with me seducing Addie's husband, nothing to do with the fact that it was obvious I was going to sleep with him, nothing to do with me making Wyatt an adulterer, and nothing to do with Addie's suicide being my fault. Not Addie's, but mine. I hadn't let myself think it was my fault. It was self-preservation at its best.

I couldn't speak. My tears choked my thoughts, preventing sound from leaving my mouth. I just sat there, waiting, crying, painfully existing in front of the man I knew I still loved but could never have. It was too much now. My feelings for him had caused too much pain. I had caused my friend's death because I was the "other woman", because I wanted to be. How would I ever live with that?

Wyatt lifted his hand and put it to my face, wiping the tears smooth along my skin, spreading them flat against his palm. I felt his hand try to lift my chin. I wouldn't look at him.

"Don't cry," he whispered.

"I can't help it," I mumbled, my words breathless in my throat.

Wyatt's hand resumed its place with mine.

"What I did that night was awful, unforgivable," I continued, gaining strength in my voice. "I shouldn't even be here. I don't know why I even came."

I moved to wipe my eyes, pulling my hand from Wyatt's. Wyatt grabbed it quickly and held it, not forcefully, but gently, spreading his fingers between mine, clasping it. I looked at him for meaning, but found nothing but my ex-lover staring into the blue sky, holding my hand.

Suddenly, Wyatt turned his head to look at me. I quickly looked down, boring holes into the grass as I stared, trying to keep more tears from falling.

"I love you."

I whipped my head up and looked at Wyatt in disbelief.

"Could you say that again?"

Wyatt lifted his hand and brushed the slowly falling tears away from my face. He said nothing as he reached for me and pulled me close to him. My body shivered. For ten years I had waited to hear those words. I had no response. I couldn't raise any words from my mouth. I clutched Wyatt, holding him tight. Neither of us resisted or moved from the other. We sat in silence, clinging to whatever part of the other we could.

Finally, Wyatt spoke again, whispering into my ear.

"I don't think we should see each other again."

"What?" I said loudly, pushing Wyatt away to look at him. "What are you saying? I don't understand."

"This is too much to ask for," answered Wyatt.

"I don't know what you mean?" I was truly confused.

"I mean, go home, Lesley. Go back to your normal life. Leave all this tragedy behind you."

"But what about you?"

Wyatt kissed my lips lightly, gently holding my face as he responded.

"I'll be fine."

Wyatt pushed himself up off the ground and started walking away. Ten feet out he stopped and turned.

"I wasn't lying when I said I wasn't at the house when she died. I saw her from the beach." He paused. "During our fight she ran out of the house. I tried to follow her from the house to the beach. I didn't see her go in, but I thought I watched her fight the waves. I must have. When I didn't see her anymore I panicked. I looked for her, but I couldn't find her anywhere, so I left. When I came back, Richie told me she was dead. I didn't know she was going to kill herself, Lesley. She had done this before. But she came out of the water that time. I called you, remember?"

"Yes."

Wyatt turned and began walking away, stopping again, this time not turning around.

"Lesley, it wasn't our fault. Just remember that, okay? It wasn't *your* fault."

Wyatt began walking again, this time not stopping, following the diagonal of the cemetery to its exit. I followed his lead, walking back over the expanse of the cemetery. Halfway to my car I looked back to see if Wyatt would follow me. He was still walking toward the exit, unmoved from the path he had chosen to take. When I got to my car I looked back again, hoping he would come after me; one last embrace perchance. But nothing. Wyatt blended in with the landscape. I couldn't see him any longer.

I started my car and proceeded to the reception wake.

When I got back to Wyatt and Addie's house most of the funeral party had left. After eating cold sandwiches and drinking warm punch, there were no spectacles to be seen. Being mostly uneventful and boring, those who had no ties to the family left first, then others in succession with their relations to the deceased and surviving. Prue had positioned herself in plain view of the door, so when it opened and I walked in, Prue made a beeline to her ex-sister-in-law.

"You've been gone for quite a while. Most everyone has left."

"I didn't feel like coming straight here from the cemetery. I drove around a little. Is Wyatt back yet?" I wanted to avoid him.

"I thought he rode back with you."

"No. Why would he?"

"Because he had no other way home!"

"What?"

"Didn't you notice there weren't any other cars there?"

"I wasn't thinking about anyone else's car! I just wanted to leave!"

"We have to go back and get him. Lesley, I can't believe you – "

Just then Wyatt walked in the door.

"Oh, thank God you're all right!" exclaimed Prue. "Who brought you home?"

"No one. I walked."

"You walked all the way from the cemetery? I can't believe it! Lesley, how could you just leave him there?"

"She didn't leave me. I wanted to walk home. I told her to go on without me."

"Oh." Prue turned to me. "You didn't say he wanted to – "

"It doesn't matter now," interrupted Wyatt. "Who all's still here?"

"Well," replied Prue, "most everyone has left. But Lesley's mother is still here, Sheriff Roberts, Mr. & Mrs. Garvey, Sue Lampin, Adam Walker, I'm not sure who else. Oh, and of course Addie's mom. Actually, I wanted to talk to you about Alma. I got a call from the museum. The African folklore exhibit is arriving early and I'm in charge of it. Wyatt, I want to stay, but I've spent most of my career doing field research to put this exhibit together. They really need me to go back tonight."

"It's okay, Prue," said Wyatt, hugging his sister. "I'll be fine."

"It's not all right," Prue answered. "This couldn't have happened at a worse time. I can't believe this."

"I know."

"Look," continued Prue. "I didn't want to leave until I saw you. I'm worried about Alma. She's not leaving until tomorrow and I don't think it should just be you two in this house tonight. So I was thinking maybe Lesley could stay tonight and help out."

"No. I don't think that's a good idea," I interjected. "I don't want to make anyone uncomfortable."

"Who'd be uncomfortable?" asked Prue.

"Prue's right," said Wyatt. "You should stay the night. I don't know how to handle Alma. With you here, the night would go smoother."

"Wyatt, are you sure?" I asked.

"I think I'd feel better if someone else were here." Wyatt saw Sheriff Roberts waving him over. "Excuse me. I think I'm being beckoned. You two decide what you like." Wyatt walked over to Sheriff Roberts, shook his hand, then turned around and made his way to the stairs, and eventually his bedroom.

"Please, Lesley. I have to leave now. Just stay one night."

"I suppose it wouldn't hurt anything."

"Of course not. Thank you sooo much." Prue hugged me, then opened the front door. "My bags are already in the car. If Wyatt comes down tonight, tell him I'll call him first thing in the morning, when I get home."

"Okay."

"Lesley, I know I've been on edge these last few days. I'm sorry if I was a little pushy. I was just trying to help Wyatt."

"I know you were, Prue. It's okay, really."

"I am sorry."

"You better hurry or you'll never make it home."

"All right. Come see me when you get a chance."

"Okay."

With that, I shut the door and focused my attention on the guests that were left. Only a handful of people remained. I served each of them coffee and warmed what sandwiches were left. When there was no conversation left to say, each remaining mourner took his leave, my mother being the last one, and I, with the help of Mrs. Daugherty, cleaned abandoned paper plates and napkins, soaked stained coffee cups. Exhausted from the day's events, I walked Mrs. Daugherty to the guest room, then found my own guest quarters on the sofa. I covered myself with two blankets and sunk deeply into the sofa's pillows, falling asleep to the sound of warm air being blown through the vents of the living room.

Around midnight I awoke suddenly to the touch of lips on my forehead. Believing I was dreaming, I continued to lie on the couch, relishing in my dream kiss, until I heard the sound of hurried banging in the living room. I sat up and found the front door was open. Slowly I moved off the couch, grabbed a poker from the fireplace, and gently tip toed up the stairs. I first went to Mrs. Daugherty's room, which was closest to me, and peaked inside. She still lay sleeping and undisturbed. Closing the door quietly I walked the opposite direction I came, checking Wyatt's office, which was locked, then down the hall to Wyatt's bedroom. The door was wide open.

"Wyatt?" I said softly, then again louder and more audible. There was no response.

I walked around the room and found there was no one there. I pulled back the curtain and looked out the window to the beach. There, on the sand hunched over, kneeled Wyatt. He seemed to be crying. I watched as he let the tide come in around him, then fade back again into itself. He seemed so far away. I stood silent, trying to take in the scene. *Maybe if I'm quiet, I could hear what he's thinking.* But nothing came to me that night except the faint, distant sound of Addie's name.

.

CHAPTER 16: S.O.S

Sunday, May 26th, 1974

"Hello," a tired voice said on the other end of the line.

"Lesley?"

"Yes...who is this?"

"Lesley it's Prue. I need your help."

Lesley's heart jumped as she recognized Prue's voice. She didn't want to think about that family connection, that old part of her life. Like Wyatt, she still blamed herself for Addie's death and had tried desperately to forget the whole thing. She refused to talk to anyone about it and had distanced herself from both families, not contacting anyone since the funeral over a year ago. Now, somehow, it seemed Addie was radically changing Lesley's life in the middle of the night once again.

"Prue, what is it? It's two-thirty in the morning."

"I know. I'm sorry, but I don't know what to do. Something's happened to Wyatt."

Lesley's stomach turned suddenly at the mention of Wyatt's name. Then it began to do somersaults at the thought of Wyatt in some awful accident.

"Is he hurt? Was he in some sort of accident? Please, God, Prue tell me he isn't dead!"

"No, it's nothing like that," reassured Prue. "Wyatt's had some sort of breakdown I think. I need you to come up here and try to fix him."

"Try and fix him? I don't understand. Why me?" Lesley was becoming annoyed. Since Wyatt was not dead and he hadn't been in a life-threatening accident, she didn't understand why she had been awakened at two-thirty in the morning for what seemed to be a private matter between siblings. If it had in actuality been an emergency, Lesley was confident that Prue would have called the local authorities for help. Instead she felt the need to call Lesley, which Lesley was positive no good would come out of.

"You're the only psychiatrist I know," pleaded Prue. "Please! I don't know what to do."

"Prue, I don't think it's a very good idea for me to come up. I'm three hours away. If it's an emergency, you should call an ambulance or the police. Someone else can help him."

"I don't want anyone else to help him. You're family."

"Not anymore," Lesley said abruptly.

"Lesley stop being selfish and get your ass up here!"

Prue couldn't believe the words left her mouth but she was starting to panic. She had always tried to speak calmly in front of Lesley, always a little intimidated by her and a little charmed. Lesley had a way with Wyatt, an intimacy that Prue was at times jealous of. More than anything she had wanted to befriend Lesley, so she tried to choose her words wisely and act accordingly, even if she sometimes wanted to slap Lesley for her egotistical ways. Tonight was no different, but Prue calmed herself a little and tried a different tone.

"Look," Prue began again. "I need your help. I don't want to call anyone else and I don't want help from anyone else. This town already thinks Wyatt's a freak. Please, Lesley. I'm asking *you*."

Angered by this nosy little sister, but also unknowing of what else to do, Lesley agreed.

"Okay. I should be there around six."

The phone clicked suddenly and Prue sat there listening to silence.

It was about six-thirty when Lesley pulled into the driveway of what had once been Addie and Wyatt's home. She sighed as she got out of her car and made her way up the winding walk. Prue was standing in the open doorway. Lesley didn't know what was waiting for her in that house and it frightened her. She had thought of nothing else but of seeing Wyatt as she drove to Point Caneissa – how he would look, how he would sound, what they would talk about. It was all a mystery that would be solved in less than ten steps. Now nine, eight, seven, six...

When she reached the house, Lesley found that Wyatt had fallen asleep on the couch. Prue, being ever the hostess, led Lesley into the kitchen and began making coffee, trying to explain what had happened as she measured the ground beans.

"I don't know what to think about all this," said Prue. "I'm not even sure what happened."

Prue pressed the brew button and sat down across from Lesley at the kitchen table.

"I don't know if I'm confused or tired," Prue continued. "Something is seriously wrong here."

Prue leaned back in the wooden chair and sighed, closing and rubbing her eyes. Lesley could tell Prue was drained, sitting silent and thoughtful, not at all like her normal Prue-self.

"Why don't you start by telling me what's going on," began Lesley. "What happened, what was so urgent, that made you call me?"

"If you didn't want to be here, you didn't have to come," snapped Prue.

"I recall not really having a choice in the matter," Lesley said sharply. "Anyway, you're missing my point. I can't help if I don't know what's going on. Remember, *you* called me, and here I am, selfish ass and all." Lesley paused. "I'm going to assume, Prue, that your shortness with me is your exhaustion coming to the surface, as long as *you* remember I'm fairly exhausted myself."

Prue understood Lesley's meaning. In no condition to start a verbal war so early in the morning, Prue nodded her head in compliance.

"Agreed. I'm sorry."

"It's alright," answered Lesley. "Let's just get back to why I'm here. What happened? Wyatt seems fine now."

"Wyatt is not fine. I think he's delusional."

"And what, exactly, do you mean by 'delusional'?"

"He's seeing people that are not there."

"What people?"

"Addie."

Lesley's heart jumped. Addie's name had not been spoken to her in a year and the sound of it made her ache. To remember Addie – that part of Lesley's life her friend had filled, the behavior that had led to her death – it was too overwhelming to think about. If one dwelled on such things the result would be the loss of one's mind. At least that's what the safeguarding side of Lesley's brain had convinced herself.

When Lesley arrived home after Addie's funeral she went around her apartment and began to gather items that reminded her of Addie: old pictures, letters, records, home movies, clothes, books, etc. It would have been easier to leave everything and move. But she did it, clearing out boxes of memories from her home and office, filling in the empty spaces with newly bought trinkets and knick-knacks, taking pictures of new friends to fill a photo album. And soon, the pain dulled to an ever-present ache that her body became used to and that her mind forgot she had.

But then, a thought – a sharp tinge of memory suddenly coming to the surface reminding you every once in a while the pain is still there – and then it's gone again.

Lesley felt her memories flooding in on her at the sound of Addie's name, but then they subsided as quickly as they came. *Strange*, she thought. Lesley didn't know what to think. But then she noticed Prue staring at her and realized she had been sitting silent for no reason, at least none Prue would know.

"Are you okay?" asked Prue.

"I'm fine," answered Lesley. "Just a little thrown, I guess. I didn't expect to be talking about Addie."

"We're not talking about Addie. We're talking about Wyatt."

"I know. It's just that you said her name and – you know what, it doesn't even matter. Let's talk about Wyatt. Tell me what happened."

"Are you sure? Maybe you should lie down for a while. You look a little pale. Maybe it's your blood sugar again."

"I'm fine. Once I get some coffee I'll be even better."

"If you say so." Prue got up and walked to the coffee maker. "Five minutes left."

Lesley noticed Prue was limping slightly.

"What happened to your ankle?"

"A casualty of last night," answered Prue.

"So tell me what happened."

"It's hard to say, really," began Prue, keeping guard over the brewing coffee, "but I think Wyatt's been hallucinating. Maybe the old stories of this house are getting to him."

"And what makes you think that?" Lesley was becoming slightly interested.

"He asked me if I believed the legend about this house – if I believed it was haunted."

"And what did you say?"

"I told him no, that the stories were untrue. Just stupid ghost stories to make kids scared. That's all they were."

"I seem to remember a time when you *did* believe in them," replied Lesley, smiling.

"I was a child then. You can't tell me that when you were little, if even for a little bit, you didn't believe in any of the ghost stories."

"Maybe a little bit. I used to alternate my route home from school so I didn't have to walk by this house," laughed Lesley. "Persephone's house."

"Yeah. Wyatt asked about her too."

"Persephone?"

Prue nodded her head.

"He wanted to know what Persephone said about the house, if she ever said anything about it being haunted."

"Did she?" Lesley asked with a sly smile.

"No!" snapped Prue. "Why does everyone think she was a bad person?"

"I didn't say she was."

"You didn't have to."

"Come on, Prue, you have to admit she was a little...eccentric, even if she was your friend."

"I don't have to admit anything."

"Well, then, we won't get very far, will we?"

"Whatever, Lesley."

The coffee maker beeped and Prue jumped at the piercing sound. She spun around, turned the machine off, and started searching for coffee cups.

"A little jumpy for someone who doesn't believe in ghost stories," Lesley teased.

Prue chose to ignore the comment, feeling Lesley smiling at her, holding back giggles. After finding mugs and pouring coffee, Prue returned to the kitchen table, leaving a coffee cup in front of Lesley and reclaiming her spot across from her.

"Wyatt believes the house is haunted," Prue said softly.

"That's ridiculous," replied Lesley.

"That's what I told him, but that's what he believes. He says sometimes late at night he sees Addie."

"He what?" Lesley almost spit the hot liquid in Prue's face. Instead, it dribbled down her chin as she tried to contain her emotion and swallow at the same time.

"I know. It's crazy, right? But that's what he believes. That's why I called you. He's not right, Lesley. There is something seriously wrong with him. He has this crazy story about you, him, and Addie. Plus his new drawing project is extremely disturbing – graphic images of a troubled fantasy."

"He talked about us?" asked Lesley, a hint of panic creeping into her voice.

"Yeah. Why? Is it true?"

"I don't know. You'd have to tell me what he said."

"What are you doing here?" A loud, firm voice entered the conversation. Lesley could feel Wyatt standing behind her.

"Prue called me – "

"I called Lesley because I was worried about you," Prue interrupted.

"Why? I'm fine now. I just needed some sleep."

"I don't think so. I think there is something really wrong here," Prue pleaded.

"Wyatt, why don't you tell me what happened, from start to finish," said Lesley, in her most therapist-type voice.

"No." He pointed to Lesley, then himself. "We are the reason this is happening to me. We caused this."

Only part of him believed what he was saying. Mostly Wyatt blamed himself for Addie's death, not Lesley. Sure, she did contribute a small amount to the happenings of that night, but Wyatt knew that he was mostly to blame. It was *his* actions, not Lesley's, that aided in Addie's suicide. If it had been Lesley's actions, Addie would have gone straight to the lake as soon as she saw the two of them in the living room. It was only after Wyatt had professed his feelings for Lesley that Addie acted on her delusional impulses. Wyatt knew he was to blame and he didn't want to bring Lesley into the insanity that had since haunted him. He wanted her safe and away from these personal demons that had taken up residence with him. Wyatt would have said anything to get her out of the house, even if his words hurt her, even if they pained him to say.

"I think you should leave. I don't want you in this house any longer. You shouldn't have come here. Please go."

Wyatt stayed for a moment, waiting for either woman to lift herself to her feet, but neither did. He could tell Prue was unmoved at the issue, wanting Lesley to stay and "fix" her brother. Lesley, on the other hand, was afraid of him. He watched her as she sat, head forward, slightly down, never raising it or turning it his direction. It was as if they were married again, having had a fight, and Lesley paralyzed with anguish over a situation out of the control of her hands, not knowing where to turn or what to do. That, he always knew, was something that tortured her. Wyatt threw his hands up in the air and sighed, walking over to the couch in disgust at the loss of control in his life. He sat with his head in his hands. Prue followed, waving Lesley to come with her.

Reluctantly, Lesley obeyed.

The twosome ended up next to him, Prue sitting on the couch beside Wyatt while Lesley stood behind them, hands gently resting on the back of the couch. Prue decided to start the intervention.

"Okay, Wyatt, tell Lesley what's wrong."

"She knows what's wrong." He didn't lift his head. Prue nodded at Lesley to sit next to him. Instead, Lesley chose the coffee table as her chair, taking the furthest corner away from him.

"Lesley, why don't you try?" Prue got up and began slowly walking the room, forcing Lesley to connect with Wyatt.

"Okay, Wyatt, tell me what happened last night."

"Why? You won't believe me."

"Tell me anyway."

"Ask Prue. She was here."

"I'm not here for Prue, I'm here for you. Now tell me what happened."

"No," Wyatt whispered, closing his eyes and leaning back into the couch.

"Unbelievable," groaned Prue. "How selfish can you be? I mean, here we are, trying to help you through whatever this is that you're going through and you're acting like a complete infant!"

"That's enough, Prue!" snapped Lesley. "I think we all need to take a breath and calm down."

"I'm fine," said Prue.

"No you're not. You're exhausted and scared and too close to the situation, none of which makes for a good intervention."

"Aren't you too close to the situation?" asked Wyatt.

Lesley didn't respond. Wyatt stared at her, silent. Lesley grew uncomfortable. She did feel too close, too vulnerable, and it made her mad. Lesley looked back at Wyatt, holding her ground.

"Prue says you think you see Addie sometimes, that you saw her last night. Is that true?"

"Prue was here last night. Why don't you ask her? Maybe she's the one that saw Addie and this is all just an elaborate ruse to confirm some childhood fantasy." Wyatt flashed a devious smile at Prue.

"Is that true?" Lesley turned her focus on Prue.

"I don't know what I saw last night," Prue answered, glaring at Wyatt. "I'd had a couple shots of vodka – "

"A couple?" interrupted Wyatt.

"Look," retorted Prue, "after the conversation we had last night you're lucky I didn't admit you into the closest psychiatric ward!"

"I'm not crazy!" snapped Wyatt.

"Okay, you're not crazy. You just every once in a while see your dead wife walking around the house. That sounds sane to me!"

"All right! That's enough!" shouted Lesley. "This is ridiculous. The two of you are acting like children. This isn't a competition of who's right or who's crazy. Now, I was awakened at a very early hour to come to a place I had hoped to never come to again by my ex-sister-in-law to help my ex-husband through some traumatic happening. By all respectable means I don't have to be here, but I came anyway because you needed my help, and, so help me God, if either of you acts out again, I am leaving this house, driving to the nearest hospital and telling the on-call psychiatrist to send two ambulances here to retrieve you and admit you both for a 72 hour suicidal watch, restraints and all!"

Prue dropped into a chair in the corner, stunned. Wyatt just smiled and laughed under his breath.

"Lesley – "

"Hush!" Lesley interrupted Prue. "Now, we're going to sit here and work through this, okay?"

"Okay," answered Prue. Wyatt remained silent, smiling coyly at Lesley. Feeling like her younger self again, Lesley returned his smile, then focused on Prue.

"Prue, tell me what happened last night. Did you see something? Wyatt seems to think you did."

"I saw a blur. That's it. It could have been anything. I was groggy. I'd been drinking. It was nothing."

"It wasn't nothing," answered Wyatt. "Why is this so hard for you to believe? You of all people. You study folklore and myths – and Persephone – I thought you would understand."

"I'm sorry, Wyatt. I just can't."

"Okay," responded Lesley. "That's enough of that. Prue, I think it's time for you to go."

"What?" responded Prue, a little shocked, and hurt.

"Why don't you go into town and get some breakfast," said Lesley, walking over to where Prue was sitting, gently pulling her out of the chair. "I would like to stay here and talk to Wyatt alone."

"But I'm the one who called you. I'm the one who wanted you here. Besides, nothing's open until noon. It's Sunday."

"Then go to church. I'm sure Father Halse would love to see you." Lesley paused and lowered her voice. "I need to focus on Wyatt now. I need to try and figure out what's causing all this for him."

"But I want to know what's going on."

"Prue, for once in your life stop meddling," said Wyatt. "Just go somewhere."

"I was just trying to help." Prue started pouting and it was hard to tell if she was serious. Lesley put her arm around Prue, and began walking her to the door.

"I think it would be best if you left for a couple of hours. I'm feeling a tension between you and Wyatt and it won't help him tell me what's really wrong."

"I'm feeling a tension between the two of you," retorted Prue.

"Look," retaliated Lesley, "you don't have to go anywhere. Go down to the beach, take a nap, go for a jog – it doesn't matter." Lesley opened the front door. "Just for a couple of hours. Take a drive. See some old friends. Spend the day shopping in South Haven or maybe Holland. Just go!"

"Fine. But I'll be back before noon."

"Whatever you say."

Prue grabbed her coat, left her keys on the key hook, and picked up the blanket curled on a chair outside on the porch. She turned to make her last demands and heard the door shut before she could speak. She was now on the outside, unable to look in.

Wyatt and Lesley waited to begin talking until they were sure Prue had left the porch and was far from eavesdropping proximity. Lesley stood in the corner of the room by the window while Wyatt watched her from the couch.

"I think she's gone," said Lesley as she lifted the curtain away from the window. "I don't see Prue anywhere. She must have walked down to the beach." Lesley continued to stand in front of the window, unmoved, silent, staring out into the tall beach grass and long-stretching blue sky. She hoped that they would remain silent, that she wouldn't have to delve into her past – their past. But Lesley knew by the way Wyatt was watching her, reading her every move, her wish would not be granted.

"So, are we going to talk," started Wyatt, "or are you going to stand there all day?"

"What would you like to talk about?" Lesley asked calmly.

"You tell me. You're the psychiatrist, remember?"

"Cute. *Know* that I didn't want to be here." Lesley hated it when Wyatt became playful just at the moments she wanted something.

"You're here now so you might as well get crackin'. Shrink me," teased Wyatt. "Besides, Prue will be angry if you don't have anything to tell her, seeing how she so desperately wants to know what's wrong with me."

"You seem very sure of yourself, Wyatt. Especially when I *know* there's something wrong here."

"And how do you know that?" scoffed Wyatt.

Lesley stared directly at him.

"Because I know you, and something is definitely off." Wyatt turned his body away from Lesley, his face tightened with anxiety. "What, no snarky comeback?"

"I don't feel comfortable talking about this with you."

Lesley felt a rush of triumph, petty as it may be, and began slowly walking toward Wyatt from her far away, dim corner.

"You felt just fine about sharing whatever 'this' is with Prue last night. Why not kiss and tell to me?"

"It's not like that," Wyatt said softly. "You weren't supposed to know about any of this."

"Well, I'm here now, so I might as well 'shrink' you, right?"

Wyatt didn't say anything. A smile crept over Lesley's face. She made her way to Wyatt, standing in front of him – the closest she had been to him all day. Finally, seeing his face looking down and away from her, she decided to sit next to him. Her body faced him as she spoke.

"Look, I know this is uncomfortable and sudden and neither of us really wants to be here right now but we are, so let's just talk, okay? Nothing has to happen. We'll just talk."

Wyatt nodded his head in acceptance.

"So, how 'bout the weather? Nice, huh?"

Wyatt laughed, keeping a smile as he spoke.

"Yeah, I guess."

"There you go!" Lesley said, lightly punching Wyatt in the arm. "I miss that, that laugh of yours."

Wyatt leaned in and placed his hand on Lesley's face.

"I miss this smile," said Wyatt, stroking Lesley's cheek with his thumb. Lesley hadn't even realized she was smiling. She leaned into his palm lightly, then moved away from his hand.

"Wyatt – "

"I know," he whispered. "I'm sorry. It's just hard for me…"

"Do you want to tell me what happened?"

"Not particularly," smiled Wyatt. "But I suppose you have more of a right to know than anyone else."

"I have no idea what you mean by that," answered Lesley, her voice slightly squeaking as she shook her head.

"Well, let me clear it up for you. It all started the day of Addie's funeral," began Wyatt. "That night, actually. I know in the cemetery I told you we should go our separate ways and not see each other anymore, but that night, when Prue asked you to stay, my heart jumped at the idea of you being here with me. I wanted you here. I prayed that you'd stay. And I breathed again when you agreed."

"But you didn't even talk to me that night," protested Lesley. "You wouldn't come anywhere near me. You wouldn't even look at me. You left me alone down here to deal with stragglers and leftovers." Lesley began to wonder what new little mind game Wyatt was trying to play on her. She was determined not to fall for it. "How can you say you wanted me here when your actions so clearly spoke otherwise?"

"You're wrong," answered Wyatt. "I couldn't bring myself to be near you in front of all those scrutinizing eyes, so I waited. I waited until there was no sound of judgments being whispered over cups of coffee and the house was dark. I waited until Alma was asleep. I came downstairs to see you but you had fallen asleep, too. So I watched you, like I did when we were married. I watched your body breathe slowly, the rise and fall of your chest, soft and rhythmic. You smile when your hair falls on your face. Did you know that?" Lesley shook her head no. "I didn't think so," continued Wyatt. "You brush it away unconsciously, but every once in a while I brushed it away for you, before you could get to it. I did the same when we were married. I liked that it hadn't changed – that you hadn't changed." Wyatt reached for Lesley's hand and, with Lesley not resisting, placed it in his own. "I kissed you that night."

"You did?" questioned Lesley, a little breathless and shocked.

"I did," confirmed Wyatt. "I took your hand, then kneeled down and gently kissed you on your forehead. I didn't want to wake you."

"That was you? I remember that."

"You do?"

"Yeah. I remember feeling a kiss on my forehead and it feeling so real. But when I opened my eyes, there was no one there, so I thought I was dreaming. I can't believe it was you."

"Dream kisser at your service," joked Wyatt.

"Why did you leave?" Lesley asked, truly puzzled by what all this meant.

"Because of what I saw."

"And what did you see?"

Wyatt became very still and rigid.

"I saw Addie."

"Wyatt – "

"I'm not crazy," Wyatt interrupted. "I know what this sounds like, Lesley, and believe me, I've thought a lot about it and tried to explain it away – made me think maybe all that stuff we heard as kids about this house was true." Wyatt paused and looked over at the staircase. "It sounds crazy, but I swear to you, I saw her, standing right over there in the same exact spot she was standing when she found us together just a few nights before. I was shocked – "

"Among other things," interjected Lesley.

"I didn't believe it at first either, Lesley. I just stared at this thing, this image of my dead wife standing fifteen feet away from me, and then she ran."

"Where did she run to?" Lesley gently mocked.

"To the beach," answered Wyatt, not paying attention to Lesley's disbelief. "Then to the water, then she was gone."

"Did you ever stop to consider you were hallucinating?" asked Lesley.

"If that's the case, then I've hallucinated an awful lot over the past year."

Lesley didn't respond. She paused and looked around the room. On the mantel Lesley found the framed photographs of Wyatt's life, most of them containing Addie at his side. Across the room on a chair was a blanket, one Addie always wrapped herself in when Lesley came all those months ago to "talk" to her. Eyes wandering to the kitchen, Lesley found the mug she had been drinking from. It was a small gift from college she had given Addie their first Christmas together. The house was filled with Addie.

"I see you still have a lot of Addie's things around the house."

Wyatt tilted his head back and laid into the couch.

"It just seemed wrong getting rid of them. This is her house, too."

"Not anymore," Lesley said quick and firmly. "Addie doesn't live here. Addie isn't here anymore."

What a novel statement, Wyatt thought. As if he didn't realize Addie wasn't "*here*" anymore". How easy it seemed to think of her that way. If only he could believe that. He wanted to box Addie's things away, but something always prevented him. Wyatt always found an excuse – a work deadline, an errand that had to be done, a shower, a nap. The simplest task – putting items in an empty box – and he couldn't do it. Wyatt couldn't explain it. But then again, this was Persephone's house.

"Easy for you to say," replied Wyatt. "You don't live here. You don't know."

"Maybe that's part of the problem," offered Lesley. "Perhaps you can't move on because you have all these things surrounding you, constantly reminding you of Addie."

"I don't know," said Wyatt, breathless and distant.

"I think it would be good for you to take her things down, maybe give them away. It's part of moving on. Right now you're in denial. Having all these things here keeps Addie's memory here, keeps her here in your mind. After Addie's death, all the things in my apartment that reminded me of her haunted me. I couldn't get her out of my mind. But those feelings began to go away after I boxed everything up."

"Sounds like denial to me."

"It's called moving on. I recommend it."

"Boxing all of Addie's things away won't change the fact that she's dead."

Lesley dropped Wyatt's hand.

"I didn't say it would."

Wyatt said the words so coldly, unemotional and detached, almost as if he had never known Addie, never cared for her, never loved her – a person of topic in a passing conversation. A therapist stating facts. It made Lesley a little jealous to hear him speak so disconnected, but she pushed it aside and marched on.

"I'm just suggesting that taking away some of Addie's things may relieve the ever-present thought of her from this house. It's not healthy. It feels so dark, cold, and gloomy in here."

"That's how Addie was. More so than either of us ever knew."

"You're probably right about that," agreed Lesley. "Addie was so hard to read there at the end. I think that's partially why I acted the way I did." Lesley brought her legs up and folded them to her chest, her arms hugging them. "I couldn't tell if she still loved you, and I felt somebody should."

"Thank you," smiled Wyatt. "You have no idea how profoundly that changed my life, how that made me see exactly how things were."

"I'm not sure if I understand what you mean," responded Lesley.

"Is that all you really think this is?" asked Wyatt, trying to change the subject. "That Addie's still so vivid in my thoughts and surroundings that I've manifested some kind of existence for her?"

"Could be," answered Lesley. "The mind is a very powerful tool. Under stress or duress it's amazing what the mind can do."

"Maybe you're right," said Wyatt. "Lord knows, with everything that's happened, I've tried to get into Addie's head. Instead, maybe she's gotten into mine." He looked over at Lesley. "So, I'm not crazy?"

"Maybe just a little," teased Lesley.

"I'll take it," said Wyatt.

"I still think you should see someone," suggested Lesley. "You really need to talk these issues out with a counselor."

"I could talk to you." Wyatt tried to take Lesley's hand again, but this time she pulled away.

"Wyatt, we've been down that road before, and it ended…tragically."

"Maybe you could suggest someone for me," proposed Wyatt, clearing his throat and retracting his hand, trying not to seem hurt by Lesley's reaction.

"I'll give you a name and number before I leave."

Lesley leaned her head against the couch and stared at Wyatt. She felt lighter for some reason, like something had been lifted off her soul. Lesley wondered if it had something to do with helping Wyatt. She had actually helped him this time, and it felt really good – not like she had the upper hand, but that they were equal. Wyatt felt like her friend again, easy and relaxed. She felt at ease, enough so she decided to ask a question she had waited a year to ask.

"Wyatt?"

"Yeah?" He had been looking at her the entire time.

"Since we're kind of on the subject, that night, after I left, where did you go? I mean, I know you weren't here when they found Addie, so where did you go? Why did you leave?"

Wyatt sighed and looked away from her, then took a deep breath.

"I had hoped you'd never ask that question."

"Why not?" Lesley didn't know if she should be afraid or offended. She was leaning towards offended.

"Because it might hurt you," answered Wyatt. "And that's the last thing I want to do to you."

"Tell me anyway," commanded Lesley.

"If that's what you want." Wyatt waited for her to change her mind but Lesley said nothing, sitting silent, waiting. "I left that night," Wyatt began, "because I didn't want to be here anymore. I didn't know what else to do. I searched for Addie, not believing that I actually saw her go into the water – I mean, who would do that? – but I couldn't find her. The alternative was too hard to face, so I left. I wasn't going to any particular place, but as I drove, part of me wished that everything would be okay – that Addie would be fine, waiting for me in this house – and part of me wished I would just keep driving and never come back. Neither happened."

Wyatt got up and began pacing the room. His right hand was halfway in his pants pocket with his thumb on cusp of the pocket, shifting back and forth as if he was drumming on his thigh. It was a nervous tick, the first sign of real nervousness – something Lesley hadn't seen in Wyatt in a long time – which made Lesley even more anxious and uncomfortable.

"I drove all night," Wyatt continued. "I must have, though I don't remember much of the drive. When I couldn't drive anymore, I stopped and fell asleep. I didn't know where I was and I didn't care."

"Where did you end up?" asked Lesley.

"Silver Beach."

"In Saint Joseph?" Wyatt heard the small panic in her voice.

"Yep," he answered calmly.

"How did you end up there?" Lesley asked, nervously searching for clues.

"Like I said, I don't know. I just drove and ended up there."

"Oh."

"It's what I found there that surprised me the most. Shocked me, really."

Lesley said nothing. She didn't even move. She sat lifeless on the couch, staring at her knees, almost knowing what was about to come.

"Maybe it's not such a coincidence that I ended up there," Wyatt went on. "During our fight, Addie told me something, this unbelievable secret."

Lesley held her breath.

"At first I didn't believe her. I drove all night not believing her. But Addie was right. I saw it with my own eyes. She was telling the truth."

"What did Addie tell you?" breathed Lesley.

"That I had a daughter."

Lesley closed her eyes, causing a tear to roll down her cheek. She didn't open them. She couldn't bring herself to look at Wyatt.

"Why did she tell you?" Lesley whispered.

"Because I told her I loved you," answered Wyatt from across the room. He had stopped in front of the window and now stood staring into the Michigan sky. Wyatt couldn't look at Lesley. He didn't want to see the pain he was causing her.

"Why did you tell her that?"

"Because it was the truth."

Neither said anything for a short moment, then Wyatt, trying to make Lesley understand, began again.

"It was kind of magical, that morning. I woke up on the beach. I had fallen asleep against my car and the smell of breakfast cooking woke me up. I didn't know where it was coming from so I followed the scent up the cliffs and found my way to this little bed and breakfast – The Bleaker Inn – and sat down at one of the tables outside. Then, all of a sudden, I was covered in water. When I looked up, there was this little girl, about eight or nine, kneeling in front of me picking up broken glass." Wyatt turned his head and looked directly at Lesley. "And she looked exactly like you."

"Except for her eyes," added Lesley, not opening her own.

"Except for her eyes," affirmed Wyatt. "The most beautiful little girl in the world kneeled before me and stared back at me with my own eyes. I can't tell you what an incredible feeling that is, seeing yourself in your own child."

"I wouldn't know," whispered Lesley. Wyatt didn't hear her.

"It put everything into perspective for me," continued Wyatt. "I saw how hard it must have been for you when I left, why you didn't come to me when my parents died. I understood the nervousness I saw in you when you found out Addie and I were dating, and the sadness in your voice when we talked about her pregnancy – the understanding you showed to her when she lost the baby. I had built up all these tiny resentments towards you over the years, all these failed reasons not to love you, and they all melted away as soon as I looked in that little face."

"Don't say that."

"But it's true."

"I don't care if it is true," snapped Lesley. She opened her eyes, but looked away from him. "I don't want to hear it."

"But it's all right now. I understand everything."

"You understand nothing," insisted Lesley. "Giving Grace away and not telling you was the hardest thing I've ever done in my entire life! Don't take that away from me by trying to tell me it was okay – that everything will be okay – that everything is okay! It's not, and it never will be. Not now, now that you know. Nothing will ever be the same. Nothing *can* ever be the same."

"But don't you understand what I'm telling you? I'm telling you I love you! That I've always loved you. That I always will love you!"

"Because I gave our child away?"

"In spite of that!"

"Well, mercy me! Aren't I the lucky one?"

"That's not what I meant."

"No, what you meant was that a lesser man would hate me, curse my name at the very thought of me. But not you! No! You fall deeper in love with me every minute of every day. Well, I'm sorry, but I just can't handle that."

Lesley got up and went to the kitchen table, pulling her car keys from her purse, then made a beeline for the door. Wyatt ran to the door and put his weight against it, grasping the door handle.

"You can't leave like this," argued Wyatt.

"Watch me!" yelled Lesley.

"I won't let you go," Wyatt shouted. "I love you too much to let you go again!"

"Stop saying that!" Lesley pulled on the door handle but Wyatt wouldn't let it go. Tired from fighting, Lesley took a step back, the weight of her exhaustion making her body sag slightly. "Don't you see?" she pleaded. "This 'thing' between us – this never-ending torrid love affair we keep hanging onto – I'm tired of it. I want it to be over."

"What are you saying?"

"I'm saying I don't love you!" blurted Lesley. She took another step back, taking in the weight of her own words. "I don't love you, Wyatt."

In shock, Wyatt let go of the doorknob. Lesley grabbed it, turning it and pulled it open, pushing Wyatt to the side. She ran to her car, almost knocking Prue down as she came up the walk from the beach. Prue called out to her, but Lesley didn't answer. Tears were streaming down her face as she opened the door to her car and threw herself in, searching for the ignition through blurry eyes. Panicking that Wyatt would follow her, she finally found the ignition and quickly started the car, throwing it into reverse, then drive, and sped away. Lesley knew she had lied to Wyatt – that she still loved him – but knowing and living with the fact that he knew her secret – that he had found Grace – and he forgave her and still loved her was more than Lesley could handle. The worst thing she had ever done in her whole life and he still loved her. *How could he still love her?* Lesley drove as fast as she could, tears clouding her view the entire way home.

When Prue reached the house Wyatt was throwing pictures of Addie on the floor in a pile.

"Wyatt, what's going on? I just saw Lesley speed off."

"She left," answered Wyatt plainly.

"What do you mean she left?"

"She left!"

Wyatt answered with such force it made Prue take a step back. Wyatt paid no attention to her reaction and walked over to the chair holding Addie's blanket, picked up the folded cloth, and threw it in the pile.

"What are you doing?" asked Prue.

"Addie doesn't live here anymore," answered Wyatt with grit in his tone. "And neither should her stuff." He walked over to the kitchen, picked up the mug Lesley had been drinking from, and threw it away. "There are boxes in the basement. I want all her things boxed up." Wyatt walked back to the living room, passing his sister again without looking at her. "You can start in the nursery," he said coldly. "Take it all down. I don't want anything left."

Prue slowly started up the stairs not knowing what to think. She had no idea what had happened but was too afraid to ask her brother for details and too afraid not to do what he asked. When she reached the top of the stairs he yelled one more command at her.

"While you're up there, start calling around and find a place to donate all this stuff. I want it gone by tomorrow."

Prue didn't see where Wyatt went but she heard the basement door slam. Then there was silence.

CHAPTER 17: THIRD TIME'S A CHARM

Wyatt

I left Point Caneissa.

It took me a month, but I moved away from my hometown, selling or donating most of my belongings. I only kept what I needed – art desk, canvas, pencils, pastels, paint and chalk. Everything else was a constant and painful reminder of the choices I had made and their effects. Addie's things were gone within three days of Prue's arrival, all given away to local charities and goodwill organizations. I wondered, while the different trucks and vans came to collect their swag, if the new consumers of this merchandise would know that the previous owner was deceased – that to these objects she held so important, so dear, she was dead and buried, her memory never haunting them as it did the others living among them. I had hoped in time that like these objects, I would come to view Addie in the same way.

The children's cartoon network I had worked for in San Francisco decided to branch out into illustrated and graphic novels with a few comic books based on the various cartoon TV shows they produced. Knowing that I had experience in the comic book world, they asked me to come work for them at this new division based in Chicago. Greedily, I accepted their offer, not only because I desperately wanted to work, but because it would again put me in the same city as Lesley. If I couldn't be with her, at least I could be near her and know that she was okay.

Work wouldn't begin for another month – the company still rounding up as many top illustrators as they could – so I took that time as my own, finding an apartment, working on my own illustration projects, and going to counseling, like Lesley had suggested. Once a week I would drive into the city for my appointment with Dr. Walsh. And once a week I would pass the building Lesley lived and worked in as I entered and left this great metropolis that would soon be my home. But I never stopped. She didn't need to know I was there. Not yet, anyway. For now, all I needed to believe was that she was going on with her life in a normal fashion – that she was happy. Eventually I would put myself in her way, not forcing myself in her life but just letting her know I was there. Then, in due time, maybe she would come to me. That was the only way I was ever going to get her again. Lesley would have to come to *me*, like she did in college, like she did that night a year ago. I couldn't force her into seeing that she loved me. She would have to realize it on her own. And whatever happened after that, Dr. Walsh tried to make me see, I would have to live with.

"I think you're right," said Dr. Walsh, scribbling notes on the pad in front of him. "Lesley does seem like the type of person who resists working through confrontations once she perceives herself forced into a situation she cannot control. But once calm and able to rationally think through what has happened, I don't think she will come to you with professions of love, even if she does come to the realization they are true. I think, with everything you have told me about your relationship with her, that she will want it to be over, that she will move on. And I suggest the same for you."

"I understand that, Dr. Walsh, but don't you think she has a right to know?"

"A right to know what? How you feel about her? How you've moved your life once again, in part, to be near her? How our sessions are mostly focused around her?"

He was treating me like a child. It reminded me of the way Prue sometimes talked to me, only with more superiority and smugness.

"Not only that," I argued uselessly, "But things about Addie, about that night and what my life with Addie was truly like."

"Perhaps," answered Dr. Walsh slowly. "But that is for another time."

Three months went by and I did as Dr. Walsh had instructed me. I didn't contact Lesley. I didn't even try. Even with my studio uncannily being two blocks down from where she lived and worked, I kept my distance. And then Dr. Walsh asked me the question I didn't know I'd been waiting for.

It was the beginning of September, and what little trees grew in the city, the leaves began to change color and fall to the ground like large globs of orange and red paint. It was the only way you knew trees even existed in the city. Normally the leaves and branches blended in with the buildings and sidewalks and the small patches of grass set aside for recreation. But in September there was no denying their existence, the red and orange popping out against the gray and black. For one month the city was alive, living and breathing naturally. Not even cloud-smashing skyscrapers could deny the beauty of fall, its colors able to be viewed from even the tallest of buildings. It gave me hope that even in the hardest, most rigid of places, life still existed, life went on.

Dr. Walsh sat in his chair, note pad in hand, as I stood against the window looking down into the city. Neither of us had said anything in five minutes, so I had begun to count the fading trees when he finally spoke.

"I think some of the things we've discussed today have been very interesting," Dr. Walsh began. "In fact, over the last few weeks I've seen great progress in your ability to deal with the traumatic events over the past year and a half."

"Thank you," I responded, not turning my head from my counting game. I was up to twenty-five. "I've tried to listen to what you've said over the past couple months and incorporate it into my life. I've tried to move on as best I can. It's still hard, though. I wonder if I'll ever be able to get past all this completely."

"Well, let me ask you this." Dr. Walsh leaned over, placing his note pad on the coffee table and returning his pen to his jacket pocket. "If you had it all to do over again, would you?"

"No," I answered quickly.

"Because of Addie's death?"

"No," I answered again.

"Then why?" he questioned.

"Because I wouldn't want to put Lesley through the pain of it all again."

"Interesting," Dr. Walsh said to himself.

"Not that I wanted Addie to kill herself or that I would want that again, it's just that, looking back at our relationship, Addie wanted specific things in life. She had this idea of how her life should be – perfect husband, perfect marriage, perfect children, perfect family – and when things didn't go the way she thought they should, she couldn't handle it. She wanted me to fit in this perfect puzzle she had created for herself, but I didn't, and the more she forced it, the more we broke apart. It wouldn't have mattered if it was me or some other guy she tried to force into her puzzle. She would have self-destructed eventually."

"That's very insightful, Wyatt."

"Thank you." I turned and faced the room now. "As for me, Addie was just a replacement for Lesley."

"How so?"

"Well, in physical attributes, they were complete opposites, which is why it took me so long to realize my true actions. To me, I thought that I had picked a woman who was completely different than Lesley. But they were more alike than even *they* would probably admit."

"In what way?"

"In lots of ways. They liked the same movies, music – hell, they were both psychiatry majors for crying out loud. They both knew how to manipulate a person, only Lesley seemed to be able to do it in a good way, a healthy way that usually ended up solving whatever problem you had and making you feel better about yourself or the situation. Addie, on the other hand, always seemed to foul things up somehow. Probably because her manipulation was more self-centered."

"And you came up with all these realizations on your own?"

"Give credit where credit is due, doc!" I answered with a smile. "Trust me. I listen to what you say. It's soakin' in."

"And what about Lesley? You said that Addie would have self-destructed regardless of what man she would have put in her life. Don't you think Lesley would have fared the same heartaches without you?"

"No."

"Why not?"

"Because I *was* the direct cause of her heartache. I chose to leave her all those years ago and that decision has caused all this pain and turmoil for her since. If she had chosen someone else, her life would have been completely different. She wouldn't have suffered through all this mess."

"One could argue that even if she did choose another man to love, he may have left her also, causing her the same heartache."

"That may be true, but that man – stupid as he may be for leaving her – probably would have left her alone instead of reappearing in her life consistently, constantly reminding her of their life together and rekindling her emotions for him. And I highly doubt that man's next wife would end up killing herself over the unrequited love of her husband's ex-wife."

"Valid point," Dr. Walsh responded with a smile. "Extreme circumstances, indeed." He leaned over, picked up his note pad, and took his pen from his jacket pocket. "Well, Wyatt, like I said before, you've made tremendous progress. Your rational thought process just now proves that you've taken accountability for your actions but that you also see the accountability in others actions regarding the misfortunes in your life and that you don't place fault where none is to be found."

"Are you kicking me out?" I asked jokingly.

"Not quite yet," answered Dr. Walsh. "But I do believe it would be okay to contact Lesley now, if you still wanted to."

"Really?" My heart began to race.

"You have unfinished business with her, it seems, and you can never truly move on with your life until you tell her what you just told me. As you said some weeks ago, she has a right to know."

"Thank you, Dr. Walsh." I grabbed my coat and began walking to the door.

"Wyatt," Dr. Walsh said shortly. I stopped in mid gallop. "I would not corner her, if I were you. If you surprise her someday with these revelations you have come to, she will feel threatened and she will reject you and what you say."

"So what do you suggest?" I asked, annoyed and frustrated.

"Let her come to you."

"And how do you suggest I do that?"

"I don't know. That's up to you to devise. But I guarantee, if you corner her with all this, she will run and you may never see her again, losing your chance forever. However, if you put yourself in her way, casually meeting her by chance, her friendship for you may allow you to confide in her and finally move past all this."

"Put myself in her way."

"Yes."

And that's exactly what I did. However, it didn't quite work out like I planned. I spent a month buying coffee at the corner donut shop on her block. I spent my lunches walking past her building or loitering in front of it on a bench pretending to look at the sketches in my briefcase. For dinner I chose a different restaurant every night, all within a five-block radius of her building, but still no luck. I never saw her. I began to worry that maybe she had moved or something terrible had happened to her, but my fears were relieved when I called her office and the sprightly Jane answered, "Dr. Lesley Trilmon's office". It seemed that I could not force fate into a chance meeting, but then fate took over for me.

It was now November and the city had seen its first snowfall – a dusting really. In the early hours of the morning tiny snowflakes had blanketed Chicago, but by 9am it had all melted or turned to little piles of slush. The city was wet and cold, the wind whipping around the brick and mortar buildings as if they didn't exist. All the leaves had fallen and blown away and there was nothing left to protect the city's residents from yet another hard mid-western winter. Soon the Chicago River would freeze, then the edges of Lake Michigan. I had succumbed to the fact that the season for my chance meeting with Lesley had ended. The weather had turned so that just standing still outside for more than ten minutes made your fingers hurt. I could no longer sit outside her building or go for lunch hour walks up and down her street. Sure, I could still go in the morning to the donut shop on her corner or frequent the restaurants around her building, but with winter settling in, getting to these places would become increasingly more difficult, and cold. No, it was best that I put away my plans and schemes and wait until spring. Then, if it wasn't raining, I could spend all day outside in front of her building if I wanted to. Okay, maybe not *all* day. But I never made it to spring. Fortune smiled upon me much sooner than that.

It was a Tuesday. I was walking from my apartment to the studio and was grateful that the snow had mostly melted before my commute. About three blocks away I stopped and joined a group of travelers waiting to cross at a light, all heading to various work destinations – a huge blob of people waiting on a light to turn green. There was no one direction we were all facing, so when a light did turn green, half the blob shifted forward or sideways, pushing through stalled bodies as they ignored the personal space of those who were unmoved. The blob moved left and right, and I moved with it, waiting for my walk to turn green, when someone pushed through me, causing me to fall, and someone to fall with me.

The person fell beside me, knocking my arm which caused my grip on my briefcase to loosen, letting it slip from my hand to the ground. When it hit the ground it opened, the slight wind around us picking up a few of the sketches inside and plastering them against the legs of the crowd around us.

"I'm so sorry!" said the voice behind the scarf in front of me. And though the face was turned away from me, the hands frantically trying to collect the contents of my briefcase, I could tell it was a woman. I closed my briefcase quickly and joined this woman in her quest.

"It's all right," I tried to assure her. "It's not like you meant to fall on me, or did you?"

"You caught me," she laughed. "How else is a single woman in the city supposed to find a man?"

"I seemed to have foiled your plan."

"Drat!"

The woman continued grabbing the pieces of paper, and though I could not see her mouth – or her face, for that matter – I knew she was smiling. Then she turned quickly and handed me my sketches.

"Wyatt?"

I looked up at the woman. She was directly in front of me. The scarf was up to her cheeks, but it could not hide the familiar face behind it. I was elated.

"Lesley!"

"What are you doing here?"

"I work here."

"What?" Lesley looked confused as she stared at me. Then her focus moved to the papers in her hand. "Oh, Wyatt! Your sketches! I'm so sorry."

Water and dirt began to seep from one page and soak into another until all of them began to stick together. I took the sketches from Lesley's hands and laid them on top of my briefcase, then helped my ex-wife up to her feet.

"It's okay," I reassured her. "These are just copies. I keep the originals at the studio."

"That's a relief."

We stood there awkwardly for a moment, the crowd again closing in around us while we kept a foot of distance between us.

"Do you want to get a cup of coffee real quick?" I asked, hoping I didn't seem too eager.

"Sure," Lesley answered. I could tell from the way her cheeks moved that she was still smiling. "But I'm buying."

This time we moved with the mob and headed to the coffeehouse just across the street.

"I just can't believe you're here," said Lesley as she set two cups of coffee down on the table. I had been sorting through my slush soaked sketches trying to salvage what I could. "I really am sorry about you're sketches, Wyatt. Are you sure you didn't lose anything important?"

"It's fine," I tried to reassure her again. "Like I said, I keep the originals at the studio, for just such an occasion."

"That's good," she smiled. "Because I would hate to think that I had ruined – "

"Again, it's fine." This time she took the hint.

"Right. So, you're working here in Chicago. How's that going for you?"

"Good. The cartoon network I worked for in San Francisco is heading up an illustrated publishing house here in Chicago and asked me if I wanted to be a part of it."

"That's great. And do you commute into the city?" she asked, taking a sip of her hot coffee.

"Uh, no. I live just a few blocks away from here, up on Wacker Drive."

Lesley spit her coffee into her cup.

"You live here?"

"Yeah."

"How long?"

"Since the end of June."

Lesley placed her cup gently on the table.

"Since June." I didn't say anything. "Why didn't you call me? Why haven't you come to see me?" The shock in her voice was laced with sadness.

"I didn't know if you'd want to see me. After our last encounter, I wasn't sure if you'd ever want to talk to me again, let alone see me."

"Right," agreed Lesley, dejected. "I guess I did kind of leave things up in the air. But you could have called me. I would have talked to you, listened to you." I didn't say anything. I didn't know what to say. I just knew I didn't want to mess anything up. "So, things are going good for you?" she asked, a little more bounce in her voice.

"Things are great. Work is going really well. I sold most of my stuff to move out here, start anew. Gave the house back to Prue – "

"Well, that's good," Lesley interjected. "That must be a relief all in itself."

"Yeah. It's nice not to be tied to it so much anymore. Real cleansing. Dr. Walsh says getting rid of the house and moving here was probably the best thing I could have done."

"Dr. Walsh? You know Dr. Walsh?"

"He's my shrink."

"He's your therapist?"

"I go to him once a week. Why? Do you know him?"

"He's a colleague of mine. We confer with each other every once in a while, meet up at seminars."

Now I realized how Dr. Walsh seemed to understand Lesley so much. He knew her.

"Not that it is any of my business," started Lesley hesitantly, "But can I ask you what you talk with him about?"

"Mostly Addie." I could see the fear recede from her eyes. "He's helped me to deal with what happened, with her death."

"How so?"

"Well, he's helped me see and understand how Addie really was."

"And how's that?" Lesley sipped her coffee nonchalantly, trying hard to bring her therapist-side out. She sounded like Dr. Walsh. But I knew, as she barely drank from the mug in her hand, she was nervous. Unfortunately, so was I.

The truth. That's what I had waited all these months to tell her. What's that proverb – "...know the truth, and the truth will set you free...". Jesus made it sound so easy. But this was the opposite of easy. The truth had bound me for so long, I wasn't sure I could actually let it go. But I suppose when you're the Son of God, the truth is irrelevant. It just is. But I'm not the Son of God. I'm just a mortal man, who loves a mortal woman – who doesn't love me in return – who blames herself for the suicide of her best friend, the secrets of which have and will continue to profoundly change her life. The truth is never easy. It is always hard and ambitious.

"Wyatt?"

Lesley's voice woke me from my reverie. I didn't know how long I'd been sitting there in silence, but I knew it had been long enough to make the air between us feel awkward.

"I'm sorry," I said quickly. "It's just a little unsettling to finally be talking about this with you."

"Well, to be fair," responded Lesley, "We really haven't been talking about anything."

"I know. But I want to." I set my sketches down and pushed them to the side of the table. I wanted and needed Lesley's full attention. "There are some things I've been meaning to tell you, things about Addie that may tie up any loose ends you might have."

"I don't have any loose ends," Lesley said quickly. "I've put that part of my life behind me."

"I know when you're lying, so don't think you've deceived me into believing that. You may say you've moved on with your life, but I see the pain in your eyes when I say her name."

"Then don't say it."

I paused for a moment, knowing that Lesley was becoming defensive, but I was determined now to move on. Defensive or not, I had a purpose after all.

"Addie was a delusional person."

"She was not," Lesley defended.

"Yes, she was. Lesley, you think you know everything there is to know about Addie, but you don't."

"Enlighten me then."

"Addie believed her life needed to be a certain way, that people and things needed to be a certain way."

"That's not delusional, Wyatt. That's idealism, and we all do that."

"Not to the point of self-destruction!"

People turned away from their morning papers and looked at us with annoyance hanging on their faces.

"Keep your voice down," demanded Lesley. "Now calmly, and quietly, try to explain to me what you're talking about."

Hard and ambitious. I took a deep breath and began again.

"Did I ever tell you about Addie's suicide note?"

"No." Lesley was genuinely surprised. "I didn't think she had left one."

"In truth, it wasn't a suicide note – just some writings she had accumulated over the week before she died. A fantastical dream, really. She had spent seven days holed up inside the nursery writing down every thought she had concerning this dream she kept having. When the police searched the house after they discovered Addie's body, they found the nursery room floor littered with Addie's ramblings. They covered the room from wall to wall."

"I had no idea."

"Neither did I. When I read them, I couldn't make any sense of them. I recognized a story from a book her grandfather wrote, but the story was grossly changed and somehow you and I ended up in it." Lesley said nothing but questioned me with her eyes, so I continued. "None of it made sense to me. I even tried to draw the images Addie described, but they led me to no answers and only fueled my growing depression."

"The sketches Prue mentioned."

"Right. I thought Addie was blaming me for her actions, but I was wrong."

"What, then?"

"It seems that Addie wanted me to fit into this perfect illusion she had created in her mind, an illusion she desperately tried to create in her real life. And it worked, for a little while. She manipulated me into what she needed without me even knowing it. But when I didn't fit anymore, when I started to break away, Addie couldn't handle it and she started to self-destruct. All Addie wanted was for me to be what she thought she desperately needed – a perfect husband equaling a perfect life. I couldn't be that for her and those writings were her plea to me."

"But you said something about me being in her writings. She must have put some kind of blame on me."

"No." I answered quickly. "If anything, I think she looked up to you. I think she wanted to be you, or be like you at least."

"That's ridiculous," laughed Lesley. "Addie was perfect in her own way."

"I don't think she would agree with you. She saw you as someone special, someone unlike anyone else she knew, and she envied that. She saw how people acted around you, wanted to be near you. She wanted that. Did you ever wonder why Addie went after the same things you had? Me for instance. Only she was determined not to lose them."

"I still don't believe any of this. Addie was her own person. She got what she wanted because *she* wanted it. Not because I did."

"Oh, really?" Lesley shook her head in disbelief. "Did I ever tell you why I married Addie?"

"No, but I do vividly remember a conversation about that subject in the library at Columbia."

"So do I," I said smiling. "You are the sole reason I married Addie."

"What do you mean by that?" Lesley almost looked offended.

"You told me to go to San Francisco because it was the best thing for me. You said anyone that loved me could see that, which meant you loved me, even if you didn't say it."

"Wyatt – "

"Now, just hold on. Let me finish." Lesley sat back in her chair, waiting for my conclusion. "I knew you loved me and I tried to show you I felt the same way, but you denied me. You didn't even let me try and it angered me, which kind of played right into Addie's hands."

"In what way?" asked Lesley, looking completely confused.

"I would have left Addie right then and there if you would have told me you loved me, but you didn't. So when I saw Addie out the window, I chased her down. I hadn't planned on asking her to marry me, but then she said the exact same words you had said to me about leaving for San Francisco. And because I thought she loved me like you did – because I wanted you or someone like you to love me – I asked her to marry me. It was later that I found out she stole those words from you. She must have known even then that I loved you, and desperate to keep us apart."

"Wyatt, I'm just finding this all hard to believe. She could be a bit of a pest at times, but Addie always seemed like she had it all together. There were no cracks until the very end, and even those are understandable because of the loss of the baby."

"She didn't even tell me she was trying to get pregnant," I blurted out. This, out of all of Addie's actions, was the one that angered me the most. It was the one that hurt the most.

"That can't be true," Lesley countered. "I could swear Addie told me you had been trying for a baby, or at least she alluded to it when she told me she was pregnant. I mean, she said you were so excited. I thought, or assumed, the baby was planned."

"That was a decision Addie made all on her own," I tried to make clear. "It wasn't something we decided on and planned. Addie just took it upon herself to change our lives again. Don't you see, Lesley," I said as I grabbed her hand. "My life with Addie was full of manipulations that I played right into because she knew what not to do. With every story you told her about us, you schooled her in 'the art of Wyatt'. Addie tried to make me fit into her puzzle, but I didn't. There was just one thing that always prevented me from being what she wanted me to be."

"And what's that?" Lesley asked.

"The fact that I loved you, that I always loved you."

"Wyatt, I told you I didn't want to go down that road again."

"Just hear me out. It will only take a minute."

"Fine," sighed Lesley. "You have one minute, then I'm changing the subject."

"Fair enough."

I paused to gather another truth-telling breath. But how much truth would I burden her with? Dr. Walsh was right. If I pushed too much onto Lesley, she would feel as though she was backed into a corner and bolt, just like she did all those months ago. I could see it in her eyes now, her fear at what I was about to say and the small twitches of her eyes looking at the various exits in the coffee shop – a desperate way out. I wanted to tell her how I felt. I wanted to tell her that I loved her, that I wanted to be with her and start our life again. I wanted to tell her I would do anything for her, do anything to be with her and that I felt like a shell of a man without her. Even when I was with Addie, being around Lesley made me feel like myself again. There were awkward moments, sure, but those were only because I was afraid to admit my true feelings for Lesley. I was afraid of being rejected. I loved her. I wanted to be with her. That was it. But how could I tell her that without her bailing on me? I couldn't. So I didn't.

"Addie knew what was coming," I tried to explain, holding back my feelings with every word I spoke. "That's why she acted quickly. That's why she always acted quickly. She knew that we once loved each other and that somehow got warped and twisted in her mind. Lesley, Addie wrote about you and me before that night, before we kissed, before she found us. Please don't blame yourself for what happened. Her world was falling apart – partially by her own doing – and she couldn't take it anymore, so she ended it. That's it. No cataclysmic event setting tragedy into motion. Addie self-destructed because she *was* self-destructive."

"And Dr. Walsh, he agrees with you?"

"Yes," I assured her.

"You showed him these 'papers' Addie wrote?"

"Yes."

"Hmm." Lesley looked over at the wet pages sitting on top of my briefcase. She touched the top one and tried to peel it away from the others. "So, what are these sketches for?" she asked, changing the subject like she promised.

"It's kind of a new idea we're working on. They're for a graphic novel."

"What's it about?"

"Ironically, they're inspired by Addie's writings and my drawings of them."

"Really?"

"Yeah. Dr. Walsh thought it would be good for me to work through some of my feelings by drawing them out. I don't know how it turned into a graphic novel but the whole process has been very cathartic."

"What's the novel called?"

"*Dream Weaver*. It's about a girl who pretends her dreams are real only to find when she grows up that she's somehow woven them into existence, and they've gone very wrong. I haven't worked out the ending yet, but I'm getting there."

"Maybe everything will turn out all right for the girl," Lesley added optimistically.

"I don't think so."

"Will it at least have a happy ending?"

"I don't know," I smiled. "I'm still waiting to see."

Lesley looked down at her watch.

"Ooh, it's late! I've got to get to a meeting downtown." Lesley stood and put on her coat. I followed her action. "It was good seeing you, Wyatt. And I appreciate what you told me here today. I don't know what to do with it all yet, but I'm sure when I have more time I'll sort through it all. We should get together again sometime. Maybe have lunch."

"That would be great."

"I'll call you, or you could call me. We'll figure it out."

"Sure." I didn't believe her. I knew there would be no lunch.

"Okay, then. I'll see you."

Lesley turned to walk away but I quickly grabbed her sleeve and pulled her towards me. I couldn't let her leave without knowing how I felt. I just couldn't. Not again.

"Lesley," I whispered in her ear, "I know you said you didn't want to travel down this road again, but I need you to know that I still feel for you the same as I did six months ago, the same as I did a year ago, seven years ago, eleven years ago, fourteen years ago – my entire life. That road, broken as it may be, will always be open for you. I'll be there at the end of it, if you ever feel like taking a walk."

Her arm went limp and I let it go. Lesley shifted her body weight into the direction she had been heading and walked away, not looking back as she left the coffee shop, and made her way downtown.

I knew I'd never see her again.

"Oh, my God!" I said, startled, as I opened my door to head downstairs to retrieve my mail. "Lesley, what are you doing here?" It was a week into the new year, almost two months since we talked in the coffee shop.

"Trying to get up the nerve to knock on your door," she answered. "Such a simple thing, knocking on a door, but I just couldn't force my hand to move in the slightest forward and back motion – not even for a faint rapping on the door I knew you wouldn't be able to hear. I guess fate kind of stepped in for me."

"You still haven't told me why you are here."

"Uh, I just wanted to see how you were doing."

"You couldn't do that over the phone?"

"No." Lesley looked down to the floor and took a deep breath. "The truth is, I've been doing a lot of thinking about our conversation in the coffee shop. It must have been really hard to go through all that by yourself. It must have been really hard to tell me. I know it was, especially since you didn't get the answer from me that you wanted."

"I don't expect anything from you, Lesley."

"But you should," she answered, looking up at me. "You see me differently in all this than I see myself. I'm not completely innocent."

"Yes, you are," I demanded. "I told you, you had nothing to do with Addie's death. I thought I made that clear."

"You did," she retorted. "But I still had a hand in all *this*." Lesley moved her hands and arms in a circular motion, as if trying to give significance to the space we were standing in.

"Lesley – "

"Wyatt, look – you had an opportunity to tell me why you did the things you did and the result of those actions – seemingly, Addie's demise, but somehow of her own fruition. Now, perhaps if I hadn't made certain choices in *my* life, Addie's life could have been spared."

"Lesley – "

"No, Wyatt. You got to tell your tale, it's my turn to tell mine."

I leaned against the door and sighed. I wasn't sure if I was up to listening to Lesley try and explain why Addie's death was her fault. It seemed like we'd been playing this game for too long now, back and forth, back and forth. But I wanted to be near her, so I entertained this newest venture.

"Do you want to come in?" I offered.

"No," Lesley said quickly. "Right here in the doorway is fine." She took a step back, almost afraid to come in.

"Okay, then. What's this new revelation you want to tell me?"

Lesley paused, standing in the doorway, looking as though she was about to squirm out of her skin. Her face, though, told a different story. Her eyes showed that her feelings had been hurt, tears just barely gathering at the surface. I felt like an ass now at my comment. She obviously had something important to say – something painful. I opened my mouth to speak but Lesley lifted her hand in protest. I heeded her warning.

"Up until that point, the day you left me was the worst day of my life. I didn't know what to do with myself. I cried for days. Then I got angry and told myself I didn't need you. And then I threw up. A lot. That's when I found out I was pregnant, which then became the worst day of my life – not because I was pregnant, but because I was all alone. I had no one to tell. I couldn't tell *you* because I had no idea where you were. You didn't want to be found. Besides, I had already signed the divorce papers. Appealing to you felt like a useless cause and a baby didn't make it any better. I couldn't tell anyone at school because most everyone assumed that even though you were gone, we were still together, and I didn't want to be looked down upon." Lesley looked down to the ground. When she looked back up, her eyes let go of the tears her previous motion had tried to hide. Her voice broke when she spoke again. "I couldn't tell my parents because they didn't even know you had left."

"I'm sorry you had to go through all that alone. I'm sorry *I* put you through that. I should have been here. I was stupid."

"You didn't know," she said quietly. "But I had to tell someone. Days began to feel like years. It was too big a secret to keep, so I told my mom. That was my first mistake."

"What do you mean?"

"I should have gone to find you, Wyatt. Instead, I suffered. Our baby suffered. You have no idea what I did, what I went through – what my mother put me through."

"Lesley, it's okay," I tried to comfort, without actually hugging or touching her. "It's over now. I know everything."

"But you don't!" Lesley protested. "The hell that I went through, the hell that I put our baby through – the hell that I let that woman put us both through! You have no idea how we suffered! My own mother wasn't even concerned for me – just concerned how it would look if her unwed daughter came home pregnant. So she hid me away at my grandmother's house, forced me to wear a girdle, and made sure I ate the same amount of food as I did before I became pregnant."

"How could you let her do that to you, to our child?"

"Because I was alone, Wyatt! And I was scared. I didn't have anyone else to turn to. She is my mother, after all."

"Not a very good one."

"Be that as it may, she's the only one I have. At the time, she was the only one I thought would help me. And in her own warped way she believed she was looking out for me."

"In what universe – "

"Wyatt," Lesley interrupted, placing her fingers on my lips to stop their movement, "I just want to get through what I have to tell you and then go. It's not something I like to talk about or elaborate on. I'm only telling you because you have a right to know. You are Grace's father after all, even if we're not a part of her life."

"Lesley, I'm not angry at *you*." I tried to assure her.

"I know," she answered softly. "Just let me tell you the rest, and then I'll go." I made no motion to stop her, so she continued. "I went on like that for months, every day in agonizing pain as my growing body tried to push out what the world was pushing in. I was always hungry. I barely gained any weight. My only relief was at night, when no one could see me. I would run my hands over my stomach and feel Grace's tiny kicks. They gave me joy and relief, but also sadness."

"Why?" I asked, not meaning to interrupt her, but curious.

"Because I knew she wasn't mine to keep. Another thing my mother had taken care of in spite of my protests."

"You wanted to keep Grace?"

"Yes."

"But why? Despite everything your mother did, she was right about giving Grace away. It would have been so hard for you, so hard for Grace. Why live that life of hardship when you knew there could be a better one for both of you?"

"Because she was the last thing I had that was yours. I didn't want to give that up. I didn't think I could."

We both stood in the doorway, silent. We looked away from each other. I couldn't look at her, not because I was angry or disappointed at her actions, but because here was a woman who had loved me so much she would have put herself through a life of hardship and heartache just to keep a part of me with her. She would have sacrificed everything she ever wanted just to see our daughter's face every day and know that she was mine. I couldn't bring myself to say anything. I hated myself more than ever.

"In the end," Lesley began softly, "It didn't matter anyway. My actions proved I couldn't be her mother. She came early, because of what I did to my body – how I tried to hide her from the world. They probably would have taken her away from me anyway, if Mr. and Mrs. Lynn hadn't agreed to adopt her. She was the smallest baby ever born at that hospital. They didn't know if she was going to make it, but she did, despite what I did to her. That day, the day she was born, became the worst day of my life, and still is. Though now, the reasons having grown in number, make my decision even harder to bear."

"Lesley – "

"I never saw her," Lesley continued, not letting me talk. "I'm glad you did, though. I'm glad you got to see her."

"I am too," I agreed. "But this doesn't change the course of events over the past two years. I don't know why you think it would."

"Yes, it does," Lesley protested. "It has everything to do with it. Wyatt, when you called me after your parents died, it was my mother who spoke to you, made you believe that I didn't want to see you. I tried to speak to you, to say something, but I was just so stunned at everything that was happening. When my mother hung up on you I had made the decision to come to you. You needed me and I loved you."

"Why didn't you come?"

"Because my mother convinced me not to. She was right, Wyatt. Your whole world was crashing down on you. I couldn't throw a baby into the mix."

"The way you tell it, I probably wouldn't have even noticed."

"You would have noticed," Lesley answered, a sly smile creeping up on her face.

Lesley was right. I would have noticed. I noticed everything about her. I would have seen the small change in her curves and known something was wrong. I would have felt the restraint as I hugged her or the awkwardness as she spoke, trying to keep her secret. And despite my world crashing down on me, I would have tried to gain the knowledge of her secret, and loved her all the same when found out.

"You're right," I conceded. "But you should have come anyway."

"I know," she whispered.

"I would have loved you."

"Even knowing everything you know now?" Lesley looked up at me, trying to hide the hope in her eyes.

"It doesn't change how I feel about you."

"Ugh, God, Wyatt!" Lesley stumbled back a little as she spoke. "Why do we do this to each other? It's not right. It's not fair. We can't deny ourselves the truth anymore. Our stubbornness and pride got in the way of what we both knew was right. We let our childish insecurities and selfishness blind us in what we truly wanted – of *who* we truly loved – and it messed everything up."

"But we can make it right, now."

I stepped closer to Lesley and pulled her body against mine, pressing my lips to her ear.

"Please, Lesley, let's not be selfish anymore."

I felt a tear drop fall from Lesley's eye to my cheek, run down the course of my neck and soak into the collar of my shirt. I placed my hand on her cheek, pulling her lips closer to mine, and, without resistance, I gently kissed her.

"Okay," she murmured.

I pushed the door open and led Lesley into the apartment, leaving the door to close behind us on its own.

CHAPTER 18: WILLOW TREES AND OTHER HAUNTINGS

Lesley

"Hello! Anyone home?"

I peeked my head around the front door as I opened it and stepped into the living room. I saw Prue's Mustang in the driveway and hoped that she was home and not out with my mother finding last minute wedding errands to run, just in case they missed something or happened to change their minds. My mother and Prue had become fast friends over the last couple of months, planning the entire wedding themselves. You wouldn't think there would be so many details to attend to for a small wedding, especially a second marriage to the same person. But leave it to Prue and my mother to find extravagance where none was needed. Like the florist, for example, staking poles in the beach grass along the pathway to the lake for hanging baskets overflowing with pink, blue, and lilac hydrangeas, or each of the chairs lined in small rows along the beach with their own nosegay of petit pink and white roses. I hated to think of what was on the side of the house I couldn't see. When I pulled up I saw movers unloading round and rectangle tables along with what looked like pieces of a dance floor. I would try and avoid that side of the house until after the wedding.

I also noticed while driving up that Wyatt's car wasn't in the driveway. He wasn't here yet. I was a little disappointed. I know it's bad luck to see the bride before the wedding, but I wanted him here with me anyway. We'd had enough bad luck in our lives to last many lifetimes. What was a little more?

I set my bags down and walked around the room, pulling the curtains open throughout the downstairs, letting light fill the open space. It was brighter than I remembered. Looking around the house I tried to forget the last time I was here. It was hard, really, to explain what transpired in the months between then and now. So many wonderful things had happened since then, but those few moments before all this, before my new life, I wondered if I would ever get over them. I wondered if I'd ever feel comfortable in this room again. This room, where Wyatt told me he loved me, where Addie found Wyatt's love lost, and the possibility she never possessed it to begin with. I looked around the room and noticed it had no color to it. I never really paid much attention before. Completely white. Perhaps there were too many emotions living in this room, one emotion never outweighing another, letting a color of violent red or tranquil blue shine through. No. Just a white-hot swirling bed of emotions that lingered there despite the passing of time. *Why had I come back?*

"Lesley!" I heard the delighted voice of my soon-to-be sister-in-law, again.

"Hi, Prue," I answered with restraint, trying to hide the growing nervousness in my voice as I watched through the window laborer after laborer bringing what seemed like mountains of decorations from delivery vans and moving trucks.

"I didn't even hear you come in." Prue walked over and hugged me tightly. "I didn't expect you until later. How long have you been here?"

"Not long," I reassured her. "Just long enough to open the curtains. I hope you don't mind. It was a little dark in here."

"Not at all," she smiled. "I would have done it myself, but I just haven't had the time. It's been non-stop directing since I got here this morning."

"This morning? I thought you were driving in last night."

"I decided not to since you said you were staying at your parents' last night. I guess I just didn't want to be in this house all by myself."

She tried to stay calm and indifferent as she spoke, but I could see the fear creeping onto Prue's face. She didn't want to stay in the house by herself because she was scared, and I didn't blame her. It was the same reason I had chosen to stay with my parents. If Wyatt wasn't here, I didn't want to be either.

"I can understand that. I wouldn't want to be by myself in this big house either." We both smiled with a small laugh under our breath. "Have you talked to Wyatt yet?" I asked, desperately wanting to change our line of conversation.

"No. Have you?"

"This morning he called. Said he had a few things to finish up at the studio before he could head up."

"I hope it's nothing that might delay the wedding," Prue huffed, folding her arms against her chest. Her eyes narrowed as she spoke to me, almost as if she was looking through me at the preparations outside but also at me. "We have a tight schedule to maintain. I don't want to keep the guests waiting. And I hate to think what mood this would put Alice in, after all the hard work we put in to this."

Apparently, Prue was now on a first name basis with my mother.

"My mother will be fine," I assured, standing a little more straight, unrelaxed, firm. "Besides, Wyatt said he would be here no later than three and the wedding doesn't start until five, so we'll be fine. There's nothing to worry about."

"Still, maybe I should call him, just to make sure."

I put my hand on Prue's shoulder.

"He's probably already left. Don't worry. Everything will go according to plan."

"You're right," Prue smiled sweetly, though I could tell she was just trying to appease me. I knew once she left me she would find the nearest telephone and call Wyatt, sure that he hadn't left yet. I wanted to be there as she hung up the phone to an unanswered call, just to say, "I told you so", but that wouldn't help anything and only add to an already over-stressed Prue. "Calla lilies," Prue said sharply as she looked through me again and out the window. "I didn't order any calla lilies. Oh, lord, they're going to ruin everything!" Prue began stomping her way toward the door.

"Where are you going?"

"I'm sorry, Lesley, but I have to go and fix this. Obviously someone is going to have to oversee these buffoons. I don't know why I thought this would be fun, like a vacation. I feel like I'm at work."

"Only they're not carrying in priceless ancient pots and tablets. They're just flowers, Prue." I tried to hide my laughter under my breath.

"Ancient African antiquities or pink and white roses, they're still all important to me," snapped Prue. She stopped a foot away from the door, her back still towards me.

"I know they are," I said gently as I walked forward, placing my hands on Prue's shoulders and moving close to give her a firm, half-hug. "And I'm glad they are. If they weren't, I wouldn't be getting this perfect, beautiful wedding. Thank you, Prue."

Prue's shoulders relaxed and her stance became more loose.

"Well, I should be getting outside."

"I was hoping to lie down for a little bit. All this excitement is beginning to wear on me. Should I put my things in the guest room?"

"No!" Prue turned quickly in the open doorway and let the screen door snap closed against her back. "I mean, I already put your dress and veil and everything in the master bedroom when it arrived this morning. I thought you'd be more comfortable in there, with the room being bigger and having the full length mirror and dressing table."

"Oh, okay. I guess I'll just head up and get settled in."

Prue opened the screen door and backed herself out of the house.

"I'll just be outside if you need anything," she called as she bounced down the steps and onto the brick path leading to the driveway.

I turned and looked up the stairs. Gathering the few belongings I brought with me into the house, I began my ascent, bypassing a room I was extremely familiar with to arrive at one that was completely foreign to me – one I never really wanted to enter. This room was Addie and Wyatt's room. For me it always would be. I had no right to be in this room. But I opened the door anyway.

My dress and veil were hanging on the full-length mirror in the corner next to the dressing table. It was the only thing new in the room. I could tell because it was the only thing in the room that didn't have a thin layer of dust on it. The room was empty, except for the furniture, and even then it was sparse. Wyatt had been telling the truth. He'd gotten rid of most everything he owned. And I imagined the room was exactly how he left it – cold, dark, and empty. It felt wrong being in this room, getting ready for my wedding in this room. There was no happiness left in this room, Addie's room. It wanted to stay sad, but I was determined to change that.

I put my bag at the end of the bed, then walked over to the line of windows on the opposite side of the room. This room was on the corner of the house and had a line of windows that wrapped from one side of the room to the adjacent wall forming an L. The full-length mirror was in the corner that joined these two walls. I started at one end, throwing open curtains and opening blinds until I found myself on the opposite side of the room, light pouring in from everywhere. The sun reflected off of the dust as it settled, picking out tiny glimmering spots of red, yellow, and blue. I wondered, as the room became calm again, why the other colors of the rainbow refused to make an appearance. Then I saw my wedding dress, and forgot everything else.

I walked over to the clear garment bag, took it in my hands and unzipped it, removing the dress and placing it on the bed. I began removing my clothes quickly, eager to put this coveted dress of all dresses on, then paused to look at myself in the mirror. I studied my naked reflection, the sunlight hitting it from all directions. I didn't care that all the windows were open and that from the ground you could probably get a good look at my breasts. If you were in a nearby tree you could probably see the whole package, but it didn't bother me. I looked at myself in the mirror and wondered if anyone could see a difference in me – if Wyatt could see a difference. I ran my hands along the curves of my body. I could see a difference. I walked over and picked up my wedding dress, stretching my arms up and letting it fall over my body. Hopefully the dress wouldn't notice the shift in my curves since the last time I had tried it on. I turned and looked in the mirror for confirmation.

The sun shone off the pearl-colored satin which created a kind of haze around the smooth fabric as the dust finally reached the floor. The entire dress was made of this soft, silky satin, at least the first layer of the dress was. You could really only see the satin, in all its loveliness, around the bust of the dress. The rest of the dress was draped in a very fine gauze that hung down but also floated around the dress at the same time. The gauze met the bust of satin in an empire waist, framing my breasts and following up the sides to form small, sheer capped-sleeves that went over my shoulders and down my upper-back until it met the empire waist again and formed a long, flowing train. The bust had embroidered flowers with pearls around it – not too many, but just enough to add detail. I studied myself in the mirror. The dress hugged every inch of my body. It had always been a form-fitting dress, but it was even more so now. I looked at myself from the side, smoothing the gauze until it lay in the right places. I was quite happy with my profile, the gauze floating and moving the way it was intended and the train flowing from my back to the floor. I turned forward again and walked closer to the mirror. The bust of the dress left little to the imagination. I felt like Olivia Hussey in *Romeo and Juliet*, my breasts pushed up and on display. I wondered if it was because they had begun to swell. It didn't matter what the reason. I looked absolutely beautiful, radiant even. Every last inch of me.

I looked over at the clock on the nightstand. It was one-fifteen. I yawned, thinking how silly it was to be tired in the middle of the day. But I did have a long day and evening ahead of me, so I removed my beautiful dress and laid it gently down on one side of the bed, then crawled in on the other side underneath the covers. Goosebumps began to pop up all over my body as it tried to warm the cold, defunct bed sheets. It felt weird, unnatural lying in Addie's bed, but I told myself it would only be for a few moments. My body relaxed and my eyes, heavy with sleep, closed as I tried to remember all the things I had to do before the wedding, preventing any long-term occupancy of this bed. Then it all faded into nothing.

I love you.
Don't leave me.
I'll never leave you.
Addie!

"Addie!" I shouted as I shot up from the bed, gasping for breath. As I tried to breathe in deeply I couldn't shake the distinct feeling that someone had been watching me, touching me. I glanced down at my arm and found red markings pressed into my skin, quickly dissipating. I looked around the room and noticed the curtains nearest the door were fluttering in the wind. The window had been opened. I searched the room for Wyatt, even for Prue, but no one was to be found. I was still all alone in Addie's room. Remembering I was still naked, and feeling very vulnerable, I quickly got out of the bed, rushed to the other side of it, and threw my wedding dress on, this time not taking the time to notice every curve or smooth every wrinkle. I looked at the nightstand. It was two o'clock. Wyatt would be here in an hour. I walked over to the dressing table and began doing my hair. I decided to put only half of it up, letting my curls naturally fall down my neck and back. Something quick and easy. I didn't want to take any more time than was needed. I wanted to be downstairs when Wyatt got here. I wanted to marry him as soon as possible. And then I wanted to go home. I didn't want to be here anymore. Coming back to this house had been a bad idea. I quickly finished my hair, the process taking all of ten minutes, and grabbed my bag from the bed, leaving the clothes I had shed earlier on the floor in front of the mirror.

At the top of the stairs I kicked my bag, letting it tumble haphazardly down. Then I picked up the skirt of my dress and swiftly followed the path of my luggage until I was safely in the living room.

"Are you okay?" yelled Prue, meeting me as I turned the corner into the living room. I could tell by the way the pillows were strewn across the floor that she had jumped off the couch and ran towards the stairs.

"I'm fine," I assured her, releasing the extra fabric of my gown to untense my fingers. I wanted to seem relaxed.

"Good God, Lesley! I thought you had fallen down the stairs."

"No, that was just my bag. I kicked it down the stairs."

"Why didn't you just carry it down?"

"I couldn't. I had to hold my dress. I didn't want to trip and fall."

"And what? You couldn't wait for Wyatt to bring down your luggage?"

"I thought it would be easier this way, less time-consuming. Now all my stuff is down here and he can just put it in the car when he gets here instead of having to look for it after the wedding."

Prue cocked her head and stared at me, her eyes narrowing as I spoke.

"I don't have time for this," she said quickly as her body shifted, her arms thrown up into the air. "I have to get ready. I'll be in the guest room if you need me." Prue took a few steps forward, then stopped on the first step to turn and look at me. "Are you all right, Lesley? You seem a little jumpy today. Is anything wrong?"

"No," I breathed. "I guess I just have a small case of the wedding day jitters."

"You?" laughed Prue. "That, I do not believe. Strong, confident Lesley Lindaugh doesn't get jittery over anything."

"It's Trilmon," I firmly corrected.

"I guess it is," agreed Prue. "And it will be again." Prue stepped down and reached her hand out to me, grabbing my wrist and squeezing. "I'm really glad that you're my sister-in-law again, though I've always felt you were my sister, even if it wasn't legally binding at the time."

I placed my free hand on top of Prue's and smiled, caressing it gently. I never knew she had felt that way about me.

"Thank you, Prue."

Prue let go of my wrist and made her way back to the stairs, this time continuing her ascent. She yelled down to me as she jogged her way up.

"Like I said, I'll be in the guest room if you need anything."

"I should be fine," I yelled back. "I'm just going to be here in the living room."

"Whatever you do, don't let Wyatt see you!"

And then I heard the door to the guest room slam shut.

I walked around the living room. The curtains were still open and I could see what movers and workers were left were putting the last finishing touches on the pathway down to the beach. A catering truck pulled into the driveway behind Prue's Mustang and began unloading what would soon be dinner. I caught a glimpse of the cake. Five tiers, each one being carried by a separate worker. Five tiers. How many people were coming to this wedding? I told Prue I wanted something small, something intimate. Not like the first time Wyatt and I got married. That was a spectacle for our parents. Everyone in town – everyone they ever met, it seemed like – was at that wedding. And I whole-heartedly bought into the idea that it needed to be like a fairytale because it would be the best day of my life, and you only get married once. How untrue that dream was. It's unfair there are no fairytales depicting real life. Maybe Wyatt could draw one, if only to give future generations a fair chance. I would try to remember and suggest it to him on our honeymoon.

Wyatt. My life with him now came very easy, as if we had never separated all those years ago. I guess in a way we didn't, always remembering the other, trying, in many ways, to get back to each other. It's sad that it took so long to happen. Even sadder that certain people became casualties in their own war of love. I tried not to think of those people, not only Addie but of Sam and Travis. And most days I didn't, choosing to focus on my life now, my life with Wyatt and how happy we were finally, together. And some days…

A tear fell down my cheek. I was picturing their faces, each one different and beautiful in its own way. I tried not to think about them. I tried to picture Wyatt's face and the day he asked me to marry him. It was April, five months ago from this day, and I remember listening to the rain outside my bedroom window as I lay in bed waiting for Wyatt to get there. We were supposed to have a romantic dinner earlier that evening but he had called and said he would be late and didn't know exactly what time he'd be in.

"Maybe you should just stay at your place tonight," I offered.

"No," Wyatt answered quickly. "I haven't spent an evening away from you since you showed up that day on my doorstep. I don't intend to start now."

I smiled even though I knew he couldn't see me.

"Okay. I'll see you when you get in."

There was a pause

"I love you, Lesley." His tone was serious and took me a little off guard.

"I love you, too, Wyatt."

"Bye."

And he hung up.

I laid in bed awake, waiting, wondering what could be keeping him so long. Wyatt never worked this late and it began to make me worry. Something had to be wrong. At the end of our conversation, his words were so firm, like he was trying to convince me that he loved me. I had heard that tone before. It was always proceeded by his leaving me. That was it. Wyatt wasn't coming home to me. He was leaving.

I began to panic. I flung the covers off of me and ran to my closet, grabbing the first pair of pants and shirt I could find. As I was struggling to put my left leg in the right pant leg, I heard the front door to my apartment open, then softly close. I threw the shirt and pants back into the closet then quickly made my way back to the bed and under the covers. I caught my breath and tried to lay relaxed so that Wyatt would think I had been sleeping.

Wyatt came into the room and slowly removed his clothes, gingerly placing them on the trunk at the end of the bed so as not to wake me. Then he lifted the covers and crawled in next to me, moving one arm under me while the other wrapped around me. He took a deep breath, letting out his tension as he exhaled, his body relaxing as the air escaped him.

"What took you so long?" I tried to whisper, though it seemed I failed, Wyatt's body jumping slightly at my question. "I was getting worried."

"Nothing to worry about," he answered. "Just some loose ends that needed to be tied up. It's all taken care of now."

"What loose ends?" I questioned. I couldn't help but be a little panicky. I felt I had been down this road before, and at the end of it, I had been left alone.

"I'm kind of glad you're up."

"Why's that?"

"I was offered a job in New York."

My heart stopped.

This wasn't happening. Not again. Not after all we'd been through! We were finally happy. This couldn't be happening again!

"A publisher in New York called me earlier today," Wyatt continued. "They heard about what we're doing here in Chicago with the graphic novel projects and wanted to do something similar, only faster. They wanted an earlier launch date than we had, so that's why they called me." He paused, waiting for me to say something, but I didn't, I couldn't, so he continued. "They figured if they hired someone who knew how to run things – how to get it started and see it through to the end – then they'd get their product out on the shelves before we did. It'd be faster than hiring someone with little or no experience."

"Sounds reasonable," I squeaked. "Was it a good offer?"

"Yeah. A *really* good offer. Lots of zeroes."

"So, are you going to take it?" I held my breath, bracing myself.

"No."

"No?" I was shocked. I thought for sure his answer would be yes. "Why not?"

"Because of this."

Wyatt unfolded his hand and placed it six inches away from my face, his fingers grasping a diamond ring.

"Wyatt, what is this?" I was too nervous to assume anything.

"I love you, Lesley. I want to marry you, live my life with you, have fat, round-faced babies with you. I want to grow old with grandbabies that look just like you. I want to spend every waking moment with you because I know what my life is without you and I can't live like that. And when it's time for me to leave this earth, I want to die in your arms knowing that everything I did in my life I did so that I could be nearer to you."

"Oh, Wyatt…"

"Lesley Ann Lindaugh, will you marry me?"

"Yes!" I shouted. "And it's Trilmon."

"So it is."

Wyatt placed the ring on my finger as I rolled over to face him, kissing him once my hands were free.

"If you told the other publisher no, what took you so long in getting home tonight?" I assumed now that the romantic dinner for two had been planned so Wyatt could pop the question. I was curious as to what would make him cancel such a significant dinner.

"I've been on the phone all day with the execs in San Francisco. They had no idea there was any competition for the graphic novel market. It's a fairly new concept and they thought they had a hold on it. We've been talking strategy all day. I couldn't just walk away without tying up loose ends. And it seems my loyalty has paid off."

"What do you mean?"

"They offered me a raise. A big one."

"That's wonderful, Wyatt!"

"Yeah, once they heard what their competition was willing to pay me, they doubled it. Plus they said they'd publish *Dream Weaver* as their third graphic novel series."

"Really?"

"I know. Can you believe it?"

"Do you think this could be the start of our happy life together?" I asked.

"I don't know about you," Wyatt said, pulling me closer into his body, "but I was pretty happy the day you showed up on my doorstep." He kissed my lips, moving down to my neck. "And I've been happy ever since."

That was a happy night, and since then I had been waiting for this day to arrive. This wedding day meant something different than the first one. This day represented a real, honest choice. There was no young love or hyperactive hormones pushing two people to the altar. Wyatt and I had chosen each other because we loved each other, because our lives separately had only fueled a growing want and need for the other. This day was about us and what our life was about to become, burgeoning and changing due to unforeseen surprises. As I looked out the window at all the people scurrying about, I tried not to think about how my small, intimate wedding was turning into a three-ringed circus. I found a chair in the corner of the room and sat in it, tilting my head back and closing my eyes, letting the room go dark and my mind run free.

I love you…

I felt a kiss on my forehead. "Wyatt!" I gasped as I sprang forward. I opened my eyes to find my ex-husband, now fiancé, soon to be husband again kneeling in front of me.

"Lesley, calm down! It's just me."

"I'm sorry," I answered breathlessly. "You startled me."

"I didn't mean to wake you. I just couldn't help kissing you. You look beautiful."

I smiled, leaning in to hug Wyatt, then pushed him away.

"You're not supposed to see me before the wedding. It's bad luck."

"I think we've had enough bad luck to last a lifetime. What's a little more?"

"I said the same thing to myself this morning," I laughed. "Just don't let Prue know you saw me. She'll flip."

"We wouldn't want that," he snickered. Wyatt grabbed my hands and pulled me up, leading me to the porch door. "Come with me."

"Where are we going?"

"It's a secret."

"But what about Prue? What about the wedding?"

Wyatt stopped at the door to turn and look at me, cupping my face in his hands.

"I promise Cinderella will be back in time for the ball."

"Okay," I accepted, my resistance melting away in his hands.

"Now, keep your eyes closed."

"My eyes are closed, Wyatt. My eyes have been closed for what I'm going to guess has been the better part of half an hour."

I was becoming irritated. I had no idea where I was or where we were going or why. And it was becoming increasingly difficult to walk in my wedding dress, seeing how both of my hands were being occupied by those of my soon-to-be husband's, rendering me completely unable to hold up the ends of my dress and amplifying my vulnerability to tripping. Wyatt was leading me somewhere. I could tell we were outside now, the train of my dress snagging the ground every few steps. Plus Wyatt hadn't stopped or paused to open a door since we left the car. And it was hot. I tried to follow the turns we made since we left Persephone's house, but I lost myself on my mental map after two left turns, a right turn, and what felt like a U-turn. I was truly lost.

"We're almost there," reassured Wyatt.

"Good. I don't know how much longer I can walk in this dress."

"You should have worn a different dress then," he taunted.

"Excuse me for thinking I was getting married today! But I guess it's my fault, really, seeing how one should always be ready to go on an adventure at the drop of a hat, for no other reason than because you asked."

"I promise it's just a few more feet."

I jerked one of hands out of his grip and tried to cradle my stomach as he continued to drag me along.

"Wyatt, it's August and I'm sweaty and tired and if you don't stop soon I'm going to throw up on you."

"We're here," Wyatt announced abruptly.

"Can I open my eyes?"

"Not yet."

I felt Wyatt move closer to me, taking my face in his hands, and kissing each of my eyelids once.

"Okay. You can open your eyes now."

I opened my eyes and looked around. We were in the middle of a hay field, surrounded by a line of trees on all four sides. In the distance I could make out the roof of an old barn that was shifting over its crumbling walls. It looked like it was floating in a sea of golden grass. I knew exactly where we were. I looked up and through the massive limbs I could see the sun trying to make its way through the long branches of an enormous willow tree. In a field that had been heavily cultivated by generations of Trilmon men, this tree was the only thing that Wyatt's great-grandfather had left standing. It was our childhood refuge, the old and rotting wood from the tree house Wyatt's father had built as a child still in its bough, broken but clinging to its branches. Just on the other side of the northern line of trees stood Wyatt's childhood home, one newly built, unlike the family homestead his grandparents had lived in which was on the other side of the southern line of trees. To the west was the inner workings of Point Caneissa and, eventually, the lake. The east side was inland woods that stretched for an undetermined distance. I was always too afraid to venture into them to see where they would lead. But this place, this spot under this beautiful old willow, this was my favorite place in the world.

"What are we doing here?" I asked, truly puzzled.

"A-hem," a voice coughed from behind the tree. I stepped to the side and found Father Halse standing patiently in the old tree's shade.

"Wyatt, I don't understand."

"I wanted to marry you somewhere special, a place that was important, significant to us. When I think of you and home, I think of this place and summer baseball games in the field or meeting after school to do homework. Building snow forts around the tree or sneaking out at night to look at the stars and talk about whatever was on our minds."

"I remember talking a lot about girls under those stars," I jabbed. "In particular, Mary Jane Obermeijer."

Wyatt took my hands and placed them on his chest.

"I didn't know it at the time, but I fell in love with you under this tree all those years ago, and I want to marry you in this spot because I know you fell in love with me here, too."

"But what about the wedding? Everything's been planned. I mean, I saw them setting up a dance floor this morning."

"Your mom and Prue will get their wedding. But this," Wyatt gestured to the willow tree and the field surrounding it, "this is just for us."

"Okay."

"Well, then, should we get started?" asked Father Halse as he met us at the side of the tree. Wyatt nodded his head. "Let's begin. We are gathered here today to join this man and this woman in holy matrimony…"

"I assume you two will not be late to the ceremony," Father Halse shouted to us as he made his way through the field. "I have an evening mass to perform at seven o'clock sharp."

"We'll be there," yelled Wyatt.

"With bells on," I laughed.

Father Halse shook his head in disbelief and continued his long walk to the edge of the trees, and eventually his car. We lost sight of him about five hundred feet out, just halfway before the line of trees.

"I can't believe we did it," I whispered. "We're married!"

"Yes, we are, Mrs. Trilmon," Wyatt said as he kissed me. "I mean, Dr. Trilmon."

"I don't know," I sighed. "Mrs. Trilmon is sounding better and better every minute." Wyatt pulled me in and kissed my forehead, closing his arms in around me. "You want to know a secret?" I asked.

"What?"

"I always wanted to make-out with you under this tree."

"What?" Wyatt laughed.

"All your friends used to bring their girlfriends here on Saturday night and make-out. I always thought you brought Mary Jane Obermeijer here to do the same thing. Maybe other girls, too."

"Again with Mary Jane Obermeijer," joked Wyatt.

"Well, she was your girlfriend, and all your other friends were doing it, so I just assumed – "

"You assumed wrong," Wyatt interrupted. "You will be the first girl I will ever have made-out with under this tree."

"Really?"

"Really," affirmed Wyatt. He placed one arm around my back and one arm under my legs, lifting me quickly off the ground. "Now the field, that's a different story." I punched him in the shoulder, hard. "Ow!" he yelped as we fell to the ground. I landed on top of him. "I was only kidding."

"You better be," I threatened, glaring as I spoke. He placed one arm around me again and the other on the ground next to him. Wyatt shifted, then rolled, and within a second, we had switched positions. He hovered above me, his beautiful face looking into mine.

"I promise," he whispered. "I love you, Lesley." He kissed me gently, as we lay under our tree, happy, married, and in love.

"Where the hell have *you* been?" bellowed Prue as we walked up the driveway along a never-ending line of cars. It was now six-thirty. "Do you know how long we've been waiting? Do you feel any sense of obligation to those people down there waiting for you? I had to open the bar and start serving hors d'oeuvres so people wouldn't leave. And Father Halse – I won't even start with him."

"We're sorry, Prue," Wyatt chuckled. "I guess we lost track of time."

"What are you two doing together anyway? The groom is not supposed to see the bride before the wedding."

"That's my fault," answered Wyatt. "I kind of ambushed Lesley."

"It doesn't matter now. Let's just get this show on the road."

We walked down the pathway behind Prue until we reached the lined chairs on the beach. People were walking around with drinks in their hands and cocktail napkins containing mini pigs-in-a-blanket, shrimp, and cubes of cheese.

"Places everyone!" Prue yelled. "They're here."

"Finally," I heard someone huff from the blob of people. My mother glared at me as Wyatt and I walked down the aisle to no music. The string quartet Prue hired had to leave at six. My father sat next to her looking slightly amused.

"Since I now only have twenty-five minutes before evening mass," sighed Father Halse, "we're going to do the short version."

"I can't believe this," my mother complained. I couldn't help but smile.

"Do you, Lesley, take this man?" Father Halse paused for an answer.

"Oh," I said surprised. "You weren't kidding when you said short." I tried to make him laugh, but Father Halse's expression stayed very serious. "Yes. Yes I do," I giggled.

"Wyatt, do you take this woman?"

"Yes." Wyatt winked at me when he answered.

"Then by the power vested in me by the Holy Trinity, I now pronounce you man and wife. What God has placed together, let no man put asunder. You may kiss the bride."

By the time Wyatt was done kissing me, Father Halse had already left, and so had half our guests, though they were making their way up to the reception.

"I'm not going to ask you where you've been," said Prue as she pulled a piece of straw grass out of my hair, "or what happened to your dress." I looked down at my beautiful dress and found that though I had done a fairly good job at keeping it clean, it did have little tears in the thin gauze with short pieces of hay poking out. "I'm just glad you two are here." Prue leaned in and hugged me. "And that you're my sister-in-law again." My mother came up behind me and joined our hug.

"Young lady, I am not amused by your antics today." Prue and I tried to let go, but my mother held us all together. "I spent a lot of time and money making this day perfect for you, for the *second* time. I expect better behavior from you." She let us go and turned to my father and Wyatt. "Now, let's all get to the reception. We have people to greet."

My mother took my father's arm and headed up the walkway to the house with Prue following like a lost puppy. Wyatt took my hand and kissed it, leading me slowly up the path to a party neither of us cared about attending.

When we reached the side of the house which had been designated the reception area with tables, a bar and a dance floor, the band began to play *Yesterday*. Without hesitating, Wyatt led me to the empty dance floor. As he held me, swaying my body with his and the music, I wondered if people thought it strange for us to dance to such a song on our wedding day. But to us it made absolute sense. As we danced, I paid no attention to our guests, the waiters, or the music, really. I just wondered if Wyatt would take me back to our tree tonight, to the place where we really got married, and lay with me under the stars and dream.

"Just so you know," Prue interrupted, "I went ahead and called the airline and changed your flight to tomorrow." Wyatt stopped dancing and when I looked up, I found only a handful of people left sitting around us. How long had we been dancing? "I didn't know when or if you guys were coming home," Prue continued, "so I called the airline to see if maybe you had decided to skip the wedding and just go to Hawaii. But they said you weren't there, so I changed your flight to tomorrow, found your luggage and put it in the master bedroom upstairs. I hope you don't mind." There was a slight sting to her tone.

"Not at all," answered Wyatt. "We kind of left you no choice, really. But we don't have to stay here tonight, Prue. You've done so much already. Lesley and I can go back to Chicago tonight. I mean, we leave from there tomorrow anyway."

"Don't be silly," Prue said quickly. "It's late. I'm sure you're tired and I don't want to worry about you two getting home safely. Besides," she added, a little hesitant, "I don't want to be in this big house all by myself anyway."

"I understand," I said softly, taking Prue's hand. I more than understood.

"Well, it's getting late," said Wyatt, pretending to yawn as he put his arm around me. "And we have to get up early tomorrow to head back home. We better get to bed." Wyatt put his other arm under my legs.

"What are you doing?" I shrieked as Wyatt swept me up in his arms.

"To the threshold," he announced.

"Good night, Prue," I laughed. I waved to her as Wyatt carried me away.

"I've never actually slept in here before," I said as Wyatt carried me into the master bedroom.

"Who said anything about sleeping," Wyatt said as he threw me onto the bed, taking off his suit coat and unbuttoning his shirt as I bounced up and down on the mattress. I squealed as he jumped on the bed next to me, taking me in his arms and reaching for the back of my dress. I couldn't help but laugh.

"Wait," I said, trying to push his arms away from me. "Just wait a minute."

"I don't want to wait a minute," Wyatt mumbled, kissing the side of my neck.

"I have something I need to tell you."

"Are you going to tell me how pretty I am? Because I already know." He continued kissing the side of my neck.

"That's definitely not what I was going to tell you," I laughed as I tried to push him off me. "But you are looking kind of like a girl, with your hair all shaggy and hippy-like."

"I thought you liked my hair longer," he whimpered. He looked truly hurt.

"I do," I reassured as I ran my fingers through his sandy brown hair. "But I got you to stop." He rolled onto his back.

"Okay. What is it that you need to tell me? And it better be good. You're interrupting my wedding night."

There was no easy way to say what I needed to tell him. I leaned back on my elbows and took a deep breath.

"I want you to know that what I have to tell you is something I would never keep from you and I was just as surprised as you will be when I tell you. It's something I didn't plan. It just happened."

Wyatt sat up and stared at me.

"Lesley, you're scaring me. What's wrong?"

"I haven't been feeling well lately. My energy's been drained and I'm tired all the time and I've had a hard time keeping food down, so I decided to go to the doctor. That's where I was yesterday before I headed up here."

"What did he have to say?"

"Wyatt, I just want you to know that I didn't plan this. I would never do that to you. I know how much it would hurt you if I did, and I would never do that."

"You said that already. Now just tell me what the doctor said." His eyes were clouding over with fear. I hoped anger was not about to join them.

"He said…" I paused. My heart was racing. Tears began to form in the corners of my eyes. I was scared I would hurt him. I was scared that he'd hate me. Wyatt took my hand and placed it in both of his. I could tell he had no idea how to read me, and that made him more afraid. I couldn't take it anymore. I lowered my head as I spoke. "He said…he said I'm pregnant."

"Really?"

I did not look up at him for fear of what I might find in the expression on his face, but I shook my head in confirmation. Wyatt let go of my hand. That was it. I knew it. He was angry with me. But then he reached for my face and lifted my chin up, kissing my lips. He made his way down my neck to my collar bone and stopped, pulling the capped sleeves off of my shoulders, then moving to the back of my dress. He unbuttoned each button, then slowly pulled the gown down, his fingers gently brushing against my body as it became available to him. Wyatt threw the gown into the corner of the room and I laid there naked, vulnerable. He placed his right hand gently at the base of my neck and leisurely traced a pathway to my stomach. His hand rested there, then slipped to the side, his other hand wrapped the other side. He hugged my waist tightly as he placed his lips just below my belly button, kissing the slight bump his hand had just rested on. Then his lips began to follow the path his hands had made, stopping when he reached my chin.

"This," Wyatt whispered, "is the best day of my life."

Wyatt kissed me, soft at first, then more impatient as he attempted to remove the rest of his clothing. I embraced him as we kissed, and his hands found me again, eager to explore my changing body.

"What about Heath, or Heather?"

"Heath?" laughed Wyatt. "Is that even a name?"

"It's a name!" I defended, trying not to smile at the fact we were lying naked in bed talking about baby names. "If you're so good at picking names, you name one."

Wyatt reached over and placed his hand on my stomach.

"How about Emily or Emma?"

"What if it's a boy?"

"Wyatt Jr."

"Wyatt Jr.? Are you kidding me?"

"What's wrong with that?" Wyatt laughed under his breath, trying to hide that he was a little hurt by my reaction, even if his initial intension was a joke.

"Really, Wyatt? You need me to spell it out for you?"

"I'll spell it out for you!"

Wyatt attacked me under the covers, tickling what sensitive parts he could reach in spite of my kicking. He grabbed me and pulled me close to him but I managed to wiggle my way out, laughing as I grabbed a blanket and ran to one of the corners of the room. Wyatt jumped out of bed, quickly tied a sheet around his waist, and headed in my direction. I tried to run, but he caught me, and we fell back to the floor.

"Wyatt stop!" I pleaded through giggles.

"Say we can name him Wyatt Jr."

"Never!"

"Say it!"

"Okay, okay! I concede. If the baby's a boy, we can name him Wyatt Jr."

Wyatt stopped tickling me and held me loosely on the floor as we laughed and tried to catch our breath.

"What's that noise?" I asked as my breathing calmed and the sounds of the house could be heard again.

"What noise?"

"That singing or humming. You don't hear it?"

Wyatt paused and listened to the air around him.

"I don't know what that is." He whispered. "It could be Prue."

"Maybe we should go check on her."

"Why?"

"Don't you think it's weird that she would be singing in the middle of the night?"

"Fine," gave in Wyatt. "Let's go." Wyatt picked me up and we quietly walked together to the bedroom door.

When we opened the door, we found Prue at the other end of the hallway, standing in the doorway of her room.

"What are you doing?" asked Wyatt, forcing his whisper down the hallway.

"I was coming to check on you," answered Prue.

"We were doing the same thing," I added.

"Do you hear that singing," asked Prue.

"Yeah," answered Wyatt. "We thought it was you. Where's it coming from?"

Prue said nothing, but pointed to the nursery. We all began slowly walking toward each other. The nursery door was directly in the middle of the hallway. After what seemed like ten minutes of painfully restrictive walking, we met in the middle of the hallway in front of the nursery door.

"You two stand back," Wyatt commanded. "I don't want either of you getting hurt." Wyatt turned to his sister. "Prue, if something happens to me in there, I want you to get Lesley out of here, okay? You get her out of here."

"Okay," whispered Prue.

Wyatt opened the door and stepped into the room and...nothing. He looked around but there was nothing there. The room was completely empty. He pushed the door open more so Prue and I could see.

"What *is* that?" I asked. My voice cracked as I spoke.

"I don't know," answered Wyatt. "Prue?" Prue just shook her head in amazement and disbelief.

We stood motionless, Wyatt in the middle of the room and Prue and I in the doorway, staring into the corner of the room, listening to the sound of a female voice singing an airy, distant lullaby while the wooden floor crackled under the movement of an absent antique rocking chair – one Wyatt had given away more than a year ago, along with everything else from Addie's nursery.

THE POSTLUDE: FRIDAY, MAY 25TH, 1973

Addie

I woke up and found the room lit with moonlight. I had slept the entire afternoon and now it was evening. I wondered if Lesley was here. Rising from the rocking chair, I slowly made my way in the dark through the nursery, unlocking the door and letting the light from downstairs flow into the room. I heard noises – indistinct noises. Curious, I made my way downstairs, stopping as I turned the corner. There was Wyatt, making love to his ex-wife, my best friend, in my own house! I couldn't speak. I just stood there and watched as the actions became more progressive. Lesley flipped her head and her eyes met with mine.

"Addie!"

My mind couldn't take it. I ran up the stairs and locked myself in the nursery, trying to make sense of everything that was happening. The lines of reality had become blurred, even more so than when I was dreaming. And because of this, after sobbing hysterically and letting my imagination flow where it wanted, I went to the pages of fantasy – written in my own hand – lying around me on the floor. I sifted and sorted until I found a halfway blank page. When I found a pen, I began to write, not a dream, but my perceptions of reality.

WHY DON'T YOU LOVE ME WYATT???

I dropped the pen and cried, my body falling limp onto the floor. It was too exhausting, my dreams, my life. All I wanted was for Wyatt to love me. I hadn't felt him love me in such a long time. I began to wonder if he ever did. I tried to remember the last time I felt he loved me, the last time he tried to protect me from myself. The more I thought, the calmer I became. I could hear Wyatt outside the door trying to figure a way in. He was talking to me, telling me he was leaving me – how he loved Lesley and not me. I couldn't let him leave. He was ruining everything! Everything I worked so hard to create was falling apart. How could I make him stay? Then I remembered Grace.

I told Wyatt everything. I had tried to give him a child. Lesley didn't even want his child. Lesley gave her away. Why couldn't Wyatt see that I loved him? I unlocked the door. I didn't know why. He didn't believe me. I wasn't ready to see him yet. Wyatt entered the room. I tried to run but he stopped me, tried to hold me. But he failed. I broke free.

I didn't have a plan to make Wyatt love me again. But then I remembered the day at the water.

I didn't know where to go when I reached the water. I could hear Wyatt behind me, calling to me. I didn't want to see him; I wasn't ready to see him. I couldn't think straight. All I could see was Wyatt holding Lesley's head as he devoured her mouth; Lesley on top of him, writhing in pleasure. I began to run again. I plunged myself into the water and began swimming out. I stopped and touched my feet to the bottom. *Still halfway up. I need to go further.* Every few feet I would stop and see if I could still touch the lake floor without being completely submerged. I decided that when I could no longer touch the bottom, that would be enough space between me and Wyatt. When I reached that point I would stay there a few minutes, then swim back to shore and wait for Wyatt to pick me up and take me inside. He would love me then, as he used to, because he would realize what his life would be without me. I submerged myself. No sand. I was at my predestined point.

I waited, treading water until it was time to go back to shore. I could hear Wyatt calling to me from the beach. I tried lifting myself above the waves to see him. I made the faint impression of his body against the lights of the house. I continued treading. I wanted him to suffer, his thoughts in agony at the possibility of losing me. After a few more minutes I began to feel the weight of my nightgown drag me beneath the waves. Frantically I pulled the straps off my shoulders and slid the wet satin down my body. It didn't work. Something was pulling me under. I tried to swim upwards, pushing against the water with my hands. A wave pushed me up and I felt the night air against my wet face. "Wyatt!" I inhaled water as my plea was broken by the undertow pulling me down. I kicked my feet as hard as I could, my legs pumping the water around me. "Wyatt!" I screamed as another wave pushed me up, the humid air burning my throat as it fought with the cold lake water trying to fill my lungs. The undertow pulled me down again as I tried to grasp and pull at the surface of the rushing water, but my fingers passed through with no resistance. Another wave pushed me up and I opened my mouth again to scream for Wyatt but no sound came except for the uncontrollable coughing my body forced from my lungs, trying to expel the water. My body was choking me. I tried to breath. I tried to look around and consciously find an image that would be my last – something that I could focus on, something about this world that I had loved – ANYTHING! I tried to see Wyatt. I could still faintly hear him, his calls muffled by the water filling my ears. But I couldn't see him. I couldn't even see the water around me or the stars above me or the moon. I could see the lights from the house, orange and yellow, burning separately in all the windows, then coming together in just one, small flickering flame. I pulled at the water as it yanked me down, my eyes open with that flicker burned into my vision. I thought I felt the night air against my cheek – my eyes seeing that flame, convinced it was my house – but it wasn't, and as my lungs compulsively tried to suck in the warm air only to find water, my body began to convulse. I tried again to reach for the surface, but everything was starting to go black, even the tiny flame. I grew tired of fighting against the current and I felt myself begin to fall. In the darkness I saw white flashes – no images – just white hot flashes that for a second gave me hope that maybe I was saved. But then I felt a pop, then warmness, then nothing, my naked body settling on the lakebed sand.

Wyatt didn't save me. He didn't even try. The story books were wrong – there is no prince charming, no happily-ever-after.

Acknowledgements

Special thanks to Bryan Palmer and Kristen Wessesler for their time spent tirelessly reading the many drafts of this novel, for their suggestions, opinions, and for putting up with my never-ending questions. To Lorrie Palmer who spent a Saturday afternoon in February looking as beautiful as she always does, braving the thirty-mile-an-hour wind coming off the torrent waters of Lake Michigan in order to produce the perfect cover picture. And again to Bryan Palmer for photographing such wonderful pictures to choose from. To Gideon Fisher for designing more than one awesome book cover. To all my family and friends for your support. And a big thank you to Sally Boyer for proofing this aspiring writer's work and for your encouraging words. Thank you all.

About the Author

Paige K. Palmer holds a Bachelor's degree in English with a concentration in literature from Indiana University at South Bend. She currently lives in Northern Indiana with her husband and daughter, spending what free time she has writing. Ms. Palmer is fervently writing her next novel, *Going on Thirty*, despite complaints from her laundry room. *Broken* is her debut novel.

For more information about Paige K. Palmer and her work, visit www.paigekpalmer.com, email her at paigekpalmer@gmail.com or check out her Author Page on Facebook.

www.ingramcontent.com/pod-product-compliance
Lightning Source LLC
Chambersburg PA
CBHW071302170626
46809CB00001B/329